DANGEROUS
ATTACHMENTS

VILLARD BOOKS • NEW YORK • 1995

DANGEROUS ATTACHMENTS

SARAH LOVETT

All rights reserved under International and Pan-American
Copyright Conventions. Published in the United States
by Villard Books, a division of Random House, Inc., New York, and
simultaneously in Canada by Random House
of Canada Limited, Toronto.

Villard Books is a registered trademark of Random House, Inc.

Library of Congress Cataloging-in-Publication Data
Lovett, Sarah (Sarah Poland)
    Dangerous attachments / Sarah Lovett
        p.   cm.
    ISBN 0-679-43559-X
    I. Title.
PS3562.0873D36   1995   813'.54—dc20   94-46947

Manufactured in the United States of America on acid-free paper

98765432

First Edition

This book is for my mother, Eleonor Marie Tompkins Poland,
and my father, Joseph Fairfield Poland

and for Jacqueline West

and for Timothy Thompson, true friend, best editor

ACKNOWLEDGMENTS

I WANT TO acknowledge all the people who helped in the creation of this book. First, my heartfelt thanks to Peter Miller, my delightful and astounding literary manager; Jennifer Robinson, who helped build from the ground up; and everyone at PMA Literary and Film Management.

For their support, savvy, and guidance, I'm very grateful to my editors David Rosenthal and Leona Nevler.

My admiration and thanks to Miriam Sagan and the Edit Femmes: Carolyn Gilliland, Melissa White, Sally Sommer, Kath Lee; also, Peggy van Hulsteyn, March Kessler, and Susan York.

My gratitude for the generosity and wisdom of psychologists

Stephen Poland, Ph.D., Robert Klein, Ph.D., Susan Cave, Ph.D., Samuel Roll, Ph.D., and Gayle Zieman, Ph.D.

Special thanks to Jim Burleson, Deputy Director of Training at New Mexico's Department of Public Safety.

Many thanks to Lawrence Lee Renner, Philip Aviles, and E. Kevin Lattyak at the New Mexico Department of Public Safety Crime Lab.

Elizabeth Guss, Connie Warren, Bob Gallegos, Pat Lopez, and Michael Maestas deserve recognition for their patience and willingness to teach; so does Charlie Overcash at the Corrections Academy.

I'm also obliged to consultants Ron Schultz and Sally Butler; and to my co-workers and companions at the penitentiary: Suzanne Johnson, Jesse Ferguson, Tina Alarid, and Ann Harvey.

To Donny Opper and Joff Pollon: I appreciate your efforts, guys.

Thanks Alice, for all the ups and downs.

Muchas gracias to my friends and fellow authors, Lew Thompson and Bob Klein.

DANGEROUS ATTACHMENTS

ONE

El chacal, the jackal, stood on the second tier of cell block one and stared down at the activity on the floor below. In the common area, four inmates were playing a round of bridge. A fifth inmate sat rigid in front of the TV and whispered to Brooke, a regular on *The Bold and the Beautiful.* The jackal sighed; an honest day's labor was rare in this world.

He closed his eyes and silently recited the words of St. Ignatius Loyola. "Teach us, good Lord, to serve Thee . . . to toil and not to seek for rest; to labour and not ask for any reward save that of knowing that we do Thy will."

It was a lesson most of the occupants of CB-1 had not yet learned. And there were other lessons: thou shalt not steal . . . thou shalt not kill.

He turned back to gaze into an open cell. The small square of window was already charcoal gray. Each day another two minutes of daylight were lost. It would keep on that way—getting darker and darker—until the winter solstice.

Day and night, just like his own two selves. He'd grown so used to them, he hardly noticed the transformation anymore. Day getting shorter. Night, longer and longer, ready to take its due.

It was the killing that made him split apart in the beginning. Or maybe the split was the reason he had begun to kill.

Thou shalt not kill. Finally, after doing so many bad, hurtful things, he had learned: thou shalt not kill.

Unless you are doing His will.

> *To labour and not ask for any reward*
> *Save that of knowing that we do Thy will.*

The jackal had been offered a task, but had not even considered it, until the Lord intervened. The Lord said, "Accept the task, jackal, and be rewarded." *His will be done.*

The task was to kill. Not a senseless, selfish kill like some of the men had done, like he himself had done a long time ago. This kill was part of the Lord's divine plan.

On earth as it is in heaven.

The reward was great: it would become the crowning glory of his work for the Lord.

He sighed and gazed down at the sheet of paper he'd been clutching in his right hand. Things had been going so well.

But then, a snafu. Somebody was nosy.

And now, he had twice the work.

One hit had become *two* hits.

The second name was written in pencil, faint but legible. His own handwriting. Over and over. Just the way the nuns had taught him to write *Be sure your sin will find you out*—on the blackboard one hundred times.

The second name covered the page ninety-seven times. The jackal thought it was an odd name. He took the stub of pencil from his pocket, licked the tip, and smoothed the sheet of paper over the rail. In minute script he added the last three repetitions: Sylvia Strange Sylvia Strange Sylvia Strange.

——

SYLVIA STRANGE TURNED from the frontage road that ran parallel with the interstate. From this distance, the building ahead looked businesslike, industrial. Closer, it became what it was, a prison with dirt-encrusted windows and gleaming perimeter lights. On her right, a pockmarked state historical sign announced the Penitentiary of New Mexico, founded 1956.

She approached the intersection going forty, swerved to avoid a jackrabbit, and swore as the Volvo slid to a stop over loose gravel. Scrub chamisa, prickly pear cactus, and occasional soda cans dotted the fields on either side of the road. A lone cottonwood towered over the flat desert landscape. In the distance, the Sangre de Cristo Mountains gave off a dull blue gleam under winter sun. South Facility, medium security, was a quarter mile to her right. On her left, a prison service truck idled by the cutoff to the maximum facility. The driver smacked his lips at her, then lit a cigarette.

She accelerated past the sewage treatment facility, past the fire trucks. Ahead, she could see the entrance to the PNM Main Facility surrounded by heavy link fencing and spirals of razor ribbon designed to slash a man to pieces. She approached it with familiar emotional discord, equal parts apprehension and fascination. Today, her thoughts were colored by too little sleep, too much caffeine. Even on the best days, it was impossible to view the Main Facility without thinking about the nation's most brutal prison riot. In 1980, thirty-three inmates had died—some tortured and mutilated—at the hands of other inmates.

The silhouette of a guard was visible in the window of the large beige tower looming over the prison's entryway. Sylvia stopped at the speaker embedded in a concrete post set in the center of the road.

"State your name and business."

"I'm Dr. Strange, here for attorneys Cox and Burnett." Her voice sounded husky, unused. She cleared her throat.

"Park in the lot to your left."

A third of the spaces were filled. She pulled into a slot shaded by a naked cottonwood and facing a trailer with a sign: FAMILY HOSPITALITY CENTER. A few flakes of snow drifted down to settle on bare earth.

Sylvia drew her briefcase from the Volvo and locked the doors. Her gray wool skirt had ridden up her thighs as she drove. She smoothed it down to the low edge of her knees and buttoned her burgundy suit jacket.

As she approached the reception outbuilding, she caught sight of her own reflection on the tempered glass. At thirty-four, she was tall, lithe, and moved with ease thanks to the weekly ballet classes she'd hated as a teenager. She had inherited her father's lean limbs and broad shoulders as well as her mother's large breasts. Thick brunette hair grazed the collar of her jacket; she wore it loose, slightly layered, brushed back from a prominent forehead. Wire-rimmed sunglasses shaded her eyes and intensified the angles and planes of her face. She walked quickly, her heels clacking on the cold asphalt. When she entered the building, she was twenty minutes early.

Several correctional officers, stragglers on the morning shift, were clustered in the reception area. The admitting C.O. glanced at Sylvia and immediately refocused. As he slid the sign-in sheet her way, he gave a low whistle. "You a lawyer?"

Sylvia's smile was cool. She was used to male attention, knew how to deal with it, but the rules were different at the pen. She signed her name and noticed her hands were shaky. "Psychologist," she said.

He glanced at the sheet. "Strange?" He grinned. "That's strange."

"Yeah, isn't it?" Sylvia smiled back mechanically; since kindergarten, she'd heard every possible pun on her name. Be kind to your local C.O., she thought.

"Doc! Haven't seen you in a few!"

Sylvia recognized the voice before she turned and beamed at a mischievous guard named Leroy. She shook his hand and said, "How's Holly?" Leroy's wife worked as a court clerk at the Santa Fe Judicial Complex.

"Holly's fine, just got promoted," Leroy said.

Sylvia watched him smooth the skin on the ring finger of his left hand. When he gave her a mock salute, she noticed a faint band of white; he'd left the wedding ring at home.

Leroy winked. "You gonna tell us who's crazy in there?"

Sylvia winked back. "Does Holly know you pocket the ring when she's not around?"

Leroy turned bright pink and his buddies hooted. When he regained his composure, he said, "I'll get you for that, Doc."

As Sylvia walked away, she smiled. "I'm counting on it, Leroy."

She felt internal gears shift as she passed through the metal detector, down the short hall, and through the exit. She had crossed into another world.

She waited impatiently in the small concrete anteway while the heavy link gate slid open with a groan of resistance. This was the worst part, the first taste of no-man's-land between metal barriers.

A sparrow landed between the diamond-shaped discs of a loop of razor ribbon. The bird chirped before flying off again. Sylvia advanced through the gate and walked toward the doors to Main's lobby. As she glanced up at the two-story fortress, she tried to remember exactly which soot-crusted window was the psych office.

—

THE ROOM WAS tiny, crammed with filing cabinets and two metal desks. Sylvia set her briefcase on the desk nearest the door. A potted plant was suspended from a web of macramé over a heating vent. Wilted leaves shuddered in the forced-air breeze. A list of phone extensions, in case of emergency, was tacked on the wall. Just in case.

She sat, snapped open her briefcase, took out several pencils, and selected the slim accordion file labeled LUCAS SHARP WATSON NMCD #36620. A blue folder contained routine incarceration documents as well as Watson's main jacket. Date of incarceration: August 28, 1992. County: Bernalillo. Determinate Sentence: 6 years. Crime: voluntary manslaughter. Twenty-one-year-old Lucas Watson had brutally beaten a forty-year-old migrant worker to death in a barroom dispute. Both men had been drunk; they had argued over money. No one had claimed the body of the victim. Watson had served three years of his sentence.

Sylvia wondered what he looked like—no photograph was included in the file—and felt a slight anticipatory edge in her stomach; it was always the same when she met a penitentiary client for the first time. Thank God he wasn't a Death Row inmate; she wasn't up to a terminal case this morning.

The thickest folder was green and included Watson's personal history as well as investigative reports on family members, and statements from employers, even schoolteachers. One fact caught Sylvia's attention: when Watson was six years old, his mother had committed suicide—a .22-caliber bullet through her head.

She skimmed the information and the note Herb Burnett had scribbled on a yellow Post-it. "Dear Sylvia, Glad you can take over for Malcolm. Lucas Watson is up for parole next week. Sorry for the rush job. How about dinner, *chez moi?*"

The red folder held a psychological assessment by Dr. Malcolm Treisman, Sylvia's senior associate up until the previous summer when he'd been diagnosed with cancer. Malcolm's death, two weeks ago, had been a blow to family, friends, and associates. It had left Sylvia with the feeling she was ghost-walking, only half present among the living. The fact that Malcolm had also been her lover sharpened her grief.

The dull ache in her temple spread across her forehead. She had just pulled a bottle of Anacin and a notepad from her briefcase when there was a knock and the door opened. Lucas Watson, accompanied by a C.O., stood framed in the doorway. He was about six feet two and wiry. His blond hair was shaved close to the skull; small scabs were visible beneath the stubble. He moved with shoulders slightly hunched—a taut inmate strut—to reach the chair in front of Sylvia's desk. As he sat, he met her gaze. His pupils were light blue, almost cloudy; they reminded her of someone who had suffered snow burn.

"Good morning, Mr. Watson."

"Lucas."

"Lucas." She smiled. "I'm Sylvia Strange." She glanced at the C.O. who had remained in the doorway. "We're okay."

The C.O. fingered his name tag: ANDERSON. "If you need me, I'll be outside."

She waited until the door closed before she spoke. "Your lawyer, Mr. Burnett, told me you requested an independent evaluation. Can you tell me why?"

Lucas shifted, hips pressed toward the desk. His tongue slid over his teeth and tiny beads of perspiration were visible on his upper lip. "For the parole board."

"Do you think your caseworker can come up with a feasible plan?" Sylvia asked. Each inmate was assigned a caseworker. When applicable, he or she was responsible for the formulation of a parole plan—the nuts and bolts of parole—including potential living situation, employment, and available treatment programs.

Lucas fixed her with his cloudy eyes and nodded.

"Good. Before we begin, I need to remind you that I can't guarantee confidentiality. Whatever we talk about in this office, I'll be sharing that information with your lawyer, and ultimately, with the parole board."

He nodded again, his body humming with motor tension, fingers drumming the arms of his chair.

Sylvia noted a dark substance under his first and second fingernails. Her guess: dried blood. When he was stressed, Lucas probably scratched the scabs on his scalp.

She said, "Because we only have this one meeting, I want to touch base with you about what's going on in your life. Later, I may ask you to complete some short tests. How did the test go with Dr. DeMaria, by the way?" The Minnesota Multiphasic Personality Inventory, MMPI-2, had been administered by one of the prison psychologists.

Suddenly, Lucas Watson's face darkened with concern. "What did she say about me?"

"Are you worried about what Dr. DeMaria might have said?"

He leaned forward and lowered his voice to a conspiratorial whisper. "She doesn't like me because I know who she really is."

"Who is she, Lucas?"

"One of *them*." He cocked his head, raised one eyebrow as if they shared a secret, and smiled.

The MMPI raw data were in Albuquerque being scored and analyzed by a firm that specialized in the computer calculation of psychological tests. When the results were faxed to Sylvia, she would use the profile and the report as part of her evaluation. But even without the results, she was beginning to get an idea where Lucas might show scale elevations. There was an irreverent saying among prison psychs: Two, four, six, eight, who do we incarcerate? On the MMPI those clinical scales measured depression, deviance, paranoia, schizophrenia. Lucas Watson was acting a wee bit paranoid.

For the next hour, the interview confirmed her first impression. He was guarded, hypervigilant, and alert to the most minute power shifts. But to her surprise, he treated her like an ally.

Watson expressed remorse when she asked him about the murder. Perhaps he felt repentant. Or perhaps, she could assume he had certain antisocial personality traits such as narcissism, manipulation, and deception.

When she was silent, it bothered him, and he leaned closer to the desk until Sylvia could smell a faint blend of industrial soap and sweat. "I want to show you who changed my life," he said. He unbuttoned the neck of his prison-issue shirt and worked his way down his sternum. The ceremonial care he took reminded Sylvia of a religious devotee. Slowly, he revealed his chest.

She stared at the tattoo over his heart: an intricate map of blue, red, green. The Virgin floated on a cloud. Red roses crowned her bowed and mantled head. Her hands were clasped in prayer. Her face—dark eyes, aquiline nose, rosebud mouth—was a study in ecstatic joy. The Madonna's ascension.

Sylvia had seen tattoos on inmates. They were part of the uniform, part of the antisocial mask. But this was no prison-issue job.

"Gideon made her."

"Gideon?"

"The artist."

"She's beautiful." As she stared at the tattoo of the Madonna, Sylvia felt Lucas clutch her face with greedy eyes.

He said, "You're like her."

She met his gaze. Light gleamed off the gold cap that covered his left canine. He took her silence for disapproval.

"I didn't mean to offend you." He sank down in the chair and buttoned his shirt.

"I'm not offended." Sylvia's expression remained neutral while she contemplated pieces of the puzzle that was Lucas Watson. Anxiety, fear, guardedness, alliance, devotion, the Madonna . . . She said, "I'm interested in hearing about your mother."

Lucas nodded as if that was the question he'd been waiting for. "I want you to know . . ." his voice dropped to a whisper and he placed his palm on his chest. "This is my mother's face on my heart." His words were laced with hidden meaning, a paranoid's secret language. His eyelids lowered like reptilian hoods, and he refused further comment.

Sylvia let the silence stretch between them. Finally, she said, "I'd like you to do a few drawings." She gave him two sheets of clean white paper, a number two pencil, and asked him to draw a kinetic family—each member in action. On her notepad, she recorded his intense concentration, his excellent visual motor function and pencil dexterity and line flow. Watson labored intently—tip of pencil to mouth then back to paper—and Sylvia's mind wandered for a moment. Since impulse control was a critical issue, she would administer the Bender, and then the Rorschach. Although she was curious what a complete test battery would reveal, there would not be time for the Thematic Apperception Test or the WAIS-R before the session ended. She heard Watson cough and glanced up in time to notice the twitch near his left eye.

He slid one sheet of paper across the desk. She saw three figures isolated to the sides of the page—one clearly patriarchal and dominant—in triangular relationship.

"My old man," Lucas murmured with an oddly perverse smile.

Sylvia knew that Duke Watson was the state senator for District 9, which included Bernalillo and Sandoval counties. The man had a flamboyant reputation as a progressive politician who managed to keep the Old Boys happy, even with the adverse publicity caused by having one son in the joint. Lucas had drawn his father with a violent, predatory mouth; he wielded a phallic cane. The other two figures in the drawing were smaller—a male and a female—but just as bizarre. They were stick figures with egg-shaped heads and detailed facial features. In each case, the eyes, mouth, and ears were overworked and prominent. Paranoid touches. Those were skeletal bodies supporting swollen thoughts.

"My brother Billy. And Queeny." He pointed to each.

From the files, Sylvia knew Watson's brother had a criminal record; his sister Queeny was adopted. She said, "In the drawing, what's your brother doing?" She wanted to probe further, to learn more about the relationship between Lucas and his brother and sister.

Lucas didn't answer her question. Instead, he leaned over the desk and peered intently into Sylvia's eyes. "I read the book you wrote. The one about inmates and their stories."

She had published a single volume two years earlier. It was based on inmate case studies, and it contained some of the most dramatic stories she'd heard from prisoners. Sylvia wasn't surprised he'd brought it up—inmates sometimes did. But why now? She had the strong feeling she'd passed some sort of test. She wanted to keep him talking. She said, "I'm flattered."

"Reading your book made me think you know my secrets." Lucas was growing more agitated by the second; his speech was now disjointed. "You know that guy who thought he remembered something wrong from when he was a kid?" Sylvia felt herself drawn into the drama of the moment. She realized she was holding her breath, afraid that the slightest rush of air might break the intimacy.

Instead of words, Lucas offered Sylvia a second drawing. It was a surprisingly accomplished pencil sketch of a woman's face.

Lucas balled up his fists and forced out the words, "My mother —that night, she was in front of the mirror—" He shook his head frantically. "She was so angry—so angry with me—"

He broke off when the alarm on Sylvia's digital watch emitted a high-pitched bleep.

The muscles around his mouth shivered, his hands flew upward involuntarily, and he shot up from the chair. He crumpled the drawing in his fist—"You fucking bitch! You're just like all the rest of them!" he screamed—and slammed it down on the desk.

Blood spattered Sylvia's cheek and hand; the metal edge of the desk had lacerated his wrist. She saw his face tighten into a mask of rage, and she sucked in her breath preparing to defend herself. Her eyes scanned the door, but the shadow on the other side of the window had disappeared; there was no sign of the C.O.

As Watson propelled himself forward, Sylvia's voice tore loose from her throat. "Lucas!"

He shuddered and backed away. Blood marked a thin trail on the floor.

Sylvia inhaled sharply. "Lucas. Sit down."

His breathing gradually slowed over the next thirty seconds as he regained control. He refocused, seemed to take in the room, and finally, Sylvia.

"I'm sorry," he whispered. He started to offer his hand then drew back in dismay as the blood on his arm registered. He released his fist, exposed the paper he held, and worked the ruined drawing flat against the desk. "Please . . . you've got to help me. They're going to take me out."

"Who?" Sylvia demanded as the door opened, and C.O. Anderson barged in.

Anderson said, "I had to handle a ten-code in the hall. You got a problem here?"

"He cut himself," Sylvia said quickly. Her own pulse was racing, the adrenaline rush had left her drained. "He needs medical attention."

"I'm fine," Watson protested, staying wide of the C.O. as he moved to the door.

Anderson glanced at his blood-soaked arm. "You need stitches." He looked at Sylvia. "Are you done? Can I take him to the nurse?"

"Of course," Sylvia said. She knew she sounded angry; the C.O. gave her a pained look.

When they were gone, the pressure in her head became so intense, she felt sick to her stomach. She stared down at the penciled drawing, torn and stained with blood. Suddenly, the lines came into focus and she realized she was looking at a drawing of her own face.

TWO

THE NOISE LEVEL in the gym was deafening: the screech of rubber soles on prefab flooring, explosions of conversation, and the heave of the H-VAC. Inmates—about thirty of them—stood around in tight groups. Most were arranged by color: brown, white, black.

Lucas Watson worked out alone allowing no one to trespass within striking distance. He had chosen this spot. Without turning his head, he could sense each man's position.

As he pumped iron, he seemed oblivious to the surgical dressing, now blood-soaked, that covered his right wrist. His jaw was rigid, and sweat gleamed off his face as he pumped one hundred and twenty pounds overhead. By the time he had finished the set, his entire body was drenched.

About ten feet away, a beefy Hispanic inmate named Roybal was using the incline press while an Anglo kid spotted for him. Roybal's bald head gleamed and his muscles bulged, swollen and purple. He said something to the kid who untied a delicately braided leather band—love necklace and crucifix—from the older man's throat. The kid placed the band on the floor next to the bench. Roybal began his next set.

Across the barnlike room, a two-on-one basketball game was underway, the players yelling at each other in Spanish. Three guards and a worker from Physical Plant Services stood on the sidelines examining a pothole in the gym floor.

A shrill whistle echoed throughout the gym. As Watson stood and lowered the barbell, *her* face filled his imagination: Sylvia.

He grimaced. The meeting hadn't gone right. He needed to make her understand about the others—that for him getting out was life or death. He knew she was different. She was the only one who could understand; that's why he'd chosen her.

So what had gone wrong? He tried to replay the scene, but the memories would not solidify. He caught only bits and pieces. The sound of her voice. The precise color of her hair and the way it curled into her brown chocolate eyes. The full curve of her breasts beneath the blouse. Just picturing her made him feel better. It would all be over soon. When he was out, he'd take her to dinner, and let her know what she meant to him.

Lucas imagined the restaurant. There would be a red rose against the stark white tablecloth. The waiter would wear a tuxedo, serve rare sirloin steak and baked potato . . . he would have to find out if she preferred champagne or wine.

The whistle sounded again and Roybal and the Anglo kid moved toward the door. Watson kept one eye on the exiting inmates, the other surreptitiously on the thin braided band that Roybal had left behind on the floor.

Roybal was one of them—a dangerous neighbor from CB-1—

and he had to be handled. Lucas had been looking for an opportunity to take care of Roybal. Maybe this was it.

He put the barbell on its mount, then moved casually across the gym floor to the necklace. When he knelt down to tighten his shoelaces, his fist closed tightly around the crucifix. He felt the cool and satisfying strength of silver and turquoise. Fist to mouth, he quickly bit the crucifix from the band, slid it under his shirt, and found the opening of his leather pouch. With two fingers he tucked the cross away, now a part of his personal collection. Still keeping a distance between himself and the others, Watson was the last inmate to leave the gym. He stepped out into the east yard and harsh sunlight.

The metal door clanged shut behind Lucas, and C.O. Anderson moved deeper into the shadows of the building. Anderson's eyes had contracted to a squint, his mouth drooped open very slightly. He watched Lucas cross the brown stubble field toward Main's cell blocks, and he knew the bitter taste in his mouth must be hate.

—

THE FEMALE C.O. didn't speak to Lucas Watson as the metal gate rolled open and he entered cell block one. She held her breath until he'd gone—not because he smelled—because something about him made her fear contamination.

None of the men in the block acknowledged his existence as he passed their cells, but he felt their hyena eyes on his skin when he climbed the stairs.

He reached the second tier and looked down over the rail; all eyes veered away. He entered his cell, closed the door, and squatted on his bed.

His fingers caressed Roybal's silver crucifix as he removed it from his pouch. The man lived just two cribs down the row. Lucas knew Roybal would begin to watch him with growing fear. Justifiable fear.

Lucas did not fuck around with his enemies.

Roybal and the others understood that. They'd seen what happened to inmate Devane when he'd challenged Watson's power.

Burly, robust Boy Devane had been transferred from Cruces with a bug up his ass. Six months later, Devane was nothing but a sack of shit and bones. The official lie was cancer. Lucas liked that . . . his work being compared to cancer.

He began his whispered chant of clipped sounds, grunts, and the name Roybal, Roybal, Roybal . . . His eyelids fluttered as he visualized rats devouring Roybal's intestines. Watson's fingers tightened around the cross as he felt the presence of his protector, the Madonna. As long as he had his pouch, she would keep him safe until Sylvia freed him from this torture.

Time evaporated behind his throbbing chant—*"Rat's going to eat his way out your asshole, Roybal"*—and he ignored the increasingly vocal protest along the block, until something metal slammed against his cell door. He heard the whispered threat—the disembodied words—through the grill, "You better stop that evil shit, man."

The speaker hid his face, but Lucas knew the voice belonged to Anderson. He was a hack now, but Lucas remembered when Anderson's father used to work for Duke. Did odd jobs, hauled trash, stuck his hand down the toilet, unclogged a pipe. Menial labor. Anderson had been afraid of Lucas twenty years ago. Now they were all afraid of him; they were all out to get him.

"Fuck you," Watson hissed. He barely heard Anderson's reply.

"In your face, Lucas . . . we'll parole you in a box."

—

WEDNESDAY DAWNED CLEAR and cold. Thick icicles fringed the roof and draped the windows. The scent of neighboring woodstoves lingered on the air. Sylvia woke with the first light of morning. There was only a fleeting sleep to leave behind, and dreams, none remembered.

Rocko, her runty, wirehaired terrier, eased himself gingerly off the king-size bed and followed Sylvia down the hallway that bisected the house. He'd been named for Johnny Rocko, the gangster who always wanted more in the movie *Key Largo*. Sylvia thought her dog resembled Edward G. Robinson, the actor who had played Johnny Rocko. Both man and dog were short, stout, and dark. Each had a gravelly voice and a comical sexiness. The terrier stayed close to her heels, and she spoke to him as she walked. "How's it going, big guy?"

On Tuesdays and Thursdays, her days were scheduled around forty-five minute sessions with her clients. Wednesday was a day when she could often work at home preparing for court cases or completing paperwork.

She showered and dressed and applied light makeup. Then she made the mental shift from her private life to work.

In the small room that served as her study, she adjusted the tensor lamp until the light shone directly on the papers and books covering her desk. Sylvia moved aside three volumes of the *Journal of Forensic Psychology* and a half-finished letter to her mother. She picked up the well-worn copy of Allison, Blatt, and Zimet's *Interpretation of Psychological Tests* and opened the cover to see "Malcolm Treisman, 1969" scrawled in fine black ink. She placed the book on the shelf next to *Attached to Violence: A Study of Attachment Pathologies in Adult Inmates*. Author: Sylvia Strange, Ph.D.

Over a cup of coffee, she again found herself thinking of Malcolm and their impassioned discussions, fights really, that lasted late into the night. He'd been a pit bull when it came to his theories.

"The madness smorgasbord. Take your choice—organized or very, very messy. Either way, they're more persistent than we are. The truly evil ones do a much better job of hiding behind the mask of sanity." The memory of his voice was as clear as if he stood again in her office wagging an admonishing finger, spouting his theory of evil, endlessly fascinated with the deviant mind.

Sylvia shared that obsession with deviance and evil. She'd stood at the edge of the light; faced enough of her own demons to know the border between normal and deviant was razor thin in places.

While he ranted, Malcolm would pace like an obnoxious caged bear. He had his uniform—a favorite leather jacket, faded jeans, and high-tops—and his arsenal of questions. He took his professorial stance. "Is Kernberg right when he structures malignant narcissism with aggression? Are those patients untreatable?"

"Don't be pompous, Malcolm."

But he'd never back down. "Don't change the subject. Tell me which case studies you'd choose."

"They choose me."

"That's right, Sylvie and her inmates. Only thirty-four, and she has a dark island to keep her fascinated."

She withdrew from the memory. Lately, she'd been losing herself too easily—in the past, in unwelcome dreams, and in her work. It scared her a little, this ability to detach and act by rote.

At ten o'clock, she opened the file on Lucas Watson; she had an in-depth social history, her notes, nothing recent on the Rorschach or the WAIS-R. The Albuquerque firm had already faxed the scores of the MMPI-2. She had just enough information to complete an evaluation for Burnett, but he wasn't going to like it. She closed the folder, deciding to avoid work a bit longer.

She pulled on sweatpants, jacket, wool hat, and hiking boots. Shading her eyes from the glare, she stepped from the warmth of the house into bitter cold. The wind slapped her face as she caught the trail that angled steeply up the saw-back ridge. She'd traveled three hundred yards when Rocko trotted past and took the lead. They walked eagerly, woman and dog, covering ground until Sylvia was breathing almost as hard as Rocko. The icy air tore into her throat and lungs.

From the ridge top, the village of La Cieneguilla spread out below like a board game. Great cottonwoods lined the shallow river. A rancher's windmill stood guard over miniature goats, cows, and horses. The adobe bricks of the ruined colonial church were crumbled, returning to the earth. Sylvia's own house was clearly visible, almost within reach, and at the same time a thousand miles away.

This was a scene she remembered from her childhood—her father standing by her side as he explained the historic significance of the valley. He'd been a plain man, skin weathered by desert and ocean, bones too large for his skin. He stood straighter whenever he told her stories about the land, this place. A small settlement of Spanish families had arrived more than two hundred years ago. The windmill was built at the turn of the century. The original walls of the graceful white adobe—their home—had sheltered weary stagecoach travelers on the old spur trail. Ironically, the red bricks that lined the adobe's long, shady portal had been part of New Mexico's original penitentiary, built in 1885 near the railroad tracks in Santa Fe. When the old pen was torn down in the late 1950s, the used bricks had been abandoned; Sylvia's father had collected several truckloads.

Danny Strange had always loved to work with his hands. The military didn't change that. Building, planting, tending were all part of his basic makeup. When he returned from a tour of duty in Southeast Asia—something rarely spoken of—he seemed to need to dig his fingers into earth. Sometimes Sylvia found him kneeling that way, as if he were holding on. She had been only three when he left, six when he came home. But she knew his eyes were different; they mirrored everything he'd seen.

For the next seven years, her father's spirit had wasted away until he finally disappeared. Absolutely, without a trace. Sylvia had never stopped searching for answers to the questions her father left behind.

—

SHE COMPLETED MOST of Watson's evaluation by late afternoon, ran a hot bath, and poured a tablespoon of olive oil beneath the spigot. The yellow globules shivered like mercury. She set a half glass of Merlot on the edge of the tub and lowered herself under scalding water until only her nose, nipples, and knees were exposed to cooler air. Her skin flushed pink, and she felt drugged by the wet heat.

But she couldn't quite let go. Something she'd seen—or more precisely, something she hadn't seen in Watson's file—kept nagging at her. She felt certain that Lucas had suffered some type of childhood trauma in the years that led up to his mother's violent death. Sexual abuse? Severe physical abuse? Abuse was such a common theme among inmates, you could almost consider it a given. But there was no evidence of it in Lucas Watson's file. Not even a hint in the medical or school records. In fact, according to his files, Lucas had a *Leave It to Beaver* childhood. Except for suicide, all very nice and normal. As if someone had erased even the slightest stain on the past.

She finished her wine. At some point, Rocko's urgent bark broke the stillness—probably a coyote on the prowl—but he quieted after Sylvia called to him. She never saw the stranger's face at the bathroom window. She didn't feel his eyes. Minutes evaporated and she closed her eyes, almost easing into sleep.

It took her a moment to register the knock at the front door. The bathroom was dimly lit. She scraped her hand against tile when she sat up abruptly in the tub.

Rocko growled from the hallway, and Sylvia left a quick trail of water on the Saltillo tile floor as she draped a robe around her body and pulled it tight. From the living-room window she could see the driveway and a dark blue van parked directly behind her Volvo. She must have been dozing when the van drove up. She considered ignoring the intrusion until she caught sight of its source. Even in late afternoon half-light, she could see a man in a florist's cap, a bouquet of long-stemmed roses clutched in one arm. Shit. She knew who sent roses.

She let the window louvers snap back into place and walked reluctantly to the front door. On the third try, the dead bolt key finally turned. She had intended to replace the lock last week. Since Malcolm's funeral, the smallest tasks had become impossible to accomplish.

She opened the door a few inches, leaving the safety chain in place, and Rocko strained to fit through the crack. When he was unsuccessful, he made a beeline for the dog door in the kitchen.

The young man shifted crimson roses aside and peered down at a list on a clipboard. His face was hidden behind black sunglasses, a four-day beard, and a baseball hat with the Marcy Florist logo.

"You've got the wrong house," Sylvia said. Her flannel robe felt damp and cold against bare skin. She wished she'd thrown on clothes before answering the door.

"Don't think so." The delivery man turned his gaze on Rocko as the terrier sprinted around the side of the house.

Sylvia studied his profile; even with the glasses he looked vaguely familiar.

Rocko lunged at black boots while the man held out the bouquet like a peace offering. "Sylvia? That's the name on the order. Sylvia Strange."

Roses had to be Herb Burnett. He'd been after her for years—he had even asked her out in high school—and he never seemed discouraged when she said no. Sylvia sighed as she slid the chain off the catch and opened the door far enough to accept the flowers. A white envelope fluttered to the ground. When the man reached to catch it, Rocko nipped his hand.

"Oops, sorry." Sylvia pulled the terrier back by the collar.

The delivery man offered her the envelope pressed between two fingers, then ducked his chin so brown eyes gazed over the sunglasses. His lips pulled into a smile. "You have a nice afternoon, pretty lady."

"Hold on, let me get my purse," Sylvia said.

He was already halfway down the drive. "Don't worry about it."

Sylvia heard the van pulling away as she tore open the envelope. One sentence had been carefully printed on a plain white card—*Some things are just meant to be.* No signature. Sylvia set the roses on the kitchen counter. Was Herb being cryptic, hackneyed, or both? Jesus, his timing was bad; roses made her think of funerals. She didn't bother to put the stems in water. Instead, she tossed the bouquet on the kitchen counter, flicked through the Rolodex, and dialed. The receptionist asked her to hold and it was three or four seconds before she heard the familiar nasal voice.

"Sylvia? I was just thinking about you."

Sylvia stared at the roses, phrasing her first question, but Herb filled the silence.

"Hey, you got something for me?"

"I'll have Lucas Watson's evaluation ready tomorrow. I'll drop by your office so we can go over it. Eleven all right?"

"Better yet, meet me for lunch at the SantaCafé, twelve-thirty."

"I can make it at twelve-forty-five. But Herb, let's get one thing straight."

"What's that?" His voice was careful.

" 'Some things are just meant to be' . . . it's inappropriate."

Herb was silent for several moments. "Am I missing something here?"

Sylvia sighed. "I'll be very clear. I don't feel comfortable with you sending me flowers. As far as I'm concerned, our relationship is strictly professional."

When he didn't respond, it dawned on Sylvia that he might have no idea what she was talking about. "Didn't you send me a dozen roses?"

"Well, hey, you should know me better than that," Herb sputtered. "I don't send flowers, I write love letters. Remember that one in the ninth grade?"

Sylvia bit her lip; she was embarrassed, but more than that, she felt fear spreading out from her abdomen. She closed her eyes and retrieved the face of the delivery man from her memory—his smile, his eyes.

"Hey, maybe it was your ex-husband. I'll never forgive you for marrying someone else."

"I'll talk to you tomorrow, Herb. Sorry for the misunderstanding."

She hung up the phone, scanned the phone book, and dialed

again. Her pulse was racing. A woman answered after two rings, "Marcy Florists."

"I just received an arrangement, a dozen roses, and I'd like to know who sent them." Sylvia rattled off her name and route number.

"Hold on a sec and I'll check."

Sylvia drummed her palm against the counter while the woman searched her records. After more than a minute, she came back on the line.

"Jerry said he didn't deliver any roses out your way. Are you there?"

"I'm here," Sylvia said. "What kind of truck does your driver use?" She pictured the blue van parked in her driveway.

"Ummm, a white van with red writing on the side. Is there a problem, miss?"

"No, sorry to bother you." There was a definite problem, but nothing the florist shop could solve.

The roses were still wrapped in their paper, stem tips trapped in plastic vials. Sylvia forced herself to pick them up, and a sharp thorn cut through the paper and stabbed her finger. She sucked at the wound.

Standing in the brightly lit kitchen, she fought the nervous edge in her stomach, then snapped off the overhead light. She slid her hand along the smooth wall, and felt the switch that controlled the outdoor flood. Everything flashed into view—the salt cedar lurched and lashed at the wind, tarantella shadows danced against the coyote fence—but all she saw was the unbidden image of a tattoo of the Virgin.

THREE

"You're missing a goddamn finger?" Rosie Sanchez sat up in bed and hit her head on the walnut headboard. *"¡Qué pendejo!"* she murmured, not quite free of the receiver's audio range. "Is Main under lockdown? I'll be right there."

She hung up the phone and slid her short legs off the bed. Her husband, Ray, had already donned his plaid bathrobe, and he was searching for his slippers. His wife had held the job of penitentiary investigator for more than seven years. The stress had done in her predecessors, but she seemed to thrive under pressure. Ray had never met anyone who loved her job as much.

In the kitchen he made instant coffee while Rosie, hastily

dressed in a beige suit, nylons, and heels, sat impatiently at the table tracing the red-check design on the tablecloth.

"Would you believe this?" she mumbled. "Somebody stole a finger—chopped it off a hand!" She gazed wide-eyed at her husband as if she didn't believe it herself.

Ray raised his eyebrows, "I believe it." He poured boiling water into two mugs of coffee and added sugar to one, milk to the other. By now, he was used to his wife's middle-of-the-night crises. There was never any doubt that Ray would always calmly stand beside her. He stirred both cups and handed Rosie the mug that said, I'M THE BOSS!

"I don't need this." Rosie brought the edge of her hand against the table in a karate chop. "I do not need Angel Tapia being cut up alive like fresh meat."

"Who's fresh meat?" a new voice asked.

Rosie looked up and saw their sixteen-year-old son, Tomás, standing in the doorway. His dark hair stood out from his head, his eyelids drooped heavily from interrupted sleep.

"Look who's sleepwalking," Ray smiled.

Rosie clucked her tongue, "Ay, hijito, I'm sorry we woke you. Go back to bed."

"I want to know who's fresh meat."

"I was just talking about work, Tomás. It's a gang-related thing, a knifing."

"Harsh," came the sleepy reply before Tomás padded on bare feet back to his bedroom.

Ray pulled two pieces of raisin toast from the toaster oven and set them on a blue flowered saucer. He selected marmalade from several jars of jam on the refrigerator shelf, put out a butter knife, and waited for his wife to eat.

She took a small bite, pushed the plate away, and kept her voice low. "The 1980 riot—when I started in 1987, they were still talking about it like it was yesterday. Not so much the murders, or the rapes, but the missing bodies, the missing parts." She brushed crumbs from her lips before continuing. "An arm here, a foot there. If it starts all over again . . ." She curled a strand of frosted hair around her thumb. She looked up at Ray with her dark, glamorous eyes.

"Most people choose a normal occupation, Rosita." Ray felt his muscles contract, caught himself, and shrugged. She was tough. Every day she did a job most people wouldn't touch. Bloody shanks, syringes, and faded balloons filled with contraband—they were all part of a day's work. She had Polaroid snapshots of the carnage. Somehow, she was able to tolerate and process daily encounters with the worst side of human nature. Ray had long since given up trying to understand that side of Rosie. He just loved her. Ray clutched his hands together, unconscious of the gesture.

—

THE PNM INVESTIGATIONS office was overheated and smelled musty. Rosie sighed; it was only 9 A.M. and already she'd been at work for six hours. She took off her reading glasses and stared at the tape recorder. Inmate injuries were commonplace; but this unauthorized "amputation" had occurred in the penitentiary hospital where Angel Tapia had been quarantined for measles. Definitely not routine. She pressed rewind on the tape and let it run for fifteen seconds. The interview with penitentiary nurse LaRue had gone reasonably well considering the woman had been on duty for more than thirty hours. When she let up on the rewind button, her own recorded voice filled the office.

"How strong would someone have to be to cut off a finger?"

LaRue coughed on tape. "Scissors are sharp. You could do it."

There was a long pause and the faint inner workings of the worn recorder were audible before LaRue continued. "He used a rubber ring as a tourniquet. He left it on the stump and injected a digital block before cutting. That's what was in the hypo in the trash. You saw the scissors, wiped clean."

"We're talking about someone with medical expertise," Rosie said.

"Anyone who's worked outside as an E.M.T. could handle it."

There was a light tap on the door, and then a young woman entered, her tanned arms stacked with folders and logs. "Here's the stuff you asked for," she said as she let herself out again.

Rosie pulled a list off the top and scanned names—inmates who had worked in the hospital during the past six months—at least a dozen.

The tape was still running. Sanchez: "Can you account for the missing dosage?"

She found the date she wanted in the stack of log books and thumbed slowly through the pages.

LaRue: "Not absolutely."

The tension roller gear on the tape cassette was tight, and the machine whined rhythmically under Rosie's voice. "So the drugs could easily have been collected over time?"

She stopped the tape. She had just come upon a second list, the last group of patients seen at the pen hospital before Angel Tapia's pinkie was severed from his right hand. One name had appeared on both lists: Lucas Watson. Just this morning, she'd seen an incident report . . . She found it again tucked under a thick notebook.

It had been filed by C.O. Jeff Anderson. Yesterday.

> Inmate Lucas Watson cut his wrist during the course of a meeting with
> a psychologist. I did not witness the incident with Dr. Strange, but I took
> the inmate to the penitentiary hospital where he was given five stitches.

Dr. Sylvia Strange. Rosie chewed on the corner of her lower lip. Her friendship with Sylvia dated back to that scorching summer's day when the thirteen-year-old *gringa* tried to talk her way out of a fight with a *pachuca*. The *pachuca* happened to be Rosie's younger sister. Sylvia had ended up with a nasty shiner and a bloody nose. She still had a way of getting in the middle of trouble.

Rosie fingered C.O. Anderson's incident report, then she picked up the phone and dialed a number from memory. She needed to talk to someone who specialized in *crazies*: her longtime *gringa* friend.

"I was just walking out the door." Sylvia sounded tired.

"I need a favor. Can you meet with me this afternoon?"

"After three-thirty. What's this about?"

Rosie paused. The guard tower was visible through thick, dusty windows. The smell of sewage from the prison's wastewater treatment plant wafted through the seams of plaster and glass. Someone whistled from the courtyard below. "You evaluated Lucas Watson?"

"Sure." After a very brief pause Sylvia sighed. "Don't try to be coy, Rosie. What's going on?"

"A delicate investigation," Rosie said, screwing up her face as she spoke.

"The evaluation—"

"I know," Rosie interrupted. "It's privileged information."

"I'll see you in your office at four."

Before leaving for the meeting with the deputy warden, Rosie fast-forwarded the tape for several minutes until she found the last of the interview.

"What about the stitches?" Rosie didn't like the brittle pitch of her voice on tape.

"He's no plastic surgeon, but he did the job. He had to pull the skin back, gouge the bone, pull the flap back over, and then stitch."

Rustling sounds of paper and fabric; LaRue sneezed.

"Who do you think did this?" Rosie had asked.

LaRue had stared at the overexposed shot of Angel Tapia's right hand with thumb, three fingers, and a bloody stump where his pinkie should have been.

Rosie Sanchez pressed stop on the tape recorder. Silence filled the room until the distant sounds of conversation and ringing phones intruded from beyond the barred windows and the closed door. She sifted through the file folder again, found an eight-by-ten color photograph—the second photo that LaRue had seen.

She pressed play, and her voice asked another question of the room.

"There's no way this is the work of the same person who severed Angel's finger?" Rosie knew the logical answer but needed to hear someone else say it.

LaRue had glanced away from the image. She'd read the attorney general's Riot Report, and she'd seen some photos of the aftermath. She was a nurse; still, she had to force herself to stare at the picture of a human torso, naked, charred, and severed. "I wouldn't think so. This guy was cut in half with a blowtorch, wasn't he?"

—

It was 12:40 when Sylvia walked into the large courtyard of the SantaCafé. A mosaic of yellow leaves peeked through snow patches. The branches of the great cottonwood tree were bare and gnarled. Inside, the elegant hostess led the way to a table in the back room next to the fireplace. Sylvia slid out of her coat and warmed her palms against the cast iron grate. Her hands were too sturdy for her slender wrists, fingernails squared off close to the fingertips, palms roughened by callouses: working hands. At the moment they were busy, muscles tense. During the drive over, she had rehearsed her questions for Herb. He could be a pain in the ass, but he wasn't stupid; he'd known that Lucas Watson was a psychological disaster area when he asked her to do the evaluation.

"Good news, Sylvia! Thanks to you and me, we got that acquittal on Allmoy."

"Hello, Herb." Sylvia selected the chair that faced the center of the room and sat. She'd evaluated Herb's client, Joseph Allmoy, a man accused of murder. It had been clear that post-traumatic stress disorder factored into the equation—four months before the murder Allmoy had himself been brutally assaulted and held hostage during a robbery. His rage had been internalized until it erupted during an argument with a neighbor. The day after Malcolm's funeral, Sylvia had appeared in court as expert witness for the defense.

She looked up to see Herb offering her a big smile and a red rose. She drew back when he brushed the bud along her cheek.

"Enough with the roses." Sylvia raised both palms to Herb impatiently and shook her head; the man just didn't get it. She turned to the waiter who was hovering at their elbows. "Coffee, please. Black."

"Something from the bar, Mr. Burnett?" The waiter spoke clearly, occasionally remembering his British accent. Like most waiters at Santa Fe's trendiest restaurants, he was young, beautiful, androgynous.

"Why not?" Herb flashed Sylvia a boyish smile. "Absolut with a twist and a splash of soda. Oh, and give this rose to the hostess with my compliments."

When they were alone, Sylvia leaned back in her chair and said, "I'm glad to hear about Allmoy's acquittal."

"Me, too. I didn't have the old smoking gun, but I did have a sensational expert witness. Keep this up and you're a shoo-in with Kove and Casias."

How the hell did Herb know about the job offer? Sylvia had just completed a laborious interview process with the firm whose psychologists held the state's forensic contract. She was in the first stages of contractual negotiation with the firm; an offer would be a definite notch in Sylvia's professional belt.

"It's still a small town," Herb said with a grin. "And you're still the best thing in it."

Sylvia shrugged off the clumsy compliment, crossed her arms, and looked expectantly at Herb.

For a moment, his expression settled into seriousness, longing, and his eyes searched Sylvia's face. Beneath their deep mahogany surface, her irises were flecked with warm gold. The small scar near her left eye was a shade lighter than her skin. Her lips were parted just enough to reveal teeth a little bit crooked. He had a sudden urge to kiss her.

Instead, he said, "You always look terrific." But he read her impatience and switched gears with a question. "What's eating you?"

"Tell me about Lucas Watson."

"What's to tell? You're the shrink."

"How long has he been your client?"

When he frowned, Herb's forehead creased like linen and he peered out from under a mono-brow. "Duke Watson is my client, has been for years. The governor just appointed him chairman of the Interim Tax Committee." Herb's voice softened, and he eyed Sylvia thoughtfully. "Are you aware of that?"

Sylvia absorbed the information: Duke Watson now held a position of influence over every commercial enterprise in the state. Perfect for a man who had a reputation as a rabid control freak. Even better if the governor wanted to pass the torch on to him in the next election.

Herb bit into a bread stick and crumbs fluttered into his water glass. "I took Lucas as a client with the manslaughter trial, three years ago, as a favor to the old man."

"I read Malcolm's evaluation."

"Yeah, but the judge wouldn't admit the expert testimony." Herb grinned. "Judge Mahoney. The honorable fartbag thinks you guys are nuts."

"Has Lucas had a full psych battery since the trial?"

Herb eyed Sylvia silently while a busboy delivered vodka and coffee. When he was gone, Herb said, "Are you going to tell me what's going on?"

"Just one more question." Sylvia took a sip of coffee. "Why did you wait until the last minute to call me?"

"Hold your horses, what are we talking here?"

"You knew that the parole hearing was coming up."

"Hell, 'Late' is my middle name."

Sylvia's expression hardened. "Did you think I might do a lousy job because I've been distracted by Malcolm's death?"

"Oh, come on, Sylvia, I knew you'd do a great job."

"Herb, don't bullshit me."

"Shall I take your order?"

Herb spit a tiny spray of vodka from his lips. He turned to face the flustered waiter. "Surprise me, pal. I'll take the chef special, whatever, the daily."

"A green salad," Sylvia said.

The decibel level in the restaurant had gone up as more customers streamed in for lunch. Tables were clustered in small rooms of what had once been a Territorial hacienda. Now, the old well shaft was covered with a sheet of thick Plexiglas set in the floor of the bar, and plates arranged with chile wonton and cilantro squab tacos were served from the stainless steel kitchen.

Using crayons supplied by the restaurant, Herb began doodling notes to himself on the white paper tablecover.

Sylvia spread her fingers on the table. "Your client has some major problems."

Herb snickered. "You know how guys in the joint are, Sylvia. Lucas has done his time and he deserves a break." He turned to stare as a young woman in a knit dress walked toward the bar. "If you want, you can talk to my paralegal. He's dealt with Lucas on most of the prep for the hearing."

Sylvia pulled a manila folder from her briefcase, and set it on the edge of the table. "Here's the evaluation."

"Great."

Sylvia spoke slowly. "There are no signs of organicity or schizophrenia or a schizophreniform disorder, and, apparently, there are no auditory or visual hallucinations."

"Hey, that's good, isn't it?"

"But the MMPI indicates that Lucas suffers from persistent, nonbizarre delusions—somatic, grandiose. There's also a high degree of paranoia . . . an inability to relate to others—suspicious, defensive, that sort of thing. I'm guessing a paranoid personality or delusional disorder. Mix that with a good dose of antisocial traits and you've got a potent combination."

"That sounds like everybody in the joint." Herb thrust his napkin on the table.

"I want Lucas Watson transferred to the psych unit in Los Lunas. The man needs help. I intend to collect more data, spend more time with him—then I can come up with a valid treatment plan. I'll do a complete test battery, comprehensive physical and mental—"

"We don't have time." Herb tapped his index finger against the cocktail glass. "Let's keep it simple. After he's out, then maybe Lucas can get some counseling." He winked.

Sylvia shook her head. "Lucas is a time bomb, and there's no telling when he'll explode. I'm recommending a psych transfer, not parole."

"A transfer!" A purple crayon disappeared into Herb's lap.

"He's been incarcerated for three years. We're talking an extremely stressful environment. His scores have deteriorated. A certain amount of paranoia is normal for inmates, but Watson's scores aren't even close," Sylvia said.

"I think *you're* the one who's paranoid," Herb said. "You spent a few hours with my client and you got spooked."

Sylvia pressed one hand on the folder. "If I'd never met Lucas, if I'd worked completely from the MMPI, my recommendations wouldn't change. Any professional in my field would come to the same conclusions. Raw scores aren't subjective."

"Bullshit. He's no more crazy than any of those guys."

She snapped a fork against the table. "Lucas thinks everyone's trying to kill him."

Herb shut down. "You're making a mistake."

Sylvia didn't answer.

He took a deep breath and maneuvered his jaw like a man who had just taken a punch. "It's ironic . . . Lucas was convicted because he wasn't crazy. Now you're telling me he's too crazy to make parole."

"Listen, Herb, during the evaluation, the man flipped out, sliced his wrist, and almost attacked me." Sylvia stood. "My evaluation is clear; Lucas needs help. If you have questions, call me at my office. But whatever you do, I recommend you get a complete battery on Lucas."

As Sylvia stood, the waiter delivered Herb's second Absolut on a tray. She reached for the glass, drank, set it down half-empty in front of the lawyer, and walked away.

—

Rosie followed Angel Tapia's gurney down the hall, her left hand grasping the cold metal. Now that his fever had broken, Angel was on his way to protective custody at North Facility, a five-minute trip from Main by van. It was a question of safety—in case whoever had amputated his finger decided to cut off another one— and a new environment seemed like the healthy choice.

She glanced down at the thick bandage covering Tapia's hand. His naturally tawny skin—now covered with peppery red spots— had gone gray. His eyes were protruding black marbles.

"Angel, just try to remember for me. If you close your eyes, think back."

"Nada," Angel whispered.

"¿Tiene miedo?"

"I don't remember."

Rosie sighed and touched his shoulder. "Was it a rival?" she asked quietly. Angel wasn't a hard-core gang member, but if he'd gotten in between something, Rosie knew he'd never break his silence.

"I'm sick," he said.

Actually, Angel's "contagious" quarantine for measles was over as of today; he was no longer considered dangerous to others, but Rosie didn't think he would appreciate the irony of the situation.

The young nurse pushing the gurney from behind mumbled a complaint about inmates and their overactive imaginations. Angel Tapia tried to raise his head and then groaned with the effort.

He ran his coated tongue over chapped lips and whispered, *"El chacal,"* his voice so faint Rosie had to lower her head and hold her hair off his face.

They had reached the end of the hallway and the door to the medical sally port. The nurse stepped away from the gurney and stared through the thick square of window cut into the exit.

"What, Angel?" Rosie prodded gently. "I couldn't hear you."

"El chacal."

Rosie squinted in concentration. *"¿Qué? ¿Chacal?* You saw a jackal?"

Angel shook his head and pressed his cheek with his good hand. His fingers moved to his forehead, and he tried to force a smile. *"Sueños* . . . dreams, but it seemed so real." He held up his bandaged paw.

The door opened, and two C.O.s moved Angel's gurney down a ramp to a waiting van. Rosie watched the double doors slam on the vehicle when Angel was safely stowed away. As she turned and walked toward the stairs, she thought, it ain't over 'til the fat lady sings. Too bad there weren't any fat ladies doing time in Main.

—

THE METAL SCRAPED and groaned and Sylvia jumped as the interior gate in Main's corridor slid open.

"Hey, Robot, how's it going?" Sylvia smiled at the balding, middle-aged man. Like so many inmates, Emilio Rodriguez had earned a special name in the joint; among the prison population, it was more real than the one on his birth certificate. In his case, the moniker resulted naturally from his mechanical, dronelike gait, and his reputation as a cold-blooded killer.

"Hey, Dr. Strange. It's going. How about yourself?" Robot waved his dust rag.

Sylvia raised an eyebrow and smiled. For Robot, the greeting was effusive; he was clearly pleased about something. "I'm all right."

She braced for the heavy clang of the metal gate as it snapped shut behind her. She'd interviewed Robot several times, by court order, and she liked him—although she'd never turn her back on the man. He had an eighth-grade education, the median for inmates, but he was quick, and he had a sense of humor. He was also an acknowledged kleptomaniac. After one session, he'd actually escaped with her reading glasses; she still didn't know how he'd managed that trick.

"Don't leave that necklace lying around," Robot said with a wink.

"If I lose it, I'll know where to find it. See you later, Robot." Sylvia laughed. She was through the second metal gate and starting up the stairs when she almost collided with Rosie Sanchez hurrying from the bisecting hallway.

"Hey," Sylvia said. "Sorry I'm late, but I couldn't find a locksmith who actually kept business hours."

Rosie smiled. "Your timing is perfect. Why a locksmith?"

"A sticky dead bolt at the house."

The two women took the stairs together; Sylvia slowed her stride to match the shorter step of Sanchez. Neither spoke until they reached Rosie's office.

"Coffee?" Rosie asked.

"Sure."

Rosie was petite, only topping five feet by an inch or so, but stiletto heels added another three inches. Bottled copper strands were artfully woven into a thick head of dark-brown tresses.

She poured two cups of viscous fluid from Mr. Coffee, opened two packets of Cremora, and dropped one into each cup. "I know you take it black, but this is industrial strength."

The heat in the office was off and the temperature had dropped a good ten degrees. Rosie flipped on lights, removed a notebook from a square vinyl chair, and motioned for Sylvia to sit. At almost the same instant, the phone rang.

Rosie perched on the metal desk and cupped the receiver to her ear. "Rosie Sanchez." Immediately, she recognized the voice on the end of the line: Matt England. "Hey, kiddo, I was hoping you'd ring me back." She'd known England since he moved to New Mexico from Oklahoma eighteen years ago. "You guys at state police hate pen business, but I need your help." She crossed her legs, scribbled Matt's name on a Post-it, and held it out to Sylvia with an apologetic shrug.

Sylvia scowled as the name returned a striking, weathered face to memory. Matt England had testified for the prosecuting attorney during a controversial murder trial. Malcolm had testified for the defense as an expert witness. England had made no effort to mask his dislike and distrust of psychologists during the trial. It was the typical bias of law enforcement: psychologists are psychos, just like their clients. Long after the defense won, England continued to give Malcolm the cold shoulder. More recently, England was a state's witness during the Allmoy trial. Once again, he had appeared for the prosecution while Sylvia worked defense.

Rosie's suddenly edgy tone brought Sylvia back from her thoughts.

Rosie said, "Matt, you were around during the riot. We've had an incident—maybe more than one—with a missing body part." Now Rosie had his full professional attention. "You'll love this, but I can't talk now, so I'm going to have a packet delivered to your office." Rosie shot Sylvia a quizzical glance. "I promise I'll get back to you, Matthew," she said as she hung up. "Why were you making such a face? Do you know Matt?"

"We were on opposite sides of the fence in court."

"Aha," Rosie tipped her dark eyebrows. "Your gain, his loss." She shrugged. "Sorry about the interruption."

"What's this about a body part?"

"I'm getting to that." In one easy motion Rosie was off the desk, sinking into the chair. "Since we're both dealing with issues of confidentiality, I'll ask you something generic. What kind of guy gets his rocks off cutting up bodies?"

"Dead bodies, I hope?"

"Actually, no."

Sylvia frowned. "You want a profile of a Mr. X who dissects living victims?"

"Dead and living," Rosie interrupted. "I don't know if he just preys on the living, if he just scavenges, or if he kills, too."

Sylvia raised her eyebrows. "Come on, Rosie, you can do better than that."

"Last night, we had some unscheduled surgery—an inmate's finger was removed without his consent."

Sylvia eased back against the chair. "Well, shit," she said softly. "I guess the surgeon wasn't Dr. Kildare?"

"This thing may go back as far as the riot," Rosie shrugged. "Arms and legs disappeared, not to mention entire bodies. There were murders that were never pinned on anyone." It took her ten seconds to continue. "About a year ago, an inmate lost most of his nose in a gang fight. We figured it was kept as a trophy by his rivals. I still think it was. But then a hand was cut off in a metal shop accident three months ago. When the doc wanted to stitch it back on, it never turned up." Rosie swiveled in her chair and stared out at bleak daylight through wire grid. "The natives are getting restless; all of our facilities are pushing their legal capacity, and we've got inmates sleeping in the dayrooms. If we don't find the bad guy soon, we may have another riot."

"Are you sure it's an inmate? Could it be a C.O.?"

Rosie looked askance. "That's possible."

"Could it just be a gang revenge thing?"

"That's very possible, but, for the moment, let's assume we've got a weirdo on our hands."

"In that case . . . a paranoid schizophrenic, a dissociative disorder, a borderline personality, any antisocial type with a game plan—take your pick." Sylvia spread her fingers, palms up. "Without more to go on, a profile would be as useful as a Ouija board. On second thought, a Ouija board would be better." She tipped her head. "Maybe you've got an anthropophagite on your hands."

"Anthro what?"

"A cannibal. Albert Fish—you remember *The* Cannibal—allegedly ate fifteen children. He killed them, cut them up, and one he even stewed with carrots and onions."

"You're having fun." Rosie stuck out her tongue and silently gagged.

Sylvia touched her fingertips together, lost in thought. "There are rumors all over China that the bodies of 'cultural enemies' were devoured in remote villages, and the Khmer Rouge—well, you get the picture."

Rosie pulled open her drawer, found an open package of sun-flower seeds, and popped a handful in her mouth. She said, "Tell me more."

Sylvia continued, "In various cultures, primitive man probably consumed the body of an alien or enemy as part of some religious rites. You'd eat part of your kin's corpse to absorb magical powers. It was a form of tribute, always about the transfer of life energy, always about power."

Rosie picked up one sunflower with two fingernails and placed it on her tongue. "You think that's what Jeffrey Dahmer was af-ter? Power?"

Sylvia said, "And it's one way to be really intimate with some-body else."

Rosie made another face. "What if someone is just collecting the parts?"

"Then we're talking headhunters. The collecting of trophies is fairly common among modern-day sociopaths; usually the victims are dead."

Both women were startled by a knock. "Yes?" Rosie said, turn-ing abruptly.

The door opened and an inmate peeked inside. His head was bald except for a dark tuft of hair behind each ear. He looked like one of the seven dwarfs, Sleepy or Sneezy . . . or Happy, because he was smiling.

His watery eyes darted back and forth between the two women. "I just wondered if you had any waste in your basket."

When Rosie nodded impatiently, he entered and moved toward

an overflowing metal trash can set in the corner of the room. The whisk and rustle of paper was a constant in the background as the inmate carefully, methodically emptied trash into a large black bag. When he moved toward the remaining trash basket under Rosie's desk, Sylvia stood so he could reach his target.

Rosie stared at the man's elflike face. "You're—?"

"Elmer Rivak." He beamed at Sylvia as he carried his load to the door.

"That's right, cell block one. Thanks for your diligence, Elmer." As the man closed the door, Rosie touched Sylvia on the arm and whispered, "Elmer doesn't look like a mass murderer, does he? I think he's got a crush on you."

Sylvia raised both eyebrows and shook her head. "Lucky me."

Rosie sobered suddenly. She chose her next words with care. "What if I found a connection between these incidents and Lucas?" She stared at Sylvia with cat eyes. "Is Lucas capable of dismembering people?"

Maybe. Sylvia frowned. She was more than curious, but for the moment, she kept her mouth shut. She knew her friend; Rosie would want to trade information. But it was up to Herb Burnett to decide if Sylvia's evaluation of his client would be released to corrections department authorities. She and Rosie walked a constant tightrope where a verbal misstep meant a possible violation of client confidentiality or institutional security.

"I know it's not scientific, but Lucas makes the hair on my head stand up." Rosie shivered. "And the fact that he wasn't here during the riot doesn't eliminate him as a suspect." She pulled a thin file off her desk and waved it in the air. "There have been some incident reports . . . concerning him. Do you know what I'm referring to?"

Sylvia shook her head almost imperceptibly. "Are these reports something his lawyer would know about?"

"Probably. He spooks the other inmates. They don't like to get near him. He's been accused of giving his enemies the 'evil eye.' He put a spell on an inmate named Roybal two days ago, and poor

Roybal is in sick bay shitting himself to death. Doesn't that sound like a man who wants to take the power of his enemies?"

"I'll tell you this much," Sylvia said. "I'm going to push hard to have Lucas Watson reclassified and transferred to Los Lunas where he can get intensive psych treatment." She paused, then said, "If you want, I'll do some 'psycho-magic' and help you find your body snatcher."

"There's something I've got to tell you . . ." Rosie's tone was dead serious. "*Jita*, be careful."

Sylvia waited.

Rosie said, "Someone's been asking about you. My ears tell me that your name is spoken in the yard, in the cell blocks. I don't know who is talking or what they say, but it scares me."

FOUR

THE AIR IN cell block one seemed thick with tedium and desperation. Beneath the spare mattress pad, Lucas felt the concrete slab pressed against his back. The cell walls seemed to swell, visibly shrinking the already claustrophobic space. Through the grill, he saw ten square inches of wall. He heard voices raised, a chorus talking back to the tube. It scared him that he couldn't remember which day it was; he groped mentally for clues. The soaps. *One Life to Live. Days of Our Lives. The Young and the* Fucking *Restless.* The smell of fish . . . Friday.

There was one way he could always escape captivity. He rubbed his pouch over his chest, caressed the Madonna, and with each breath disappeared in his own flesh, deep into the boy named Luke.

His mother smiled at him. She was standing next to the ironing board, and she was barefoot, naked except for a gauzy white slip. In her hands she clutched a child's cowboy shirt. Her hair fell loose to her shoulders, tendrils damp against high cheekbones.

The boy Luke reached out to her, and because he was only five years old, his arms clutched her knees. A sweet smell filled the air. *Mama.*

Her laughter washed over the boy like a great wave.

Mama.

The boy felt her hands on his tiny shoulders when she pushed him away. He fell backward, his face collapsed into a scowl, and both his arms reached out hungrily.

Maamaaaa, bed!

Like a silent actress, she touched her finger to her mouth, and the light reflecting from her wedding band exploded in a dance of gold fire. A bead of moisture spanned the distance from lip to finger; for an instant her spit bridged the space between word and touch. When the boy's mother snapped her finger to the iron and the triangle of hot metal sizzled, he saw the bad word spill from her lips.

"No."

A harsh, black rage vibrated through the boy's fragile body. He threw himself against his mother's legs. He clawed, scratched, screamed until the pressure in his skull became too intense and everything turned gray. And quiet.

When the boy came to, he was in his mother's arms. In her bed. And the warmth, the warmth was heaven . . .

The pain of a severed synapse stole the memory from Lucas and the claustrophobia of CB-1 intruded once more. But the texture of the pouch kept him from spinning out. It was slick and warm, a reassuring opening for his fingers. He found his mother's wedding ring, tightened his fist, and the gold band cut into his flesh. He closed his eyes. "Mama."

It took him a moment to realize he'd spoken aloud. After a second exploration of the pouch he found the lock of hair. These were the treasures he massaged against his belly, round and round, until he ejaculated into his other hand.

So good. The warmth . . .

He gripped the pouch until his breathing returned to normal. He stretched, so relaxed that he was able to ignore the hard mattress beneath him. When he sat up in the bed, his hand brushed against something sharp; the manila folder.

This morning, Mr. Lawyer had feinted left and right. "What happened when you talked to Sylvia?" Mr. Lawyer had probed. "Did it go okay? Did something happen? What questions did she ask?" Lucas opened the lip of the folder and slid the pages out until the letterhead was visible.

Mr. Lawyer didn't really want to let his client see the evaluation. So he said. But Lucas could see the lies as they spilled from Mr. Lawyer's thick lips, and he always got what he wanted from the Herb. All he had to do was mention compliance monitors, the Duran Consent Decree, and prisoners' rights.

He glanced at the scroll of letters against the page then held the paper to his face and inhaled. He picked up her scent very faintly. Sylvia—her face merged with his Madonna. He sucked in visions of the woman. He imagined the taste of her and believed he could track her anywhere in the world with only this fragile sensory path as guide.

Eagerly, he began the work of reading. He hunched over the pages focusing on each word, each line. "The purpose of . . . Tuesday, November 16 . . . critical evaluation." As he worked his way through the report, his breathing became labored and his pulse quickened. Occasional flashes of light exploded in front of his eyes like fireworks. He forced himself to continue, but he was not prepared for the impact of her words: ". . . no immediate evidence of organic syndromes . . . probable magical thinking . . . shift from a moderately paranoid state to severely erratic behavior not inconsistent with delusional (persecutory) psychosis

. . . although the interview was prematurely terminated . . . seek a transfer to a treatment facility. At this time, I strongly recommend against parole."

The rage surfaced like a shark. He fought the shuddering emotion until the heels of his feet were lifted from the floor.

———

"I'M GLAD YOU could fit me in on such short notice." Mrs. Young smiled nervously and shifted her weight on the rose-colored couch.

Sylvia returned the smile. "You can adjust those cushions to make yourself more comfortable."

"Oh, thank you." Mrs. Young fluffed several pillows.

The woman was an emergency referral from Dr. Albert Kove. Mrs. Young's husband of six months was under indictment by a federal grand jury, and her stepson was in jail for stealing the family car.

She denied needing therapy, but casually mentioned frequent suicidal thoughts. Albert Kove's notes to Sylvia stated that Mrs. Young had spent several weeks in rehab for substance abuse. By the end of the session, Mrs. Young admitted that she used to have a slight problem with alcohol. She also expressed intense anger at her husband because he was verbally abusive. Sylvia made notes: establishing therapeutic rapport was first on the list, negotiating a treatment contract was next. That was assuming the woman kept her second appointment. At 5:50, Sylvia scheduled Mrs. Young for the following Monday morning and walked her to the stairway that led down to the open courtyard garden and the parking lot.

The second-story Territorial-style offices appeared to be deserted, but Sylvia had the uncomfortable feeling that she wasn't alone. The hall was cold and drafty and prematurely darkened by the low arc of winter sun. She always found the lonely building disquieting; she'd been surprised by an off-schedule janitor more than once. As she returned to her office to lock up for the day, the ticking of the old radiators sounded like footsteps.

Sylvia made a mental note to call Albert Kove and thank him for the referral. It was a good excuse to touch base, in case Kove or Casias had any questions about the pending job contract. Sylvia realized how important the possibility of a new professional partnership had become since Malcolm's death. The urge was there— to move on and to forget. Nothing like a little denial.

Rush-hour traffic on Cerrillos Road was congested as usual. For several blocks, the Volvo was trapped between an old school bus and a U-Haul truck, both belching clouds of black exhaust. Sylvia jumped between radio stations to keep her hands busy. The thought of the roses still made her very uneasy.

At the suburban mall that marked the south end of Santa Fe, she turned west onto Airport Road. Her thoughts returned to the session with Mrs. Young. Borderline personality disorder? The woman had a history of relationship instability, identity disturbance, and, possibly, self-damaging behavior. Sylvia made a bet with herself: Mrs. Young had attempted suicide at least once in her adult life.

The Volvo's engine whined as Sylvia shifted belatedly into third gear. Her mind hadn't been on her driving. It was a constant in her profession, a hazard of the psychological trade—the never-ending evaluation of information; weigh, sort, sift. It was a continual distraction from daily tasks. It was a soft light you could never quite turn off; to do so might mean someone's life.

She did not notice the blue van following a half block behind. Its distance didn't vary as she drove past trailer parks, prefab apartments, a Tibetan stupa with colorful streamers dancing in the wind, and the golf course. Sylvia maintained a speed fifteen miles over the limit until the bump of dirt road marked the home stretch. A ridge cut off the last light of day, and, for an instant, headlights illuminated a windblown tumbleweed before it continued on its violent course.

The blue van pulled off the road and stopped at a place where high school lovers often parked after sunset.

—

WIND SCOURED THE concrete walls of the penitentiary, and each new gust seemed to gain velocity. Above the plaintive sound, C.O. Anderson heard the low growl and stopped in his tracks. Except for the wind and an occasional cough or snore, cell block one had been quiet. But now he heard the moan of a dog. Anderson's skin puckered with goose bumps as he traced the sound through the shadows to Lucas Watson's cell. He walked on the balls of his feet and stopped short of the grill. Anderson squinted, adjusting his vision, and he saw a dark form pressed into one corner. Watson's eyes seemed to glow. Hot fear rose from Anderson's feet and flushed through his body. He clicked on his radio and whispered.

"Hey, Manny. Anderson. I think we got a problem here. Number eighteen."

Inside the cell, Lucas Watson shot forward like a bullet, ricocheted off the sink, and hit the wall with a blunt explosion of air.

"Sonofabitch, get me some backup quick!" Anderson screamed into the radio.

Watson slammed his head against concrete. There was a damp, solid sound each time flesh met stone.

Anderson heard footsteps and yelled, "I'm going in!" as C.O. Erwin Salcido lumbered toward him. The door to the cell slid open and Anderson moved in carefully. His stomach heaved when the copper stench of urine hit him full-blast. Watson was still repeatedly drilling his own skull into the wall.

"Fucking *pendejo!*" Erwin said, wedging his bulk through the door. "Don't get too close, *Jéfe.*"

Anderson heard the scratch of the radio and then Erwin hollering for medical in CB-1. With one eye on Watson, Anderson took in the condition of the cell. A carpet of cornflakes covered the floor. The box was a chewed mess in the sink. Paper floated in the toilet, the red stamp of CONFIDENTIAL bleeding color. Anderson's foot slid on something wet. He looked down quickly and saw more paper smeared with a film of feces. "Shit," he said stepping over it, inching closer to Watson.

Inmates in cell block one were shouting now, banging shoes against the bars. The sound almost covered the sickening thud of Watson's head.

Erwin Salcido stayed just behind and to the left of Anderson.

"All right, Watson! Take it easy, man!" Anderson moved forward as Watson slumped for a moment, his hands on his bleeding skull. Then Watson raised his eyes until he was staring at Anderson. Flecks of spittle hung from his chin, his lips curled into a snarl. Anderson did not move a muscle. Neither did Erwin Salcido.

Suddenly, Watson screamed so loud that Anderson's ears rang with pain. All three men crashed to the floor, Anderson carried by the force of Watson's body, and Salcido thrown off balance. An animal smell filled Anderson's nostrils as his head slapped sharply against the pipe beneath the sink. His arm hurt; he kicked away from Watson. Erwin struggled to regain his feet.

A sharp ache shuddered into Anderson's calf. He hollered, and turned to see Watson with his teeth sunk deep through pants and flesh. "Ah, Jesus," Anderson wailed. He imagined bone hitting bone. He flashed on AIDS and rabies.

Just then, Erwin landed like a blubbery whale, full force, on top of Watson. There was a sickening snap, and Anderson dragged his wounded leg free.

Before Anderson pulled himself up, he saw the pouch. It was under his nose. Watson's prized possession. He scooped it into his freckled paw as backup arrived.

They had to gas Watson before they could get his hands behind his back, put the cuffs on, and pull him from the cell. The din coming from neighboring inmates was deafening as it echoed off the old concrete walls of CB-1. Six tennis shoes, eleven socks, three briefs, and four pairs of pants were flushed down cell block toilets that Friday night.

After the shakedown, the contents of Watson's cell were listed on a separate sheet and attached to the incident report and use-of-force forms filed by all relevant personnel. Contrary to persistent rumors, Angel Tapia's pinkie was not located anywhere in the cell.

Erwin Salcido filed his report with Lieutenant Cobar, contents as noted:

corn flakes
1 box ritz cakers
toothpaste + brush
jergens lochun
soap
pills looking like aspiren
some pages from a doctor report
some other mail
P.S. after he bit C.O. Anderson he tried to eat some
    paper + he did

Later that night, as Anderson dozed fitfully, alone in the officer's lounge, he remembered those few moments before the bite when Lucas Watson stared back at him with mad dog eyes. Anderson had not been able to move his feet. He had been frozen in place by the malevolent force of Lucas Watson.

—

THE PENITENTIARY ADMINISTRATION offices were deserted, the hall lights dim on Saturday morning. In the psych office, Sylvia collected a thick stack of notes and drawings. She'd just finished a two-hour interview with a schizophrenic, a nineteen-year-old convicted rapist, whose functioning was rapidly deteriorating; penitentiary cockroaches were sending him messages with their antennae. His lawyer wanted him reclassified and out of general population. With luck, he was bound for the psych unit at Los Lunas.

Her mind still on the session, Sylvia left the office. On the stairwell, boots clattered behind her and a hand clutched her shoulder. She turned abruptly to find herself face to face with a C.O. It took her several seconds to register his name: Anderson, the officer who had accompanied Lucas Watson to the evaluation. She was unnerved by his disheveled appearance. Forty-eight-hour shifts were not uncommon at the pen, but this man looked as if he'd been worked over by a grizzly bear.

She flinched as Anderson pressed a manila envelope into her hands. "You for-for-forgot this," he stammered.

"This isn't mine," she said. *Be careful, jita.* The hair on the nape of Sylvia's neck stood up.

Anderson wouldn't touch the packet. "Keep it. If he gets it back, he'll do more bad things."

She felt as if she was holding liquid metal the way the C.O. kept backing away from the envelope.

"You're a doctor," he said.

Sylvia stared at the towering, dish-faced man. His skin was flushed and rivulets of perspiration ran down fleshy, freckled cheeks. He smelled of fear—acrid and rank.

She extended her hand, and the envelope. "Whatever this is, give it to the investigations office—"

"Don't you get it?" Anderson snapped. "Lucas read your report."

Sylvia stared at the guard, trying to take in his words.

"It made him crazy."

"What are you talking about?"

"You know." Anderson gaped at her, his upper lip tight and paper white. "They didn't tell you?" He jabbed an index finger in the air above the envelope. "You keep it," he whispered. "You're the only one who knows."

Sylvia watched him turn and limp up the stairs.

With the bulky envelope in her hands, she stood alone for several seconds deciding what to do. Then, resolutely, she tucked the packet into her briefcase, pivoted, and walked toward one of three gates that would slide open to the world outside the prison. Her curiosity had won out.

—

IT WAS LESS than nine miles from the penitentiary to downtown Santa Fe. During the fifteen-minute drive, Sylvia's gaze returned repeatedly to the envelope on the passenger seat.

The office lot was full, but she outmaneuvered a man in a Porsche and parked on the street near the corner of Chapelle and McKenzie. Sylvia gathered up her briefcase and the envelope and walked the short block to her office. The air had snap and carried the savory punch of a piñon fire. She moved briskly through the dormant courtyard garden and up the stairs of the historic two-story adobe. Her office was the third on the right. She unlocked the door, dropped her briefcase on her desk, and stared at the envelope. Just as she slid an ornate brass blade along the paper seal, the phone rang.

"Dr. Sylvia Strange? This is Duke Watson."

Even behind the white noise and static, Lucas Watson's father sounded like a man who was accustomed to being obeyed. Sylvia felt cornered, instantly exposed, as if he'd been spying on her. She dropped the envelope.

He continued, "Sorry about the connection, but I'm in my car." His voice was inaudible for a moment, then, "—haven't met, I felt I could call—some sort of misunderstanding. I'd like to take you to lunch so we can clear things up."

"I'm sorry, Mr. Watson, but we don't have anything to discuss."

Electronic snow obliterated reception for several seconds before the Duke's voice reappeared. "—love my son—a bad mistake four years ago, but—his debt."

"Mr. Watson, this phone connection is extremely poor, and this conversation is inappropriate. You're familiar with the parole process. The ultimate use of any psychological evaluation is between your son and his legal representative."

"I hear you just fine, Dr. Strange." The line was silent for a moment before Duke continued. "How's this? Can you hear me now?" He kept his voice as even as a mowed lawn. "You and I both know that you can influence my son's future."

Sylvia tried to focus from Duke Watson's perspective. He was a political animal. His criminal son had cost him votes, and worse, had stained his name. The fact that Duke had risen as high as he had was a testament to his determination, his savvy, his connections. Now, he was being groomed for the next gubernatorial race. Problem: In political circles, having a son who was labeled "crazy" was worse than having a son who had been convicted of manslaughter.

"Dr. Strange . . . are you still there?" His voice was soft.

"I'm here."

In a new, businesslike tone of voice, Duke said, "I'm asking you to drop the reclassification issue. I'll see that my son gets the care he needs, the best care possible."

Sylvia paused, considering her words. "I think I understand some of your concerns, Mr. Watson, but your personal wishes are not my business—your son's welfare is."

There was a pause while Sylvia waited for Duke Watson's response. Instead, she heard the soft click as the receiver was replaced.

She walked into the bathroom and ran a glass of water from the tap. The face staring back from the mirror looked pale, the eyes were sharp, as she considered the phone call.

Duke Watson was setting high stakes on her ability to influence his son's fate. True, Santa Fe was a small town, but Herb Burnett could bury her report so that repercussions with the parole board would be minimal. Minimal unless C.O. Anderson was right, and Lucas Watson had flipped out. Sylvia set the glass on the sink, clicked off the overhead light, and stood in the dim light.

Her heartbeat accelerated. A fine sweat broke out on her skin.

Within minutes, the anxiety subsided, but two unpleasant thoughts lingered.

The Watson family was . . .

In a word: ominous.

And she could easily get in over her head.

She crossed her office to her desk, sat, and reached for the half-opened envelope. A small package was tucked inside. Like the petals of a flower, Sylvia pulled back the layers of tissue until a small leather pouch was revealed. It was secured by a ribbon and the leather had an oily sheen from repeated handling.

Sylvia worked the ribbon loose—using the tip of her pencil, carefully avoiding touch—and stretched the neck wide. The contents of the pouch spilled onto a sheet of white paper, and she studied the objects. There were eight: a gold wedding band, a leather thong strung through six human teeth, a tangle of hair, a smooth brown stone, a silver and turquoise cross, a bundle of delicate bones, a tiny clay figurine, a chewed stub of a blue pencil. With a shudder she recognized the pencil as the one Lucas Watson had chosen during the evaluation session. When she shook the pouch a tiny sprinkle of white chips shimmered out. At a closer look, Sylvia realized they were the clipped remains of fingernails. Still, there was something else caught in the leather, and the pouch was softly extended around the bottom edges as if a form held it in place. At first, she didn't differentiate it from the skin itself, but her fingers probed and pushed and a ninth item slid out of the pouch. Dark and dried like an old apple, the ear was so weathered, Sylvia didn't immediately recognize it as human.

FIVE

THERE WAS A waiting list for Sunday brunch at Tortilla Flats, but Rosie was already seated in a booth. She raised a lipstick-stained coffee cup and smiled when she recognized Sylvia.

"Coffee for me, too," Sylvia told a waitress. She slipped out of her coat and tucked it over the edge of the seat. The air smelled of spices and tortillas, and neighboring tables were filled with parents, teenagers, and toddlers.

"What's up?" Rosie asked.

"I'm in a tight spot," Sylvia said as she slid into the booth. She waited while the waitress set a huge platter of stuffed tortilla, beans, rice, and a side of grease-puffed sopaipillas in front of Rosie.

"I ordered a burrito," Rosie said. "I couldn't resist."

The waitress placed a clean cup on the table and poured coffee from an insulated pot. Sylvia dabbed at the base of the cup and a small brown stain spread out onto the napkin.

"Share these with me," Rosie said pushing the basket of sopaipillas and a plastic squeeze-bottle of honey toward Sylvia. "I'm listening."

Sylvia set the envelope containing the pouch on the table. She let the baggie slide out onto Formica. Through the slightly opaque layers, it was impossible to identify the contents.

Rosie pointed to her full mouth and wrinkled her nose quizzically. After she swallowed, she said, "What is that?"

"I didn't bother to put it back together," Sylvia said. "I didn't want to screw around with evidence." She watched while Rosie slit open the plastic runner with a polished nail and surveyed the contents of the bag. From an adjacent booth, a three-year-old tossed a wadded napkin over the Formica divider; it bounced off a salsa bottle and fell into Sylvia's lap. She aimed it gently back in the direction of the child.

"Is this what I think it is?" Rosie asked pointing at one corner of the bag.

"An ear?" Sylvia kept her voice low and ignored the large woman, probably the mother of the three-year-old, who glared at the two women.

"Where the hell did it come from? Whose is it?"

Sylvia took a swallow of coffee, brushed a strand of hair from her eye, and stared at the overweight mother until the woman turned back to her family.

She held up her thumb and said, "First, I'd like to avoid getting my source fired. Second," her index finger joined her thumb, "I'm not at liberty to speculate on the ownership of the pouch. It should've gone directly to you in the first place."

"Why didn't it?"

Sylvia dropped her hands to the table, tore off a piece of sopaipilla, and leaned forward. "Because he was scared." The crispy golden dough disappeared between her lips.

"Who is the damn source?" Rosie stabbed at her burrito, tore into the soft tortilla with her fork, but she didn't bother to eat.

"One of your C.O.s," Sylvia said.

"One of my boys? And the pouch belongs to Watson?"

Sylvia's features settled into a neutral mask. She tipped her cup and glanced at the brown ring of fluid trapped in the bottom. "I want to know exactly what happened with Lucas." The cup fell back into the saucer with a clatter.

"You're handing me a severed ear, but you won't tell me which C.O. gave it to you, and I'm supposed to tell you the details of an active investigation?"

"Yes, I'm giving you the damn ear," Sylvia whispered. "I shouldn't even do that much." She paused and took a breath. "Anderson. He's your C.O."

Both women sipped coffee, and then Rosie nodded slowly. "It happened Friday night; Lucas went berserk. The doctor says psychotic break. He's medicated now. He had a copy of your evaluation; that seems to have been the trigger."

Sylvia slammed her spine against the vinyl seat cushion.

A busboy chose that moment to refill coffee cups and water glasses, and Rosie put her arms around her plate protectively. "I'm not finished," she said. When he disappeared with his coffee pot, Rosie relaxed her body and exposed the plastic baggie tucked next to her breakfast plate. "If this is a human ear, then I have to seriously consider the likelihood that it came from my body snatcher."

"It's human," Sylvia said.

"What's the rest of this stuff? A ring, hair, teeth . . . a gallstone? *Jesus.* It's a medicine pouch, isn't it? I've seen Native Americans who keep something like this."

Sylvia lowered her voice. "A medicine pouch . . . or a collection of trophies."

"How nice," Rosie deadpanned.

Unconsciously, Sylvia caught a lock of hair in her fingers and twisted it tight. "Quantico's Behavioral Science Services Unit differentiates . . . organized killers take their victim's wallets, rings, keys—anything that might help the cops. Later, they use those souvenirs to relive the *glow*. Disorganized killers might collect hair or body parts to make a blender pick-me-up."

Rosie stuffed a last bite of sopaipilla into her mouth. "Sylvia, please . . ."

"I see it two ways," Sylvia said abruptly. She raised her index finger. "It's a mojo or medicine pouch used to ward off or to inflict evil." She lifted her middle finger. "It contains trophies that can be traced to victims."

Rosie made a face and said, "The only thing that isn't in the pouch is Angel's missing pinkie. What? You've got that look!"

Sylvia stared at the pouch. "If this belongs to Lucas then my guess is category number one: mojo pouch. He's paranoid and he needs something to ward off the psychic evil all around him." She shook her head. "What will you do with all this?"

"Send the ear over to the D.P.S. Crime Lab. Then I'll question Anderson to see if I can confirm who the pouch belongs to. If I connect Lucas with Tapia's missing finger, I'll call in the state police and notify the parole board." Rosie crossed her arms under her breasts and stared at Sylvia. "But after last night, I don't think Lucas has a prayer with the board. I saw your evaluation, Sylvia. Lucas will blame you."

Sylvia nodded. "Sounds like he already has." Not to mention his father, she thought.

Rosie pushed her plate away and reached for her purse where she carefully stowed the baggie and its contents. "I promised Ray I wouldn't miss the entire football game—the Boys reaming somebody."

"Brunch is on me."

"Thanks." Rosie slid her way out of the booth. "Want to come watch football?"

"I'm going to do some work on your body snatcher." Sylvia held up a hand. "By the way, in your office you mentioned a missing hand, a missing nose. Who lost an ear?"

Rosie punched an arm into her down overcoat. She caught her belt and pulled it tight at the waist. "As far as I know, nobody. An ear certainly seems like something you'd miss."

—

SYLVIA STOOD IN the hall in Main's hospital and peered through a window. The tiny treatment room was empty except for a small examination table and a porcelain sink. The next room was just as small and packed to overflowing with a nurse, a C.O., and an inmate.

Sylvia left the treatment area and continued down the hall to the room where Angel Tapia had been quarantined when the body snatcher struck. The door was open and the room contained a hospital bed stripped of bedding, a chair, and built-in metal cabinets that lined the wall opposite the door. The trash had been emptied, the floor had been mopped, and the room smelled strongly of disinfectant.

Sylvia entered, closed the door, sat in the chair, and looked up. The ceiling tiles were water-stained and corners had begun to curl. She imagined that Angel Tapia knew those stains by heart. There was nothing else to look at if you were lying down, nothing except the green floor, the green walls. She idly pondered institutional green; was it a product of World War II surplus?

She closed her eyes and focused on the muffled voices coming from the treatment cubicles. A female voice carried through plaster and concrete block. Otherwise, this room was a world of its own where Angel Tapia had been locked away. The nurse, LaRue, had taken a very long dinner break. And C.O. Anderson had monitored hall traffic.

Sylvia opened her eyes, stood, and turned panning all four walls. Whoever removed Angel's finger had planned his crime in advance, he'd also been flexible—

She froze and stared at the stainless steel cabinets. She could see her reflection. Or actually, she saw her hair and her eyes. The rest of her face was obscured by a dull film of . . . what? She stepped close enough to run her index finger across the surface. A gritty powder had collected on her skin. She sniffed: Ajax? Some kind of cleanser. But it was on too thick to be left over from a routine scrub. She finished her examination of Angel's quarantine room and left the hospital.

Sylvia found Main's inmate services meeting room deserted although an empty cigarette pack, the smell of smoke, and the scrawled greeting—WELCOME FRIENDS—on the blackboard were all evidence of an earlier AA, NA, or spiritual meeting.

She dumped a stack of files on the long wooden table. The prison's psych offices were in use all day as part of an annual mental health screening. For her purposes, she preferred the barnlike atmosphere of the meeting room; she wanted to spread out.

She sat in a worn vinyl chair and placed a two-inch-thick orange file on her left. Two years ago, a colleague who specialized in the treatment of post-traumatic stress disorder had interviewed members of the pen's general population who were Vietnam veterans. Sylvia had a copy of his abbreviated reports; they included general findings, brief statistics, and a list of interviewees.

The competent amputation of Angel Tapia's finger clearly indicated the cutter had some medical background. The possibilities included a nurse, an E.M.T., an army medic. She didn't know of any medical doctors doing time . . . or veterinarians, for that matter.

On her right, Sylvia set down a massive manila envelope. It contained a report authorized by the state's attorney general, February 1981. Subject: Known and suspected predators during the 1980 riot. Some were now dead, others had been transferred, a few had been released. But a half-dozen of the men were alive and well in Main.

For the next two hours, she read and reread documents. She scratched almost-illegible notes on a memo pad: name of each victim and every known detail of the crime, psych diagnoses of known predators. Several words were circled, others crossed out, and arrows pierced clouds. At a certain point, her thoughts lost their thread of logic and drifted like paper boats on a lake. She stayed almost immobile as minutes ticked by until she suddenly reached for her notes and scribbled *Man with a mission.*

If Rosie's instinct was correct, if the body snatcher's collecting dated back to the riot, he was in for the long haul. He wasn't in a hurry and his attacks were not random. His work was important; details were important. Specific parts? Perhaps a right hand was more important than a left, and a pinkie more important than a thumb. Or perhaps Angel Tapia's pinkie was what mattered? His mutilation was certainly premeditated. Sylvia was convinced the body snatcher's mission made perfect sense—to him if to nobody else.

She heard a horn honk outside the building, glanced at the clock, and wasn't surprised to find another hour had passed. Lost hours had become routine lately.

She went back to her notes and stared at the phrases she'd circled. *Sunglasses crushed, mirror smashed, chrome surface dulled, window soaped.* These were details from three different crime scenes where body parts went missing.

She stood, stretched, and walked to a window. Outside wire and glass, the sky had darkened; the clouds were chunks of charcoal. Sylvia's spine ached, so did her head. She leaned a shoulder against the wall, removed her glasses, and massaged her temples. A rhythmic noise, like a fountain or a gurgling brook was coming from somewhere outside the building. She couldn't locate its source, but it had a calming effect.

Her eyes followed the repeating pattern of the wire grill that was two inches from her face: right in front of her nose. Neat, even, methodical; not flashy, not exceptional in any way. Just like Angel's stitches.

And then she saw her own reflection in the glass and smiled.

Sylvia retrieved a pack of Marlboros from her purse and tapped out the one remaining cigarette. She found matches and lit up.

She had an off-the-wall theory. *He doesn't like to see his own reflection. The snatcher is shy. Why? A deformity?* She didn't think so; not an external deformity, anyway. Could it be as simple as self-loathing? Religious penance?

The smoke tasted wonderful.

Last spring, the day Malcolm revealed he had cancer, she'd bought a pack of Marlboros. He told her it was a stupid, obvious way to defy her fear of death. She agreed. Now, she only smoked when she was alone; she coveted her secret habit.

She stubbed out the last of the cigarette when she heard a door close somewhere at the other end of the hall. That was followed by shuffling footsteps, probably a C.O. cleaning up.

She left her files and notes in the meeting room and strolled down the deserted wing. An inmate artist had executed a mural on the walls. The murky colors—black, gray, red, brown, purple—always reminded Sylvia of somebody's drug nightmare. Dark dreams of shadows, monsters, and demons against a nihilistic landscape. To look was to touch the mind of the artist—to look was painful.

"Hello," someone called out quietly.

Sylvia had reached the end of the hall. To her right, behind a glass wall, a desktop publishing system sat unused. The room was empty.

Who had said hello? Sylvia's attention turned to the open doorway opposite the office. It led into a large room, now almost completely dark. The sound of the fountain was audible again, but now it was more like a purring cat. And it seemed to be coming from inside the room.

Sylvia inched toward the main door and the stairs. Not water, not a cat, but breathing. Somebody breathing.

The door swung open abruptly and someone stood in shadow. A hulk of a figure.

"Nobody's supposed to be here now."

Sylvia caught her breath as a door slammed at the other end of the hall. She felt trapped. The figure moved forward into the light. He had the ruddy features of a redneck. C.O. Anderson.

"I'm locking up. Let's go."

Sylvia's muscles didn't respond immediately when she willed them into motion.

She found her voice and said, "I'll get my things."

She strode down the hall to the meeting room and began to gather up her files. It registered immediately: the pages with her notes were gone.

—

THROUGH THE 600 MM lens, Billy Watson could stand forty feet from the house and see Sylvia Strange in her kitchen. She was in perfect focus. Her dark eyebrows shaded deep-set eyes. Her unruly hair was tucked behind her ears. On her chin she had a faint dimple. And her neck looked creamy white except for the slash of shadow in the hollow.

The Volvo was parked at an angle in her driveway, and lights glowed from the living room, kitchen, and study. The electric halo illuminated patches of juniper and piñon surrounding the house, but the light didn't reach his hiding place on the south side. He had set up his tripod under a small cottonwood near the coyote fence. The moon, what there was of it, was shielded by clouds. There were no street lamps this far out of town, the nearest house was a quarter mile across the river, and his blue van was hidden behind juniper and scrub. If she looked out her window, she'd only see a tree.

The tripod held the lens steady even though his hands shook in the thirty-degree air. Through the viewfinder, the world flushed yellow-orange, and a golden Sylvia stood in front of the sliding glass door. He could see the tip of her nose, her lips were open, and she was singing to herself.

He squeezed off two shots as she disappeared from the frame. Then, before he was ready, she was back. The whole thing felt like ducks popping up and down at a shooting gallery. Deep in concentration, he bit his tongue. The next time she stepped into frame, he just stared at her, focusing, refocusing. "Yes, baby, yes . . ." he whispered in the darkness.

He hadn't planned to come here. At home, he'd been restless, angry that everyone was calling his brother crazy. He knew better; Luke wasn't nuts, he just knew how to keep them off balance: they were scared.

Billy remembered one time when he was in third grade and Luke was in fourth. Luke had refused to talk to the nuns the entire day. He had clamped his mouth shut and smiled when Sister Antonia and Sister Margaret cuffed his ears and made him kneel on concrete. The next day, when Billy tried the same trick, it took one slap from Sister Margaret before he was blubbering and acting like a crybaby.

At home tonight, his sister Queeny was sick again. And what was worse, the old man was yelling at that lawyer Burnett. Luke would've smiled at it all, but Billy was still just a crybaby. So he'd gone out to cruise, out for a six-pack, and found himself on the road to her house.

Since he'd delivered the roses, he always parked in the same spot. It was a good place to smoke, finish the beer, watch. Seeing her tonight had prompted him to take his camera out of the trunk. He was good at photography—it was the only thing he'd enjoyed in high school. You could set up your own secret world through the viewfinder. The pictures would be a gift for Luke.

He wrapped his arms around his chest and paced. His breath came out in smoky wisps. When he happened to look up, he saw that the cloud cover was breaking apart and that stars had appeared, gleaming like glass shards. He lowered his eye to the viewfinder.

She was back in his frame, moving a pile of books, adjusting her robe around her hips, and then she disappeared. Five seconds later, she walked across the face of his lens, stopped, and turned toward the window. Billy smiled. He watched her reach into the refrigerator and pull out something—milk. She drank directly from the carton and splashed liquid down her chin, onto her chest. He saw her jump back and shake her head. He was ready when she opened her bathrobe and reached for a towel to dab the milk from her breasts.

Billy squeezed the camera's trigger—yes—got her. Just like a lover, her head was tilted, dark hair framing her face, lips parted. He could feel the excitement when he shot her through the wall of the camera.

—

LYLE LOVETT CROONED a blues ballad at low volume while Sylvia sang harmony. She put the carton of milk back in the refrigerator, grabbed an Oreo from an open package, and wiped crumbs from her mouth. She found a bottle of Stoli in the freezer, and drained the bottle when she poured herself a generous shot. She carried the vodka to her study.

On her desk, the test results for an overdue evaluation were strewn everywhere. She found her reading glasses in a tiny drawer built into the back of the desk and adjusted them carefully on the bridge of her nose. She took a swallow of vodka, and stared at her notes, but she found she couldn't concentrate; she was distracted by a guilty conscience. After a few minutes, she picked up the portable handset and dialed a number.

"Monica?"

"Sylvia? I've been meaning to call you." The slightly breathless tone, the uneven cadence, were typical Monica. Malcolm Treisman's widow hesitated for a moment.

"How are you doing?" Sylvia asked.

Monica sighed. "Oh, all right. No, not really all right, but you know . . . what about you?"

Sylvia pictured the other woman's slender, girlish body, perfectly cut blond bob, pert features. Monica was one of those people who depended on others to keep things running smoothly. Her life always seemed to fall into place—until Malcolm's death. Sylvia stopped herself from her tendency to dismiss Monica; their relationship was different now. Monica had been the one to care for Malcolm in the last months of his illness. "I'm okay," Sylvia said.

"I've thought of you often since the funeral."

"I've been so busy—"

"You don't have to explain," Monica said quietly.

It was the silence that gave her away. She knows, Sylvia thought. She knows about Malcolm and me. There had been no husband's confession from Malcolm, of that Sylvia was certain. Monica and he were already separated when Sylvia began her professional partnership with Malcolm. For all his faults, Malcolm wasn't a man who manufactured drama for its own sake. And Sylvia had taken great care that their affair remain private, unspoken. Still, it was clear Monica Treisman knew that Sylvia had been in love with her husband.

Breathless again, Monica said, "I was going to call you. I need your help."

Sylvia, caught off guard, said, "Anything. What?"

"It's Jaspar." After a quick beat, Monica jumped into the phrase like a person who starts a dance step on her left foot. "He's having such a hard time with his father's death."

Sylvia stood up and paced the few feet the room would allow. She shook her head, saw herself maneuvering mentally, gaining a professional distance. She sat back down. "What exactly? Nightmares?"

"Yes, every night. And he wet his bed last night, too. He's afraid of the dark now, *really* afraid." Monica stopped and started, the anxious tremor punctuating her words. "Oh God, Sylvia, he's all I have . . ." Now the words dangled helplessly.

"Monica, are you and Jaspar seeing anyone? I can recommend a good child psychologist."

"I don't want a good child psychologist." Monica carefully mimicked the last three words. "I want you to spend some time with him."

"Me?"

"He'll trust you," Monica said.

"It makes much more sense for Jaspar to see a stranger," Sylvia said. "I don't want to get into dual relationships here, and ethically—"

"Don't give me ethics or dual relationships." Suddenly, the wispy voice was replaced by a command. "I know who Malcolm would trust with his only son."

That was it; Sylvia understood there was no way she could refuse. "All right," she said reluctantly. "But if it turns out I think he needs some actual therapy, I'll give you several names of qualified people who work with kids."

"Fine."

They agreed she would stop by the next afternoon. As she hung up the phone, Sylvia remembered the last time she and Malcolm had made love. In this house, on her bed.

For an instant, the sound of his voice replayed in her head. A joke; he'd told a joke, and she'd laughed so hard her stomach hurt.

How's your aptitude for fucking? She'd said that.

Malcolm had sat up and raised one eyebrow. Then he'd rolled over onto her body, let his weight press her against jade-colored sheets.

He had never once said he loved her.

Sylvia worked at her desk for another hour until the typed lines on the pages blurred into tiny rivers of ink. In an unconscious gesture of concentration, she pulled her dark mane of hair away from her face, then closed her eyes.

Rocko's canine ears picked up a dull thud outside the window, and he gave a low growl. As Sylvia straightened, he let loose a soft woof that exploded into wild barks. She snapped off the tensor lamp and closed the window blinds. Before last week, she wouldn't have been so easily spooked.

—

LUCAS WATSON HAD a dream that night. Curled up in his cell, he went back to his mother's bedroom and let the sunshine warm him. It poured through the windows like caramel, lending the room its liquid edge. He examined his face in her vanity mirror, touched the half-empty bottle of White Shoulders, ran his fingers over the sheets still bearing her imprint. He thought the house was empty until she whispered his name. A great sadness washed over him, and he realized that she would die a second time. He crawled onto her bed, pulled his knees to his chin, and began to suck his thumb. When he woke, his face was wet.

Three days later, on the Wednesday before Thanksgiving, the three-person parole board, appointed by the state of New Mexico, reviewed sixteen penitentiary inmate cases for possible parole. Lucas Watson was not allowed to leave his padded cell. He could only imagine the wide echoing room furnished with folding metal chairs. The men who wore suits and severe expressions. The proximity to freedom.

After a short conference—with references to the biting incident and certain relevant psychological material—Lucas Watson was denied parole.

SIX

It had been snowing for half an hour, thin flakes that left a dull sheen on the ground. Lucas Watson moved away from the window. How long had he been segregated in Main's hospital? He knew Thanksgiving had come and gone, and it seemed like he'd been in this place a very long time.

When he stood, his knees trembled from the effort. He turned right and touched battered knuckles to the wall. Its dirty sheen matched his skin. He returned to the wired window that offered the only view from the tiny padded cell. Moonscape. It was time to find his pouch, time to get out. He was in danger from them, caged, and everything that connected him to the world, and to his mother, was inside that tiny leather bag.

Using two fingers he gently stroked the Madonna on his chest. He caressed her cheeks, her aquiline nose, her hands clasped in prayer.

"Sylvia," he whispered.

The confusion, the pain, the rage increased in steady increments. Why had she fucking betrayed him?

He began his chant for protection—*Mater noster*—but it was no good without the pouch. Lucas groaned and his eyelids shot up abruptly.

At 11:00 that morning, he was returned to his regular cell in CB-1. Two hacks accompanied him through the connecting corridors. C.O. Anderson watched while they removed the cuffs, checked the cell, and locked it down.

When the other guards had gone, Lucas whispered to Anderson through the grill. "You took something that belongs to me." Watson's forehead was a mass of bruises and scabs, one eye was swollen shut, and he had a cold sore in the corner of his mouth.

Anderson stared at a spot behind Watson's head.

"I want it back," Watson spit. Anderson felt saliva strike his face. Finally, he let his gaze settle on the inmate.

"I gave it to the head doctor," Anderson said. Lucas made him feel small and impotent, and it went all the way back to when they were kids. The memories were vivid. Anderson would be playing outside, waiting for his dad to finish work at the Watson's house, and he would hear the noise coming from inside. It was Lucas having a tantrum, screaming at his mother until he was blue in the face. Then it always got real quiet for a while, and afterward, Luke always had a wicked look in his eye. More than once, he'd chased Anderson down and pelted him with a BB gun.

Anderson said, "The shrink. I gave it to her, and she took it. Now she'll take care of you." His mouth twisted to a sneer as he turned and walked away.

—

THOUGH HE WAS only six years old, Jaspar Treisman wore the look of a world-weary traveler. His neatly cut fringe of sandy hair erupted in a cowlick over his forehead. His bright blue eyes seemed too large for the delicate features of his face. The faint moustache of milk above his upper lip added a Chaplinesque touch to his serious countenance.

He sat in the front seat of the Volvo next to Sylvia and watched her while she drove. When she glanced his way he avoided eye contact; he pressed his nose to the passenger window and his breath left condensation on the glass. She turned off I-25 at the Lamy exit and pulled into the Country Store for gas and refreshments. The parking lot was filled with cars, holiday weekend business. Jaspar declined the offer of ice cream or Coke. He was polite, but withdrawn.

"We've still got about ten minutes to go," Sylvia said as she pulled out into traffic.

"Okay," Jaspar nodded. His voice was small and noncommittal. Tucked behind the seat belt and shoulder strap, he looked like a tiny man.

They drove past the new subdivision projects with their signs advertising affordable country living. Jaspar stared at the giant yellow Caterpillars and steamrollers pushing earth. The growl of machinery and diesel fumes filled the car's interior. Even a four-day weekend didn't slow the developers down. Sylvia opened her mouth and then closed it again. She couldn't think of anything to say. When they bounced over the railroad tracks, Jaspar turned in his seat to gaze out the rear window.

"Do you see a train coming?"

Jaspar shook his head. "They don't go as fast as cars."

They were silent as the car rolled past the Lamy overpass and the turnoff to the village of Galisteo. Sylvia had been considering the best approach to open up communication with Jaspar. Although he'd been told his father was dying, Malcolm's cancer was already acute when diagnosed; death had come soon after. Often, children Jaspar's age believed their own thoughts or actions had caused the death of a parent. She gazed at the boy, saw Malcolm's style reflected in his son, and decided not to push—let him take his time. She opened the window and breathed in icy air. The sky was cloudless and cobalt blue. Hard, brown earth slid up to the distant horizon and rose suddenly to form jagged ridge backs and the blunt nose of the Ortiz Mountains.

"Did you know that people hunt for gold in those mountains?" Sylvia asked.

Silence.

"Is it too cold for you, Jaspar?"

This time he responded with a shake of his head. He picked up the small pack at his feet and held it in his lap. "There were Indians here?"

"Un huh. Anasazi, I think. Anasazi Indians."

Jaspar considered this.

"They were ancient people, anyway. I know that for sure," Sylvia said.

"Who told you?" Jaspar's tone was polite, but now there was a note of curiosity.

"My father."

"Oh."

Sylvia searched for the off-road clearing, slack barbed wire fence, and NO TRESPASSING signs that marked the Lamy swimming hole. They came to a stop in a swirl of tire tracks in the dried earth.

Jasper looked around with a quizzical expression. "This is it?"

"Lock your door, and don't forget your fanny pack." Sylvia put the key in the back pocket of her jeans and buttoned her jacket. Wind intensified the cold outside the car. "Ready?"

"I need my hat on," Jaspar said.

"Where is it?"

Jaspar peered carefully in the pockets of his green mackintosh. "Don't know." After some searching, they discovered the wool hat stuck to a strip of Velcro on Jaspar's sleeve. It was the first time Sylvia had heard Jaspar laugh since his father's death. It was a soft, quick sound that touched her. She joined in with her big laugh then pulled the hat over his ears and buttoned his collar.

"There."

The highway was deserted, no sign of traffic from north or south, and it stretched out to infinity over flat earth. Overhead, a twin-engine plane sketched a lopsided figure eight in the air; it appeared to be exactly the same size as a crow coasting below.

They hiked across the road, slipped through the barbed wire, and negotiated a trail around rocks and trees. Jaspar trekked silently, eyes to the ground. He found some cicada shells and a raven's feather and put these items carefully into his fanny pack. He pointed to three tiny holes in the ground. Sylvia explained that they were left by the cicadas when the insects came out of the ground at the end of their dormant cycle. Jaspar absorbed the information without comment.

As they walked, Sylvia felt the muscles in her legs contract and release. It was a good sensation, freeing, as if she'd been static for months. She waited while Jaspar added pebbles and some withered purple juniper berries to his collection.

"Keep your head up now."

"Why?" Jaspar looked up at the sky and then at Sylvia.

"We're getting close."

"What is it?"

"You'll see." Sylvia held out her hand. After a moment's hesitation, Jaspar put his fingers inside hers. They walked side by side toward the cluster of giant boulders in the distance.

"There might be arrowheads," Jaspar said.

"We'll find those later. Right now, look up."

At first there were just rocks, thick and gray, broken and tumbled into fantastically massive shapes, but unmarked by humans. Jaspar pointed to a boulder that pressed into the side of the cliff

face. Sylvia followed the direction of his small finger and saw RUDY
WAS HERE! splashed in spray paint.

Jaspar tugged on Sylvia's jacket. "Is that it?"

When Sylvia didn't answer, Jasper turned back to the rocks. He
was squinting in the sunlight. He curled his fingers over his eyes
like binoculars and stood very still. "There's a hand," he said suddenly.

Sylvia nodded. She pointed to the dark palm print, fingers out-
stretched, pressed over the sandstone. She moved her arm six
inches to the right. "There's a snake," she said. Jaspar stared at
the zigzag lines. "And I think that's a man."

Slowly, Jaspar took in the magic of the rocks. Moments before,
there had been only shadows. Now spirals, horses, and lizards appeared. There were dozens of pictographs and petroglyphs; he lost
count as the ancient forms multiplied and it seemed as if bare rock
was nonexistent.

They circled and climbed and hunted for new rock creatures. As
they searched, Jaspar had questions.

"Are these very old?"

"Very."

"A hundred years old?"

"Some are even older."

"How much older?"

"Hundreds and hundreds of years."

"How many hundreds?"

"Ummm, at least six or seven."

Jaspar pressed his own hand against the rock. They had circled
back to find the first palm print. It floated on the sandstone fifteen
feet above their heads. A raven cawed from his perch at the top
branches of a piñon. Wind whistled down through the boulders,
carving and blasting bits of stone. With each gust, a crevice widened, a crack deepened. Sylvia stood shivering, eyelids closed. Everything was ancient in this place, and everything was somehow
sacred. The raven squawked and Sylvia opened her eyes.

"I wish my daddy could come here," Jaspar said.

Sylvia took his hand. The therapist in her knew the appropriate answer, but the woman chose silence. The raven cawed again and soared out of view.

Jaspar led the way back to the car. When he bent down to scoot under the wire fence, he let out a cry. For a moment Sylvia was sure he'd been cut on the barbs, but he opened his dirty fingers and displayed his found treasure. Instead of an arrowhead, it was a sea shell. Sylvia stared at the perfect pink and brown spiral. She wondered where on earth it had come from. When she looked up, Jaspar was smiling at her. His face was streaked with dirt, his skin glowing from sunshine, and a snowflake—seemingly as out of place as the shell—stuck to his cheek and melted instantly.

—

THE RUMOR BEGAN like a glint of silver on the edge of the horizon, a whispered wave building muscle and speed: the riot was coming. Inside the medium security South Facility an agitated whitecap licked at the cinder-block corners of the barbershop, the store, and the chapel. At the maximum security North Facility, a prefab fortress constructed in response to postriot litigation, a floundering, watery panic flooded pod after pod of the twelve housing units. Inside Main, by the time inmate Daniel Swanson reached the hospital, CB-4 and CB-5 were engulfed in a tidal wave. Inmate Swanson had cut off his own penis with a file. This was not news—it was Swanson's second attempt at self-mutilation. What had started the wave, what set off the panic, was the fact that Swanson's severed penis had not been found.

During yard time, inmate Swanson was in the habit of leaning against the chain-link fence near the baseball diamond, conversing with Jesus. He'd chosen that spot to perform his amputation. No one knew how long he'd been there, fingers like a clamp on the metal fence, blood draining from his crotch, down his legs, staining the brown, stubby grass.

Rosie watched as Swanson was placed on the stretcher and

wrapped with blankets. "Take it easy, Daniel," Rosie said. "You're going to be okay."

"I want it back," Swanson cried. "He said I couldn't, but I want it back!"

"Who said?" Rosie asked. She was crouched, holding his hand, keeping pace with the stretcher.

"J-J-J-Jesus said." Swanson swooned.

A line of inmates had gathered ten feet away from the scene. White and brown skins were polarized and Rosie saw jittery eyes staring from impassive faces. She whispered to one of the C.O.s, "Get Swanson the hell out of here, and get Colonel Gonzales. Now!"

A two-hundred-pound Anglo inmate raised his fist like a flag. A second man—this one skinny and white—parroted the militant gesture.

Rosie recognized them both as members of the pen's smallest major-league gang, the Aryan Brotherhood. The ABs stood opposite four wiry homeboys. Rosie started to ease her way toward the chain-link fence, and she signaled the C.O.s on the field to move with her.

Two of the C.O.s walked directly toward the first line of inmates; Rosie swore under her breath and whispered, "Back off, guys."

But they didn't.

The sun glinted off something metal; Rosie could see it in the skinny white inmate's hand—she prayed it wasn't a shank.

She heard barking dogs—reinforcements on their way—too distant to save this moment. Without another thought Rosie called out in a loud, clear voice that nobody could miss. "Well I'll be damned . . . a penis!"

It was oddball enough to throw the tension off center for twenty seconds while everyone regrouped. By then the metal gate opened, whistles blew, and the dog team was on the field.

Rosie walked calmly out the gate, stumbled on asphalt, and almost wet her pants. She didn't notice the lean, blond inmate who watched the action from a distance, but Lucas Watson noticed her.

One hour later, Main Facility was under a twenty-four-hour lockdown. During the shakedown, no evidence of the missing penis was found.

———

ON WEDNESDAY, THE parking lot of the penitentiary was full—the usual result after a lockdown when all privileges had been suspended. Billy Watson joined the steady flow of visitors.

The large visitors' room was crowded and noisy. Billy got a Pepsi from the machine, sat in one of the vinyl chairs, and drummed his fingers. Led Zeppelin's "Stairway to Heaven" was playing in his head. Even though it was cold, some couples and little kids stayed out in the yard that butted up against the room. Billy watched a baby crawling on dirt. Then he turned to stare at the guard standing on the other side of the grilled doorway. As if on command, his brother appeared. The guard ran his hands over Luke, under his arms, between his legs. The whole time, Luke didn't look up. His hair was matted over a thick scab, and a long gash mapped his cheek.

"I got my eye on you," the guard said.

When Luke was inside the grill, Billy pulled him toward two chairs in the far corner. They sat. "What happened? What did they do to you?"

Lucas ignored the question and peered intently at Billy. "I need you to do a job."

"Whatever it is, no problem." Billy squirmed against the hard plastic chair. He would do anything to please his bro, but Luke was different now. He seemed all dried up like a husk of something. Billy forced himself to look straight at his brother. Those blue eyes took him right back to when he was five years old. Little Billy's chore: *You will keep that dog chained securely to the post, otherwise he will kill the chickens.* That was a job Billy was proud of— until the day he forgot to double-check. They found the chicken house filled with blood and feathers; feathers stuck to the dog's mouth when Duke beat the whimpering animal to death.

Lucas took the whipping for his brother, same as all the other times. Billy remembered. He squeezed the chair with his fingers and asked, "What you want me to do? Name it."

Lucas smiled, and leaned close to whisper what was needed. He smelled sour and sickly.

Step by step. They went over it together, and then Billy repeated the plan just to make sure it was in his head. He was concentrating so hard, he almost forgot to give Luke the pictures of Sylvia Strange.

—

THE SNOW STOPPED the next morning. Before dawn, Billy left the house his old man had bought in Bernalillo eighteen years ago—right after they'd moved from the adobe—the suicide house.

He pushed the Corvette to sixty-five on the dirt and skidded around the corner heading south toward Albuquerque. The old van was shit, but the 'vette was cool. He was following the river now, his eyes open for cops. He knew where they hung out, and they knew him. Mostly, they left him alone.

Billy lit up a cigarette and sucked on a can of Budweiser. It would be a good day to rip off a car. A fat, black crow spread its wings and flapped away from a fresh kill on the shoulder of the road. Bare cottonwoods draped the river, and the water flowed brown and rough.

He passed a sign that read: DRIVE SLOW AND SEE OUR TOWN NOW, DRIVE FAST AND SEE OUR JUDGE LATER.

—

PERIMETER LIGHTS STAYED on all day at the penitentiary. The daylight was gone by 5:15 when Lucas Watson swallowed a razor blade. Although his manner was passive, his blood pressure was high and he showed signs of anxiety. The PNM nurse decided that transporting Watson to St. Vincent's hospital in Santa Fe was a good idea. Arrangements were made, and the hospital was warned that the penitentiary was sending an inmate for X ray and treatment. This inmate could be considered dangerous. C.O. Salcido and a rookie C.O. named Barclay escorted a handcuffed Watson to the emergency room at the hospital. ER was backed up with a three-car collision and a drug overdose—a lively Thursday night. Dr. Paul Huffy placed Watson in a private examination room along with the two correctional officers.

"He swallowed a razor blade?" Huffy queried curtly.

"A safety blade," Salcido clarified.

The doctor was exhausted, worried about a three-year-old with severe scalp lacerations, and the razor blade was a standard inmate trick; it usually did surprisingly little damage.

"Most likely it's going to pass on its own," Dr. Huffy said as he left the room.

The three men sat waiting, Watson on a bed and the two C.O.s propped on hard metal chairs. At 6:45 a young woman offered coffee to the two C.O.s. With orders to Watson to stay put, they left the room.

Dr. Huffy took time between setting a broken arm and stitching head lacerations to check on the prison inmate. When he opened the door, he found himself alone with the handcuffed Watson who was sitting quietly on the bed.

"Oh, Jesus!" Huffy's cheeks shivered when he bellowed, "Where the hell did those guards go?"

Watson shrugged his shoulders.

"Only in Santa Fe!" Huffy snapped in disgust. Just last week two felons had stepped out of a sheriff's transport vehicle while it idled at a stoplight. Cuffed and shackled, they'd still managed to evade recapture for three days. He slammed the door and returned less than a minute later with both C.O.s looking sheepish.

At 7:59 Watson complained that his hands were numb. His movements were sluggish and sickly, and he seemed to be in some pain. C.O. Salcido refused to remove the inmate's handcuffs.

Five minutes later, Watson asked to use the toilet. Both C.O.s accompanied him to the bathroom two doors down and then waited in the hallway. Nurses bustled by, rolling patients on gurneys. A female doctor was speaking Spanish to a child. The same young woman who had brought the officers coffee stepped out of an office and smiled at Salcido. "It's a zoo tonight," she said.

C.O. Salcido heard a dull thud. He wrenched open the bathroom door. Lucas Watson lay rigid on the floor in a puddle of his own vomit. Great shudders wracked his body, his lungs sucked air, his eyeballs bulged out and rolled up under his lids.

"Shit! Get him out—" Salcido began, but he was silenced by the great noise of wrenching metal, shattered glass, and screams. Forty yards away, a pickup truck had just smashed through glass and plaster and slammed into the lobby adjacent to the emergency room.

C.O. Salcido yelled to a nurse for help with Lucas Watson. A woman dressed in surgical greens responded. She pushed her way into the bathroom as C.O. Barclay restrained the seizing inmate.

Even over Watson's harsh, guttural spasms, they heard the explosion of gunshots from the lobby. A woman shouted, a child screamed. C.O. Salcido charged into the conflict like a snorting bull.

C.O. Barclay watched Salcido disappear, but the nurse's order brought him back to attention.

"Get the cuffs off!"

"I can't—"

"Get them off before he dislocates both shoulders."

Barclay groped for the keys on his belt. Sweat ran down his face and throat as he tried to fit the key into the cuffs.

The nurse glared at Barclay. "Keep him down! He'll thrash his head!"

"I can't do both—" the key turned and the cuffs came off. "Oh, shit, he's turning blue!" Barclay moaned.

"Keep him still! I'll be right back." The bathroom door closed hydraulically behind the departing nurse.

C.O. Barclay clamped one hand on the jerking inmate's shoulder, the other on his hip. He wasn't ready for the shock of impact when Watson's body bucked and cracked upward. Barclay's jaw snapped behind the force of Watson's skull. Barclay gulped blood.

"Fuckin' pig!" Watson grunted as he jammed his head into the lumpish guard a second time.

"Ummmmph," the breath shuddered out of Barclay like air from a pierced inner tube.

Watson closed his fingers around Barclay's neck and dug his nails into skin. He leveraged his weight and smashed the C.O.'s head into the edge of the toilet.

Barclay went limp.

At the same instant, the nurse stepped through the door and saw a blood-soaked inmate staring back at her with white eyes. She stiffened in fear, but Lucas had her by the hair before she could scream. His body poised like a hitter, hands clamping hair instead of a bat, he slammed her into the wall and she went down.

He stuffed the unconscious C.O. into the shower stall, tore off the nurse's surgical top, and left her limp body where it had fallen. He slipped her shirt over his head, opened the bathroom door a crack, and peered out into the hall. He could see two nurses huddled behind the reception counter, their attention riveted on the sliding glass doors and the lobby directly beyond.

For an instant he stared, too. Under the glaze of fluorescent lights a bright yellow pickup truck looked like it was eating its way through plaster. A doctor, her white coat flapping, yelled orders. Two or three other people huddled over someone on the glass-strewn floor.

Lucas forced himself to walk out of the bathroom, and ten feet down the hall, he slipped into a curtained treatment bay.

Yellow eyes stared back at him. An old man was propped up in a wheelchair; a tube protruded from a hole in his throat.

Lucas inspected the wheelchair-bound man. "You're my ticket out of here, old man," he whispered. He heard raised voices.

Dr. Huffy's voice boomed out from the damaged lobby, "The cops are on their way!"

C.O. Salcido's voice exploded angrily, "Get down! Spread your legs!"

"You're fuckin' nobody! You're all fuckin' nobodies!" Even from a distance, Billy's voice was slurred and raw.

Lucas growled; they'd caught his brother.

He couldn't wait; he pushed the wheelchair. The ancient face rolled up at him, red eyes bulging. The tube in the old man's throat jerked like a straw as it sucked in and out of the fleshy hole.

Watson pushed the man past a nurse comforting a child, past a room where someone was crying, and through the door marked EXIT in hot red letters.

He moved briskly toward the west end of the ER parking lot. When he reached the last six car slots in the row nearest the hospital, he let the wheelchair go. It rolled forward—the old man straining like a landed fish—and bounced off a truck's fender.

At least three sirens wailed angrily. The sounds grew closer by the second.

The overhead street lamp was out; Watson's feet crunched broken glass. In the dark it was hard to see the colors of the vehicles. The blue Capri was parked second to last. Lucas found the key under the front bumper. He unlocked the door and slid behind the driver's seat. The map was on the seat next to him. Clothes, fast food, and a bottle of whiskey had been stashed on the floor. He was ravenous. He clamped a Big Mac between his teeth, turned the key, and felt the rumble of the engine in his bones.

SEVEN

Rosie spun out, struck a pose, and then whirled back into Ray's arms. She had her shoes off, the heels too high for dancing, and her stockinged feet moved easily to the funky beat of Los Lobos. Ray, though short and round, was the perfect dancer; he always made his partner look good. For most of their married life, Rosie had been Ray's principal dance partner but he'd been known to kick up his heels with various cousins, nieces, and even Abuelita Sanchez. Ray let out a whoop as he dipped Rosie back and planted a kiss square on her mouth. Laughing, Rosie led her husband off Rodeo Nites' dance floor and back to the small table where Sylvia was sitting.

"I'm getting old," Rosie said. Sylvia shook her head and pointed to her ear. Rosie tried again, forcing her voice over the loud bass beat of the music, "I'm getting too old to stay up past midnight."

"In that case, I'm dancing with Sylvia," Ray said.

Sylvia protested as he pulled her from the chair.

Rosie waved. "Just let him lead!" She watched her husband gliding Sylvia across the floor. Her friend was at least five inches taller than Ray, but the two still made a cute pair. Rosie was glad to see Sylvia laughing, having fun.

She eased her feet into magenta heels and glanced toward the bar. Through the smoke and press of bodies—for a Thursday, it was packed—she glimpsed a familiar face. She lost him in the crowd. When he reappeared following a majestic blond female, Rosie recognized the twice-broken nose and dark head of Matt England. It was easy to spot him for a cop. The authority of his presence couldn't be left at home with the uniform.

The woman tugged him toward the bar.

"Yo, Matt!" Rosie tried to catch his attention. He and the blonde were speaking—arguing?—and then Matt turned away and left her at the bar.

Rosie saw him exit Rodeo Nites. She pushed her way past urban cowboys and followed her friend out the door. The cold assaulted her skin and cleared her head.

"Hey, England," Rosie called.

He was hunkered against the stucco wall, both hands stuffed into pockets. "Rosie?" He returned her grin with an embarrassed smile that melted away fifteen years. She almost expected to hear a *gee whiz*.

Instead, Matt spit out his chewing gum and said, "What are you doing here?"

"Dancing with Ray. What's your excuse?" Rosie arched an eyebrow toward the bar's entrance. Two men were entering just as Matt's date appeared; they both turned to appraise her butt.

"Angelique," Matt said. It came out more like an apology than an introduction. "Angelique Harvey, this is Rosie Sanchez."

As Rosie extended her hand to meet Angelique's limp hand-shake, she got a whiff of smoke laced with expensive perfume. Neither woman spoke. With ample opportunity to survey Ms. Harvey's lithe body in skintight jeans, off-the-shoulder bandeau, and leather jacket, Rosie placed herself a mental bet—the clothes, the muscles, and the mane were all the result of a very recent divorce. The blonde gave Rosie a cool once-over.

To fill the silence, Matt spoke loudly. "Angelique's brother works at the lab with Gausser."

"Really?" No doubt Hansi Gausser, who ran the state crime lab, had fixed Matt up with Angelique. Gausser was terrific at his job, but completely inept at anything else, especially matchmaking. Pull in your claws, she told herself.

Rosie took Matt by the arm and navigated him to the edge of the walkway. "Did you look at the file I sent over?"

Matt frowned. "Missing body parts . . . I think the whole thing smells like gang bullshit." He shook his head slowly. "I'll tell you who to talk to . . . one of the honchos during the riot be-longed to the Aryan Brotherhood. That dude knows everything that's going on. Bubba Akins, a real sweetheart, remember him?"

Just as Rosie was about to answer, Ray stepped up and deliv-ered a punch that connected with Matt's shoulder.

"Time to try a few hands among friends."

"My poker's rusty, Ray," Matt said.

"Hey, all the better," Ray laughed.

Sylvia stood several feet away, arms crossed over her chest. An-gelique ignored Sylvia, but greeted Ray with a smile that was sixty degrees warmer than anything she'd flashed Rosie.

"Matt, have you met Sylvia Strange? She's an old friend—"

"I know who she is." Matt's voice sharpened with sarcasm, "She wrote the book on inmates who love too much." For the first time, he looked directly at Sylvia. "I see you got your acquit-tal on the Allmoy case. Remind me to get your phone number. I'll give you a call when he murders someone."

"Screw you," Sylvia said flatly.

Rosie grimaced and watched Sylvia stride toward her car. "Matthew, you little brat." She shook a finger at him. She heard Sylvia's car door slam.

"What?"

"You know what." Rosie waited while Sylvia's Volvo slowed on its way out of the lot.

Sylvia leaned her head out of the window and called to Rosie. "I'll give you a ring tomorrow." She glanced back at England and mumbled, "Macho fuck."

Rosie found Matt waiting beside his pickup truck. She leaned against the fender of the Mazda parked in the next slot. "Why were you so rude? I'll never forgive you."

"Yeah, you will." He crooked a finger, motioned her close enough to hear his confidence. "Did you ever hear me talk about the jackal?"

Rosie's butt slipped off the Mazda and she caught herself. She stared at him, stunned. "The jackal?"

"Right after the riot, that's when I heard about him."

Rosie shook her head. "The jackal existed fifteen years ago?" She sighed. "I only heard about him today from Angel Tapia."

Matt raised his eyebrows. "After the riot a snitch told me, '*El Chacal* was scavenging.' "

"Does that mean what I think it means?"

"Collecting miscellaneous body parts? Isn't that what jackals do —scavenge?" Matt grinned. "Interesting, *no?*"

"Was your source reliable?" Rosie asked.

"Under normal circumstances, yes. But OD'd on Thorazine ain't exactly normal." Matt frowned, "If the jackal existed, the dude was invisible."

From inside the truck, Angelique leaned across the seat and rolled down the driver's side window. "Can we go? I'm tired." She sounded angry.

"In a minute." Matt kept his eyes on Rosie. "I'd like to help you track him down."

El chacal. As far as Rosie knew, the name wasn't on file, but she'd run a thorough check tomorrow. She patted Matt on the arm and said, "Thank you, officer. And you try not to wear yourself out tonight, ya hear?"

Matt laughed as he climbed into the truck.

Ray was waiting in the Camaro when Rosie slid behind the steering wheel. She took a swipe at the tiny baby shoes suspended from the rearview mirror and said, "Thanks for waiting, handsome."

As she pulled her car into northbound traffic on Cerrillos Road, Ray remarked, "What was that between Matt and Sylvia?"

Rosie shook her head. "Professional animosity. I could wring his neck."

"Just stay out of it, Rosita."

Rosie clucked her tongue against her teeth. "What did you think of that babe?"

Ray belched. "I never knew Matt was such a lady killer."

"He's the lamb, and she's the wolf," Rosie said. She drove cautiously, on the alert for drunk drivers. Ray gave a noncommittal snort.

"I could tell you liked her," Ray said.

"I could tell you did, too."

Ray sank down in his seat and his belly expanded. "She's not my type."

Rosie laughed, "You'd better say that." After a pause, she added, "She's totally wrong for Matt."

Now Ray pulled himself up in the seat and ran his hand over his head. "Whoa! Here we go."

"What's that supposed to mean?" Rosie jerked the wheel, and the Camaro swerved to avoid a Range Rover. She swore softly in Spanish.

"*Nada*," Ray said.

Rosie shot him a look and said, "Don't nuthin' me. What are you trying to say?"

Ray rolled his eyeballs theatrically. "Why did I open my big mouth? One look at her body, and she's good for at least one thing Matt needs."

Much to his surprise, Rosie didn't respond. She kept her eyes on the road, a thoughtful expression on her face. At the intersection of St. Michael's Drive and Cerrillos Road, a high-rider with HIGH ROLLER painted on tinted windows ran the red light. Rosie jammed on the brakes and missed a collision by inches. Ray could smell burning rubber.

Suddenly, Rosie's beeper went off in shrill alarm. Ray read off the digitally displayed phone number.

"Colonel Gonzales," Rosie said.

"And I thought we might have one night without trouble."

—

DUKE WATSON ROSE from the governor's dinner table, apologized to the state's first lady, and took the phone call in the immense walnut-paneled library. Fresh hothouse orchids, petals delicately brushed mauve and peach, graced the Louis Quatorze desk. Their stems were contained in a Steuben vase. Duke separated a single stem and held the flower to the light; he saw a network of almost invisible veins.

"Duke? It's Herb."

Duke waited. He was still able to breathe, talk, smile. He smiled, but his eyes were fish eyes, void, lifeless.

"It's not good," Herb said. "I just heard from the state police. Lucas escaped." When there was no response from Duke, Herb continued, "There's more."

The orchid stem snapped in Duke's hand. "Billy."

Herb Burnett swallowed. God, he hated to be the messenger of bad news. Especially to a man who'd already suffered so many tragedies. He said, "Apparently, Billy stole a truck and drove it through the lobby of the hospital. Lucas got away, but a security guard had a gun, and Billy's in custody."

"And you're on your way," Duke said quietly.

"That's right . . ." Herb never knew what to do when the Duke froze up. He always felt like he was swimming alone in a very dark, very dangerous ocean. Now, he simply confirmed Duke's directive.

Duke hung up the phone and walked to the stone fireplace where he lifted a framed photograph from the mantle. It was a portrait of the governor, his handsome wife, their braces-and-ponytail daughter. The perfect family.

He examined the picture for a long time and then repositioned it with care.

On the way out of the library, he tossed the damaged orchid in a hand-pounded copper basket and replaced his smile for the governor and his wife.

—

It was close to midnight, but the streets were busy as Sylvia drove up Cerrillos Road. She slowed as she approached each intersection; her reactions were fuzzy after two drinks and no dinner.

At the corner of Cerrillos and Rodeo roads, the Volvo crawled to a stop behind a line of cars. Two state police cars were angled across the road, red lights pulsing. Sylvia's hands went cold; they must be looking for drunk drivers. She groaned—she'd had enough law enforcement for one evening—and rummaged in her glove compartment. Beneath a pile of papers and maps she found her proof of insurance, registration, and a stick of Dentyne. As soon as the gum was in her mouth she slapped her face with her fingers. She couldn't believe two drinks had made her tipsy.

The line of vehicles inched ahead. A uniformed officer leaned into the window of each car, another held a flashlight that he aimed through windshields, a third gripped a rifle. With a dry mouth, Sylvia eased the Volvo to the head of the line.

"Good evening, ma'am." The light scoured her car's interior. "This is a roadblock. Where are you headed?"

"Home. La Cieneguilla."

With a nod, the officer said, "We're searching for an escaped inmate, ma'am."

Sylvia shivered and instantly pictured Lucas Watson. "Do you know who it is?"

The officer leaned close to her window and shook his head. "Someone from the hospital."

Sylvia asked, "The state hospit—?"

But the officer had reached out one quieting hand; the other went to his left ear. Sylvia realized he wore an earphone and was listening to the radio clamped to his belt.

He moved several paces from her car and she took a breath. The state mental hospital was located sixty miles to the northeast in Las Vegas, New Mexico. There were some extreme cases in the hospital's violent ward. Not the kind of guys you wanted to run into late at night, when the lights went out.

The officer moved past her car again and she was about to repeat her question when he said, "Be careful, ma'am, and lock your doors."

—

LUCAS LAY CURLED on her bed, his face buried in her white silk blouse, his thumb in his mouth. Had he been resting for minutes, hours? He wasn't sure because his thoughts had been lost in the past, back in that other time, back on that other bed. He tasted salt, a tear. He'd been crying.

The shower continued to drip, a maddening, methodic sound. He counted each drop, caught himself, and bit his own arm. His skin was pink from scrubbing, it tasted of soap and powder. The scent made him think of pretty women on TV who worried about their laundry.

Clothes, books, baskets, cosmetics, jewelry, notebooks, pages—all were strewn around the bed. Her dresses were scented with her, a musky perfume. Panties, shoes, sweaters—everything smelled of her.

But no pouch.

He selected each item with care: black silk panties, black bra, black stockings. And bloodred fuck-me shoes.

———

SHE TURNED OFF the gravel road onto dirt, maneuvering the car to avoid ruts and ditches. The dark shapes standing so close to the roadside were cows. She could almost reach out to touch them. In the pasture, two horses pressed their heavy flanks against a wire fence. The car hit a pothole and old metal shuddered. Across the river, the Calidros' two-story house was lit up, surrounded by a pool of light from the arc flood suspended thirty feet in the air. Sylvia navigated the Volvo toward the lighted portal of her own house. She set the brake, cut the engine, and listened to the soft ticking of hot steel as it cooled.

The gate sagged open at an angle, and Rocko didn't respond to her whistle.

"Damn mutt," she muttered. As usual, he was out after some bitch in heat. Sylvia avoided the patches of snow that had hardened to ice on the flagstone walkway. She inserted her key in the front lock. From inside, she heard the phone ring.

EIGHT

In the shadows of semidarkness, he waited. Her key in the lock made a scraping noise that strained his nerves. His mouth filled with saliva, his mind with anticipation—a warm tingling zap of electricity that traveled to his groin.

Lucas Watson jumped at the sudden intrusion of the telephone. Each ring seemed to build in intensity until, abruptly, her voice filled the room. The effect was hypnotic until Lucas was jarred again by the electronic beep.

"Sylvia? Pick up, it's Rosie. Are you there? I've got to talk to you right away. Call me as soon as you get in; it's an emergency."

The voice ended as precipitously as it had begun, and the dial tone agitated Lucas Watson. He stepped back several feet expecting the door to open. When it didn't, he jammed his bare foot down and felt glass shatter. There was no pain as the skin of his right heel slid wet against tile. Carefully, he set his cheek to the wood and listened.

———

THE RINGING HAD stopped. Sylvia tried to turn the key in the lock, but nothing happened. She pressed her ear against the door and strained to decipher words amplified by the answering machine. She felt a splinter from the coarse wood stab her cheek. Her breathing sounded loud in her ears. From inside the house there was a blur of sound and then a low decibel hum. She glanced down at the key, tried it again. With pressure from her wrist, it caught, bent, and broke.

She held the detached base of the key in her hand; just that morning, she'd stopped at a locksmith shop and had the damn thing reground. She stepped away from the door and stared at the fused lock.

Alcohol and fatigue had combined to dull her senses and increase her frustration. She wanted to climb into bed, pull the covers over her head, and sleep. *Fat chance.* The back door was locked with a dead bolt; that key was inside a drawer in the kitchen.

Rodeo Nites had been a mistake, and she was tired and cold. She frowned and considered breaking a window to climb through. Unfortunately, they were all triple pane and expensive.

Her body tensed. She turned and stared at the door. Had she heard something? An icicle cracked suddenly from the roof gutter and impaled itself in a bush. She turned back toward her car and whistled for Rocko. The only response was a dog barking in the distance.

Enough already. She would drive to Rosie and Ray's, apologize for the late hour, and spend the night on the couch.

—

LUCAS BOLTED TO the small window that offered a view of the portal and the driveway. He saw her back away, and fury and frustration propelled his body toward the door. Driven by emotion and reflex, he didn't feel the pain of impact. The wood trembled but held. He braced to throw himself again, but stopped suddenly. If he acted now, he could reach her.

He sprinted toward the rear of the house where he had broken in; years of pent-up energy suddenly unleashed catapulted him through the gaping glass hole.

The Volvo roared to life and accelerated. At a flat-out run, Lucas stayed parallel with her car. His fingers scraped across the Volvo's bumper. His breath was coming in ragged gulps. He held on, stumbled, kept pace for another twenty yards. Then he hit the invisible wall and felt his muscles seize up. He veered off, his foot snagged a gopher hole, and he stumbled forward.

The stolen Capri was two hundred yards from her house. Hours ago he'd concealed it between a cluster of salt cedar and a scrub oak. He jumped in.

The engine caught, and Lucas scraped gears and bit his tongue as the sedan slammed over ruts and moguls. He was traveling blind, headlights off, straining to catch sight of her car in the distance. There was a sharp washboard rattle as the car crossed the cattle guard. Her taillights came into view a quarter mile ahead.

—

SYLVIA DOWNSHIFTED AND the Volvo slowed to a crawl. Her mouth tasted sour and her clothes smelled smoky. She pushed in the cigarette lighter, and then she reached into the glove compartment in search of a smoke. The rough metal edge of the old dash sliced her finger; it was surprisingly painful.

As she sucked blood from the cut, she remembered to check under the passenger visor. A pack of Marlboros fell to the floor.

Sylvia groped under the passenger seat, felt the cellophane pack, and flipped a cigarette loose. The lighter popped up in the dash. She held the glowing tip to the Marlboro and inhaled with nervous pleasure. She accelerated, turned left.

Traffic on Airport Road was light, few cars in either direction. As she shifted into third, she caught a flash of metal in her rearview window; it was gone when she looked again. A bolt of fear traveled her spine. *We're searching for an escaped inmate, ma'am.* The cop had never actually said the escapee was from the state hospital.

The golf course appeared on her right. Unnaturally green turf gleamed under lurid artificial lights. On the other side of the road, the gravel yards, welding shops, and junkyards formed a rural-industrial moonscape. Sweat had broken out on Sylvia's face and she cracked the window for air. Headlights flashed in her rearview mirror. Highbeams. They flashed again. And again.

Sylvia tried to shake her mounting fear. It was probably some drunk or a teenager out for a cruise.

She sped up. Fifty-five. Sixty. Sixty-five. Seventy miles per hour over asphalt and ice patches. The other car stayed right on the Volvo's bumper. The speedometer was edging toward eighty—too fast even for an alert, totally sober driver.

The other car pulled alongside. She glanced over. At first, all she saw was the silhouette of the driver. When the interior of the other car was illuminated momentarily by flashing lights, Sylvia felt sick. The sharp profile, the hollow cheeks, the buzz cut: *Lucas.*

His car veered closer, forcing the Volvo toward the gravel shoulder of the road. To avoid the ditch, she had to pull back onto asphalt. The crunch of scraping metal made Sylvia grit her teeth.

Her hands jerked off the wheel when the sedan smashed into the Volvo's door.

The Volvo careened off asphalt, bounced along the shoulder,

and skidded on a patch of ice. Sylvia fought to keep the tires turned in the direction of the skid. The steering wheel shimmied dangerously as the tires hit dirt. A ditch materialized in her headlamps. She screamed and wrenched the car toward the road.

But Lucas forced her Volvo back onto the soft shoulder.

Three times her Volvo took the impact of the speeding sedan. Although the vehicle was built like a tank, it suffered from each blow. Her left headlight was blown, a grinding noise seemed to be centered in the transmission, the steering wheel shimmied steadily, and metal must have torn loose under the hood.

She was racing for the flashing red lights on Cerrillos Road. She gauged the distance to the intersection at a quarter mile now. The sedan cut straight into her fender.

The Volvo spun out in a mad spiral, Sylvia's skull smacked metal, and she felt a sickening flash of pain along her neck.

Lights, a sense of everything happening in slow motion, a glimpse of Lucas Watson's crazed face. For an instant, she thought she really did see him laugh, but that was impossible. It was dark, all happening too fast, and the sedan driven by Lucas was sliding in the opposite direction.

The Volvo completed its three-sixty rotation. It skidded to a stop and Sylvia slumped over the steering wheel. *Oh Jesus.* She took several labored breaths, did a quick mental inventory, and sampled blood; although she'd bitten her lip in at least three places and she had a crashing headache, she seemed to be in one piece.

But what about Lucas?

Sylvia couldn't see his car anywhere. She drove slowly, shakily toward the roadblock.

"Turn off your engine!"

It took Sylvia a few seconds to realize the officer was addressing her. She opened her car door.

"Keep your hands in view!"

She stumbled when she stood. She looked at the young cop and said, "You don't understand."

"Get out of the car!"

———

WHEN LUCAS SAW the flashing lights of the roadblock, he swung the car into a parking lot between a liquor lounge and a trailer park. He wasn't ready for the rush of blood through his carotid arteries. He felt as if the skin over his body was expanding grotesquely, bloating like a balloon from the pressure. He slammed open the car door, collapsed on the icy pavement, and regained his feet slowly.

He wasn't sure if he called out, but a woman answered. Lucas tried to focus. The woman wanted to know if he was all right. Was he all right?

Sylvia had come back for him.

"Hey, are you sick, mister?"

Lucas fell against the side of the car and wiped a hand across his face. He barely made her out, standing in front of a neon sign.

Sylvia . . . she's such a bad girl.

"Why don't you come in for a drink, hon?"

Her legs were long, and her voice was husky. He called out, "Sylvia!"

"Who the hell is Sylvia? I'm Lorraine!" She was laughing, moving toward him, weaving slightly as she walked.

Lucas heaved himself up using one arm and the pressure increased in his head until he was certain his skull had cracked. He vomited suddenly.

"Gross!" The woman backed away and fell against the brick steps that led to the lounge. Her face pulsed with the light of flashing neon.

"Bitch!" Lucas bared his teeth and slithered forward like a snake on ice. His fingers closed on the coarse fabric of her skirt.

The woman screamed, and she scratched at him, long fingernails scraping skin from his face. For a moment, he loosened his grip, and she galloped on all fours through the door of the lounge.

Lights flashed on in the trailer, and he heard voices behind him. As he turned, three men emerged from the lounge. One of them shouted something and there was an explosion of sound and light. The bullet struck the sedan and Lucas threw back his head and screamed Sylvia's name. Then he shot forward between two trailers, dodged a human form, and kept running. His bare feet left a trail of bloody prints.

NINE

"As far as you know, nothing's missing?" Criminal Agent Matt England sat on the edge of the chair with his arms folded over his chest. He looked like a rock, solid and impenetrable, in a sea of chaos. The overturned couch was flayed and disemboweled, a mass of foam, feathers, and fabric. Tiny bits of blue and white pottery covered the floor like aquamarine sand. A brass standing lamp lay prostrate against an end table. Magazines, books, video-tapes, and a rubber dog bone were scattered like flotsam.

Sylvia stared at her living room, held out both hands, then shook her head. Ray Sanchez set one giant hand on her shoulder and squeezed to lend her strength. She glanced at him gratefully, and he felt renewed concern; she was pale as milk, and she was trembling. When Matt sent him a look—a silent command to wait outside—Ray shook his head.

"It's okay, Ray," Sylvia said softly. "I'll be okay."

After a moment, Ray nodded. "If you need me . . ."

"Thanks," she murmured. When she was alone with Matt England she pointed at a dark smear on the floor. "Is that his blood?"

"We'll find out. We've already collected samples," England answered. He fingered the keys on his belt while he spoke.

"I wasn't ready for this." Sylvia's voice dropped. The first sight of the damage had left her stunned and feeling violated.

"Do you know who's responsible?" Matt England asked.

"You don't?" Sylvia heard her anger breaking through. "Lucas Watson walked away from St. Vincent's hospital last night. I know it's not your job to make assumptions, but who the hell do you think did this?"

"Matt?" A uniformed trooper appeared in the doorway. He cleared his throat, kept his eyes on England, and said, "We're ready."

England gave Sylvia an appraising glance. "I'd like you to follow me, but don't touch anything."

Sylvia willed herself forward, but her body resisted. Instead, she slumped against the wall and pressed both hands to the cool plaster. The truth was, she didn't know whether she could cope. She wondered if she was coping now.

"Do you need to sit down?"

Matt England's voice sounded far away. Sylvia felt sick, angry, and on the verge of losing control. Only her rage gave her the energy to follow England down the hall.

The destruction was worse in her bedroom. Her bedspread was turned down and wrinkled as if someone had slept on it. In the center of the duvet, Sylvia saw her clothes laid out neatly: her stockings, her black lace brassiere and silk underpants. Red velvet high heels had been placed on the floor. She sniffed something strange—the air was infused with a distinctive metallic odor.

The trooper and a female forensic evidence technician stood near the bed whispering in hushed tones. Sylvia stared at them dumbly. For a few seconds, she couldn't swallow. Since entering the house, she had been aware of her own growing discomfort. At first, the sensation was a vague tightness in her stomach, then it seeped up to her chest, and finally, it took her by the throat. Instead of her clothes, it might easily have been her own body arranged neatly, lifelessly, on the bed.

England blocked her further entry into the room and nodded toward the wall at the base of her bed. "He left you a message."

At first she only saw the watercolor in the shattered frame, the carved wooden *Dia Del Muerte* figurines, and the massive armoire. It took her a moment to make out the words written in red lipstick on the armoire's mirrored door. She began to read: "Once you spill the first—"

"Once you spill the first blood, there's no turning back." England's voice sounded unnaturally loud. "Do you know what he meant?"

Sylvia shook her head, but she still couldn't speak. She locked the sentence in her memory and allowed England to usher her out of the room. He stopped at the bathroom door and let her look inside. A lab technician was seated on the edge of the porcelain tub brushing surfaces with dark powder. Sylvia examined her own bathroom as if it belonged to a stranger. The shattered cosmetic bottles and their contents—the creams, the lotions, the shampoos —that were coagulating on the floor formed a Rorschach pattern. Damp towels hung like drapery over the toilet.

Detachment felt safe.

"He took a shower." She registered surprise that her question had come out as a statement. Matt England nodded.

They returned to the living room, and the patrol officer brought coffee in Styrofoam cups. Sylvia gulped the scalding liquid and glanced at her watch. It was already 6 A.M.; sunshine penetrated the east-facing windows and spilled onto the floor. When she kept her eyes on that spot, it was possible to believe nothing was wrong. That square of tile seemed normal, the way the rest of the house had always been before last night. She drank more coffee, sipping this time, and turned to find Matt England watching her. He was seated on the chair again.

Sylvia faced him. "He urinated in the bedroom?"

England rubbed a hand through short graying hair. Deep lines stood out around his eyes; his tanned face looked faded and dull. "You're the shrink, you tell me."

"He marked my clothes and the bed with body fluids—urine and semen. Did you find any shit?"

"No." England reached into his jacket pocket and pulled out a roll of Life Savers. A thin ribbon of wrapper trailed from his hand. He knocked a green candy off the roll with his thumb, popped it into his mouth, and then offered the pack to Sylvia. "You must have a pretty good idea what he was after."

She pictured it then, the pouch, leather soft and dark with the oil of fingers and constant fondling. It had been like a worry bead for Lucas Watson, tucked away in the dark corners of his consciousness. It meant so much to him, he would commit violence to get it back. But he hadn't just come for his pouch; his behavior in the bedroom had convinced her of that. The clothes laid out so carefully on the bed, the masturbation, the lipstick message—all impressed her as elements of a private ritual he was acting out.

Matt England's voice disturbed her thoughts like a stone on water. He said, "I'd like to hear about your drive home from Rodeo Nites." He held a small tape recorder in his hand and clicked it on.

"Don't you have better things to do?" Her voice was shrill. She began collecting broken glass from the antique picture frame on the floor near her foot. Her great-grandmother's Italian eyes gazed into space. Sylvia didn't feel the cut until beads of blood collected under the glass fragments in her palm. This was the third time in a week that she had injured her hands.

Matt England set the tape cassette down and began to reach out toward her.

"Don't!" Sylvia froze. She stared at her hand as if someone else had gathered the collection of broken glass.

He didn't speak. Instead he held up a wastebasket and Sylvia emptied her palm. He left for a moment and returned with a wet paper towel. She pressed it against the wound. He questioned her with professional concern. "You going to be all right?"

It was tempting to laugh, or cry, or scream, but somehow she gathered the self-control that had threatened to shatter as cleanly as the glass frame. It covered her now like a second skin. She took comfort in the familiar and repeated the sequence of events as she remembered them from the time she left Rodeo Nites. England held his questions until she was through. What route home did she take? What did the first cop at the roadblock tell her? Had the lock given her trouble before?

"I meant to get it fixed weeks ago—" Her voice trailed off as the realization hit her. When she spoke again, her voice was flat. "He was in the house while I was at the door."

Matt England cleared his throat and bit off a yellow Life Saver from the pack. "That's my guess. He broke a window in back."

"Jesus, I can't . . . can we go outside?" Sylvia stepped out, saw the familiar landscape, scrubbed hills, cottonwoods, and took several deep breaths. The fresh air was jarring and felt clean. Ray was standing near Sylvia's car; his face wore a quizzical expression. She waved at him and followed England into his unmarked Chevy. He started the engine and turned the heat on full. Sylvia aimed the closest vent toward her chest, felt the hot air, and closed her eyes. England looked at the woman seated next to him. She hunched forward in the seat, her face shaded by the visor. England felt his own fury at her emotional defenses dissipate as he realized his courtroom adversary was now another victim. She puzzled him. He knew she wasn't someone who let her guard down easily, and yet her vulnerability was tangible. He felt a twinge of regret for the way he'd treated her at Rodeo Nites.

"What?" Sylvia asked. "You've been staring at me."

"A security guard and a C.O. caught Billy Watson at the hospital. Apparently, he helped his brother escape."

"Thanks for telling me."

"Why don't you tell me about the pouch?"

Sylvia was silent for a moment before she said, "Because Rosie already told you." She crossed her arms.

Matt England spoke quietly. "I don't give a damn about your house. I'm worried about what he would have done to you. What he still wants to do to you. That message on the mirror was fairly graphic."

"Lucas Watson didn't come here to kill me."

Matt England almost choked on his Life Saver. "You don't think he's dangerous?"

"Oh, he's dangerous; but he came here to tell me something, not to murder me."

The scorn in England's voice was thick. "What did he want you to know . . . that he's from a dysfunctional family unit? His father works hard to keep that fact a secret." Matt was well acquainted with Lucas Watson's father. The senator from District 9 had a habit of using law enforcement when and how it suited him.

"Lucas needs help."

Matt gave a short humorless laugh, "No shit. But I don't think this was just a cry for help, Dr. Strange. I recommend you look into an alarm system for your house. Soon."

Sylvia pressed her forehead against the passenger window. She could smell coffee on her own breath. From the corner of her eye, she saw a patrol car. Another vehicle pulled into the driveway.

"Stay here," England said brusquely. "I'll be right back." He was gone for several minutes. He conferred with an officer, then disappeared inside the house. When he returned he pulled the door open with too much force. "They just apprehended Lucas Watson behind the country club less than a mile from here. Looks like he was on his way back to find you."

———

WIND SENT CLOUDS scudding across the moon as the van transported Lucas Watson and two correctional officers to pod 3-B North Facility. He'd been questioned all day by the state police, Rosie Sanchez, and others whose faces he couldn't remember. It was almost a relief to arrive at Maximum; at least he'd be left alone. The C.O.s guided him through the medical sally port next to Administration. When Watson stepped out of the van, handcuffed, his first sight was a metal fence and razor ribbon three layers deep. Although he'd heard about North Facility, Maximum, he'd never seen beyond the walls. One C.O. spoke into a radio, and the sixteen-foot-high gate slowly rolled back to reveal a diagonal walkway that was completely encased to form a caged tunnel. Beyond the tunnel, in the yard, a dome of branches was draped with animal skins. It was a sweat lodge used by Indian inmates.

Watson saw a small square building constructed of naked concrete blocks to the right of the yard: the death house.

The three men kept walking.

When they reached the orange steel doorway to the housing unit, the C.O. on Watson's left pressed a black button and stated his business through the intercom. There was a loud buzz and the C.O. pushed the door open. Inside, meshed windows on pod doors revealed a concrete wasteland.

Someone tapped metal on glass, an officer in the control booth overhead. Shoved from behind, Watson entered the strip cage beneath the booth. He felt eyes on him, at least five pairs of eyes, and at the same time, he heard the long thin sound of keening, the sound that passed for music in housing unit 3-B. It rose like a ribbon echoing off ten-inch prefab concrete walls, and, because there was no escape, crashed down again in despair.

Lucas blocked out the sound. He'd never be broken by this place, by these enemies. In every fiber of his body, he knew he'd have his pouch back soon. This escape had failed, but there were other ways.

TEN

When Rosie passed the officer's lounge, the afternoon C.O. shift briefing was in full swing. The lieutenant on duty was announcing a temporary halt to repairs on the roof of North's gym. Civilian workmen had been mending leaks at both the Main and North facilities. "Security clearance will remain as is for the next five days. The workers' names are on the list, and no replacements will be allowed—no exceptions—without written approval from the warden's office."

Rosie groaned; all she needed were more outraged inmates who couldn't get their daily exercise. She blocked out the uninspired drone of the lieutenant's deep voice, caught a glimpse of brown uniforms, bored expressions, and blue plastic chairs, and sighed. She was frustrated by the lack of progress on what she now called the jackal case. She wasn't getting hard information from her standard informants, but the grapevine was simmering: *The joint's gonna blow, man.* And despite the unrest caused by the missing limbs, despite the pen's population running at an all-time high, the warden had stuck his head in the sand like the governor's ostrich.

Rosie rapped on an open door and entered the office of Colonel Gonzales.

He looked up from the white mountain of reports on his desk and waved a hard square of chewing gum at Rosie Sanchez. "I quit smoking," he announced. He was in his early fifties, a medium-sized man who still packed his uniform with muscle. His hair was brown and thick except where an island of scalp was starting to show on top. The smile was leisurely, but the eyes never slowed.

Rosie sat in the single chair facing his desk. "Does gum help?"

"Nicorette. Nope, it doesn't help a bit." He leaned back in resignation, and his belly pressed over a thin brown belt. "So, what are we going to do about our unhappy campers? I got a bad feeling, a déjà vu from 1980."

"We farm out about two hundred inmates so we're back to normal overcrowding, we separate gang members, we fix the gym. Then we find out who's causing the trouble; who chopped Angel Tapia's finger, and what happened to Swanson's penis. When we do those things and answer those questions, we cool things down." Rosie crossed her legs and drummed the metal arms with her fingernails.

"You got a plan?"

"I'm on my way to interview Bubba Akins."

Colonel Gonzales snorted. "Areeyyyan Brotherhood!" He popped the gum into his mouth and made a face. "That sonofabitch breathes on you, you die. But Bubba was locked up tight in North when Angel's pinkie took a walk."

Rosie smoothed a wrinkle in the ankle of her stocking and nodded. "Most of his Aryan brothers weren't."

The colonel patted his breast pocket automatically before remembering he had joined the ranks of nonsmokers. He frowned and said, "You think his white boys are doing it? Bubba's never been a snitch."

"Why do you think I came to see you?"

"You missed me?"

She put both hands on the colonel's cluttered desk. "Bubba Akins saved your life during the riot. If anybody knows his soft spot . . ." She left the sentence dangling, waiting for Gonzales to push away the memories of his forty-eight hours in hell.

Colonel Gonzales fingered a tuft of dark hair sprouting from the well of his ear. "He's got a squeeze . . . Sugar, or Shug. He's crazy about her. She's trouble—got caught with a coke balloon in her mouth, got her name rubbed off the visitor's list."

"Anything else?" Rosie stood.

"Yeah. He saved my life because I always gave him a fair deal. But he killed at least three inmates with his bare hands. Don't forget, Bubba's an asshole with his own brand of justice." Colonel Gonzales removed the wad of gum from his mouth and tossed it toward a trash can. With a splat, it landed an inch below the outside rim and stuck.

At the door Rosie turned and said, "By the way, José. Was it doctor's orders?"

"What?"

"To give up smoking?"

"Are you kidding?" José Gonzales shook his head thoughtfully. "Who listens to the doctor?" He threw Rosie a rueful smile. "My wife's."

———

THE PERMANENTLY SUNBURNED bulk of Bubba Akins filled the doorway of the examination room of North's hospital. He shot Rosie a puzzled look and slapped his fat thighs. "I thought I was gettin' a shot or somethin'."

Rosie stood and motioned to a chair. She held her breath when Akins sat, but somehow the wood accommodated his great mass. "I wanted somewhere we could talk without interruption," Rosie said.

For a moment there was only the sound of his labored breath. His nose had been pulverized so many times it lay flat against his doughboy face.

Rosie examined him carefully. The perfect white supremacist, she thought: mean eyes, florid skin, the body of a giant oak. A chill ran down her body.

As if he read her thoughts, Akins shot her a lewd smirk. "I can't think of anythin' you and I have to talk abou' . . ." He dropped the phonic at the end of a word like he was too lazy to keep his lips working.

"Wrong, Bubba," Rosie answered.

Bubba Akins's response was to shrug his thick shoulders and rework his lips into a wet grin.

"You earned yourself a reputation," Rosie said.

Bubba's grin widened.

"Too bad that reputation can't help you on visiting day." She returned his smile. "I hear you've been talking to the compliance monitor."

The smile didn't waiver, but Akins's blue button eyes hardened.

"I thought maybe we could make sure there's no mix-up with Shug." Rosie kept her voice steady, then she crossed her arms and waited for the thought to sink in. She could almost hear the whine of Akins's brain grinding away on all three cylinders. She began slowly, "It's so long ago now, and since I wasn't here . . . I need someone with an accurate memory of the riot."

"Yeah . . ."

Rosie felt her way around the approach to Akins and decided direct was best. "I need to know about *el chacal*. The jackal." To her surprise, Akins laughed, a breathless snorting hoot.

"Yeah . . . the jacka'. People been lookin' for him for years. You want to know who lifted that pretty little beaner's finger?" Bubba Akins shifted his bulk to the edge of the chair so two legs rose from the floor. "The jacka' shoulda cut off that dirty homie's dick, steada his finga."

"Who is it, Bubba?"

"I ain't no snitch." Bubba Akins shook his head, "That all the problem you got, pretty señorina?" He smiled. "I think the warden after your sweet ass, huh? You don't catch this body snatcha, this hungry ghost, the warden gonna blame you when the riot goes down." He wagged a finger at Rosie. "But, I don't know nothin'. We talk 'bout nothin'. I jus' here for a shot of somethin'."

"Does the jackal exist? Tell me who he is. You could stop another riot."

"Riot? You talkin' to me 'bout a riot?" With a finger digging at his nose, Bubba Akins said, "Talk 'bout my sweet Shug, 'stead. The lady been treated real bad. Hell of a time gettin' in to see her sugardaddy."

Rosie emphasized each word: "It won't happen again."

Bubba smiled. "The jacka' exist and he happy to see anotha riot. He got a job to do. Riot jus' make his job easier." He stood up, and his three hundred pounds redistributed themselves along his frame.

Rosie wasn't ready to let him go. When she blocked his way, she had to tilt her chin skyward to see his face. "What kind of job? You mean kill someone?"

"Yes, ma'am. He gonna take somebody out." He stared at Rosie so long that sweat beaded and dripped from under her arms. Finally, he smiled and his eyes disappeared under pink lids. "The way things go, you might tell your friend, the one with the legs, she be careful."

Rosie stopped breathing. "You mean Dr. Strange? Is he trying to kill—"

"And you should watch out for yourself, too."

"Bubba—"

"Gotta go." He moved forward and Rosie had no choice but to step out of the doorway. He said, "The jacka' don' botha me none. These days, lots of folks got a hunger for the dead." For a moment, his bulk blacked out the lights in the hall, then he turned the corner and vanished.

—

THE JACKAL LET the bucket dance against his leg as he navigated the stairway that led down to the shop areas. A new C.O. was supposed to be on day duty, but his post was empty. The jackal hummed to himself, "I did it my way."

Several inmates lounged against the walls outside the wood shop. Their blue shirts hung open, exposing white T-shirts. The piercing scream of electric saw and drill shattered the air. No one paid much attention to the jackal as he disappeared into a utility room next to the shops.

Cobwebs drifted from the sagging ceiling tiles. A soiled mattress leaned against the naked block wall. Rags were piled in one corner along with several mildewed textbooks. Home sweet home. The jackal settled himself between the mattress and the rags.

He took a square of butcher paper from his pocket and creased and folded it neatly. When he peered down into his bucket, pine fumes assaulted his nasal passages and made his normally labored breath even more difficult.

Inmate Daniel Swanson's penis, a gray morsel, drifted rhythmically to and fro in an inch of cleaning fluid. It had not aged well during the week since Swanson had cut it off. The jackal acknowledged a momentary pang of disappointment but shook off the feeling. Science was so often the collaboration of many not-so-impressive parts fused into the Lord's magnificence.

Word in the joint was that Daniel Swanson wanted his penis back. The jackal felt no remorse. If you couldn't take care of your things, you didn't deserve to keep them.

The pint of wood preservative was stored in its usual place—the hollow center of a loose cinder block. The jackal used his finger as a tool, pried off the lid and brushed the pungent oil over flesh and butcher paper.

Today, as he began his military fold, he was distracted by thoughts of his younger sister. After Nam—all that dirty business —she had been brutally disappointed in her hopes for her brother. But there was still time to change all that, to renew her faith in him.

He thought, also, of the nosy shrink. She wrote a book about inmates, and Lucas Watson had showed it around and bragged that she was going to get him out of the joint. She was a snafu, all right. But the jackal didn't kill casually these days. Maybe, if she backed off, he would let her live.

Satisfied that the treatment was complete and his new package was ready to go into storage, the jackal tidied up, took a moment to disappear inside himself, and left the utility room. Walking the hall, surrounded by a stream of inmates exiting the shop areas, he was as obtrusive as air.

—

BILLY WATSON DRAINED the last of the beer in an effort to chase away the sickening taste of cops, courts, and lawyers. Hours of interrogation with that dick-ass cop Matt England—not to mention the arraignment when he was forced to talk to his dick lawyer Herb Burnett—had made him crazy. The old man put up the seventy-five grand bail bond, but didn't show his face in public. Big fucking surprise. Assisting an escape and conspiracy. With his old man pulling strings, Billy knew he could walk.

He got out of the 'vette, slammed the door, and traversed a rough stone walkway. Broken leaves scuttled like tiny crabs across the porch of the white house on Lena Street and came to rest on the welcome mat. Curtains covered the windows facing the street, and a large sign with black, block lettering against a white plywood background hung near the door: TATTOOS. And in smaller letters, RING BELL.

Billy hunched both shoulders as if an invisible weight had settled on his leather jacket. He took a last drag off his cigarette and
tossed the butt on the sidewalk. It took him a moment to find the
doorbell, a tiny steel nipple hidden high on the edge of the door
frame. While he waited, he watched cars pulling into the parking
lot at the corner. The Sabrosa restaurant was popular with the
lunch crowd. State secretaries in high heels and tight skirts maneuvered between parked cars and potholes. A charmed snake,
Billy watched their hips dancing under winter clothes.

He rang the bell again, then opened the door and entered what
looked like a living room. Even in dim light, the furniture was
visibly threadbare. A pillow rested in the elbow of a vinyl sofa, a
braided rug covered the linoleum floor, and a pay telephone was
mounted on the wall. His attention fixed on the myriad tattoo
designs above the sofa. Snakes, skulls, and guns. Breasts, blondes,
and buttocks. Saints. Virgins.

He inhaled deeply and pushed his hair away from his face. A
feeling of sudden relief surprised him and propelled him into action. There were two interior doors in the room. He opened one
and stared at the upturned face of a man seated at a desk. The
man was whip-thin, and he had leathery skin, long black braids,
and restless eyes. Two sheets of paper, pencils, and packets of dis-
posable needles were spread in front of him. A cord extended to a
circuit in the ceiling.

"You're Gideon," Billy said flatly.

The man stared.

"You did a tattoo for my brother." He took two steps into the
room and sat down on a wooden stool. "You remember the tattoo
you did for Lucas? It was five years ago."

"You got a picture?"

Billy pulled two Polaroids from his jacket pocket.

Gideon stared down at the Virgin of Guadalupe. The fluidity of
line, the depth and perspective, the detail work—this Madonna
was beautiful. A man worked a lifetime to achieve some small

speck of perfection. Gideon knew his art was parasitic; when the host died, so did his art. He grunted in recognition. "Yeah, she's mine."

"That's what I want," Billy said.

"I never repeat anything, man. It's part of my art."

Billy leaned over the stool and shook his head. "Not this time, bro. This time it's got to be the same . . . line for line." He set his wallet on the table. A thick fringe of bills was visible.

Gideon stared at the money, then licked his lips and nodded.

—

IN THE CAFETERIA, a line had formed for chow. The jackal bypassed this, nodding greetings to C.O.s Salcido and Mora. He waved at Joseph "Greasy" Spoon, who had been running the kitchen almost as far back as the jackal's first day at PNM, May 23, 1974. The man was doing twenty and a 'bitch. Greasy twitched his left eye in greeting and leaned casually against the edge of the counter.

"You gonna add some Lysol to sweeten the stew?" C.O. Mora laughed as he cruised by the two men.

The jackal set the bucket on the counter and Greasy accepted it without looking inside. Before the jackal left, he rubbed his palm over the shiny chrome surface of the counter.

"I've told you not to do that a thousand times," Greasy snapped. "I just polished with Windex and now you smeared it." With a scowl, he turned his back on the jackal and took the bucket through the kitchen right past inmate Andre Miller, who was chopping onions, past the steaming twenty-gallon double boilers, through the prep area, and beyond the stacked crates of tomato sauce, peas, and reconstituted potatoes. In the deepest recesses of the kitchen, next to the door that opened onto the sally-port loading dock, Greasy unlocked the padlock on the old walk-in. The aroma of stale ice and Freon blasted him as the twelve-inch-thick door groaned open. At the very back, behind plastic crates of salt pork, mountains of white bread, logs of yellow cheese, and several unidentified and long-frozen boxes, Greasy paused. He set the bucket on the ground and tucked the jackal's neatly wrapped parcel in the corner of a milk crate. It matched its half-dozen neighbors in outer wrap, if not in size. Greasy stuck his finger in his ear, dug for wax, and considered. One parcel was the shape of a shoe box, another barely as big as a finger. But one tube, long and heavy and propped against a crate of wieners, must've weighed at least thirty pounds. He'd rotate the parcels soon. He liked to keep them moving from the old walk-in to the new freezer and back. Whatever they contained, he didn't want to know.

—

THE INSTANT SYLVIA opened her front door, she smelled pine and raw chemicals. The pungent smell was disinfectant. She held a shiny key in her hand. The Merry Maids had left a set in the mailbox, and this one fit the new dead bolt.

She forced herself to enter. She almost regretted refusing Rosie's offer to accompany her, but the need to face the house on her own was paramount. Rocko stuck close to her heels sniffing anything at nose level, his fur bristling with suspicion. Sylvia assessed the living room. The sofa was upright and two cushions had been reversed—to conceal lacerations, she thought—while the third was missing completely. The tile floor gleamed from scrubbing and several coats of acrylic finish. The abstract pastel canvas had been rehung on the east wall. The portrait of her great-grandmother rested in a cardboard box by the standing lamp. The cleaning crew had done their best to sort out those items that could be repaired.

Her books had been placed on the shelves of three large book-cases. Later, she would reorganize the volumes by subject. She pulled a first edition of Tony Hillerman's *Dance Hall of the Dead* off the shelf, and she ran her fingers over the now-battered jacket. She replaced the mystery between a worn leatherbound copy of Proust and a psychiatric reference book.

Two additional shelves held her collection of more than two

hundred classic videos. Most had survived intact. When she had the energy, they would be rearranged by filmmaker and decade: D.W. Griffith's *Broken Blossoms*, 1919, through Alfred Hitchcock's *Psycho*, 1960.

The room, the whole house, impressed her with its sterility. It was as if her own past had been eradicated by scrubbing, washed away with dust and dirt, all traces tossed out with pail after pail of grimy water.

In the kitchen, the smell of cleanser was even stronger. Salty, almost invisible swirls of scouring powder covered the countertop, the stove, her fingers when she rubbed them together. The refrigerator was bare except for a few assorted bottles of condiments, jam, and Parmesan cheese. The Merry Maids had left a bill for $399.00 and a note taped to the refrigerator: "The alarm company we recommend is booked for the next week but will send a rep out ASAP. We'll drop by a second set of keys for the new dead bolts tomorrow or the next day."

Sylvia folded the note and tucked it under the telephone. She poured kibble into Rocko's dish, and then she put water on the stove for a cup of tea.

She'd left Rocko in a kennel and spent four nights at the Inn on the Alameda. On Monday, after completing an evaluation in Taos, she had not returned to Santa Fe. Instead, the night had been spent without rest at the Sagebrush Inn. She had registered under the name of Norma Jean as if Marilyn Monroe and a false identity could alter past events. At least she had delayed her return for one more night.

She pressed play on the answering machine. The chipmunk song of rewind went on forever. She stood, pencil in hand, jotting notes on the pad of paper she kept tucked in a top drawer. Rosie had called. So had Monica. Albert Kove wanted to touch base about the job contract. A persistent journalist had called three times to request an interview. The last message turned her skin clammy.

The phone line had buzzed and snapped, the static complaint of a bad connection. The recorded voice was a whisper: "Do you feel me?"

In those four words she knew her caller had been Lucas Watson. Her body responded instinctively—pounding heart, sweaty palms, the sensation of oxygen rushing from her lungs to leave her breathless. Lucas Watson was laughing on tape.

"I followed you last night. Did you feel me? I watched you sleep. I walked through walls to find you, be with you."

Sylvia's mind struggled to organize, distance, regain control.

"I figured out what happened," Lucas continued. "The more you sent hate—accused me of crazy things—the more I reacted in hate. But it wasn't you, was it? It was them. They were forcing you to destroy our connection."

A deep breath, as if respiration was a labor. "Sylvia . . . you and I are just instruments . . . remember this when the future happens. Even though I'm trapped behind walls, our future is already decided."

She thought she heard the click, the hang up. She reached to stop the tape just as he breathed, "Come see me once more . . . you're the only one who can bring me back."

She snapped off the machine and lifted out the message cassette. It had been seven days since she'd walked away from her locked front door, one week since Lucas Watson had destroyed her home and her sense of invulnerability.

Now she had to face the fear, the urge to turn on every light in the house, the sense buried deep in her muscles that he might still be waiting for her. The rational knowledge that he was locked up did nothing to calm her. She sat on a stool, in darkness, and snapped her fingers for Rocko. When he licked her hand, the walls gave way and she began to cry.

ELEVEN

THE PACIFIC STORM stomped and thrashed its way from California, and by the time it reached northern New Mexico, the wind velocity was forty miles per hour.

Rosie stared out her car windshield into a black sheet of blowing snow that nearly obliterated all view of Highway 14. Reluctantly, she had given up on her usual Wednesday morning target practice at the Law Enforcement Shooting Range. Only C.O.s working tower or vehicular perimeter watch were allowed to possess firearms on penitentiary grounds. But Rosie kept a Beretta 9 mm semiautomatic at home and carried it with her in the car; she was thoroughly trained in its use. She had never had to shoot a human being but she was prepared if the worst came to be. She often wondered if New Mexico's wild territorial days—when shootouts, vigilantes, and outlaws ran rampant—were any more dangerous than the contemporary wild West.

The ominous gleam of ice was visible just ahead on the highway, and she eased her foot off the gas while a radio disc jockey predicted the storm would blow itself out within the next twelve hours. Since they were almost always wrong about New Mexico's weather, Rosie braced herself for the worst.

—

MATT ENGLAND SCANNED the open stretch of road and saw Rosie Sanchez's Camaro emerge from a screen of blowing snow. He walked through the double glass doors to the North Facility lobby after C.O. Elaine Buyers pushed open the lock-bar.

"You back again?" Elaine's henna hair bubbled on the crown and reached her waist in shaggy tendrils. "You still talking to Lucas Watson?" Her New Mexican accent was pronounced, lilting over odd syllables.

Outside, in the parking lot, Rosie was striding toward the doors. She kept her head down and England marveled at her speed in high heels. He was also amazed that she didn't blow away. He turned to Elaine Buyers and smiled. "How you been, Elaine?"

"Eeee . . . my landlady won't fix the heat in my trailer. It's like a hundred and fifty degrees all night."

England nodded sympathetically as Rosie reached the door and gave him a small wave. She shook off snow, greeted C.O. Buyers, and then guided Matt past the security station. "Sorry I'm running late. How's the investigation?"

"I spent five hours with Billy Watson on Monday. The arraignment went as predicted; he's charged with assisting an escape and conspiracy."

"I heard he's out of the detention center?"

Matt gave an ironic laugh. "Thanks to his old man and Burnett, he's been out for two days."

Rosie clucked. "Herb has his hands full with Duke Watson's family."

"So does Duke."

"The esteemed legislator from Bernalillo has the Slick Willy touch." Rosie frowned. "I doubt if he has to worry about Lucas getting more time. Within two weeks, he'll be at the Grants facility for reclassification. I think he'll get the psych transfer that Sylvia recommended. Which reminds me—"

"Hot off the comparison microscope." Matt pulled a baggie from his pocket. It contained Lucas Watson's pouch.

"The ear?"

"The ear is human but mummified. This is even better." He tossed the baggie in the air, then caught it.

Rosie eyed the leather pouch warily. "Don't tell me."

"The pouch itself is made out of an organ, probably a stomach," Matt pronounced.

"*Jesus*. Human?"

"Let's see if Lucas will tell us who this beauty used to belong to."

They waited in the small attorneys' room tucked between the facility control center and the stair that led to the yard. The room was austere, boxy, and devoid of natural light. After five minutes, Lucas Watson entered followed by a C.O.

"Hello, Lucas. You remember Matt England?" Rosie nodded to the C.O. who left the room.

Watson stood near one of four chairs. He kept his eyes focused on a point level with England's chest. His handcuffed wrists were clasped at his waist. His normally chiseled face was gaunt; it reminded Rosie of a death mask. Beads of sweat gathered on his upper lip and neck, dark hollows obscured his eyes.

Rosie set a tape recorder on the table.

Lucas watched as Matt England sat, stretched his legs, and adjusted the recorder's microphone.

"This is Criminal Agent Matt England of the New Mexico State Police. The time is 0845. Today's date is Wednesday, December 9. Present with me are Rosie Sanchez, Penitentiary Investigator, and inmate Lucas Sharp Watson, NMCD 33397." Matt cupped the back of his head with both hands. "How you doin', Lucas? How've they been treating you here at North? You settling in okay?" He had Watson's attention, and the inmate seemed to relax just slightly. "I want to thank you for your cooperation. Why don't you have a seat?" Matt paused, casually accepting Watson's lack of response, and took an easy breath. "You want to tell us about Thursday night?"

Rosie Sanchez adjusted the cassette recorder. She kept her eye on the small red light as it flickered sporadically.

Lucas said, "I already told you."

Rosie patted one of the chairs invitingly. "You know how these things go, Lucas. It's a slow process. It can drive you crazy sometimes, it takes so long to get things sorted out."

Silence.

England reached into his pocket and pulled out the baggie. He let its contents—the empty leather pouch—slide out on the bare table. They expected a response from Lucas, but not the one they got.

He reacted so suddenly, rushing forward, handcuffs slamming the table, that a gasp escaped from Rosie's mouth.

Aware of the C.O. just outside the door, Matt snatched the pouch from Watson's reach.

Lucas growled, paced a tight half circle, and turned. He faced Matt England. "It's mine."

Rosie said, "We talked to the lab, Lucas. We know the pouch is a stomach. Everything will go easier if you tell us about it."

Watson's eyelids lowered to half-mast, and his lips curled into a slow smile.

They continued their questions for another twenty minutes, but they got little out of Lucas. He became increasingly withdrawn and furtive, and eventually he began an eerie, almost inaudible chant.

Matt and Rosie silently agreed to conclude the interview.

Rosie was the first to leave the room. She stepped into the hall and almost plowed into Sylvia Strange. "What are you doing here?" she asked in puzzlement. She noticed the C.O. who stood beside the door and motioned him inside the attorneys' room.

When they were alone Sylvia said, "Lucas asked me to come."

Rosie grabbed her friend by the arm. "Are you crazy?"

Sylvia's mouth was a resolute line. After the phone call from Lucas the night before, she'd been left with two choices: allow the fear to take root or regain control of her life. She'd dealt with dangerous men before—it was part of the job—but this was the first time since the early days of her internship that she'd doubted her ability to get past her own anger and fear.

Lucas kept reaching out to her, and instinct told her there might be something more to his messages than delusional ideation and transference. She had a nagging dread that perhaps she had dismissed his fears too soon. She also had an unpleasant and melodramatic sense of foreboding.

"What's going on?" Matt England's voice snapped Sylvia from her racing thoughts.

Rosie ignored Matt. "But Sylvia, one of my boys warned me that you could be in danger from the jackal—"

Sylvia interrupted, "Lucas isn't the jackal." She moved past Rosie impatiently. "I'll explain later."

"Explain what?" Matt demanded.

Rosie said, "She needs to talk to Lucas."

"Forget it."

Sylvia set her jaw. "He asked for this meeting, and I'm willing to go in, but I damn well want some backup by this door in case something happens."

England exploded, "You're ordering backup? We're here to conduct an investigation, not an encounter therapy session where you get your head torn off!"

"Matt," Rosie warned. She sensed in Sylvia the urgent need to put demons to rest. She touched Matt's arm and said, "It's my ass on the line if something goes wrong. Do it for me . . . as a favor."

After a beat, Matt said, "What if he goes for your throat?"

Sylvia met his gaze. "I'll scream."

———

WHEN THE C.O. left the room, Sylvia found herself alone with Lucas Watson.

"Hello, Lucas," she said softly. She noticed the red light on the tape recorder. She clicked off the machine. "I got your message."

Lucas slammed his manacled fists against the wall. Sylvia forced herself to stay seated, apparently calm; the table separated them. There was a distance of less than eight feet between her and the door.

He inhaled unevenly, extended his fingers, gazed at his palm. She was surprised to see that there were tears in his eyes.

He said, "I could tear you apart." But he sounded like a defeated man.

Sylvia was aware of Matt England's face behind the mesh window. She ignored him, kept all her energy focused on Lucas.

"You left me here to die," he hissed. "You were supposed to get me out."

She said, "I'm going to do that, Lucas. I understand that you're angry, but a transfer takes time—"

He began to move again, shaking his head, mumbling. He didn't look at her when he said, "I chose you. You're supposed to understand . . . about them."

Sylvia inched forward on her chair and said, *"Them.* Who are they?"

He lifted his chin, aware of her every movement. She could almost hear him sniff the air for her scent. It was eerie the way he gazed at her from the corners of his cloudy eyes as if full sight would overwhelm his senses. She waited.

Finally he spoke. "You took away my pouch. It protects me in here."

"Protects you from what?"

"My father wants me dead."

Sylvia stopped breathing in anticipation of what Watson would say next, but almost instantly she was startled by the loud voices outside the door. Lucas turned to stare intently, and Sylvia followed his cue. A C.O.'s face filled the small window, and he mouthed something to Sylvia.

When she brought her eyes back to Lucas, she saw that he was gazing at her accusingly. He opened his mouth, then managed a half nod before his eyes went dead. Nobody home.

Sylvia tried to bring him back. "Lucas, you said your father wants you dead?"

Nothing but silence. All circuits shut down.

"You left a message for me, and I came. Lucas?"

Sylvia exploded internally; the goddamned C.O. had broken her connection with Lucas. In one instant, the paranoia had again encased him like an airtight shell.

She didn't let her anger reach the surface; her expression remained neutral as she said, "I'll get you out of here as soon as I can."

It was urgent that Lucas Watson get psychiatric care.

He spoke in a lifeless voice. "I'm tired."

Sylvia stood and watched him follow the C.O. out the door. He walked like a condemned man. *My father wants me dead.*

Rosie entered the room and Sylvia spoke abruptly, "What the hell was that about? I had Lucas talking then all that noise—"

Rosie picked up the tape recorder and said, "Bad timing."

Instantly, Sylvia recognized Herb Burnett's loud voice outside the attorneys' room. He and Matt England were involved in a heated conversation. Both women joined them in the hall.

Herb said, "What is this? Nobody bothers to tell me when they're interrogating my client?"

Rosie said, "Herb, we—"

Burnett cut her off, "What are you doing here, Sylvia?" His eyes shifted to Matt England and back to Sylvia. He was trying to gauge the situation. "Is this another evaluation? Haven't you done enough damage?"

Rosie ignored two C.O.s who were escorting an inmate past the room, and said, "Let's go outside, Herb."

Herb, followed by Sylvia and both investigators, marched through North's lobby, past C.O. Buyers, and out two sets of glass doors. Blowing dirt and snow immediately blinded them. Sylvia could barely make out Herb's shape. His overcoat slapped his thighs in the wind, and she heard his shouted words, "What were you doing with Lucas?"

Matt England guided Rosie by the sleeve to confer at a distance from Sylvia and Herb. Rosie kept her hands cupped around her face to ward off the stinging snow.

Sylvia had to yell to make herself heard. "I wasn't evaluating anyone. Lucas asked me to come. What he told me was confidential."

"You expect me to buy that? What about them?" He pointed at Matt and Rosie. "Goddamn it, Sylvia. I'm his lawyer. I need to know what he's telling you!"

"I'll talk to you tomorrow, Herb. After I get my thoughts together." She poked at the third button on his coat. "But I'll tell you this much: he thinks his father wants him dead."

Herb's cowboy hat blew up from his head, but he jammed it down with one gloved hand. He stood, mouth open, for several seconds before he said, "Bullshit! You told me yourself, he's paranoid."

"But you know the saying," Sylvia said. "Even paranoids have enemies."

—

ROSIE WAS STILL mulling over the aborted interview with Lucas Watson and the strange run-in with Burnett when she returned to her office. A new incident report quickly monopolized her thoughts. It was lying on the floor directly below the mail slot. She scanned the contents as she opened blinds and shifted directional heating vents.

Due to high winds, a power outage at the pen and surrounding areas had occurred at approximately 4:10 A.M. Backup generators had switched on according to the penitentiary's emergency contingency plan, but only after a 190-second delay.

In the middle of the night—last night!—all prison security systems had been without electricity for more than three minutes, allowing ample opportunity for a catastrophic breach of security. Rosie picked up the phone. The warden was not in his office. His secretary said he couldn't be disturbed from a meeting with representatives from Techtronics—the company that handled the pen's security—and New Mexico Property Control. Rosie hung up and bit her red nail thoughtfully. She wished she could talk to security wizard Pat O'Riley, but he'd left Techtronics last spring. His former employer had manufactured and replaced 90 percent of the penitentiary's current security system after the 1980 riot. Since installation, the new security system had failed repeatedly. Infrared barriers, locking systems, roof hatch alarms, fence rattlers, and the "hot" line were often or always dysfunctional. Techtronics was rumored to be one lawsuit away from bankruptcy. They might be out of business before they could fix everything that was wrong with prison security.

Her other line buzzed and a voice boomed from North Facility. Rosie said, "Hello, Colonel Gonzales."

"Rosie, we've got a sewage overflow in Two-A and -B. Physical services says the pipes are jammed, can't swallow all the rubber the inmates are flushing. I also got half my shift out with vehicular trouble. I just wanted to warn you it's a mess over here. I already got the word from one inmate. Don't be coming to work tomorrow.''

—

IN CELL BLOCK one, adjacent to the administration wing on the ground floor, the jackal frowned when the lights dimmed. He had capped his day poring over his most recent issues of *Omni* and *Scientific American*. There was an absorbing article on the moral dilemmas of gene-splicing, a long piece on DNA reconstruction, but most interesting of all was the story on autotomy in spiders. The jackal read and reread the paragraphs on limb regeneration and metamorphosis. He marveled at the arachnid's ability to tear off its own leg, take sustenance from its own juices, and (with luck) replace the limb. When he closed his eyes, his head filled with thoughts of biogenesis, and the scenes from last night's dream finally began to surface.

A great laboratory, lights so bright they were blinding, a black-and-white diamond pattern marking the giant chessboard floor. In his dream, the jackal saw himself enter the room and stand in front of the operating table. He wore a surgeon's smock and mask.

There was an oversize book mounted on a pedestal. A nurse appeared with a tray of instruments. Another wheeled in a tank with tubes protruding like a mechanical Medusa. "Do we have his head yet, doctor?" she asked.

The jackal was about to answer when the lights flickered, died, and flared again in CB-1.

—

A HALF MILE away, as the crow flies, C.O. Anderson slammed the thick metal door behind himself and swallowed hard. It was better if he didn't look up at the vertical tunnel of the sixty-foot tower before he approached the first row of pale orange rungs. His vertigo would kick into gear if he didn't follow his routine to the letter, and there were six sets of rungs ahead of him.

The tough leather soles of his boots clanged against metal as he climbed, and the wind yowled like a trapped beast inside the narrow tunnel. He was breathing hard by the time he reached the top and pulled himself up onto the ten-foot-square tower platform. C.O. Anderson shivered as a concrete wall of air blasted tempered glass, slid through cracks, and blew the calendar, roster sheet, and daily log from a small table.

There was no room for a door in front of the lone, freestanding toilet. Loose sheets of paper had blown up against its porcelain base.

The C.O. had to stoop down or stand on his toes to peer through the scratched windows that overlooked North Facility. The original architects must have had a sixty-inch officer in mind when they designed tower visibility levels. If a C.O. was over five feet, he or she had better be at least six feet three to see above the solid panel that separated window bands. Anderson grunted at the sharp twinge in his back, a chronic pain when he was working the tower. Blowing snow obscured his 360-degree pan of North administration's roof, the gym and main yard, psych units, housing units 3-A and 3-B, as well as the medical sally port. The grounds were deserted.

When he squinted through the white glare of electric lights, he could see the roof of 3-B and a double stretch of live alarm wire shivering against the wind. There was equipment on the roof of the gym—left over from work the construction crew was doing before they got stormed out. If they didn't reopen the rec facilities soon, they'd have a friggin' riot on their hands. C.O. Anderson smiled.

He felt a strong vibration as wind ripped at the tower. In the distance, the giant perimeter isolation zone lights flickered off, then back on, bare yellow circles against the snow.

—

ONE HUNDRED YARDS north of the tower, Lucas Watson paced his narrow cell. He did five sets of one hundred sit-ups each, and seventy push-ups on the concrete floor.

The heater wasn't working. The stench of sewage leaked through the walls. Watson forced himself to sit on the concrete bunk. He stared down at a half-written letter. After a few minutes, he stuffed it into an envelope and quickly scratched an address on the front.

The unnatural silence in the housing unit made an awful contrast to the storm outside. *Too still, too quiet, too dead.* He'd heard the rumor just like everyone else in North Facility. The nervous animal energy seeped from every man's skin; it even seeped from the walls. The riot was about to go down.

TWELVE

ON THURSDAY MORNING, the jackal kept his hand over his eyes as the truck negotiated snow and ice on the mile-long stretch of road between Main and North Facility. His first day of duty at North was not off to an auspicious beginning. The storm had done anything but abate as yesterday's weather report had forecast. The jackal sighed. His teeth were chattering and his fingers had a bluish cast. The faces of the two other porters working North settled into grim masks as ice thickened on their eyelashes.

When the truck pulled up in front of the concrete fortress, his blood quickened. He felt a thrill the moment he entered North's outer doors. He stood next to the porters in front of the glass that separated them from C.O. Elaine Buyers. Rage and frustration was about to erupt. The sparse hair on his arms stood up.

"Take off your shoes," C.O. Buyers demanded. Her voice was tight, whittled down to size by the tiny speaker set in glass. She waited while the inmate removed his shoes.

"Okay, try it now." Her face revealed irritation clamped over fear.

As the porter shuffled through the open doorway, the metal detector went off. On the third try, the whining alarm was silent. It had gone dead after a power surge.

"Shit, not again!" C.O. Buyers admitted all three porters and ran the battery-operated hand detector over the outline of their bodies about three inches from the surface of their suits.

While they waited, she used her phone to report the breakdown. "It's not just the metal detector. My radio is out, too. I don't know if it's batteries, or what!" She chopped her chin up and down as she spoke. "I did! I reported that three hours ago! They said they won't have another 'til lunch."

Dumbly, the jackal followed the other two men through the door and into the hallway that accessed offices, C.O. lounge, and the shift briefing room. The other inmates began the job of cleaning the men's toilets. The jackal would not go near the bathroom mirrors so he claimed a vacuum from the supply room.

Deafened by the harsh industrial drone, the jackal steered the cumbersome machine over the carpet. Two secretaries disappeared behind office doors. Methodically, he made his way down the hall toward the lounge where a haggard-looking C.O. slammed his fist against the pop machine. A Pepsi banged into the metal gutter. The C.O. left the room without looking at the jackal.

The jackal circled the pool table, sucked up a pile of plastic scraps behind the microwave, and then swung a left toward the vending machines. His eye caught motion outside the wall of windows covering the east end of the room. In the parking lot, a black garbage bag sped madly across ice, driven by a tempest. Other plastic bags had caught in the rolling razor ribbon that decorated the edge of Administration's roof. Shredded by wind and sleet, they waved like streamers on a used car lot. As the jackal stared open-mouthed at Siberia, the whine of the vacuum ceased, and he was surrounded by sudden silence. The stillness was so dense it was another barrier; the facility's power was dead.

—

WITHIN THE THREE pods of housing unit 3-B, in reaction to a second power surge and break, the cell doors rolled open and froze halfway. In their cells, the inmates stopped reading, pacing, eating; they waited. The C.O. making rounds inside the first pod stopped, also. For several moments, the tableau was set. Neither guard nor inmates stirred. Then, Bubba Akins peered out from his ground-floor cell into the pod's concrete gloom. Within ten seconds he had a shank at the guard's throat; he pushed his hostage through the pod door and down the hall to the locked entry of the unit's upper-level control center.

C.O. Rafael was in the bathroom when the second surge occurred. He stepped out into dim light, moved past the large L-shaped control panel, and peered through the angle of windows that provided a shadowy bird's-eye view of each two-tiered pod. All three pods were arranged around and below the control center like segments of a baseball diamond. Guards working control had at least a partial view of thirty-six cells. The windows also offered restricted sight lines of the hallway separating inmate living areas from control.

C.O. Rafael heard, but did not see, his partner request entry into the control center. He pulled the long lever that manually unlocked the control center door when electronic methods failed. He managed to radio a 10-33 before he was beaten by four inmates who stormed up the eight-rung metal stairs into the room. When the communications officer radioed back for confirmation, Bubba Akins forced his hostage to give the 10-22. *"All clear."*

Two inmates scaled the ladder to the escape hatch that gave access to the roof from control. Within another minute, they had gathered up blowtorches, staple guns, drills, and hacksaws left behind by the work crew, and they passed them down through the hatch fire-brigade-style.

The first murder of the riot took place in protective custody when a snitch was strangled by two pod-mates immediately after the power surge. Two hours later, hostages were held in all three housing units of North Facility.

A quarter mile to the east and south, respectively, inmates at the Main and South facilities remained relatively quiet.

—

LIKE A STEER in a slaughterhouse, Lucas Watson's first instinct was to escape when the riot broke out. He slipped out of his cell and crouched on the concrete balcony of the pod while Bubba Akins pushed his hostage through the door below. Watson knew that sides would be chosen and lines of battle drawn. What mattered now was the strength of your army . . . or your invisibility. Lucas Watson had no army in the joint. He was alone. To survive, he would have to make his powers work for him. He reached under his shirt for the pouch but felt bare skin. He heard his own cry of rage bouncing off the cold, angular walls. Carried by the raw edges of that sound, he bounded down the eight curving stairs to the lower level and slammed through the door to the hall. He knew the entire yard around 3-B was a steel cage. He turned in the direction of the utility rooms.

—

THE MIDNIGHT SKY streaked red as flames licked the edges of North Facility administration. Fire trucks, ambulances, helicopters, dog teams, the media, and National Guard vehicles created a symphony of chaos. The governor of New Mexico had set up a command center in North's parking lot. With the help of Colonel Gonzales, Rosie Sanchez worked to establish radio contact with the rioting inmates inside North.

—

THE JACKAL DIDN'T know how long he stayed hidden in the women's locker room. Long after the initial panic of personnel exiting the building he remained tucked between several stacks of lockers. Once, he moved to the shower stall and crouched behind boxes of building materials and cleaning supplies, but that had become uncomfortable. At some point, there was a great chemical explosion and he vomited from the fumes.

Finally, he ventured out in the hall, entered a deserted office, and climbed through a smashed window to the central yard. None of the inmates stopped him, although he walked slowly, legs stiff. He passed the body of an inmate—probably overdosed from stolen pharmaceuticals—on his way to the gym. The dead man's skin was waxy, and vomit had dried in a crust around his lips. The jackal didn't allow himself to be sidetracked by the corpse; he was a man with a mission. And besides, he might be able to return later.

Inside the cavernous building, groups of inmates were smoking, talking, sleeping. Two inmates dribbled a basketball around the slick floor. No one challenged the jackal.

—

HOUSING UNIT 3-B WAS clogged with smoke. Lucas Watson's throat contracted as he imagined the screams from protective custody across the yard.

His father was coming for him; he knew that fact in every cell of his body. The Duke had planned all of this, set up the carnage, and now it was real. It was happening. They were going to kill him.

He crouched in the corner of his cell, unsure how much time had passed. He only knew he had been hiding for hours, waiting for the moment to make his move.

Inmate gangs had already searched the unit twice. The first

time, Watson had hidden in the shower stall. The second time, he had been driven back to his cell in search of cover.

Now, someone yelled that they were torching snitches in P.C. Feet ran by, and then, moments later, he heard the sound of footsteps.

Inches away, just beyond the cell, he caught the sound of something being dragged across the wet floor. A man laughed and there were dull thuds as boots impacted against flesh. After several minutes there was only silence.

The smell was sickening. When Watson peered out, he saw blistered feet. By craning his neck he was able to look at the charred and blackened thighs, torso, shoulders, and head. A dead inmate. He slipped through the open door and examined the lifeless body; the arms ended in singed and bloody stumps.

Before he knew what was happening, two inmates shoved him back inside his cell and he felt something hard smash against his jaw. Eyeballs bulging, gasping for breath, he tried to lunge from his corner, but hands grabbed his arms and legs, and a steel pipe struck his forehead so he was blinded by his own blood. From a distant place he heard voices.

"It's the mojo man. Motherfucker."

Laughter. Another voice. "See you in hell, Watson."

And then an animal howl in crescendo, his own.

When the pipe came down, Watson heaved bile. He wanted to scream, "I know who sent you!" But the pipe came down again, and again.

He felt himself start to go out. A vision of his mother, smiling, arms open, flashed with each breath. He had one thing to ask her before it was all over. He opened his mouth and blood spurted from his throat as he whispered, "Can you forgive me?" Then there was only blackness and space.

———

IT WAS EARLY morning when the jackal entered the control booth of 3-B North. Miraculously, the list that matched every cell with the name and photo of its occupant had survived intact. He found Lucas Watson's photograph. It was a simple matter to find his cell.

He recognized Watson's corpse; in his heart, he knew the face of a savior however charred and blackened. The body had been punished. In fact, much of his work had already been done. There was a deep gash along the throat where the head lolled. Black welts, burn marks, and cuts marred the skin. A jagged pipe protruded from the body's rectum. The jackal shook his head and clucked with pity. He knelt and took the head in his hands. He wiped at the face with his sleeve. Beneath the dead skin, he knew the face was beautiful. There was life in the singed hair, and it would continue to grow after death. A miracle.

The jackal stood and set down his pail. In one corner of the cell he saw the blowtorch. He shook his head; he had no use for such a crude tool. Earlier, in preparation, he had retrieved his aluminum cigar case from its usual hiding place. Now, he unscrewed the lid and let the surgical blade slide into the palm of his hand. To the jackal's eye, the metal had a hungry gleam. He moved to the body. There was no time to waste. He'd been hired to do a job; although the jackal had not struck the death blow, the job had been completed. *His will be done.* He would take his reward, his crowning glory.

THIRTEEN

FROM HER PERCH on the edge of the bed, Rosie slammed the phone in its cradle and stamped her stockinged foot.

"You better put on shoes for that, *querida*," Ray said softly.

"*Chinga.*" It was barely a whisper, but Ray heard his wife. When she swore in her mother's tongue, business was bad.

"The riot's over, Rosita," Ray said.

Eight days ago, the riot had ended officially—after forty-nine hours—when National Guard and SWAT forces regained control of North Facility. Preliminary information on the dead had not been released to relatives for five days. Names of live inmates were broadcast to family members camped outside penitentiary grounds. Those who did not hear the names of their husbands, lovers, fathers, and sons had only the worst to fear.

The death count was twenty-nine, but official confirmation of all fatalities had still not been announced by the Office of the Medical Investigator. Matching up the body parts was not an easy job. Perhaps the jackal had been at work again . . .

When his wife didn't respond Ray prodded her, "Want to tell me about it?"

Rosie shook her head and gazed at the *retablo* of the Virgin de Guadalupe hanging on the wall; it had been carved and painted by her son, Tomás. "I'm going to mass." She felt her husband's hand on her shoulder, but she didn't look at his face.

"Why don't you confess to me first," Ray said.

Rosie glared at the big man, ready to chastise him for taking her moods too lightly, but he looked worn out. She sighed.

Ray sat on the edge of the bed next to his wife. "I'm waiting."

Rosie said, "That was the M.I.'s office. Yesterday, they released the body of a riot victim, an inmate, to his family. I can't believe it."

"Those poor people are tired of waiting for their dead," he frowned. "Why is this a bad thing?"

"That's just it!" Rosie stood abruptly and began to pace the plush carpet. "Only one man got permission to bury: Duke Watson. And that happened because he pulled strings and made deals with the Good Old Boys. The same Good Old Boys who are busy talking to CBS and NBC and the L.A. *Times* while everyone else just waits and waits and waits."

She pulled a skirt from the closet, a sweater from the drawer, tossed them on the bed, then grabbed high heels.

Ray tapped her shoulder and said, "The colors clash."

She froze and stared at her husband. Her eyes were yellow with exhaustion and faint lines etched her skin. She said, "They are still piecing together those corpses . . . that's why it's taking so long. They don't even know which of those poor boys goes where . . . *Dios mío.*"

—

LIKE A GRIM voyeur, Sylvia watched the funeral in Bernalillo. She needed to witness Lucas Watson's interment.

She had been acquainted with many of the men who survived the riot; she'd known five of its victims. Six, including Lucas. They had endured horrible, gruesome deaths and she pitied them.

Her feelings about Lucas were more complex. Pity and rage, yes. Those emotions had been accompanied by guilt: *You could have saved him.* And a fleeting relief that she wouldn't have to face him again . . . and more guilt.

Seated in a borrowed Toyota that belonged to Rosie's son Tomás, she watched from the road as the casket was lowered into a grave dug in an icy slope.

A colonial Spanish church made of mud and wood dominated the two-acre cemetery. The land was bordered by bare cottonwoods. Many of the graves were overgrown with weeds. The only sign of life was the circle of people clustered under black umbrellas seeking shelter from the drizzling rain. Sylvia identified Duke Watson by his trademark cowboy hat and boots and his position next to the priest.

A young man stood with his arm around a girl. He was dressed in a black suit that was too short in the sleeves. The girl kept her face pressed against his shoulder. Sylvia caught her breath when he raised his head. His coloring was dark, but his angular bone structure and short-cropped hair made Billy Watson the ghost of his brother. There was something else that was familiar. Sylvia slapped the dash. Billy Watson had delivered the flowers to her doorstep in November. The hat, the beard, the sunglasses had all obscured his face. It seemed so obvious, but she hadn't made the connection until now. Who knew what kind of game he'd been playing?

She guessed the girl was Lucas Watson's adopted sister, Queeny. Although Herb Burnett was conspicuously absent, there were five or six other mourners, and the murmur of prayer drifted out like a dirge.

When the services were completed, Duke Watson and the priest walked slowly toward the gate. Duke stopped short of a black limousine, and Sylvia endured a taut instant when he stared directly at her. Pressed behind the wheel of the Toyota, she felt fear. And again the crippling sense of guilt: if only she hadn't evaluated Watson . . . if she hadn't filed her report . . . if she had pushed harder for his transfer.

Duke Watson turned his back, and Sylvia exhaled deeply. Lucas had not belonged on the streets. Still, the ache in the pit of her stomach remained.

The sounds of raised voices caught her attention; the Watson family was arguing. Duke Watson stood rigid while his son moved like a man about to lose control. Suddenly Billy thrust an arm at his father's chest.

Sylvia was repulsed by Duke Watson's reaction to his son's fury. The senator turned his back, strode open-armed toward the elderly priest, and ushered him into the backseat of the limousine. He moved as if his children were nonexistent; his actions reflected a man oblivious to anything and everything not centered around himself. A narcissist, Sylvia thought as she watched the long black bullet of a car join the stream of late afternoon traffic.

Watching the incongruous juxtaposition of the shiny limo, the dirt road, and the tiny Bernalillo cemetery, Sylvia let her head fall back on the seat. She felt the cold seep into her bones even with the engine of the Toyota idling and the heater at full force.

Billy Watson walked out to the road followed by his sister. The humiliation of the encounter with his father was apparent in his posturing, his false bravado. The girl huddled beside her brother for at least five minutes before a car stopped to pick them up. Sylvia drove away soon after.

Traffic on I-25 North was heavy. Several cars with pine trees strapped to their roofs sped past the Toyota. Sylvia pushed buttons on the radio avoiding holiday Muzak and heavy-metal renditions of "White Christmas." According to a disc jockey there were four more shopping days until Christmas. Sylvia fought the lethargy that threatened to overwhelm her body. In her practice she saw the havoc the holidays inflicted on many people. This year, she could count herself as one of the season's emotional victims. She couldn't shake thoughts of the riot. She couldn't shake the guilt. If she couldn't deal with herself, how could she help her clients?

God, she missed Malcolm. He had always helped her regain her balance and clarity.

The radio had become a steady stream of static; she switched it off.

What would Malcolm have told her? That Lucas had all the hallmarks of someone suffering from an attachment disorder? That he had indeed been an extremely volatile individual? He would have said, let go, leave it alone, you've lost your objectivity; you're moving into dangerous territory.

And why was she so obsessed with Lucas? She'd dealt with inmates who were more pathological, more shrewd, more crazed.

Don't try to pin the guilt on Duke Watson to relieve your own conscience—that's what Malcolm would say.

Her car crested La Bajada. In the distance, west of Santa Fe, a strip of hot orange sunset shone like a ribbon against the horizon. By the time she reached her driveway fifteen minutes later, it was dark.

Rocko had managed to escape from the yard again; he raced to meet the car. She honked, then pulled up to her mailbox. The latest edition of the *Journal of Forensic Psychology* and several envelopes were stacked inside.

Sylvia drove the last thirty yards to her house with Rocko hounding the car. The Chevy parked in the driveway scared her until she recognized Matt England leaning against the hood.

Shit. After the funeral, he was the last person she wanted to deal with. She strode up the walkway, thrust the key in the dead bolt, and left the door ajar. England followed her inside and stood with his hands in his pockets. He seemed unaffected by the cold reception.

She said, "I need a cup of coffee."

In the kitchen, she glanced at the answering machine; the light was blinking, but she wasn't about to listen to messages with England staring over her shoulder. She thought about the tape with Lucas Watson's recorded voice. It was in the top counter drawer tucked behind a packet of sponges. She set her mail on the counter.

"How was the funeral?"

She stared at England, her dark eyes softly quizzical.

He said, "I was parked right behind you."

She emptied coffee beans into the grinder. The whine of the blades killed all possibility of conversation for several moments. Sylvia used the opportunity to inspect England. He seemed to be searching for something to say, or the right way to say it.

"You were there?" she asked as the grinder moaned to silence.

He nodded. "I also passed you on the highway. Are you always that distracted?"

"No."

England brushed his hand lightly through his hair, a gesture Sylvia recognized as characteristic. He shifted his weight back and forth between his feet as if he were finding his center against the soft sway of a ship. "If you want to get on with your life, stay away from that family."

Sylvia avoided his gaze, shook the last of the grounds into a filter, and filled the base of the coffeemaker with water. The machine began its mechanical wheeze, and the first aroma of coffee mixed with the faint scents of Ajax and lemon. "Is delivering that advice the point of your visit?"

England's eyes narrowed. "Duke Watson has already slapped a lawsuit against the corrections department; I wouldn't be surprised if you're next."

Sylvia felt the involuntary contraction of her muscles. She took a deep breath and said, "Why do you hate him?" When England didn't respond, she turned to face him. "What did he do to you?"

He massaged his neck and there was an audible crack as a vertebra realigned itself. "We've had a few run-ins."

Sylvia snorted as she took two cups from the cupboard. Steam exploded from the coffeemaker and she reached for the pot. Hot coffee bubbled over the side of the cup as she poured. She pulled her hand away and mopped up the excess liquid with a sponge.

She studied England as she slid the cup across the counter. "That's all? A few run-ins?"

"Save your therapy for your patients, Dr. Strange."

"Fuck you, Agent England. You've got an attitude problem."

He caught her off guard with his grin. His mouth was a lopsided angle against the irregular line of his nose. He pulled gently on one ear. "So I've been told."

Unexpectedly disarmed, Sylvia returned his smile. The man was attractive when he acted human.

He took a sip of coffee and said, "Why did you go to that funeral?"

"Closure."

"He was a sick bastard who destroyed your house. He would've raped and murdered you."

She was right back where she had started with Matt England—feeling frustrated and antagonistic. She guessed he felt the same way. Intentionally, she turned her back on him and sorted her mail. A badly creased envelope caught her eye. It was addressed to Sylvia Strange, La Cieneguilla. There was no route or box number and someone had scrawled "Please forward" near her name.

She slit the paper with her little finger. A single handwritten page slipped out. The top was dated December 9, the day before the riot—the day she had talked to Lucas in North Facility.

Sylvia, what I have is time. Time to sleep, time to dream. The more I dream of you the more my hate turns to love. You are my power. In another time we knew each other. Remember this when the future happens. My only crime is loving too much. We must be together or others will die.

When Matt saw her face, he took the note from her hand and skimmed the page. "Lucas?"

She nodded slowly. "This is why I needed to see him buried. I'm tired, Agent England. Can we call it a night?"

He nodded a bit reluctantly.

She walked him to his car. The moon had climbed up behind the Sangres; it was milky and subtle, a woman behind a veil. Clouds covered all but a thin strip of sky, and a smattering of stars shone like winter fireflies.

England leaned against the door of the Caprice and gazed at the tall, dark-haired woman. He sensed her personal power, and he felt an odd affinity. He also felt the frustration she always seemed to elicit from him.

"What?"

He shrugged. "I've been meaning to apologize for the way I acted at Rodeo Nites." They were standing so close, she could smell aftershave and the scent of his worn leather jacket.

She studied his face. His eyes, unreadable in the darkness, searched hers. He shook his head and reached for her shoulders tentatively. His grip was strong.

"You'd better go," she said.

He stepped back and dug his hand into his jacket pocket, pulled out a bottle, tossed it in the air and caught it. "Somebody's been drinking Wild Turkey in your driveway."

The empty bottle threw her for a few seconds, but she said, "I get strays out here. Lovers looking for a place to park, guys who want to drink a six-pack. They end up turning around in my driveway."

It was impossible to read his expression in the darkness as he climbed into the Caprice and closed the door. She said, "I know how to take care of myself."

FOURTEEN

INMATE ANDRE MILLER from CB-1 had been found stabbed in the prep area of Main's kitchen. Rosie had already secured the crime scene, then she'd called in the state cops. One of her best boys was assisting with evidence collection so Rosie was free to continue the investigation in other quarters.

She traversed the slick, soapy penitentiary corridor and approached the metal barrier that separated Main's hospital from the cell blocks. She waited while the C.O. buzzed her through from the control booth. Andre Miller was a quiet, unassuming man who kept a low profile as far as Rosie knew. She'd seen him at chow, but only because he worked as a regular in the kitchen.

She would review penitentiary log-books this afternoon to see if she could get a bead on Miller's attacker. Daily logs tracked traffic to and from recreation areas, sally ports, towers, each control center, and the hospital. They recorded who attended self-help groups, who went to art classes, who used the law library. Basements and closets were filled with illegible entries written on now-moldy paper stored in military-surplus trunks and files. The excessive paperwork was an incredible bureaucratic headache, but it was part of prison security. Rosie had already reviewed logs pertinent to the Angel Tapia–missing-finger incident. She knew exactly who was where, and when. Or, more accurately, she knew what had been entered in the logs. In real life, Rosie understood things were overlooked, left out, intentionally or not.

Recently, she'd begun to doubt some of her own theories; namely, Angel's missing pinkie and the existence of the jackal. No one could remain invisible for decades. The most obvious theory—gang retribution—was looking more and more plausible. Her only confirmation of the jackal had come from Bubba, and he had his own reasons to obscure an investigation that might be centered around racism and gang rivalry.

She had other reasons to be concerned. At their last meeting, Warden Cozy had accused her of fanning prison fires by her pursuit of a phantom monster. What if Cozy was right?

Rosie reached the hospital door and opened it to find three inmates in the waiting area; they looked perfectly healthy. Of course, a third of the pen's inmates were chronic malingerers. Anything to get out of a cell. Who could blame them? A vinyl couch occupied most of the space, and Rosie recognized Chuey "Shotgun" Martinez sprawled on one end. In the past few years, she'd questioned him several times after his halfhearted suicide attempts.

She said, "Hello, Chuey, where's the nurse?"

Chuey smiled at Rosie. The wide gap where his front teeth should have been gave him an obtuse charm. "She's gone to the sally port to send Miller to St. Vincent's," Chuey Shotgun said.

Rosie frowned. If the shank damage was bad enough to necessitate a transfer to the hospital, the assault was more serious than she'd first thought. There had been one really odd thing about the kitchen crime scene: the shiny stainless steel counter—all of it!—had been smeared with Miller's blood. She thought about that fact as she walked back toward CB-1.

The trip took her downstairs to ground-floor level, past the deputy warden's office and the inmates visiting room, and through three sets of locked gates.

Two C.O.s were in the cage between CB-1 and the central corridor. Rosie said, "Keep an eye on me." They opened both gates and let her through.

Without turning her head, she scoped out the stairway to the second tier, the empty shower cubicle, and the location of visible inmates. She acknowledged the six men who were seated around a common television set. They were watching *The Price Is Right.* One of them—she thought she recognized "Stinky" Gray—kept jumping out of his seat to coach the game-show players.

He stabbed two fingers into the air, "Hey, asshole, two bills! Two and a half bills, ducksbreath! Lookatthatfatcow! He doesn't have a clue—"

While Stinky continued his running tirade, Rosie mentally I.D.'d the others: Roybal, Theo T. Bones, Robot Rodriguez, Elmer Rivak, and Del "Loco" Montoya.

She took the keys from her belt clip and approached Miller's locked cell. She felt eyes crawl along her back and her skin twitched like a dog shedding bothersome fleas. She unlocked the cell door and used her weight to pull open the door. The first thing she noticed was the small cloth bundle in the sink. When she shook it open gingerly, a small brown finger rolled out. Abruptly, the hair on her arms stood up and she backed out of the cell and firmly closed the door. *Madre de Dios,* she murmured silently. She'd found Angel Tapia's finger. It had to be. It certainly didn't belong to Andre Miller whose skin was white as Wonder bread. Could Miller be *el chacal*?

Rosie shook her head as she turned her key in the lock. For a moment, she'd forgotten where she was. Now, she turned slowly to face the five men in front of the television. Five heads turned, five faces stared.

Without speed, Robot and Loco Montoya stood at the same time and moved toward her.

Roybal crossed his arms over his muscled chest and smiled.

Rosie gauged the distance between her position and the entrance to the cell block: forty, forty-five feet. She could hear the C.O.s talking, something about the dinner menu.

Chinga. She was getting too cocky, too stupid, letting her guard down. She could feel the tension emanating from the inmates—could see it in their bodies. Loco Montoya now stood two feet in front of her.

"What's up?" Montoya asked in a flat voice.

"Can we help?" A muscle in T. Bones's jaw twitched.

Rosie swallowed; her mouth was dry as dust.

"What'd you find in Miller's cell?" The voice sounded normal, almost friendly. Rosie's eyes shifted; the voice belonged to Elmer Rivak.

Loco Montoya said, "Maybe Miller had a recipe for quiche."

The men snickered. Loco Montoya stepped back and slid a pack of cigarettes from his breast pocket.

"Yeah," Loco Montoya said. "Somebody shanked Miller 'cause his chow stunk so bad."

Stinky Gray had intensified his television tirade. "Hey, penis head, why don't you teach her to hula? Why don't you just yank that flatulent tack? Yakkety-yak! Don't talk back, sweetheart."

Rosie heard footsteps approaching from behind. She stiffened and turned her head slightly. She saw the brown uniform of a correctional officer. Two more steps and the guard came into full view: C.O. Anderson.

Rosie breathed a deep sigh of relief.

Anderson said, "How's the game going?"

Since Rosie's entrance into CB-1, Stinky Gray's eyes hadn't left the television screen once. Now he turned and nodded to Anderson. "Going fine, but the price ain't never right."

———

Jaspar held one end of Rocko's leash, Rocko strained at the other end, and Sylvia grasped the middle. They merged with the procession that circled the baseball diamond in Train Park. Bundled up against the cold in parka, cap, mittens, and wool scarf, Jaspar resembled a short Santa Claus.

Maggie Hunt, director of A Dog's Life obedience school, circulated among her clients offering words of encouragement or clucking her displeasure. "Don't let him get away with that. Snap the leash. Release! Now say, *good boy*, and give treats, treats, treats!"

Sylvia leaned down to unwrap two layers of leash that had twined around Rocko's neck; she found herself looking into Jaspar's serious eyes. The child seemed more withdrawn than he had been at the petroglyphs. This morning, when Sylvia stopped to pick him up, Monica had quietly reported no changes in the frequency of bed-wetting and bad dreams. Again, his mother had refused to accept a referral.

Sylvia directed child and dog across the grass. For now, she would go along with the supposition that Jaspar needed a friend more than he needed a therapist. Even so, she wasn't the best choice. Since last night, her thoughts had been on her encounter with Matt and the letter from Lucas.

While Sylvia's mind wandered, Rocko took advantage of the slack and lunged for a dalmatian. Maggie Hunt appeared, grabbed the leash, and snapped, "Uh!" In response, Rocko lifted his leg and peed very close to Maggie's loafer.

A man in his late twenties matched stride with Sylvia; she thought he was Maggie Hunt's assistant until he asked his first question. "Dr. Strange, how would you characterize your relationship with Lucas Watson?"

Sylvia came to a complete stop.

"Keep moving," Maggie Hunt commanded from center field.

Sylvia tapped Jaspar on the shoulder. "Can you handle Rocko?" He nodded. She gave him the baggie filled with sliced hot dogs, then stepped away from the circle. The man followed her.

"My name's Tony Vitino. I'm a reporter from the *New Mexican*."

"I know who you are."

"I hoped you'd return my phone calls."

Sylvia had been ignoring calls from journalists for weeks—queries about Watson's escape from St. Vincent's and the riot. She'd been relieved that media interest and coverage had finally died down. Or so she'd thought.

Vitino said, "Could we grab a cup of coffee? We should discuss why Lucas Watson went to your house after he escaped from St. Vincent's Hospital."

"There's nothing to discuss," Sylvia said, turning away.

"Did you and Lucas Watson have a sexual relationship?" Vitino pitched the question, and it hit Sylvia like a fastball from left field.

She turned and jabbed a finger toward his chest. "What?"

Vitino shook his head and kept talking as he stepped backward. "You gave Lucas Watson pictures of yourself. Would you describe them as intimate?"

Sylvia opened her mouth, then snapped it shut.

"I'm talking about the complaint lodged against you with the Board of Psychologist Examiners." He cocked his head and eyed her with a mix of surprise and pity. "You don't know about this?"

She made a mental grab for bearings and then forced herself into motion. "I have nothing to say." She caught up with Jaspar and took hold of Rocko's leash. Heading toward the car, both boy and dog had to trot to keep up with her. Jaspar kept his eye on Sylvia. "Are you mad at me?"

"Of course not, kiddo." She tried to keep her voice light. "I just remembered I have to do something urgent." She unlocked the car. "Buckle your seat belt, and let's find your mom."

Tony Vitino rapped on the window as she pulled out of the parking lot. His mouth was moving, but Sylvia couldn't hear him over the noise of the heater. How the hell could Lucas get photos of her? And why was a reporter telling her she had a complaint with the board of ethics? Albert Kove was the head of the state's Board of Psychologist Examiners, the very same board that investigated grievances, ethical and otherwise. She'd talked to him this morning, but he hadn't mentioned a word about a complaint. She didn't dwell on the fact that she was very close to a contract with Kove and Casias.

After she dropped Jaspar with Monica, Sylvia drove directly to Kove's office. He was scraping ice off the windshield of his Subaru when Sylvia slid the Volvo to a stop.

"Albert!" She stepped out of the car.

Kove turned and wiped his glasses with gloved fingers. "Sylvia?" He frowned. "What a madhouse today. Who says there's more domestic violence in hot weather?"

"We need to talk," Sylvia said.

"Tonight. I've got to be across town in ten minutes."

She could barely see his eyes behind fogged glasses. "Albert, is there a complaint against me?"

"This isn't the place to discuss it."

"Who filed it?" Sylvia asked. "I've got a right to know."

Albert Kove steadied himself on the hood of the Subaru and said, "It was filed this morning by Duke Watson."

"On what grounds?"

Kove opened his car door and spoke reluctantly. "Sexual misconduct."

"That's absurd. What possible evidence—"

"Photographs." Kove climbed into his car. He removed his glasses and gazed up at her bleary-eyed. "Watson claims you sent them to his son as part of an ongoing sexual relationship."

"You're taking this seriously? You think I'd seduce an inmate?" Her pulse was racing. "Does Duke Watson think I had sex with Lucas in his cell?"

"I'll see that you get copies." Kove started the Subaru's engine.

"Albert, this is crazy!" Sylvia watched the Subaru's rear tires spin on a patch of ice as Kove drove off. Rocko barked fiercely at the retreating vehicle.

She wasn't surprised when she didn't find Herb at the courthouse complex. At the modest stucco offices of Cox and Burnett, she parked behind his red-and-black Bronco that sported an ego plate: SF LAW. She ignored the receptionist's questioning look and strode down the short hallway to his office. She entered without knocking.

"Sylvia," Herb shifted his cowboy boots off the desk, leaned forward in his chair. He clicked off the dictaphone and ran a hand through curly hair. "Did I miss something? Did we have an appointment?"

"We do now." She ignored his gestured invitation to sit. "I want you to tell me exactly what Duke Watson gave to the Board of Psychologist Examiners."

Herb coughed. "You know that's inappropriate. My client—"

"Show me the goddamn photos!"

Herb stared at her, opened his mouth, closed it, and shrugged. He pulled a manila envelope from a top drawer and slid it across the desktop. "These don't leave my office."

Sylvia forced herself not to turn away from him. She opened the envelope and pulled out four black and white eight-by-tens. They were all of her; in each, she was wearing her bathrobe, standing in her own kitchen brushing her hair, apparently smiling and talking to the camera. In the last photograph, she had her head forward, eyes cast down, and the robe was open exposing her breasts. Sylvia felt sick.

She put the pictures carefully back in the envelope and fastened the clasp. She set them on Herb's desk. In a hard voice, she demanded, "Who took these?"

Herb met her eyes and glanced away. "I think you can answer that question," he said.

She wanted to slap him. "Where did you get them?"

"They were with Lucas Watson's possessions."

"And how did they come into *your* possession, Herb?"

Herb stood. "Sylvia, I let you see the photos because I consider you a friend—"

"Those pictures were taken by Duke Watson without my knowledge, without my permission. I'm not a lawyer, but it sounds like I can get him for invasion of privacy, harassment—I'll have a warrant sworn out. I'll hit him with a lawsuit. You tell him that!" She slammed glass doors behind her as she left the building.

By the time she reached her car, she had made up her mind to do some homework on Duke Watson. She glanced at her watch: 12:40. She could make it to Albuquerque in fifty minutes.

—

THE HOURS SYLVIA spent at the *Albuquerque Journal*'s morgue were tedious but productive. She started with several stories on Watson's early political career. Jotting down notes, she scanned articles on his campaigns, his pledge to balance the state's economic and environmental demands, his efforts to modernize New Mexico's public schools. He was a champion of children's rights. A reformer. Unusual for a small-time politico. But Duke was different; for three decades he'd kept his eye on the big time.

A 1962 graduate of the University of New Mexico, Duke practiced business law in Albuquerque for several years. His political climb began after his marriage in 1970 to Lily Nash, daughter of a wealthy New Mexican land and cattle man. Sylvia found a nuptial announcement, but no photograph of the couple. Lily gave birth to two sons—Lucas Sharp Watson and William Nash Watson—within two years of the wedding.

Sylvia pushed away from the table and stretched. She wanted a cigarette and a long vacation. Even more, she wanted to know what had gone on in the Watson family for the next few years until Lily's death. Her imagination had always been potent, but it paled compared with what she'd seen in the course of her work. She could think of too many possible—and nasty—reasons why a young mother would leave two children behind in the wake of violent, self-inflicted death.

Lily Watson's suicide predated 1980 when all papers were cata-
logued and recorded on microfiche. But Sylvia eventually un-
earthed two articles among the stacks of old newspapers.

The suicide was covered in the *Journal*'s morning edition on
July 7, 1977, page four. The headline read: YOUNG MOTHER DIES. The
short article reported that Lily Watson, wife and mother, had died
two nights before between 6:30 P.M. and midnight. Her body was
discovered the next morning by a caretaker. The medical exam-
iner's office had not yet released the cause of death.

The second story—which ran the following day on page eight—
explained that both of Lily's sons had been staying with the family's housekeeper on the night of the tragedy. It continued: "Away
on business, state Sen. Duke Watson was not immediately in-
formed of his wife's death. Watson, D-District 9, was not available
for comment, but the dead woman's sister, Belle Nash, expressed
the family's shock and sorrow."

Sylvia skimmed the next column and stopped short when she
saw the article's last paragraph: "Medical investigators have deter-
mined that 28-year-old Lily Watson died from a self-inflicted bullet wound, Bernalillo Sheriff's Deputy Matthew England said
Thursday."

So Matt England had investigated Lily's death when he was a
deputy sheriff. He hadn't mentioned that fact last night. His antip-
athy for Duke Watson was almost two decades old.

She put her speculation on hold and turned her attention back
to the stack of newsprint in front of her.

Six days after the tragedy, the *Journal* ran a photograph of Duke
Watson standing over his wife's grave. Next to him, two small
boys clutched the hands of Lily's sister, Belle Nash. Sylvia recognized the colonial church in the background; Lucas had been buried in the same cemetery as his mother.

It occurred to Sylvia to pull papers for the one-year anniversary
of Lily's death.

Under funeral notices and memorials:

Lily Nash Watson, on that darkest of nights, you left us. Our
prayers for your comfort seemed unanswered until we accepted
God's will as all-knowing and ever-wise. We will meet again in
the next world. We love you. And we miss you since you went
away a year ago today.

As she copied down the memorial, she wondered who had
placed it in the paper. Duke? Probably not two boys under the age
of eight.

Lucas Watson's arrest for murder was easier to find because it
was recent . . . the murder he committed, and his trial, were un-
remarkable, except for the brutality of the beating and the fact
that his father was a state senator.

Finally, Sylvia pulled up the sole reference on William Watson.
At the age of seventeen, Billy had been arrested for false imprison-
ment.

In print, the eighteen-year-old victim told a horrifying tale of
stalking, kidnapping, and attempted rape. Three weeks later, the
charges were dropped when the victim recanted—she now
claimed to have willingly posed for the telephoto pictures found in
Billy's possession.

———

IT WAS HOT in the court as Duke Watson slammed the ball against
the whitewashed wall. "It takes balls to play squash, Herb."

Herb wiped sweat from his forehead on the sleeve of his gray
T-shirt. "Just need to get in shape."

"Fifteen-two, fifteen-four, fifteen-one."

"Don't rub it in."

Duke tossed his squash racquet in the air, caught it in one hand,
and slapped it against his thigh. "Let's get in the sauna. I need to
burn out a cold." He led the way through the low wooden door to
the locker area.

The Kiva Club was the only men's club in Santa Fe, and Duke
Watson had joined in the mid-seventies. He continued to pay his

dues because he enjoyed the squash games, and, most of all, he appreciated the gentlemen's agreements that were sealed with sweat and a beer from the lobby's vending machine—a sub rosa courtesy of the management.

The club was housed in a historic adobe complete with fifteen-foot ceilings, cracked vigas, and thick earth walls that were white-washed year after year. From the outside, the building looked like a part of the old La Posada Hotel property that was immediately adjacent. No sign; to find the club, you had to know where you were headed.

Duke folded his clothes and laid them in a loose pile in front of his locker. As he strode toward the sauna, his gut trembled, but his thighs and butt didn't budge. Herb followed the older man into the dark interior of the cedarwood room. They were its only occupants, and Duke immediately ladled water from a bucket and splashed it over hot rocks. Vapor billowed up, and Herb gasped as he sucked fiery air into his lungs.

Duke Watson took the high bench.

Herb eased his rear onto the low bench and wiped his hands over his face. "Toasty."

"That's the idea."

To Herb, Duke looked like Humpty-Dumpty. His legs were toothpicks, but above the hips he swelled into a huge egg. There was a strong chance Humpty would be New Mexico's governor by next term. A drop of sweat dripped from Herb's nose and landed on his penis; he remembered where he was.

"So, what's on your mind?" Duke asked.

"This complaint—"

"What about it?" Duke leaned back, spread his knees wide, and his genitals hung loose like a bird's wattles.

Herb said, "Sylvia saw the photos."

"How did that happen?"

"She barged into my office, screamed at me, said she'd get a lawyer."

"So you rolled over and showed her your belly?"

Herb didn't answer, and Duke's expression hardened. "It's her bad luck those pictures survived the riot. My son had them tucked inside that book she wrote."

Herb frowned. "But who took them?"

"Herb . . ." Duke spoke as if he were gently correcting an errant child.

Herb wiped the sweat from his face. He was breathing harder now. His voice was so low it was almost inaudible. "All I know is Lucas wanted a shrink for the parole board—he wanted Sylvia. Fine. You told me to keep him in the pen. I did. I killed two birds with that evaluation." He swallowed hard. "Now, he's dead."

Duke's eyes narrowed. "Neither you nor I could have prevented a riot."

Herb sputtered. "I just . . . It's just, to ruin her career—I know she didn't sleep with Lucas, and I don't like the idea of filing the lawsuit just now—"

"She was at Luke's funeral." Duke raised a finger, took a breath, then dropped his hand to the bench. "She had some kind of relationship with my son . . . she's to blame for his escape, his transfer to North Facility. In my mind, she's to blame for his death."

FIFTEEN

At 7:35 A.M., Sylvia found Matt England shooting baskets in the gym of the Law Enforcement Academy. He was bounding around the court, drenched with perspiration, doing his best to intimidate the hell out of a young recruit.

He seemed to be succeeding. The recruit didn't get many shots in before the round ended and Matt tossed the ball to a noodle of a kid dressed in gym grays.

"Take over, Waters!"

England acknowledged Sylvia, picked up a towel, and joined her at courtside.

She said, "Can we talk?"

"How did you find me?"

Sylvia shrugged. "Rosie knows half of your buddies; she did me a favor." They both stood silent for a moment, watching the athletes, then Sylvia said, "Why didn't you tell me you worked on Lily Watson's suicide when you were a deputy?"

"None of your business." The basketball shot out of the court and slapped against England's thigh. He caught it between palms, hollered, "Heads up!" and tossed the ball back into play. The kid named Waters caught it, dribbled, and scored a basket.

Sylvia stared blindly at the game; she seemed oblivious to the screech of rubber soles on varnished wood, the high-intensity energy level of the players. Matt noticed her hair was uncombed, her clothes looked slept in, and she wore no lipstick, no makeup at all. She looked like she was under stress and buckling.

He said, "I've got some brochures at home—dream vacations where you can get away from it all for two weeks."

She frowned. "I'm serious—"

"*I'm* serious. You look like hell. Get out of town, get your mind on other things. Get your life back together."

"I can't." She tipped her head forward and dark hair tumbled in front of her eyes.

"I read about the complaint in this morning's *New Mexican*."

Sylvia had started her day over an hour ago when she walked down the road to pick up her morning paper. The headline ran COMPLAINT LODGED AGAINST LOCAL PSYCHOLOGIST. The byline belonged to Tony Vitino. The article at the bottom of page one was short and to the point. Duke Watson had filed a complaint against psychologist Sylvia Strange alleging sexual misconduct with his son and her client, Lucas Watson. Watson's attorney, Herb Burnett, was quoted briefly, "The evidence is being considered by the state's Board of Psychologist Examiners."

England assessed her for an instant, not unsympathetically, then said, "Let me throw on some clothes. I'll meet you in the cafeteria."

She watched him jog back to the court to confer briefly with both recruits. By the time she reached the stairs, he had disap-peared. She exited the gym and found the cafeteria on the lower level.

A half-dozen tables were occupied in the small self-service snack area. Male and female state police recruits hurriedly con-sumed institutional-style scrambled eggs and bacon, toast, and coffee.

Sylvia had bypassed the steam trays and had just taken her first sip of coffee when England pulled out a chair and joined her at a corner table. Her eyes skimmed over Matt, tan slacks, leather jacket, and boots. "That was quick. It takes me that long to pull on a pair of cowboy boots."

He grinned and clicked the heels of his boots together. "Lucchese's. They're made with local ostrich hide, completely handcrafted, the dyes are natural."

She dredged up a smile. "Can I buy you breakfast?"

"Thanks, I ate three hours ago." He pulled a napkin from a plastic container and blotted up a small puddle of coffee near the sleeve of her sweater. She was close enough so he could see a tiny freckle on her nose.

She lifted her chin and gazed directly at him. Her eyes were almost black under fluorescent lights. She watched his tongue working behind his cheek while he considered what he would say next.

When he finally spoke, his voice was subdued. "It was the first real case I worked in New Mexico. I'd been a sheriff in Oklahoma, but I left in a hurry and took what was offered when I got here: deputy." He glanced out the window, saw a somber, cloudy sky, and frowned. "That morning, I was the first officer on the scene. I got there after a security cop showed up." He predicted her ques-tion and said, "The caretaker—he'd worked for the family for three or four years—he found her mid-morning. Called us, then he called his buddy who worked a few minutes away from the house."

Three recruits finished their coffee and walked past the table with a nod to England; Matt watched them silently until they exited the cafeteria. "It was hot that day. Sweltering. I remember it made me think of Oklahoma. Muggy, dense, big thunderheads." He frowned. "She was on her bed. You could tell she'd been beautiful."

Sylvia imagined an overheated bedroom and a dead woman stretched out on a large bed. The story fed some empty internal place in her, but her eagerness to hear it disturbed her, made her feel unclean.

He continued. "I felt it right away—something was hinky. They'd already moved evidence . . . and they'd left coffee cups on the vanity and cigarette butts in the ashtray."

"The security man?"

"And the caretaker. Later, they claimed it was accidental."

"Did Lily have any history of previous attempts?"

"Her doctor admitted she'd had a problem with downers and booze. OMI found a generous supply of Valium in her system. From what the sister said, Lily was high-strung . . . a firestorm."

"Where was Duke Watson?"

England gave her a speculative look. "According to one of his law partners, he was in Denver at the Brown Palace."

"Did the hotel confirm that?"

"A maid, a bellhop, the desk man all vouched for him—he was registered for three nights—but they couldn't swear he was there the night Lily died. There was nothing to place Duke at the suicide." He crumpled up a napkin. "That's it. End of story."

Sylvia nailed him with her eyes. "Not quite."

Matt resisted the urge to shift his butt in the hard chair.

She said, "Ten people a week tell me their stories, and I know when it's time to peel back another layer and go deeper." Sylvia inched forward in her seat. "We haven't reached the end of your story."

She waited, kept her eyes on him, and ten seconds crept by before she saw him make up his mind.

"When I got there, the .22 was a few feet from the body." Matt had lowered his voice almost to a whisper. "Later, after I was off the case, I had a chance to read the medical investigator's report; it said the weapon was found in her hand." His voice stayed even as he continued. "The hole in her face, to me it looked like an exit wound. The one in her neck looked like entry. It's hard to shoot yourself in the back of the head . . ." With his finger he traced an invisible infinity sign on the table. "The autopsy report disagreed with my opinions."

"You think he murdered his wife? What motive?"

"There was none . . . her money went in trust to her children, he never remarried, her family gave him the connections he needed."

"But you still think he killed her." Sylvia stood and gathered her things. As she left, England didn't say a word.

—

THE PENITENTIARY PSYCH office was too cold, and the jackal said so. He watched as psychologist Sylvia Strange rolled her chair a few inches along the floor, adjusted the thermostat, and rolled back behind her desk. She eyed him intently.

He had just spent the last hour drawing pictures, looking at ink-blots, and free-associating. Now, they were discussing his past.

He wondered, *Does she know who I am? If she doesn't, she lives. If she does, she dies.* He wanted to spare her; he didn't kill anymore for pleasure.

He said, "I first heard the voices in Vietnam. I killed babies and innocent women. I don't do that anymore; that's what separates me from all the predators."

It was interesting to confide in her, to tell her about himself. He knew she was smart. He knew he didn't frighten her; his dark corners didn't even make her blink. He was sorry they couldn't be friends. He had a feeling she might understand his mission in the Lord's Army.

"The voices, what were they like?" Sylvia asked.

He thought, *She wants to know if I'm psychotic.* "They were loud.

They said I should kill myself. The Army docs said they were the voices of people I'd killed. Guilt."

"Do you think that's right?"

"It seemed right."

"Is there anything else you can describe about the voices?"

"Sometimes they spoke Vietnamese." The blade was taped under his armpit. It was scalpel-sharp and bore no resemblance to a blunt, clumsy shank.

"Do you speak Vietnamese?"

"Just the little bit I learned over there."

Her questions continued. She encouraged him to elaborate and focus: Were the voices repetitive? Did they speak in complete sentences? Did they come from inside or outside?

He said, "They could've been my own thoughts. But the orders to kill came from Washington. You'd be court-martialed if you didn't obey." He smiled at her. "The voices from Washington, they weren't crazy."

He told about the shock therapy and how the voices disappeared for a while. About his second time in the hospital. About his discharge. The way she sat so quietly, accepting him, his words, made him feel better.

She was silent, leaving him space to continue.

"That's when the Lord's voice came," the jackal said simply. He could tell she was interested. "He talks to me."

"When?"

"Whenever he has important things to say." He felt the need to change the subject. "I've always been religious." It was the first lie that he'd told her, and it made him feel bad.

Her eyes were following him closely. "I'd like to hear more about the Lord's voice."

"I'd rather talk about growing up."

"You seem uncomfortable," she said softly.

"Yes. I'd really rather back up." He shifted in his chair and the tape under his arm gave way. The blade slipped down his shirt sleeve and fell out his cuff. It lodged in the seat of the chair next to his thigh. His mouth tightened. She was watching him so closely.

He closed his hand around the base of the blade; he nicked a finger as he told her he had been a Boy Scout. She was impressed. They talked about his childhood, his younger sister, and the way his pa had screamed at his ma. It occurred to him that her father may have been a soldier, too. Korea? Maybe Nam in the early years. The jackal nodded to himself; that was probably the genesis of her darkness.

"You said you started committing the robberies when you were twelve?"

"Twelve or thirteen." He felt blood drip from the cut on his finger.

"Did your sister know about the robberies?"

His sister had asked him to see a psychologist. She was worried about him, about the letters he was writing her every week.

She worried about the money—after it was delivered by one of the hacks—even when he told her an Army buddy had finally paid back an old debt.

But it was payment from higher powers for a job well done, he thought.

Sylvia asked, "What are you thinking about?"

He saw that she had her head tipped at an angle like a bird. He felt a sense of relief: *She doesn't know who I am.* "My sister."

He'd sent his sister every penny; all he needed was the head.

When the session was over, he stood and thanked the doctor.

She stood also and walked around her desk. Her hand brushed his arm just as he covered up the now-bloody blade.

"—you ever a medic in the Army?"

He heard the edge in her voice; she'd picked up his panic. *Shit, she does know who I am.* The Lord had okayed his plan; it was quick and efficient. He would put her out of her misery.

As he turned in readiness, she stepped back, and the office door opened. A woman breezed in, her arms overflowing with files.

"Oh, sorry," Linda DeMaria said. Files tumbled onto the desk.

She was a compact, perky woman with short dark hair, bright eyes, and forceful brows. "I thought you'd already finished."

Sylvia said, "We were just leaving. We'll give you back your office." She stared at the jackal. "I'll see you in the new year."

The general in the Lord's Army had no choice but to make his exit. As he reached the door, he caught the ghost of his reflection in the frosted glass and he turned his head abruptly away.

—

TWENTY MILES SOUTH of Santa Fe, Billy drove the Corvette off I-25, parked on pueblo land near the underpass, and watched a crow glide past the windshield. He pressed his head against the neckrest and closed both eyes. With the mouth of the Wild Turkey pint, he traced the dark outline of the tattoo on his chest and thought about his mother. And Luke.

His brother had been Lily's favorite and she gave him her *special time.* That made Duke furious. It made Billy jealous.

He opened his eyes, leaned forward, and stared at his own shadow in the rearview mirror. The oblong shape of his temples, dark brown eyes, and the bridge of his nose were reflected back. Since Luke's funeral, he'd done a lot of thinking. And drinking, and shooting at crows. And he'd made a decision, a commitment to pick up where his brother left off.

His gaze shifted to the heavy Army-issue Colt .45 in his lap. The old man's shooter. Billy took another taste of whiskey and pulled the trigger. *Click.* Empty chamber. He squeezed the trigger again and again. Metal against the firing pin was a good sound.

The Duke had fifty "gun" rules he'd drilled into his boys. He gave his sons guns the way other fathers gave out baseball mitts. He'd made them oil and polish fucking metal for hours at a time.

Billy dry-fired the Colt again and smiled—Duke wouldn't like it. Duke didn't like much of anything these days. He didn't like all the questions Luke had started asking six months ago. *Where were we the night Lily died? Where did we go? Why weren't we home?* Duke hadn't liked those questions at all.

And Billy wasn't sure he liked them either. He remembered the housekeeper's home. And images that flashed through his mind like scraps of a cut-up photograph. He didn't know where Luke fit into the picture. But he had one fleeting vision of his father weeping . . .

Billy got out of the car. He finished the last of the Wild Turkey, threw the bottle against a rock, and yelled at the fat blackbird circling lazily overhead. It surfed air currents like waves.

He began the quarter-mile walk to reach the arroyo, a walk he'd made many times. It was huge, a sand river that flowed from the southeast and the Ortiz Mountains to the Rio Grande. The Sandias loomed behind the mineralized Ortiz range. This was the place he loved, the place he always came to shoot and drink and work things out when they got knotted up.

Billy could see the highway in the distance. Cars crawling like ants at 10 A.M. Early to him; he'd stayed out all night to party. That bitch he'd tried to make it with had laughed at him when he couldn't finish what he started. The fact that the evening had been fucked was no big surprise. His entire life was fucked.

Here he was, hungover and thirsty in an arroyo somewhere between Algodones and Budaghers. He loaded the Colt .45, raised the gun overhead, and shot at the crow.

He missed. Another shot, another miss. He used up three rounds shooting at the damn bird.

He tore up an aluminum can with the next three rounds. He reloaded, fired at the crow again, and the bird squawked but stayed airborne.

The last bullet almost took off his right foot. He forgot where the Colt was pointed when he squeezed the trigger. Billy stared at the fresh bullet hole in his boot heel. The crow cruising overhead belted out a mocking caw.

—

AT 10:50, BILLY TOOK the La Cienega exit and cruised slowly north along the frontage road. Five minutes later, he pulled up in front of the neat, two-story house. A large sign, weathered by age, declared forty acres as the site of Blue Mountain Business Park. But no mountain was visible, and the closest business appeared to be the Santa Fe Downs racetrack, a half mile away. Billy climbed out of the Corvette, walked to the porch, wiped his soles on the bootscrape, and took the three steps in one leap. He released his fingers from the Colt .45 that was tucked into his waistband and rang the doorbell. He recognized the neat plaque mounted on the front door; HENRY ORTIZ, D.D.S. had been seared into burnished oak. Although Henry was retired now, he'd been the Watson family dentist forever. Mostly, Billy had pleasant memories of the man who had supplied candy for his younger patients.

He stepped back as the door opened.

There was a long pause, then a voice asked, "William?"

The smell of *biscochitos* and camphor washed over Billy as he stared into the dim house. "Dr. Ortiz?"

A heavyset man smiled out into daylight. He had a hound's jowls, and his skin was the color of used tea bags, but his eyes sparkled. "What's this about an emergency?"

"Sorry to bother you, sir," Billy said. "But I've got a bad toothache."

The door stretched wider and Billy entered a spotless living room. A magpie of a woman tiptoed out from the kitchen and patted Billy's arm. "Is this little Willy?"

"Billy, ma'am," he corrected shyly.

"You know Henry's retired now, Billy. How's your father?"

"Fine, Mrs. Ortiz."

"Such a fine, fine man," Dr. Ortiz murmured. He grinned at Billy. "I'll come out of retirement for you. Follow me."

"What about some cookies—" Mrs. Ortiz began.

Her husband waved a hand. "The poor boy's got a toothache, Myra."

Billy remembered the way to Dr. Ortiz's spacious office. The hall looked exactly as he remembered it from his last visit two or three years before. Nothing seemed to change in the old man's life, Billy thought. The enormous black leather dentist's chair felt just as it always had, too big, too hard. The drills, each neatly docked at shoulder level, were antiques.

"Open wide," Dr. Ortiz said. "Now which one . . . ?"

Billy said, "I don't really have a toothache. I need a cap."

Dr. Ortiz looked puzzled.

Billy squirmed in the chair, pulled his lip away from his gum, and pointed to his left canine.

"Nothing wrong with that."

"I need it capped, sir."

"Now, William, that's a perfectly healthy tooth. By the way, I could only fit you with a temporary crown."

"Would this temporary crown be gold?"

"It would look gold." He frowned, "I'm just not in the business anymore, at least, not enough to deal with labs and molds and cosmetic brighteners . . . all those modern things."

Billy found that it felt good to tell Dr. Ortiz the story of Luke's death—to unburden himself. *My bond with my brother is so powerful . . . I must have this crown. A way to honor my dead brother . . . a way to show respect.*

Dr. Ortiz turned away to the window and thought about his youngest boy—no, he'd been a man—who had died in the Gulf War. In front of his eyes, the sweep of land toward the Jemez Mountains became nothing but desert sand and wind. When the dentist finally nodded reluctantly, Billy shook hands with the man.

While the novocaine took effect, Billy closed his eyes and felt the Colt heavy against his gut. The chemistry of whiskey and painkiller had a numbing effect and the tension evaporated from his muscles.

The grinder looked like a carpenter's tool and spit bits of tooth into the air. Billy felt his skull vibrate, electric pain fired up his nerves and pulled the blood to his feet. Dr. Ortiz had always been stingy with the novocaine. Billy squeezed his eyes shut and took the pain. He remembered how Luke had always taken the pain for him when they were kids.

When the job was done, Billy paid Dr. Ortiz with two slugs from his old man's gun. Then he paid Myra.

In their kitchen, he stuffed two of Mrs. Ortiz's fresh-baked *biscochitos* into his mouth and almost threw up. It depressed him to kill—he felt sorry for himself—but there could be no witnesses to his transformation.

SIXTEEN

THE ROAD TO the ski basin curved past the massive homes of Hyde Park Estates, past a popular Japanese-style bath house and Black Canyon Campground, then continued to climb the Sangre de Cristos. Thick stands of piñon gave way to the denser forest of spruce, fir, and aspen. Ridges of dirty snow—the frozen wake of snowplows—lined both shoulders of the two-lane road. Sylvia watched Albert Kove guide his Subaru wagon around a particularly tight turn. His glasses crept down the bridge of his nose, but his grip on the steering wheel didn't relax.

She said, "Your eyes aren't open yet, Albert."

"I didn't get much sleep last night." He stifled a yawn.

"We didn't have to drive this far to find a cup of coffee."

He glanced at her quickly, then his eyes returned to the road. "I wanted a chance to talk to you . . . without interruption." He downshifted to keep a safe distance between the Subaru and a yellow school bus loaded with children and skis. "I'm worried about you."

"Albert . . ."

"Don't tell me you can take care of yourself; I've never doubted that."

"Should we even be having this conversation?" She sat up straight, and her voice gained an edge. "Doesn't it jeopardize your objectivity? As a member of the board."

Albert cut her off. "Malcolm was one of my oldest friends, Sylvia. And he cared for you as if you were his own daughter."

She eyed Kove sharply; as far as she could gauge, he was sincere —no irony, no veiled sarcasm intended.

A weariness washed over her; she was tired of her own secrets, tired of her loneliness masquerading as the need for privacy. She was exhausted . . . and she felt uncomfortably wedded to a much younger Sylvia, the girl-child who always seemed to be waiting for her father's return.

She almost blurted out the truth to Albert Kove: *Malcolm was my lover, not my father.* But the internal rush of her own anger silenced her. That wasn't the truth. She *had* lost another father.

"What?" Kove gazed at her curiously.

"I didn't say anything."

"Oh." He smiled and tipped his head.

Sylvia was reminded of the wonderful crow, an animal wizard, who often hung out on the telephone pole near her house. A rascal.

They were silent for several miles. The road wound past Nun's Corner named after the women whose car had gone over the precipice four decades earlier.

Just two months ago, these same mountains had been covered with the soft green-gold of the turning aspens. Now, the aspens had shed their leaves and the deep evergreen of pines contrasted sharply with the snowy scrim.

When the Subaru was midpoint on an S-curve, Sylvia stared out at Pleistocene alluvial fans—the western toes of the Sangres—that stepped boldly toward the Española Badlands . . . *Las Barrancas*. That sky was a clear-biting blue, but a fat black cloud hovered over the ski basin.

"When I drive this road, I always remember why I chose Santa Fe over New York or L.A.," Albert said.

"You might as well say it."

"What?"

"Whatever you got me up here for."

"Coffee." Albert smiled. "They have the world's best coffee at the ski basin."

She gave him a wry smile. "Right. Were you surprised by the article in yesterday's *New Mexican*?"

"I was surprised that you made the papers so quickly." Albert turned the Subaru into the parking lot below the ski area. "But considering the other party, I shouldn't be. So I brought you up here for coffee and some tips on self-defense." The lot was almost full, but he found a half-space beside a mound of plowed snow. They followed the short path past the "chipmunk" play area and the main chairlift. When they reached the lodge, Albert motioned to the open veranda where vendors sold coffee, doughnuts, and sandwiches.

Albert bought two coffees, and they sat and watched skiers maneuver the powdery slopes. The basin was still foggy, but the air wasn't uncomfortably cold, and the low clouds lent an atmosphere of soft intimacy.

After a few minutes, Albert said, "Duke Watson came to my office yesterday."

Sylvia kept her eyes on the distant skiers who appeared and disappeared in drifting fog.

Kove continued, "He's extremely unhappy with you." His voice was low, but that didn't lessen the solemnity of his tone. "Whatever pain he is suffering because of his son's death seems to be focused exclusively on you." After a long pause, he continued. "I know you didn't do anything unprofessional—I have great respect for you, both as a psychologist and as a human being—but this whole thing may go well beyond an ethics review."

Her face and hands felt numb.

"Do you have a lawyer you can trust?"

"I'd already planned to talk to someone—"

"Don't wait."

"All right." She didn't expect her voice to sound so insubstantial, so ill-prepared. She cleared her throat and put force behind her words. "I'll get some help."

Kove studied her face for several moments before he nodded deliberately, "Don't underestimate Duke Watson."

They finished their coffee, and, although they talked of everything except the complaint, Sylvia knew that Albert Kove continued to assess her emotional stability.

As they stood to leave, a lithe female skier dressed in a hot-red bodysuit raced by the veranda doing at least thirty miles per hour. Sylvia kept her eyes on the colorful and reckless athlete. Within seconds, the woman narrowly avoided three collisions as she skidded to a stop in front of the chairlift access.

Sylvia and Albert exchanged glances. Then, with a last look at the long, slick run and the downhill parade, they walked back to the Subaru. The return trip to Santa Fe seemed to take twice as long as the drive up. Traffic was heavier, and, more than once, Albert swerved to avoid oncoming vehicles.

He pulled up in front of her office where she'd parked the Volvo. She was surprised when he squeezed her hand for an instant before she got out of the car. She watched the Subaru merge into the slow, steady stream of traffic, and then she drove straight to the mall.

By eleven that morning, the parking lot at the Villa Linda Mall was a solid mass of cars. Sylvia drove around for fifteen minutes before she finally found a space at the edge of the lot. As she walked briskly past a young patrolman mounted on a bay gelding, she smiled and said, "You've got your hands full."

"Wait 'til you get inside."

He was right; inside, the mood of the shoppers seemed frenzied. Sylvia groaned. It was crazy to come within five miles of the mall two days before Christmas; she wanted to be home alone even though she knew that social contact was the healthier choice. She'd promised Rosie that she'd make a special effort to be festive and to shake off the weight of the month's events. But that was before the complaint and before her meeting with Kove. His warning had left her feeling the need to take action, but that didn't include Christmas shopping.

A child dressed in a Santa's cap grinned at her and Sylvia grinned back. 'Tis the season, she thought.

She worked her way toward the mall's east end where the Cinema Six offered the latest holiday releases, Santa Claus had set up house, and food kiosks were clustered around a carousel. The smell of pizzas, egg rolls, and burritos jogged her appetite and gave her energy level a boost. Food always made her feel better.

Still no sign of her friends.

Sylvia was about to grab a burrito when she heard someone call her name. She scanned the crowd and saw Ray astride a green giraffe, and Rosie perched sidesaddle on a yellow horse. The merry-go-round ground to a halt, and they stepped off.

"Feliz Navidad." Ray kissed Sylvia's cheek.

"How did you get on that thing?" she asked. "The line is a mile long."

Rosie laughed. "Ray knows the ticket man. He offered him a bribe."

Ray ducked his head and smiled. "I invited him to our regular poker night. He's been wanting in for years."

"Shop or eat?" Rosie asked.

Ray and Sylvia both answered in unison. "Eat!"

"Oy," Rosie patted her husband's paunch. "You look as though you need nourishment." She smiled mischievously at Sylvia. "And you better watch out. Some morning ten years from now, you'll wake up fat. Trust me, that's what happens to skinny people."

Ray nudged his wife. "It's a good thing I love plump women."

Rosie and Sylvia carried trays of Chinese food back to the table Ray had staked out. Fried rice, egg rolls, mushu pork, and wonton soup overflowed plastic ware.

Ray dipped his egg roll in hot mustard. He swallowed and then fanned his mouth as he talked. "So what are you going to get your *mamacita*, Sylvia?" He knew about the estrangement between mother and daughter, and he'd been trying to reunite them. To Ray, family was everything.

Sylvia gave him a look. "Listen Raymond, don't start with me." She jabbed her fork into a thick strip of pork.

He said, "It's an innocent question."

"I went to the Chile Shop yesterday and sent her the New Mexico Assortment. Satisfied, Mr. Manners?"

Ray gave her a thumbs-up sign.

Sylvia tapped on the table with her fingernails. "Who wants this egg roll?" She immediately picked it up and took a bite.

Rosie said, "God, you eat like a horse." Her mouth was full when she noticed a homeless woman digging deep in a trash container. She nudged Ray and said, "Give her some dollars, Raymond, please?"

Ray stepped away from the table, and Rosie gazed at her friend. "You were right. He's alive."

"Who?" Sylvia scrambled to catch up with Rosie.

"The jackal. An inmate named Andre Miller was stabbed yesterday."

"Miller? I don't think I know him."

"It's too late now. And he died before I could talk to him."

Rosie's words ran together, "He lived in CB-1. Guess what I found in his cell?"

"Angel Tapia's pinkie."

"Who told you?" Rosie looked crestfallen.

"Nobody."

Rosie eyed Sylvia suspiciously, and it took her a moment to get back on track. "This is the weird part: Miller was missing his little finger when he was found."

"You mean it was freshly amputated?"

"Yes."

"Where was Miller killed?"

"In the kitchen. He worked there."

Sylvia slid a fingernail between her front teeth to free a sesame seed. She licked her finger. "The kitchen has lots of chrome surfaces, doesn't it?"

Rosie nodded. "You always do this . . ."

"So did you notice anything unusual? Like shattered glass, soap on pots and pans—"

"Where we found him, the counter was smeared with blood." Rosie pictured the sheen of stainless steel obscured by reddish-brown swirls.

Sylvia said, "I've got an oddball theory that the jackal is afraid of his own reflection."

"Like a vampire?"

"Vampires don't have reflections, they have boundary problems." Sylvia shrugged. "I'd say the jackal has something in common with a vampire: lacunae in the ego."

"Speak English."

"Lacunae are holes, gaps, craters in the ego. Too little ego, too much ego."

Rosie bit her lower lip. "So the jackal has a screwed-up ego?" She broke off when her husband returned to the table.

Ray gave his wife a sharp look. Sylvia was surprised by the intensity in his eyes. There was tension in the Sanchez family, and it centered around Rosie's work.

Ray started to gather up the leftovers and empty plastic containers. He had hardly eaten anything. He said, "I don't want to hear about people who cut up other people. It's almost Christmas." He dropped the litter in a trash can and walked to the crowded carousel.

Sylvia patted Rosie's arm and said, "Ray's right. We'll talk about the jackal later. You still want that little espresso maker?"

"You aren't serious? This isn't L.A., *jita*." Rosie held two fingers in front of her eyes. "Let's split up. I don't want to know what I'm going to get."

Most of Sylvia's time was spent in lines or dodging the logjam of pedestrian traffic. She found classic videos for Rosie and Ray: *The Thin Man, The Big Steal, Rope of Sand.* Usually, she purchased her videos through a mail-order house, but this was last-minute shopping. When she spied a mini espresso machine at Design Warehouse, she couldn't resist. For Tomás, the simplest choice was a gift certificate at the CD store.

She enjoyed the shopping and found it lifted her spirits. After much debate, she decided on two illustrated dinosaur books for Jaspar. On a display rack, she noticed a children's book, *Circle of Wonder*, by N. Scott Momaday. She thumbed through the pages and loved the illustrated story about Christmas in a New Mexican village. She put it in her basket, joined the checkout queue, and paid for her final Christmas purchases.

She found Ray waiting back by the carousel. Rosie, lugging packages, soon joined them, and the three made their way out of the mobbed mall. Sylvia took a grateful breath of fresh air as they crossed the lot.

There was ice on the asphalt, and several cars executed threesixties in slow motion while helpless passengers threw up their hands.

When neither Ray nor Rosie said a word, Sylvia sighed and touched Ray. "Don't worry about Rosie."

He put his arm on her shoulder and raised his mouth toward

her ear, "*You* tell her to slow down. Maybe she'll listen to a shrink."

"What are you guys whispering about?" Rosie asked.

With his rumpled shirt and polyester jacket, and his thinning salt-and-pepper hair, Ray Sanchez looked like he owned every one of his forty-eight years.

Sylvia said, "She'll be okay. She's got you." Her mood suddenly plummeted. She had a good career in her hometown. She'd worked hard to earn the respect of friends and peers. She'd worked her ass off and Duke Watson could take everything away on a trumped-up charge.

She said, "Two clients called this morning to cancel. They read the paper." The food she'd eaten churned in her stomach. "I need a lawyer, and I'm going to talk to Juanita Martinez tomorrow at her firm's Christmas party."

Rosie said, "She'll eat him alive."

"I hope I'm there to watch," Sylvia said bitterly. She caught sight of a battered dull-blue fender dotted with snow. Her 1986 Volvo was a mess after the high-speed encounter with Lucas Watson; Sylvia identified with her car. Her auto shop had recommended a new Volvo; when she refused, they had tried to repair the damage.

Rosie had to trot to keep up with Sylvia. "How far do you think Duke Watson will go with this? Do you really think he'll base a lawsuit on vicious lies?"

Sylvia gazed down at her friend's face now furrowed with worry. "I think he's done a lot worse. I spent Monday afternoon at the *Journal* morgue; I looked up everything on his wife's suicide."

"His wife?" Rosie interjected. "What's that got to do with this?"

"If it was a suicide," Sylvia said.

Ray's eyes widened. He shifted his packages. "You think he murdered her?"

Rosie shushed her husband. "Raymond."

"I think it's possible," Sylvia said quietly. She started to tell them about her talk with Matt England but stopped herself. He'd spoken to her in confidence; she appreciated his candor.

She leaned against the Volvo's trunk and felt the cold metal, even through layers of wool. "But I don't know why."

"You're serious?" Ray lowered his voice. "Do you have any evidence?"

Sylvia shook her head. "And no motive."

"Then don't even say such a thing out loud!" Rosie said, "Duke Watson is a bully and a politician, but that doesn't make him a wife-killer."

Ray shrugged. "I've heard of weirder things."

Rosie stared at Sylvia and tried to view her objectively. She saw a woman who looked afraid, alone, vulnerable, and delicate in spite of her physical stature.

Sylvia's mouth quivered. She got into her car, started the engine, and rolled down her window. In a small voice she said, "I think I'm in deep shit."

—

THE LAST LIGHT of day barely penetrated into the dentist's office. Matt England tried to ignore his foul mood and concentrate on his job. He was careful to step wide around a coagulated puddle of blood. There was more—three maybe four quarts—on the floor, the walls, the bodies. The preliminary analysis on the wall spatter was easy. It was high-velocity impact spatter, mistlike, that had traveled a short horizontal distance.

The dentist was sixty-eight years old according to his driver's license. He had been shot once in the throat and once in the right temple. The second bullet had traveled through his right hand before it reached his brain. He'd fallen back against the dental chair, and now he resembled a prone patient.

Hansi Gausser, on call for the Department of Public Safety crime lab this week, was hunched over the dentist's body. Hansi lifted his chin, waved an arm at Matt, and said, "OMI's due here any minute. I think we're ready for them."

Matt nodded.

"Mr. Ortiz was too old to be taking out people's teeth. From the look of the place, he was retired, or semiretired. That drill's a museum piece," Hansi mumbled.

"So maybe the patient was a friend. Or maybe he was persuaded." Double homicides, especially when the victims were apparently nice, middle-class retirees, weren't everyday occurrences in northern New Mexico. The sight of the bodies made Matt angry.

"I can tell you this because I'm a genius," Hansi said. "This was one—maybe more than one—fucked-up killer."

Matt moved carefully toward the female victim. They were guessing she was the dentist's wife. She was pictured in numerous photographs around the house. She might have been anywhere between fifty-five and seventy years old. Her soft gray hair was still neatly bound into a bun. She was wearing a pink sweater and a darker pink skirt, both now drenched with blood. It was difficult to discern her facial features because she'd taken one bullet in the mouth and one in the forehead.

She was sprawled on her back, in the doorway to the office. Matt stared down at her and thought of his own grandmother. She had died peacefully, in her own bed, surrounded by family. Mrs. Ortiz had been robbed of a tranquil death.

He and Gausser had spent more than two hours on their search of the office—the video, photographs, sketches, the inventory. The conspicuous evidence had been logged, bagged, and transported to the van outside. When possible, each item would be carefully vapor-checked for prints. If they got extremely lucky, they'd get one good print to run through the automated fingerprint identification system, AFIS.

Sometimes the work got to him physically. Like now, his back hurt like hell and he had a headache. He wanted to stretch out on his own couch, zone out, and wash down a double shot of tequila with a beer chaser.

In lieu of that, he began a careful inventory of the rest of the house. He passed a fingerprint technician in the hall; gray aluminum powder covered the banister. Matt climbed the stairs gingerly.

The second story consisted of the Ortiz's bedroom, a small bathroom, and what looked like a combination sewing and guest room. In the bedroom, a double bed was covered with a hand-crocheted spread. It looked like something Matt's mother would've made. Two children were portrayed in separate studio portraits—complete with a baby-blue sky and Greek pillars—and kept on matching bedside tables.

From the looks of numerous additional photographs, the Ortiz children were now grown, with kids of their own. They hadn't been notified of the murders yet.

Gently, he lifted a gold-colored crochet doilie that rested over the head of the bed. The knots in the thread seemed amazingly delicate and much too small to be made by someone's hands. He replaced it, checked the closets, the drawers, the other rooms. Everything was neat and in its place.

From the look of her clothes, Matt knew that Mrs. Ortiz was the orderly one. She probably attended mass three times a week, and she kept track of all the children and grandchildren and their birthdays. And he'd win a bet if he had any takers that she selected an outfit for her husband each morning, and she laid it out on the bed. After all, Mr. Ortiz was colorblind; it said so on his driver's license.

He could smell the faint scent of licorice on the air. Slowly, he walked down the stairs, and he entered the kitchen through a swinging door. Mrs. Ortiz had left a tray of *biscochitos* on the kitchen counter. He sniffed the cookies, absorbed that sweet cinnamon aroma, and noticed the crumbs. Two cookies were missing; a trail of crumbs led to the door. Mrs. Ortiz was too conscientious to let those crumbs lay where they fell.

The killer had liked *biscochitos*. Matt didn't; they were too dry and sandy for his taste.

In the den, he found the patient files: thirty years' worth. He flipped through a history of patient's crowns, fillings, bridges, and caps. *A–C, D–F,* etc. . . . But he stopped at *S.* The files for *T* through *Z* were gone.

SEVENTEEN

Rosie GLARED AT the stack of reports that covered her desk on Christmas Eve. The attorney general's office was generating mountains of paper for its riot report, and the state police were conducting their own interrogations. Copies of even the most sensitive documents crossed Rosie's desk: hostage depositions, inmate interviews, medical files, and letters from enraged family members. She had lists that accounted for file cabinets damaged, vending machines destroyed, National Guard equipment used, hostage names, names of those sodomized, and names of the dead. Administration files at North had gone up in flames during the first hours of the takeover; reconstruction would take months. Fortunately, the master prison records were kept at Main. Unlike the previous riot where all records were destroyed, the master records had remained intact and had been used to account for the living and the deceased. Matching body parts was a real problem this time around. One emergency response team member, a combat veteran, had vomited from the stench and sight of the mutilations.

Rosie swallowed hard. Nightmares of the riot repeatedly woke her in a cold sweat. Ray wanted her to ask for a leave of absence, but she ignored his pleas. There was too much work to be done, and pressure from the governor's office, the Department of Corrections, and the warden was intense. The official demand was the same from each office: get the dead buried and assign blame to the living: the predators.

Piecing together the chronology of the riot through inmate eyes was the hardest task of all. Ultimately, it was the only way to answer the most difficult questions—who led the murder squads, who committed the actual killings? After the riot in 1980, almost $2,500,000 was spent to finance nine trials that resulted in twenty-five murder convictions and seventy-nine convictions for lesser crimes.

Rosie didn't know if they'd do as well this time.

Under "Inmate Interviews" Rosie had crossed off those who had already been transferred to federal and state prisons, county jails, the state hospital in Las Vegas, and St. Vincent's Hospital. Of the remaining names, several were circled. Bubba Akins was a reinterview. Since most of the inmates in protective custody (or "snitch row") had been listed as dead, she had only two names left to interview there. Before she closed her book, Rosie circled three more names to include. Elmer Rivak, Theo T. Bones, and Robot Rodriguez were not residents of North, but as porters, they'd spent the entire riot caught in the administration building.

Through a series of phone calls, Rosie established T. Bones's and Rivak's whereabouts. They were part of the work detail at North Facility. A crew of about forty inmates was still removing debris from the areas that had been burned, flooded, or otherwise damaged. Rosie left word to have the two inmates removed from work detail on December 26 for interviews.

As she was about to leave the office to question Robot Rodriguez, Matt England knocked on the door. He eased his body into a vinyl chair and gestured toward her desk. "What a mess."

Rosie set her hands on her hips. "You don't look so hot yourself."

"I can't complain. Just overworked, underpaid, and overdue." Matt England relaxed his long legs, the toes of his cowboy boots at three o'clock. "So, I had a chat with your friend Bubba Akins."

Rosie raised her dark eyebrows. "And?"

"I don't know," England said. "Bubba was one of the first out of his cell and he took the first hostage, but I can't pin much else on him. Crime lab's got their report. Bloody palm prints, latents, blood and tissue samples. Nothing nasty belongs to Bubba although the word is that he killed a homie."

Deep furrows lined England's brow as he closed his eyes. "At least it's not as bad as 1980. It took four days before crime scene areas were taped off in Main. Four days while the politicians, lawyers, and reporters were touring the freak show and palming souvenirs. God knows what physical evidence we lost . . ."

Rosie said, "Any idea when the attorney general's riot report will be complete?"

Matt shrugged. "Governor's pushing for completion by the legislative session. You can bet they're feeling the pressure."

"So am I," Rosie said. She accepted a Life Saver from England and sucked on the lozenge thoughtfully. "Bubba didn't happen to mention the jackal, did he?"

England shrugged out a kink in his shoulder muscle. "Bubba says the jackal's dead. He says he died in the riot."

"Well, of course he'd say that; you're a cop. But I don't believe it."

"Because of Andre Miller? Miller might have been the jackal." Matt England stood and stretched. His knuckles scraped against the tiled ceiling.

Rosie tipped her head and let her eyes close. "Then why did he cut off his own finger?"

"He didn't. Somebody did it for him—payback for Angel."

Rosie made a face. "What about Swanson's penis?"

"Destroyed in the riot." Matt grinned. "Or maybe Miller ate it."

"Now you sound like Sylvia." Rosie said. "She told me back in November that the jackal might be a cannibal or a serial killer who collects trophies."

"See? There's a logical explanation for everything."

When Rosie smiled, England moved toward the door and said, "Tell Ray we're playing poker tomorrow night."

"Oh, no you don't. You're sitting down to Christmas dinner, and you two will eat *carnitas* until you can't move."

"Yes, ma'am!" With his hand on the doorknob, England turned casually toward Rosie. "By the way, who else is coming to dinner?"

Rosie cocked her head and her eyes widened. "Tomás will be there with his girlfriend."

"Your boy has a girlfriend? Already?"

"He's almost seventeen. Then there's Abuelita Sanchez, and Ray's *tío* . . ." Rosie batted her eyelashes. "Do you want to bring Angelique?"

England cut her off. "Did you invite your friend Sylvia Strange?"

"Oh." A pause. "She said she might stop by. I hope she does because she needs some holiday cheer." She set her chin in the palm of her hand. "Why do you ask, Matthew?"

"Because if you didn't ask her, I was going to." Rosie's mouth dropped open and England winked. "Merry Christmas, Rosita."

—

Sylvia turned off Paseo de Peralta into the parking lot of Fern, Martinez, and Peña. As she pocketed her keys and climbed out of the Volvo, she saw Juanita Martinez marching through the firm's hand-carved front door. Juanita barely reached the five-foot mark in stockinged feet, but her size didn't diminish the terror she was able to instill in opposing counsel. Sylvia caught a flash of scarlet —ribbon and holly—in Juanita's raven hair. Decked to the hilt for Christmas, Sylvia thought as she caught up with the other woman.

"We need to talk," Sylvia said.

Juanita smiled, "Let's get a drink and—"

"Now. Please."

Juanita led the way through the plush lobby. It was overheated and crowded with partying paralegals, secretaries, and support staff. Conflicting scents of cologne, sweat, and hair gel stung Sylvia's eyes. The women continued down the hall to Juanita's office. Sylvia was ushered inside. The closed door shut out the heavy bass of Christmas rock and roll.

"So?"

"I need your help," Sylvia began. She told Juanita about the complaint and the offending photographs. She did not mention her most serious suspicions about Duke Watson. She didn't need another person suspecting she was crazy. When she was finished, Juanita leaned against her large walnut desk and considered Sylvia.

"Can I talk to the Board of . . . ?"

"Psychologist Examiners. I'll give you Albert's number."

"Are you willing to take this to court? Fight fire with fire?"

Slowly, Sylvia nodded. "I'll do whatever it takes to clear my name."

"Okay, then." Juanita shook her long hair away from her face. "If you're right, and that creep son of his, Billy, shot those photos, and if we can prove it, Duke may back off. His boys have always been his Achilles' heel."

Juanita's eyes glazed over as she said, "I'll bust his balls. Do you have your checkbook with you?"

Sylvia gave Juanita a thousand-dollar retainer.

They left the office and made their way past revelers to the huge conference room with its massive table and twenty matching chairs. She couldn't walk without elbowing past various loud conversations.

"I filed that brief on the fifteenth and—"

"They'd have to be crazy to try for a dim cap."

"It cost me a million-five for a ridge-top, but the view is fabulous!"

"I told them to screw the interrogatories!"

Sylvia couldn't take the noise level and the crowd; the wet bar adjoining the conference room was less congested. Several people mouthed greetings, and she had a brief conversation with a young lawyer she hadn't worked with in almost a year. When he alluded briefly to the ethics complaint and expressed embarrassed sympathy, Sylvia gulped her drink and excused herself. As she set her empty glass on the counter, she felt an arm insinuate itself around her shoulders.

"Hey, there, beautiful!" Using two hands, Herb Burnett turned Sylvia so she was facing him. She had her back to a very tight corner. His eyes worked their way down her body and returned slowly to her face. His whites were bloodshot and the pupils dilated and contracted. He lowered his voice, "You just missed Duke. I want you to know I don't feel good about what's going on."

"What is going on, Herb?" Burnett was the last person Sylvia had expected to run into at this party. Juanita had represented Herb's ex-wife in divorce proceedings.

"Those pictures . . ."

"Billy Watson took them, Herb. He's taken pictures of other women before, or didn't you know that?"

"Please don't be mad at me," he said. His words were beginning to mud at the edges; he wasn't as drunk as he was going to get.

"Out of my way." She tried to squeeze past him.

"You always break my heart, Sylvia. Forgive and forget?" He leaned closer, exuding alcohol fumes. "You were nicer to Lucas than you are to me, Sylvie."

Sylvia's reaction was swift and deliberate; she stomped the heel of her shoe directly down on Burnett's toe.

"You're an asshole, Herb." She left him with a flabbergasted look on his face.

—

THREE HOURS LATER, Sylvia saw the headlights flash off her living room wall. She frowned. She'd had enough holiday festivities for one day; she was in the middle of wrapping her small cache of presents, a strand of silver ribbon caught between her teeth. She switched on the porch light and peered out the front window. The car was familiar, a Bronco. When Sylvia saw Herb Burnett stumble out of the driver's side, she shook her head in exasperation.

Before Herb made it very far up the walk, a snarling mass of fur came charging from behind the coyote fence. Herb started and raised his arms defensively. The momentum propelled him backward and he landed, butt first, on the ground. Sylvia swung the door open and yelled at Rocko. The terrier gave her an injured look, then the ruff on his shoulders stood straight up, and he lunged at the inebriated lawyer's ankles.

"Rocko!" Sylvia grabbed him by the collar. "Enough!" From his horizontal position, Herb grinned up at Sylvia.

"Lookin' good." He held out a hand, too drunk to be fazed when she ignored him. "I feeeeeel good!"

"You're drunk, Herb."

"As a skunk! Christmas martinis," he said. His speech was surprisingly lucid now, as if he'd gone beyond intoxication. "Make it a double shot of Beefeater, two olives, two cherries."

For a moment, Sylvia was tempted to laugh at the absurdity of the situation. This man had pursued her in high school, he'd introduced her to Lucas Watson, he'd delivered a complaint to the ethics board, and he might be about to file a lawsuit that named her as defendant. Now he was crawling on hands and knees toward her feet. She sighed. "You're going home in a cab."

"Wait!" He managed to hoist himself. "You shouldn't be all alone here." He tried to embrace Sylvia. She kept out of reach and lured him toward the door away from his car. She couldn't let him kill somebody on the highway.

"Herb, give me your keys."

"What for, Sylvie? Mind if I call you Sylvie for old times' sake?" He stuffed the key deep into his hip pocket.

"I'm calling you a taxi."

"Okay, I'm a taxi."

They were almost to the stoop when Rocko began to bark again; the terrier charged around the side of the coyote fence.

"What's his problem?" Herb mumbled.

Sylvia didn't bother to call her dog back; he wouldn't come. She eased Herb through the door and had him positioned over the couch when she pushed him down physically. "Stay here."

"Whaaa?"

Sylvia scanned the phone book for taxi companies. She placed the call and hung up as Herb entered the kitchen.

"You got a nice bedroom," he said with a wink.

"The taxi's on its way."

"Why'd you do that?" Herb breathed closer, exhaling gin fumes. "You want to go somewhere, Herb can drive you. I got a great set of wheels."

Sylvia steered the lawyer back toward the living room; he moved like a sailboat tacking side to side. "The cab is for you, Herb."

Herb tapped the couch with his right hand. "Your stupid dog's barking again. C'mon, sit down."

Sylvia ignored him. She moved toward the window and heard Herb struggle to his feet behind her. She was about to turn around when she smelled his breath. The alcohol fumes were overpowering. She jumped as his hands slid around her waist to cup her breasts. Herb tightened his grip and kissed her on the neck. Sylvia pulled away, but he managed to swing her around, strong-arm her, and thrust his tongue into her mouth. She brought her knee up and caught him below the groin. She moved her thumb to his eyelid and pressed hard. Herb let go with a groan, a balloon losing air.

"Jesus, Herb," Sylvia snapped, "I could bring charges against you."

"I jus' stopped by to wish you a Merry Christmas."

She sighed, "You always manage to fuck things up. You never grew past high school."

". . . and to tell you, Lucas was right."

"What?" She turned, but he was through the front door before she could stop him. Herb ignored Rocko who was barking fiercely at the rear fender of the Bronco. He climbed up into the driver's seat, slammed the door, and managed to start the engine. As he drove away, he honked the horn three times.

Sylvia screamed after him, "Right about what?" Frustrated, she watched as the Bronco disappeared in the distance. She locked her door and leaned her back against cool wood, every muscle aching. When she closed her eyes, she saw her father instead of Herb. She was all too familiar with binges.

From the kitchen, Sylvia canceled the taxi. She dialed again, but no one was home at the second number. She checked the clock: 10:45. It was an hour earlier in California, and her mother would be playing bridge and celebrating the holiday with other widowed and retired women. Sylvia would call again in the morning.

Ten minutes later, when she was getting ready for bed, she saw two words scrawled in the vapor that covered the windows. HERB + SYLVIA. They were contained inside the outline of a heart.

—

As THE BRONCO bounced over the cattleguard at the end of the dirt road, Herb had to swallow to keep bile from rising into his mouth. He felt suddenly sick, could taste the alcoholic stew in his stomach, and he was cultivating a nasty headache. He lowered the window so the cold air could ease the nausea. The lights of Rodeo Road seemed to melt and lengthen into luminescent strands; they reminded him of when he was a kid night-writing with sparklers on Independence Day. The lump was growing larger in his throat, but he resisted the impulse to cry. Not the time to lose control. On the overpass above St. Francis Drive, he swerved to avoid a twenty-five-ton truck. Stupid driver, can't keep his rig in the stupid lane.

Lights gleamed from the foothills directly ahead. The signal at Old Pecos Trail turned red just as he entered the intersection; there were no other vehicles in sight. Herb smiled; he needed a drink—that's all he needed. He turned east onto dirt at the cutoff.

The Bronco was well named; it kicked and bucked over potholes like a green colt; the right road could realign vertebrae and strain muscles. Herb caught sight of himself in the rearview mirror. He scowled at his reflection—the thick bridge of his nose, the small eyes. He felt gross, ugly; no wonder a woman like Sylvia wasn't interested in his attentions. Out of your league, buddy— she always was—she's the majors and you're the minors.

Mountain Drive traveled straight for a mile, then it began a switchback ascent to the top of the ridge and home. He thought about how good it would feel if he were bringing Sylvie home. He'd met her when he was eleven, and he'd loved her a little ever since then. Was it doomed from the first moment he saw her? Probably. Everything in his life seemed to go to shit—his marriage, the kids he never saw, his work. He was a lawyer for Christsake! What did he expect? Lawyers did what they were paid to do; he'd filed Duke's complaint against Sylvie. Herb laughed, then caught himself. Don't lose control now.

He pulled the Bronco back on center and cut into a sharp turn. He'd veered perilously close to the drop-off. Shift down, grind gears, roll her over the top. His driveway was here somewhere. The car eased onto asphalt, a smooth relief. Herb fumbled for the electronic garage opener; the Bronco slowed to a stop.

The car door flew open with too much force and he half fell out, stumbled, then caught himself. The house key was on the ledge above the door where he always kept it. He managed the lock, entered, and switched on a hall light. Behind him, the door to the garage didn't quite close. The car door hung open and the space was softly illuminated by the Bronco's overhead light.

Herb was already in his kitchen, a double shot of gin in hand, when the other man rose from the backseat floor of the Bronco, slid silently out the open door, and entered the house.

Herb, barefoot now, sprawled in the white chair by his pathetic effort at a Christmas tree; sparse branches draped with clumps of tinsel and cheap red bulbs. Pen in hand, he began the outline of a letter to Duke, but the effort was too much for his boozy mind. He'd finish it tomorrow. He sipped his martini with eyes closed and thought, Don't forget to call the kids, Birdbrain.

He stood suddenly, lurched, caught his balance, and weaved his way through the house to the master bedroom. The buttons on his shirt were hard to manage, but soon he'd scattered every stitch of clothing across the plush carpet. The lights of Santa Fe flashed in his floor-to-ceiling windows. A million-dollar view. In the master bathroom, Herb turned the faucets and began to fill the Jacuzzi tub. One-hundred-degree water—that's how he liked it.

Back in the living room, he put on a CD of Steely Dan, *Asia*, and turned the music up. He wanted to top off his drink, but he couldn't remember where he'd left the gin. He did remember to check the back door; it was open. He locked it and padded down the hall toward the bath.

The wet heat eased the pressure in his neck and head. His body hugged the porcelain of the tub, and the jets massaged aches and pains. Maybe the headache would back off so he could breathe. He let his face muscles go slack. It surprised him to think there might be tears on his cheeks; he dunked his head underwater and came up for air. Maybe he could actually remember back—remember a time before he'd begun to hate himself. Was there such a time? He should ask his mother if he'd been a happy baby. Right.

The bathroom lights were controlled by a dimmer switch; a warm white glow barely illuminated the blue-tiled sinks. Through the narrow window facing west, he thought he saw stars. Perhaps the clouds were breaking up? He heard Cassie, his youngest daughter, walking in the master bedroom. It was too late for her to be up. It slowly occurred to him that his daughter wasn't really here; she was living with her mother in Albuquerque. He dunked himself underwater again to clear his head. When he came up for air, opened his eyes, the room was dark. For a moment, the man was no more than a shadow arched over the tub. Herb's recognition registered in one word: you.

The shadow pulled back suddenly, arms extended, gripping a solid rod that came rushing down with brutal force. The impact forced air from Herb's lungs and propelled his body underwater. He struggled to reach the surface, air, but the next blow crushed his skull. The water turned dark with blood.

EIGHTEEN

"Good King Wenceslas looked out on the feast of Stephen . . ."

The Christmas carol—sung in Spanish to a rap beat—echoed through the cell block. The jackal hummed along as he worked. He remembered the real words from elementary school. Ah, the holiday season, a time of reckoning, sacrifice, and redemption.

There was the business of Andre Miller. The man had forced him to strike in the open. He should have ignored the jackal's stash in the freezers. But Miller was nosy, and he'd stolen Angel Tapia's little finger—a tiny yet integral piece of a complex plan.

After so many shared evenings when they'd engaged in spiritual talk, Miller had become a Judas. Well, the jackal had taken care of that Judas in a jiffy.

Nevertheless, this was a very special Christmas because last night the jackal had received another message from the Lord. The Lord said, "The disciple is not above *her* master, nor the servant above his Lord." The jackal knew he was the Lord's servant, and now he was going to obtain his very own disciple: a female. He was glad he hadn't hurt Sylvia Strange or Rosie Sanchez. In His wisdom, the Lord had held him back. And soon, he could announce himself to the world.

He stared down at the blueprint he was working on and removed a pencil smudge with spit; the sternocleidomastoid needed work—what was a man without laughter?

He compared his efforts with the medical textbook that lay open on his bed. The trapezius would be a breeze, but the cricothyroid was another muscle altogether.

This was no simple design. Compassion, intelligence, creativity, the ability to love, all were crucial to the final product; but the will had to be intact or nothing was created. And it was imperative that *everything* be created.

He ran his tongue over his lips and sang quietly. "God rest ye merry gentlemen, let nothing you dismay, remember Christ our Savior was born on Christmas Day."

—

CHRISTMAS MORNING. SUN streaked through cirrus clouds and reflected off a lace coverlet of snow dusting cottonwoods and junipers. Piñon smoke perfumed the crisp morning air. A fat bluejay shared the bird feeder with four sparrows. Sylvia wandered the house in her robe, brewed coffee, and mixed the ingredients for a batch of cookies. She sent Rocko outside with a steak bone and he gnawed contentedly near the deck of the hot tub.

She selected a radio station playing Christmas music and called her mother. No one answered, and she imagined the sound of the telephone reverberating off pastel walls adorned with her mother's oil paintings. Sylvia had seen the condominium just once, three years ago. That visit had ended with harsh words, mother and daughter each blaming the other for past mistakes.

Sylvia hung up the phone. Less than thirty seconds later, it rang.

She dusted flour from her hands and picked up the receiver; she expected her mother. Instead, she heard Matt England's voice.

"Merry Christmas."

Sylvia laughed. "Same to you."

There was a silence before he said, "I'm having dinner at Rosie and Ray's tonight. Rosie said you might be stopping by." Matt England coughed and cleared his throat.

"I plan to," she said.

"I thought you might want to do something after? A drink or a walk or something?"

Sylvia hesitated, then said, "Why not?" Because I can give you fifty good reasons why not, she thought. The sudden aroma of cookies brought her back to reality. "Listen—"

"See you tonight," England said, then he hung up as if he sensed she might change her mind.

A walk was no big deal. Liar, she told herself.

Thirty minutes later, when the doorbell rang, Sylvia was showered and dressed. She opened the door and found Monica and Jaspar with his arms around Rocko. Several days earlier, Sylvia had agreed to spend the holiday morning with Jaspar while Monica visited her aunt at a rest home north of Santa Fe. It would give Jaspar and Sylvia time to exchange gifts. December 28 marked the two-month anniversary of Malcolm's death; Jaspar had a lot to deal with this holiday.

"Merry Christmas," Monica said. She smiled and held out what was clearly a bottle gift-wrapped in silver foil. "It's not much, really. But I want you to know I appreciate what you're doing."

Sylvia dropped her arms to her sides. It hadn't occurred to her to give Monica a present, but now it seemed like such an obvious gesture of respect. Flustered, she scrambled to recover. But it was Monica who rescued her.

She said, "I have a policy of no gifts between friends, but this year I broke my rule. Forgive me." Monica's smile was charming and warm.

Sylvia took her first real look at her lover's wife.

Dressed in a fur cloche, wool jacket and skirt, and fur-lined boots, Monica Treisman resembled a cossack princess. Sylvia couldn't resist a mental pairing of husband and wife. The vision was incongruous: the big, broad strokes of Malcolm shaded his dark, Russian ancestry, his boundless intellect, and his insatiable ego; in contrast, the delicate brushwork of Monica highlighted pale, delicate features, her attention to the needs of others, her quiet intelligence. For the first time, it occurred to Sylvia that Malcolm had been in love with his wife when he died.

The realization hit her like a blow. It made her feel jealous, naïve, inadequate. It also made her grateful that Monica had been there to care for Malcolm when he was dying.

"Open it," Monica said when they were seated in the living room.

While Sylvia unwrapped the gift, she noticed Jaspar eyeing her intently. She smiled and patted the couch. He plopped down next to her, Rocko in his lap, and waited until the foil was off. The present was a bottle of 1978 Bordeaux.

"Delicious." Sylvia smiled. "Where was I in 1978 . . . in school?"

"Malcolm bought a case years ago. It's been in the basement under cobwebs, dust, and furniture. It's drinkable until 2010."

"How far away is that?" Jaspar asked.

Monica patted his head. "Not very." She glanced at her watch. "I'll pick Jaspar up in about three hours." She kissed her son on both cheeks and squeezed Sylvia's hand good-bye.

Jaspar, Rocko, and Sylvia stood together on the doorstep while the gray Mercedes disappeared in the glare of sun.

"Want to open presents?" Sylvia asked.

Jaspar gave her a slow smile, exposing the gap between his front teeth and led the way inside.

Sylvia pointed to three packages placed on a pile of pine boughs in one corner of the living room. "That's the Christmas tree."

Jaspar sat down quietly and began untying ribbon. Sylvia absorbed the delicate lines of his face, the glow of his skin. What was it like to give birth to such a perfect child? How could anyone bear such vulnerability in their lives?

After Jaspar had unwrapped his presents and browsed through page after page of dinosaur information, he turned to Sylvia and spoke quickly. "Will you take me to see my papa?"

The request caught her off guard. Jaspar had not been at his father's funeral because Monica felt he was too young. Would she be upset if Sylvia took Jaspar to the grave? When she hesitated, Jaspar prodded, "Please?"

"This instant?" Sylvia extended both hands, palms up, in a gesture of surrender. She collected car keys from the kitchen counter and returned to the living room.

Jaspar held out a package. His present to Sylvia was encased in layers of multipatterned wrapping and great swatches of scotch tape.

"I wrapped it up all by myself," he said.

When the paper finally slid away, Sylvia stared at the shimmery triangles, squares, and circles of lacquered tissue paper in her lap.

Jaspar said, "Hold it up."

She lifted the hook made from a paper clip, and waxed threads carved silver trails in the air. The paper shapes bobbed in a gentle tangle at the end of the threads. A mobile.

"I made it just for you." Jaspar's face was somber.

Sylvia would have hugged Jaspar, but his expression cautioned her to keep her distance. She said, "Thank you, it's beautiful."

Together, they hung it in the kitchen in front of the window.

Through purple, crimson, and aqua shapes, Sylvia saw the jagged prongs of the windmill dancing in the distance. When she looked down at Jaspar, he was holding up a second package.

"This is for Papa," he said.

———

SANTA FE MEMORIAL GARDENS cemetery consisted of several acres on the north side of Rodeo Road. Sylvia drove past the iron gates, slowed the Volvo, and rolled to a stop on gravel. The grounds were deserted except for one car and several people tending to a gravestone. Jaspar was staring out the passenger window intently. Sylvia could see the tendons in his neck, but his excitement was contained.

"Do those people know someone's dead?" he asked finally.

Sylvia nodded. "Yes."

"How many dead people will fit here?"

"I don't know."

"Is it full?"

"I don't think so."

"Can Rocko stay here when he dies?"

"This cemetery is just for humans. I'll probably bury Rocko on the ridge behind my house after he dies. Shall we walk to your father's grave?"

Jaspar turned to her and his face was pale. "When you drive past a grave place, you're supposed to hold your breath."

"I used to hold my breath and lift my feet in the air." Sylvia smiled and took his hand. In her other hand, she carried a geranium cutting, bright pink, from the plant in her kitchen. They walked slowly down the road toward the area where Malcolm was buried. "There are lots of superstitions about death."

"Why?"

"Because we don't know what it is. No one is really sure what happens when we die."

"That's when bad people come to find you in the dark." Jaspar's eyes were troubled.

Sylvia brought his coat collar up around his neck and buttoned it. She was squatting in front of him. "What bad people, Jaspar? Tell me about them."

"Bad men come to steal things."

"What do they steal?"

Silence. Jaspar stared at the ground; only his quickened respiration gave away his agitation.

Sylvia spoke gently, "What was your daddy doing when he died?"

"Sleeping."

"And what were you doing?"

"Sleeping," Jaspar said. He began to kick at a pile of snow repeatedly.

"In the dark?" Sylvia asked.

Jaspar nodded.

"Are you scared something might happen to you in the dark?"

Jaspar didn't answer, but he wrapped his arms around his torso and his fingers clutched his shoulders.

"Bad men didn't come to take your daddy away, Jaspar. He was very sick—so sick that he couldn't go on living. He wanted to stay here with you, but he couldn't."

It took almost thirty seconds, but Jaspar finally raised his head to look at her. "Where did he go?"

"I don't know. Everybody dies, and when that happens, I think our souls go free and join all the other atoms and molecules, all the energy in the world—the trees, the sky, the rivers. What do you think?"

Jaspar shook his head, his brow creased with concentration. "I don't know."

She led them along a stone walkway and stopped in front of a simple square of polished granite set in the earth. MALCOLM TREISMAN. Nothing else was carved on the rock face.

"Here we are." She placed the geranium on the grass next to the rock.

They stood for a time, silent, staring at the earth. Jaspar traced the letters with his fingers. He spoke his father's name. Then quietly, he pulled the crumpled package from the pocket of his jacket and set it down on the grave.

"Do you want to unwrap it?" Sylvia asked.

Jaspar kneeled down and carefully opened his package. It was a dough sculpture, brightly painted, a squat creature with four legs. Jaspar set it purposefully on the grass in front of the gravestone. "It's a horse," he said. "Galloping fast."

When Jaspar turned to Sylvia and held out his hand, his eyes were red.

"I still cry about my father," Sylvia said. She had to struggle to hold on to Jaspar's hand as he took horse leaps over the stone walkway.

"Why?" Jaspar kept moving as he spoke. In an especially energetic leap, his hand broke away from hers.

"Because it's always hard to say good-bye." The words caught in her throat. The grave had brought back memories of Malcolm, but mostly of her own father. What it had been like to walk by his side as a child.

Sylvia suddenly realized she'd been standing still, tears streaming down her face. Jaspar watched her, and then he reached up and put his hand in hers.

When they drove out of the cemetery, Sylvia caught a glimpse of a woman adding plastic wreaths to a marble headstone. A man, so thin he seemed made of sticks, sat in a wheelchair nearby. His hand moved like a leaf in the breeze, and Sylvia saw Jaspar wave back.

———

DUKE WATSON SLAMMED the ax into a frozen chunk of piñon. With a solid crack, the wood split apart like a sheet of ice. He grabbed one of the halves, balanced it squarely on the worn chopping block, and swung again. In one strike, the piece split nicely down the seam. He split the remaining half and set the next chunk on the block. The natural smell of wood turpentine and the gas-oil fumes of the chain saw mix filled his head. He inhaled deeply and went to work on the piñon.

This load of century-old wood had been trucked down from his three-hundred-acre parcel in the Pecos. He wished he was there right now, instead of standing a stone's throw from his house. He could see Christmas tree lights twinkling through the windows.

He set up the next log, focused on the grain and struck. *Thwack.* Another log. Another split. Quickly, he worked through a dozen pieces before he stopped to pull a bandanna from his pocket and wipe sweat off his face.

Queeny's inside the house right now with her tattoos and her pierced body. Somebody's punk nightmare with her pain on display. She has everything a girl could want but she stains and stabs herself for public consumption. It's the exposure I hate. It's the idea that others can see what should remain private.

He brought the ax down for a clean cut. He set up the next log.

Billy's been gone since yesterday or the day before. I don't want him around the house anymore unless he straightens up. It's impossible to look at him—he's become the image of his brother.

Thwack. Sawdust sprayed out from under the ax blade and a pine-bark larva escaped from its wooden bed. The perfect wood was never green, always seasoned and free from knots. Duke set up a log the size of his thigh and tore it cleanly down center.

On Christmas, they call to warn me that I'm too visible in the media. Got to tone things down if I want to win the big war. They're behind me for now, but it's not the time to rock the boat.

The ax struck true and he quartered fifteen more logs. The last one was a wishbone where a branch had grown off the main trunk. He spread his feet, gripped the ax with both fists, and drove it toward the belly of the wood. The ax sideswiped the log, edged off to the left, and missed tearing off his shin by millimeters.

—

AFTER JASPAR HAD gone home with his mother, and Sylvia was alone, the depression settled in like fog between cracks. The visit to Malcolm's grave had stirred painful memories. She remembered the dreams she used to have. Her father standing deep in a tunnel. He called out to her as earth rained down and the tunnel gradually collapsed in on itself. She never made it inside, she never saw him suffocate. In the dream, like life, they were both encased in constant, entropic limbo.

She wondered what her father was doing at this instant. Was he alive? Or had he died years ago as her mother insisted? In Sylvia's mind, her father lived forever in shadowy memories and speculation. The child in her never quite let go.

He had become increasingly withdrawn and moody after his return from Southeast Asia. Still, she would have done almost anything to please her father . . . to win back his love. Because she felt she had lost it, somewhere, sometime in the years of her girlhood.

She threw on her coat and gloves and left. Suddenly, the house that once belonged to Daniel Strange had become unbearably macabre for Sylvia. It was almost as if her father's eyes watched her with some ghostly, haunting need.

—

WHEN SYLVIA AND the Sanchez family were seated at the dinner table, Ray filled plates with food. Tomás said a blessing, and eighty-year-old Abuelita Sanchez made several elaborate toasts.

"Too bad Matt's missing an incredible meal," Tomás said.

Sylvia saw Ray wink at Rosie.

Tomás looked puzzled. "I thought he was dating that blonde with the ti—"

Rosie blurted out, "Did I tell you something funny, Sylvie? Matthew lives at your old elementary school."

"Salazar?"

"He has a trailer parked on the school grounds, six blocks from here. He keeps an eye on things." She snapped her tongue against her teeth. "Quite a coincidence, huh?"

Sylvia hid a smile.

Tomás said, "Is he your boyfriend now, Sylvia?"

"Zip it, Tomás," Ray said.

The scent of *biscochitos* and *posole* mingled with the savory aroma of *carnitas*. Sylvia felt tiny arms embrace her legs under the table and looked down to find the family's newest addition, Rosie's one-year-old nephew, Miguel.

His newness in the world was astonishing, Sylvia thought. Having grown up without a brother or sister, she never took the company of children for granted. The time she spent with them was oddly comforting, like something new and shiny that didn't quite fit. She felt that way about Jaspar.

They were halfway through the meal when Rosie reached across the table and clasped Sylvia's wrist in her fingers. Rosie's eyes were melting, her skin pink from rum and eggnog, and she opened her mouth to whisper a question when Ray proposed a toast to friendship. Sylvia drank, glad the moment with Rosie was past. She knew what her friend would have asked: Do you miss Malcolm? Yes. Are you okay? No.

At 9:30, the telephone rang. A minute later, Tomás relayed a message: "Matt's on the phone. He wants to speak to Sylvia."

Sylvia felt her cheeks redden. She hurriedly excused herself from the table.

"We missed you at dinner," she said into the phone.

"I couldn't call sooner." He paused for a moment. "I'm at Herb Burnett's house."

She knew instantly that something was wrong.

"He's dead."

"What do you mean, dead?" Her words sounded ridiculous to her own ears.

"He was murdered. His skull was crushed. Probably died between Christmas Eve and Christmas morning."

"My God . . ." Sylvia swallowed, and beads of sweat broke out on her brow. "He left my house late Christmas Eve. About ten-thirty."

Sylvia heard noises in the background, and then Matt put his hand over the receiver and spoke to someone for several moments. When he came back on the line he said, "I've got to go, I'll talk to you tomorrow. Give my apologies to Rosie and Ray. Oh, and Sylvia, don't be alone tonight." Before Sylvia could respond, he hung up.

NINETEEN

Herb Burnett's house perched on an eastside ridge top. Thick adobe walls, square footage that could double for a football field, and all the Santa Fe–style trimmings announced prosperity.

The Volvo shimmied over washboard ruts on the road to the ridge. Sylvia took the last stretch in first gear and eased onto an asphalt driveway. A county sheriff's department vehicle, England's Chevy Caprice, and a Volkswagen beetle were clustered in the turnaround.

She found level ground, set the emergency brake, and stepped out into the leaden air of a storm front. To the west, low clouds were settling over the city. She gathered her wool jacket around her neck and turned to see two people standing outside the yellow crime scene tape that surrounded the open garage. One was a petite woman with red hair; she clutched a notepad. The other was Matt England. They were both staring up at the sky where two fat crows cried alarm, in high-speed pursuit of a hawk. The raptor's wings made a soft quick fanning sound as they beat the air. When the crows veered off from the chase, England turned and caught sight of Sylvia. He waved and then shook hands with the departing journalist. "Check back with me late this afternoon. I may have something for you."

As the woman climbed into her Volkswagen and backed out of the driveway, Sylvia walked over to England. He seemed edgy and nervous, and his eyes skimmed over her.

"Reporter from the *Albuquerque Journal*," he explained. "She wrote the lead in today's paper—Local Lawyer Murdered—and now she wants the rest of the story." As England spoke he found himself staring into Sylvia's troubled eyes. "I should've called you, but we've been busy."

They entered the house through antique double doors. Sylvia barely took in the foyer before they stepped down to the living room. An attractive Hispanic woman was listening to a man seated on the corner of a leather couch. She took notes on a steno pad and nodded to Matt but kept her eyes on the man.

Matt directed Sylvia down a hall to what had to be the master bedroom. A king-size water bed, dwarfed by massive ceilings, offered a floating view of the Santa Fe Basin. Sylvia scanned the room and noticed the contrast between plush carpet and bare windows.

She stared at the tiled archway leading to the bath and dressing area. The coffee in her stomach threatened to come back up when she saw the trace of blood on the floor.

England said, "According to the MI's preliminary report, Burnett probably didn't feel much after the first couple of blows." He frowned and massaged the base of his neck. "His skull was crushed with a wooden club or bat."

Sylvia nodded. She felt an overwhelming rush of sadness and pity for Herb.

"No forced entry that we can find. Burnett drank a martini, put on some music. Seems to have settled down to a leisurely bath. After it was done, the murderer took Burnett's Bronco; we found it abandoned on I-25." When England tightened the skin around his eyes, he was unreadable, a tortoise retreating into its shell. He scratched his chin and stifled a yawn. "You saw Burnett on Christmas Eve?"

Sylvia nodded. "Twice." There was an uncomfortable stillness in the room.

"When exactly?" He pulled a notebook from his pocket.

"In the afternoon, around three o'clock. That was the Christmas party at Fern, Martinez, and Peña." She examined the patterns left by many feet walking over two-inch plush. "He was drunk." She felt tired and cheerless as she gave England the details of her brief conversation with Herb and his later visit to her house.

"When did he leave?" The pen was poised above paper.

"Ten-forty. I know because after he left I tried to reach my mother in California." She took a breath. "Who found him?"

"When he didn't call his kids all day Christmas, his ex-wife had a neighbor check." He ran his fingers across the dark stubble on his cheek and kept his gaze locked on her face. "Were there any cars around your house on Christmas Eve?"

"Just Herb's." She became aware of another presence. The woman from the living room eyed Sylvia with frank curiosity as she approached Matt.

"Sylvia Strange, Agent Terry Osuna."

While Sylvia shook hands with Agent Osuna, she took in the other woman's perfect features and neatly manicured hands. Agent Osuna's manner was intelligent and assertive.

Osuna asked, "Do you know anyone who'd want to kill him?"

Matt was guiding Sylvia toward the door. She eased herself

away from the tip of his finger. "His ex-wife, half the attorneys in town, more than half of his clients, and a judge or two."

"He sounds like a great guy," Osuna said dryly.

"He was. His kids adored him." Sylvia walked into the living room and sat in a chair next to a small Christmas tree. She doubted that Herb had been on great terms with his children, but she wanted to defend the man she'd known for almost a quarter of a century.

"Watch the dust," England said following her. The house had been dusted for prints, and gray aluminum powder and black carbon powder were visible on various hard surfaces.

Sylvia stared at the tree: a half-dozen red bulbs were draped with tinsel. The house was depressing—would have been so even if Herb had not been murdered—and Sylvia didn't want to stay any longer. "What a stupid realization . . . I'll miss Herb. Even with the complaint and everything, I was actually fond of the man."

He watched her for a moment, then said, "When you're ready, I want you to look at something." He pointed to a glass coffee table and a folder she hadn't noticed before. "Go ahead and read it."

The yellow legal pad was new and only the first page had been used. It was a letter to Duke Watson, or, more accurately, the outline of a letter.

> Duke:
>
> 1) balance due/will not protest in fact encourage you to seek other counsel
> 2) unable to continue present undertaking
> 3) will not stand for harassment inflicted by you and your son
>
> Fuck you most sincerely, HB

At the bottom of the page a few words were scrawled: tell Sylvia about Jeff.

"Who's Jeff?"

Matt scratched his chin. "I hoped you could tell us."

She shook her head.

Matt followed her outside and opened the door of the Volvo.

Sylvia climbed in, started the engine, and shifted into reverse. When she turned her head again, England was motioning toward her window. She rolled it down. Light refracted off the gray-green of his pupils. Both hands rested firmly on the rim of the door, dark hairs shaded thick fingers. Fatigue clouded his features. "Look," he said, "I don't like how this is shaping up. There are too many unknowns, and it doesn't feel right." He stared out toward the city in the distance. "Until we know exactly what's going on."

"Don't worry," Sylvia said softly. "I'm scared." She remembered the last words Herb had spoken to her: *Lucas was right.*

She let out the clutch and the Volvo glided down the driveway. She understood, but she didn't need the warning. Herb's murder had made her think of Lucas Watson and how, three years ago, he had brutally bludgeoned a man to death.

———

BILLY STARED DOWN at the tattoo needle pecking his chest like a bird. Now that he'd been here twice, he was getting used to the feeling. Gideon was standing, completely caught up in his work. He was so short, barely topping five feet, that he didn't need to hunch over. Billy could see the stripe of pale scalp where Gideon parted his hair and tied it into braids. The sharp scent of the other man's sweat and the animal musk of leather blended with the smell of alcohol and hot electrical cord. Tattooed figures—a raven, a crouching cougar, a naked woman astride a Harley—covered the bare skin of both his arms. The smoking barrel of a .45 peeked out between the neck edges of his black deerskin shirt. The inked weapon pointed dead on at Gideon's Adam's apple. That made Billy smile.

Billy's own tattoo was taking shape. The man had been working around his pecs for twenty minutes. Red laced blue and brown; roses were sprouting from clouds beneath the Virgin's bare feet. Billy grunted and closed his eyes to absorb the singular sensation. It wasn't pain, more like something eating at him from inside, things left unfinished. He tipped the whiskey bottle and drank.

"You better take it easy with that," Gideon said quietly. "It's Satan's brew."

Billy ignored him. His chest burned, it was swollen and red, but the tattoo felt as if it belonged to him. He didn't want to think about his brother's tattoo on dead skin under dirt.

"Worms," he whispered to himself. The squirming image made him queasy. At least the lawyer was going to the worms, too. Herb Burnett had made the front page of the *New Mexican*. PROMINENT LAWYER FOUND MURDERED. He started to laugh and Gideon pulled the needle away and stared at him.

"You need to take a break?" Gideon asked.

"No," Billy said. His expression changed, his eyes went flat. "How come lawyers always survive shipwrecks?"

Gideon shrugged and went back to work.

"Sharks don't eat their own kind." Billy pressed his head against the high neck of the chair and set his jaw. What bothered him was that bitch doctor. Lucas was dead, and she was walking around free and easy. Doing what she pleased. Fucking whoever she pleased.

Something had changed for Luke near the end. The last time he'd seen him, when Luke was in North, he'd told Billy that Sylvia was really Lily, that she'd come back to be with both her boys.

Now, Billy had remembered something on his own. He'd remembered the morning after his mother died, Duke was yelling in their housekeeper's living room. And then he'd remembered something new: Lucas. His six-year-old brother walking toward him, trembling. When Luke opened his hand, Billy had seen an object in his brother's palm. It was a wedding ring.

He reached down to touch the tattoo on his chest and felt a pang of regret. Gideon was an artist. Even though killing got a little bit easier each time, Billy was almost sorry he was going to have to take this man out.

—

"APPROPRIATE CRISIS RESPONSE, post facto mobilization," Rosie muttered to herself. The words snapped out a counterbeat to the clack of her stiletto heels, and the sound echoed around Main's administration hall. She was angry and indignant. It was the day after Christmas for Christsake; Warden Cozy knew better than to call her back to work for a special meeting.

"Information management specialist. Bullshit specialist is more like it." Her back ached after the hour-long encounter. She hated meetings! She was part of a bureaucracy, she didn't deny it, but wallowing in its worst aspects on holiday weekends was beyond the call of duty.

Rosie nodded absently at two women carrying stacks of files. Her mind was racing. During her entire tenure as penitentiary investigator, she'd walked a very thin line politically. The warden was not her ally, nor she his. But she had friends in appropriately high places and enough clout to keep her operational . . . or so she'd assumed.

Today's meeting—Cozy rambling on about press management, public relations, legislative analysis—had left her with a bitter taste in her mouth.

Cozy had graced her with his infamous smile, part smirk, part sneer. "I know that you care as much about this institution as I do, Ms. Sanchez. I know you take your commitment to the inmates of the penitentiary seriously." He had pulled his belt higher on his belly. "The rumors that are circulating interfere with the functional level of everyone on this ship—especially after the riot —and we've got to man the oars together. I don't want to hear another word about body snatchers or escape attempts unless you've got serious substantiation."

That had floored Rosie. She hadn't mentioned one word about escape attempts. She just prayed that the warden had been speaking in the abstract.

—

SHE WAS STILL wound up when she left the prison an hour later. Chewing on her thumbnail, she darted in and out of traffic on Highway 14 and then rode somebody's tailgate down Cerrillos Road. At Second Street, she scraped rubber from the front tire when she cut the turn too close.

There was one parking space left in the lot fronting Gold's Gym. Rosie grabbed her shoes, jogged to the women's locker room, and squeezed her body into flower-covered Lycra leggings and a neon pink stretch top. She and Sylvia had made a plan to meet at aerobics class to work off holiday calories. The class was already halfway through the warm-up when Rosie chose a spot next to Sylvia in the back row. After twenty minutes of agonizing floor work followed by thirty minutes of peak aerobic exertion and a cool-down, Rosie's tense muscles finally loosened up.

For ten minutes after class, the women's locker room was crowded. Sylvia managed to grab one of the three showers. When she finished washing, Rosie took her place, quickly rinsed, and began to dry off with her leotard.

"Use this." Sylvia held out her towel. She had pulled on form-fitting jeans and a red cotton sweater. She bent over at the waist and shook her hair out. It fell naturally into loose curls. Rosie pulled her own hair gently out of a ponytail and fluffed it up. She tried to tame the slightly wild effect she saw in the mirror. As she dressed, the locker room emptied out.

Sylvia said, "I went to Herb's house." She took a manila file out of her bag.

"Why didn't you tell me you were going there? I would have gone with you." Rosie pulled on her dress and zipped it up the side.

"You had family to visit—"

"If you needed me, I would have gone with you." She slipped on her heels. "You don't reach out enough. You don't ask for support. I don't understand you."

Sylvia stood silent for a moment, then she placed the file on the bench in front of Rosie. "This is what I have so far on the jackal. Look it over. We should get together soon and talk about it; for now, everything's in there."

Rosie stared at her friend and shook her head. "Fine, let's talk about the jackal."

"I'm beginning to narrow down your choices. You'll see, I'm leaning toward a select group." She pointed to the file. "You knew one of these guys was a murderer, but I don't think you knew he cut up his victims and hid the parts. I put a star in front of his name."

"Shit."

"Another *star* is a raving schizophrenic. Even if he's not the jackal, he should be transferred to psych."

"What about the jackal's collecting?" Rosie asked.

"It's childlike regressive behavior. Most likely, he's regressing because his early life was safer and more secure. Or at least, he perceived it that way."

"You still think this thing with mirrors and his reflection is right?"

Sylvia crossed her arms and shrugged. "So far every one of his crime scenes—or at least what we believe are his scenes—fits my little theory. But that's all it is—a theory. I did find a candidate who showed absolutely no reflection responses on the Rorschach."

Rosie looked bemused, and Sylvia explained. "Reflection responses have to do with the symmetry of the cards: someone will say, this is a bat, and this is his reflection in the water. Antisocial, narcissistic guys—like most guys in the joint—tend to have lots of reflection responses. They see everything as a reflection of themselves."

Rosie still looked puzzled. "But you said this guy had no reflection responses?"

Sylvia nodded. "Right. He's masking . . . just like the jackal is covering up shiny surfaces. I put two stars by his name." She gathered up her bag and tossed her coat over her shoulders.

Rosie had to hurry to catch up with her. There were only a half-dozen cars left in the lot when the two women left the building. They walked in uneasy silence. As they crossed the asphalt, there was a sudden clatter of bottles from a nearby Dumpster. Rosie took several steps before she realized that Sylvia had frozen in her tracks.

"What?" Rosie felt the contagion of the other woman's fear.

Sylvia gazed wide-eyed toward the darkness of the alley. "Did you see something?"

"I don't know. Was it a cat? Something moved."

Sylvia shook her head. All she could hear was the heavy bass beat of the next aerobics class. Suddenly, a dark shape rose above the Dumpster, and she stifled a scream. In the dim light, she saw what looked like a homeless man. He was swaddled in rags, and she felt his watchful, accusing gaze before he disappeared again below the rim of the metal container.

Rosie shuddered. "Herb's murder has you spooked, doesn't it?"

"Yes," Sylvia replied.

"Me too."

TWENTY

At 8:05 on Sunday morning there were nineteen inmates at work in the warehouse that served as a woodworking and metal shop for Prison Industries of New Mexico. Last-minute finish work on a big contract order included oiling, staining, and the detailing on five dozen Taos-style chairs. The air reeked of turpentine and linseed oil while band saws created a steady hum.

Most of the chemical labor was taking place in the first third of the shop; a group of five inmates worked the saws at the opposite end. The detail had been selected on the basis of their efficiency and skill; this order needed to be delivered before the New Year's

Eve open house at the new offices of the Department of Corrections.

Two correctional officers were in charge of the group and they alternately stood on opposite sides of the warehouse or "floated" the floor for two or three minutes at a time. Fifteen of the inmates were Hispanic, one was black, and three were white.

Juan "Ball" Barela switched on the circular saw and hefted an oak four-by-four to the metal platform. Although he kept his eyes only on his work, he was acutely aware of the homeboys to his left and right and the two white boys—Stick and Hall—in front of him. The whine of the band saw changed pitch as wood was cut and reshaped by the blade.

At 8:20, one of the C.O.s tapped inmate Roger Stick on the shoulder. Stick cut the motor of the saw he was working and strained to hear the message the guard delivered. Finally, he nodded slowly, glanced at the young man next to him, inmate Bobby Jack Hall, and followed the C.O. to the front of the warehouse where they joined the second guard.

Bobby Jack had his plastic safety goggles low on his face, wood chips were stinging his skin; over the noise of the saws, he didn't register Stick's disappearance.

Ball Barela clicked his tongue behind his teeth and tipped his chin, and the men at his sides moved with the lethal grace of bullfighters. In one flowing turn they had Bobby Jack on his back, a rag stuffed into his mouth, and his left arm under the blade of the circular saw. Blood exploded and spattered their faces like red oil. Ball Barela clutched the severed arm and cast it across the room; it rolled to a stop in a pile of debris and sawdust. Before the C.O.s could control the three men, they had sliced most of Bobby Jack's right arm off, too.

Reinforcements arrived, but the scene in the warehouse remained chaotic until the dogs cooled things down. Several of the nineteen inmates were found outside where they had fled at the first sign of trouble. Bobby Jack Hall went to the hospital with his right arm attached by a three-inch thread of fascia. His left arm was missing.

—

WHEN ROSIE ARRIVED at the breakfast table at eight o'clock, Ray greeted her with a kiss.

"Eggs?" He waved the frying pan in his hand.

"Ummm." Rosie sighed; exhaustion had seeped into her bones like the cold. She stood by the table and traced a flower on the brightly colored oilcloth. "Where's Tomás?"

She accepted the steaming mug of coffee that Ray handed her and watched her husband turn back to the stove. From the rear, in his chef's apron, he looked chunky.

"I sent him next door to help Mrs. Flores with her bathroom pipes. Her son is working up in Taos for the week."

Rosie pulled a strand of hair from the corner of her mouth. "It's not supposed to turn colder, is it?"

Ray cracked two eggs expertly into the pan and hot grease cackled. "Sure is. Weather report said wrap the outdoor pipes and keep the faucets on drip until next year." He dropped slices of pale bread into the toaster, humming as he worked.

"Storm?"

Ray nodded and flipped one egg. "Maybe a ten-year-storm. Coming from California. Washing away all those movie-star homes in Malibu."

Rosie grunted and shuffled to the coffeemaker to refill her mug. Ray pinched her on the rear as she passed by.

"Ray Sanchez!"

He grinned at her, held both arms open, and swiveled his hips in a comic bump and grind. "Come and get me!"

Rosie brandished a finger at her husband and then collapsed in laughter at the table. After several kisses, Ray served up eggs over easy, toast, and jam. They ate in comfortable silence, and then Ray swallowed a last mouthful of egg and wiped his mouth with his napkin.

"I thought we could go to the mall and check out paint at Sears."

Rosie cocked an eyebrow and chewed thoughtfully on her toast.

"Maybe take in a matinee. Tomás might even let his parents sit next to him." Ray sloshed hot coffee into both mugs and spooned sugar from the bowl. "What do you think?"

"Tomás hasn't let his parents be seen in the same theater with him since he turned thirteen."

"So maybe he's grown out of it."

"Un huh." Rosie's response was noncommittal.

"Did you have something else in mind for today?"

She squared her shoulders and stared back at him. "I have to go in to work. For a few hours, Ray." She tried unsuccessfully to keep the defensive tone from her voice. When Ray carried his dishes to the sink with a stony look in his eyes, Rosie said, "You know I can't take the day off unless things are really under control." She cringed at the sound of dishes assaulted in sudsy water.

Ray turned suddenly. "Since the riot . . . I'm not sure you know what's important."

Rosie set her mug on the table next to her half-eaten breakfast. She smoothed her hair from her face, caught her lip between her teeth, and stood. Each movement was totally contained. She walked from the room leaving Ray with soapsuds on his arms and an angry frown on his face. When he was alone, his face fell as anger was replaced by sadness.

Rosie was almost out the front door when the call came from PNM Main; Bobby Jack Hall had been involved in an incident. And so had the jackal, *el chacal.* Rosie acknowledged the inference with dread. One of Hall's arms was missing.

She raced the Camaro's engine and reviewed what she knew about Bobby Jack Hall. He was young and pretty, maybe twenty, serving a fifteen-year sentence for armed robbery, and he was a member of the Aryan Brotherhood. Most pertinent of all, he had been Bubba Akins's "slave" when Bubba was still at Main. Rosie burned rubber coming out of the driveway.

When she reached the penitentiary, she learned that Bobby Hall was already in surgery at St. Vincent's having his right arm reattached. A search of the warehouse was under way, but his left arm was still missing. She notified the captain to let C.O. Maggie Donner do the preliminary interview with Barela; she would get to Juan and friends later. She wasn't about to get stonewalled by the homies when she had leverage she could use on someone else.

Rosie drove quickly along the narrow road that led from Main to North Facility. She glanced off to the right when she reached the turnoff for the new sewage treatment plant. Dormant equipment rimmed the leach pond like giant, parasitic insects. The stench of human waste and chemicals trespassed the tight seal of the Camaro's windows. Rosie pressed a little harder on the gas pedal. She passed just one utility truck on the half-mile stretch to North's parking lot.

C.O. Elaine Buyers welcomed Rosie into North. "Cold out there, huh?"

Rosie responded with a cursory nod. "Colonel Gonzales?"

Buyers's radio emitted a sharp burst of static and she reached for it with a scowl. "I just saw him go back to his office."

Rosie left Buyers trying to decipher a garbled radio message and marched through the door that led to the colonel's office. In this hallway, the blue carpeting remained, but the walls showed severe damage from acetylene torches and various battering tools.

Knocking twice with her knuckles, Rosie opened the door and José Gonzales's hefty form filled the space.

"I was just leaving," he said as one arm scooted her into reverse.

Rosie maneuvered skillfully on her high heels and her brown eyes grew wide. "First, we need to talk."

Gonzales raised an eyebrow. "No need, someone wants to talk to you."

"Bubba?"

"The same. He heard about Bobby Hall ten minutes after it all went down. He asked for you." As the colonel spoke, the stale scent of cigarettes hovered around his mouth. His wife's anti-smoking campaign seemed to be losing ground.

Gonzales led the way to the C.O.'s lounge where he let a quarter clang into a bright-blue vending machine. He whisked out the package of white powdered doughnuts and retraced his tracks down the hall. As he tossed the doughnuts into the air and caught them again, he said, "These are a goodwill offering. Bubba loves his doughnuts. And now he loves you, too."

They took the hall that led past Administration's control center. Behind the glass, Rosie saw an unfamiliar face staring up at six closed-circuit television screens. In the background, the bright green-and-yellow screen of the computer looked like a baseball diamond on a child's video game. Rosie knew the image would flash an alert if there was any penetration of North Facility's chief barrier.

Colonel Gonzales passed the base of the guard tower and unlocked the door that opened out to North's largest yard. The door was made of unmarred steel, replaced immediately after the riot.

Cold stung Rosie's nose and mouth. In the northwestern sky, sullen clouds loitered over the Jemez Mountain Range. She wondered if the temperature could have dropped several degrees in the few minutes she'd been inside North. The door clanged shut behind her. Colonel Gonzales stood by her side, his hands in his pockets. They surveyed the yard in silence.

There was little change since Rosie's last visit before Christmas. Some debris had been cleared from the area near the bleachers, but the yard was unused. Housing unit one faced this yard—the only H.U. in North that was currently functional. Thirty-eight maximum security prisoners had been moved here and remained under twenty-three-hour lockdown. Other state facilities had been reluctant to accept the worst of the bad.

Without a word, Gonzales strode across the dried grass and dirt to the asphalt walkway skirting Town Center—law library, chapel, education center, and visitor's center—and the gym. He still gripped the doughnuts in his hand, presenting an absurd picture,

Rosie thought. Again, Gonzales used his keys to unlock the door. When Rosie stepped into the gym, her skin tightened in the frigid air.

"No heat yet," Gonzales muttered.

"It feels like a freezer," Rosie said. It took her eyes several minutes to adjust to the dim interior. "I trust we have a reason for staying in here."

Colonel Gonzales nodded. After a beat, Rosie realized he was acknowledging a presence. Bubba Akins. The huge man sat casually on a bench staring back at them with a faint smile on his round face.

"Bubba preferred an informal meeting," Colonel Gonzales said. He tossed the packet of doughnuts into the air and Bubba caught them without moving anything but two fingers and a thumb.

"Get the bull out of here," Bubba said.

"McKevitt?" The colonel raised his voice and sent it out into the gloom. Another shape materialized, this time a guard standing about ten feet behind Bubba. "You can leave us alone for five minutes."

They waited until C.O. McKevitt closed the door quietly, and then Bubba ripped open cellophane and bit deeply into sugar. As he ate, he made the slushy sounds of hogs at the trough. He grinned up at Rosie and stuffed the last doughnut between thick wet lips. Pink skin was peeling from his nose and there were pronounced bruises shading his cheek, eye, and forehead.

"Bobby Jack been treated worse than 'n animal." Bubba spoke so low that Rosie leaned forward in an effort to hear. "Since that riot, been nothin' but shi' for my family." He smiled politely at Colonel Gonzales and nodded his head. "Thank you, Colonel, for the refreshmen'."

Rosie kept plenty of space between herself and Bubba. He loomed larger than she remembered, but his face looked battered and his eyes projected a dull weariness.

Rosie said, "So what are we going to discuss?"

Bubba shook his head and his skull swung slowly on the axis of his thick neck. "Un. I ain't discussin' to nobody. I'm doin' my studies in the library."

Colonel Gonzales spoke easily. "Bubba's got some big complaints, and he's filing with the court *pro se*."

"Tha's right. Defend myself this time."

"What complaints?" Rosie asked.

The big man waved his fleshy hand in dismissal. "Abou' my personal comfort and safety . . . but don' need to go into it now. I'll send you a copy fo' sure."

Rosie exchanged a fleeting glance with Gonzales and let out her breath. "What do you want, Bubba?"

Bubba raised his eyebrows and shook his head as if excusing Rosie's lack of social graces. "An exchange."

"What for what?"

"I wan' out of hea'."

Rosie scoffed. "I can't get you paroled."

"I didn't say parole. I jus' want to enjoy a different environmen'. I want Bobby Jack to enjoy somethin' different, too." He paused and rubbed a finger against the darkest part of his bruised face. "Texas, mebbe. Or Tennessee."

"Why?"

" 'Cause I kinda figured I'd like to live to be thirty-three."

Rosie said, "It's a nice age."

Bubba cut her off with an explosion of sharps and flats that passed for laughter. "My friends ain't gonna wait for the birthday party. We havin' a disagreement—payback time. They take care of me like tha'." Bubba snapped his fingers with a final sound. "Like they almost take care of Bobby."

Rosie waited, watching his eyes, the canny gleaming dots. "Who did it?"

"Right. You want to play or not?"

"If the game's right . . ."

"Cut me a deal."

Rosie's eyes narrowed. "What is it you've got to trade?" She held her breath waiting for the answer.

Bubba grinned as if Rosie were a hundred-pound bass dangling at the end of his hook. He worked up to words with several wheezing breaths. "You still lookin' for the jacka'?" He nodded. "Yeah, I see you are."

"He's alive, isn't he? Did he do Bobby Jack?"

"We got us a deal yet?"

Rosie tipped her head. She could see the toes of Colonel Gonzales's shoes, boot black and streaks of dust. The shoes moved.

"I think I better find C.O. McKevitt. He's been gone so long he probably got lost somewhere." The door opened briefly and a thin arm of sunlight reached in only to be severed when the door slammed shut.

"Well?" Bubba leaned on the syllable denting it in three places.

"We have a deal."

Bubba strained forward on the bench, and for a moment Rosie feared he might be coming at her, but he was only shifting his weight. "I got your word of honor as a lady." His tone was only half ironic.

"You've got it."

"And Bobby Jack?" Bubba's voice was barely audible.

"And Bobby Jack."

Bubba seemed to study his belly for several seconds, then he ran a meaty palm along the side of his neck.

Rosie couldn't wait for the fat man to speak. "So which of the guys who cut Bobby Jack is the jackal?"

Bubba shook his head. "None."

"Bubba, I need to know who did the cutting. We have a deal."

"The deal is I tell you who's the jacka'. The jacka' jus' happen to be in the right place to pick himself up another piece of meat."

Rosie asked, "Why would he take an arm?" Her voice was a whisper.

"Maybe he thinks he's Doc Frankenstein . . ." Bubba said. He scratched his chin, and white sugar dust rose in the air. "After the riot, you sure you matched up all those arms and legs?"

Rosie's eyes widened and she swallowed carefully. She remembered the scene from the movie where the mad scientist applied electric currents to his creation—smoke, lightning, and then the monster's eyes opened.

She ran a quick mental inventory: right hand, right pinkie, left arm, penis, nose . . . She was startled by the sound of Bubba's laughter; she could see his face turning red.

"You look like you believe me," Bubba said when he caught his breath.

Rosie lifted her chin. "You said the jackal had a *job* to kill someone."

"Yeah, I said that. Mebbe you talk to Anderson."

"Anderson?" Rosie scanned a mental file of inmates—several Andersons came to mind.

"Correctional Officer Anderson." Bubba grinned. "He might help you find Doc Frankenstein before the monster comes a callin' on you."

"Who is the jackal?"

"Charl' Co. My lie. That's where you'll find you a jacka'." His eyes disappeared behind fatty flaps of skin. "I can't say no more," he murmured hoarsely.

It took her a minute, but Rosie got it. *My Lai.* Vietnam.

"An' when you find that jacka'—give Bobby Jack his arm back."

———

"YOU'RE TOO LATE." Criminal Agent Terry Osuna thunked her fist on the roof of Matt England's Chevy Caprice. She leaned into his open window and plunked both elbows on the frame. "Captain Rocha and I just spent thirty stimulating minutes with Senator Watson." Osuna fluttered her eyelashes. She was standing on the sidewalk in front of the four-story Schumacher Building where Duke Watson maintained his Santa Fe offices. Matt's Caprice was parked in a loading zone.

Osuna said, "Basically we got zip. He says Billy's out of town with friends, but he doesn't know their names. He says he'll give us his utmost cooperation. He says Burnett didn't have an enemy in the world." This time she rolled her eyes and she reminded Matt of Betty Boop.

He said, "Didn't your mother ever tell you you'd go cross-eyed?" He pulled a tin of Copenhagen tobacco off the dash and popped the lid. "I had a talk with an old friend, a renowned Albuquerque P.I. who shall remain nameless. When the legislature's in session, he's been known to work as an analyst. His hobby is watching politicos screw each other from behind."

Matt sifted tobacco between his fingers and packed a wad into his mouth. "The buzz is that some members of the party think Duke may be a little hot to handle right now. They say good riddance to one son, but hello, he's got another one. On top of that, his lawyer got whacked." Matt climbed out of the Chevy and locked the door. "So I thought I'd stop by to cuss and discuss."

"Rocha isn't going to like the idea of you going after Duke alone." Osuna started to walk away, then she flashed him a smile. "But I do."

The offices in the Schumacher Building were arranged off short and thickly carpeted corridors; footfalls were prohibited. Breathing a little too heavily from the three-floor walk up, England scanned the doors on the third floor of the west wing. Number 306 was stained mahogany as were all the others. A tasteful gold plaque with black lettering and a longhorn logo had been attached at eye level: Duke Land and Cattle Co.

The door was unlocked and Matt entered. He was greeted immediately by a very efficient and very pert woman seated behind a desk. "May I help you?"

The entire wall behind her chair was lined with books. The spines ran in color series; red on the middle shelf, olive green on the top shelf, and so on. A healthy *habanero* plant bearing tiny, bright red chiles decorated a low table where the magazines were fanned across glass. Two comfortable chairs, now empty, were there to oblige visitors.

Matt showed his badge, and she reached out a thin arm and

gripped it between even thinner fingers while she studied it for several moments. When she was satisfied, she gave a quick nod and a smile and said, "You're here to speak with Senator Watson, but he has just stepped out for lunch."

Before Matt actually heard the door open, he turned and found himself four feet from Duke Watson.

"It's all right, Mary."

Matt repressed the urge to butt heads, lock horns, and settle the long-running score like a pair of rutting rams. Instead, he stayed within "butting" range and watched as Duke decided which approach he would take. The senator's subtle emotional transitions rolled over his face like fruit on a slot machine. Three lemons lined up and Duke scowled. The politician regained control almost immediately.

"Agent . . . England, isn't it?" He glanced at his watch. "I just finished speaking with your superior, Captain Rocha, and your associate, Agent Osuna."

Matt nodded. "I'd like a few more minutes of your time, Senator."

Duke Watson sighed, raised both palms in a gesture of surrender. He said, "Mary, please let me know when Mr. Cane arrives."

Mary said, "Yes, Senator." The look she gave Matt England was a blend of reproach and flirtatiousness.

Inside his private office, Duke Watson motioned to Matt to take a seat while he closed the door.

Matt chose a fat leather armchair.

Duke dropped into the chair behind his desk and his face darkened with contained emotion. "Herb Burnett's death was shocking. It makes me sick . . . and very, very angry."

Matt nodded slowly. "Burnett outlined a letter the night he died."

Silence.

"Burnett mentioned you." Matt thought the smell of aftershave in the room had intensified. He said, "Herb also referred to someone named Jeff. Do you know who he meant?"

"Not offhand. If you want to make a copy of the letter available to my office, I would appreciate it, Agent England." He started to rise. "Is there anything else?"

Matt said, "Yes," and Duke sat back down. "You know we want to visit with Billy about Burnett's murder."

"I already told Captain Rocha—"

Matt interrupted him. "I've got another case I'd like to discuss with Billy." He crossed his legs and settled deeper into the chair. "Do you know a man by the name of Gideon?"

Duke shook his head impatiently.

"He was a tattoo artist. Pretty good . . . did almost anything you'd want: roses, tigers, swastikas, well-endowed ladies, Virgins. In fact, he did a tattoo of the Virgin for your son, Lucas. Very special." His tongue poked against his gums. "But he won't be doing any more tattoos because he was murdered a few days ago."

"What has this got to do with me?"

"Did your boys used to get their teeth taken care of by Dr. Ortiz. Henry Ortiz, the dentist?"

"I knew Henry."

"Ah, then you know he's been murdered also." Matt's face hardened. "And so was his wife Myra. Both shot in the head." He let out a breath and made a show of relaxing. "You know, this job gets to me sometimes."

"Why don't you retire?"

"Henry Ortiz was retired. Did your boys have lots of cavities?"

"Henry Ortiz was our family dentist for many years. I read about his death. It's awful, but Santa Fe has changed. You know that . . . we used to have no crime at all. Now . . ."

"Do you own a Colt .45, Army-issue pistol? Senator?" Matt lifted his gaze to a polished steel sword mounted on the wall directly above and behind the Duke's head. Its bone hilt was carved with a formal Asian motif. It looked like a Japanese military or ritual sword, perhaps a trophy from the Second World War.

"Why the fuck do you want to know?" There was a long silence while Duke Watson took a breath and reminded himself he was a politician. He leaned back in his chair and set the tips of his fingers together. "I had one years ago. I'm sorry to say it was stolen."

"That's a shame."

"Yes, it is. The Colt belonged to my father. He fought in the Pacific."

"I've heard through the vine that you've got a Lee-Enfield .303. I'd like to see your collection someday."

The intercom buzzed and Duke Watson was on it immediately. "Yes, Mary."

Mary's scratchy voice was audible: "Mr. Cane is here."

"Tell him I'll be right out." Duke Watson stood and adjusted his broad shoulders inside a tweed jacket. "I hope that I've been helpful, Agent England."

"No, not yet." Matt stayed in his seat. "Tell me about Blue Mountain Business Park."

There was no question about it, the senator's mouth twitched.

Matt said, "You bought that land in 1983 as a partner with Henry Ortiz. I wondered if it's been a good investment."

Duke Watson focused on a spot behind England's head. "Your time is up."

Matt stood and moved two steps closer to Duke Watson. He topped him by four inches. "People around you keep dying, Senator. You know, if I were you, I wouldn't destroy an innocent woman's career."

The senator's blue eyes seemed to flare for an instant. Matt closed the door gently as he left the private office.

He crossed the room and Mary gave him a warm smile. He nodded to a mousy man he assumed was Mr. Cane. As his fingers were about to close around the doorknob, the door to the hall flew open, and a white male with red hair and freckles squeezed past him and into the room.

The man said, "Is he in, Mary? I just need a minute—"

"I'm sorry, but he has a luncheon appointment, Jeff." The secretary sounded like a demure bouncer.

Matt thought about the red-headed male named Jeff as he walked to his car. Inside the Caprice, he turned on the engine and sat. He hadn't intended to get on the subject of Sylvia Strange; his own outburst had taken him by surprise.

After only a few minutes, Jeff left the Schumacher Building. He got into a hot-red 1995 Mustang and drove away.

The Mustang had a New Mexico plate, and Matt caught it in his rearview mirror as the Mustang disappeared down the street: HOT-SHOT.

He smiled, pulled the Caprice out into traffic, and managed a U-turn. While he drove down Guadalupe Street, he kept a leisurely distance between Caprice and Mustang. He called in the plate number and looked longingly at Bert's Burger Bowl as he drove past the tiny stand with its outdoor umbrellas.

He kept thinking about a green chile burger with all the works while the dispatcher ran the MVD check: the hotshot was one Jeffrey Hookman Anderson, D.O.B. 6–21–66. No outstanding moving violations, two outstanding parking tickets.

Jeff Anderson. Now he had the name; the face jogged into place. Anderson was employed as a correctional officer at the penitentiary. *Nice wheels for a guy who earns $17,000 a year.* He would talk to Rosie. Then it would be interesting to keep an eye on hotshot for a few days.

—

A FAMILY OF fat, black ravens squawked from the trees as Sylvia and Jaspar crossed the Santa Fe Plaza late that afternoon. Even though the temperature had dropped to twenty-eight degrees during the past thirty minutes, a guitarist still strummed folk songs with stiff fingers, and plenty of tourists and locals strolled the streets or huddled on public benches. Three large buses sent toxic fumes into the air as they unloaded exhausted-looking skiers.

"Banana or chocolate?" Jaspar asked. He had Rocko on the end of a leash and he was being pulled toward the Plaza Bakery.

"Chocolate," Sylvia said. They had come from another dog obedience class, and the stop for frozen yogurt was a spur-of-the-moment treat. "But don't tell on me."

The shop was filled with teenagers, tourists, and several families with small children. At the table, Jaspar sucked his vanilla malted through a long straw. He'd finished half before he sat back and rubbed his tummy. "I was hungry. Don't you want yours?"

Sylvia realized that Jaspar was staring at her. "Sure." She spooned a bite of her yogurt and smiled.

"My dad liked you," Jaspar said suddenly.

"I liked your dad, too. And I miss him a lot."

"Me too," Jaspar said.

Sylvia touched Jaspar's hand with her finger. "Your father told me how much he loved to spend time with you. He told me you guys did lots of special things together."

Jaspar twisted his straw around one finger until the thin plastic cracked. His round eyes latched on to a tiny child who crawled across the floor. "We made things," he said finally. "Trains, and an airplane, and stuff like that."

"I'd like to see those trains sometime. Will you show me?"

Jaspar nodded, his head tilted forward so Sylvia couldn't read his expression. The last of the malted gurgled up through the straw. Sylvia waited for the inevitable and sure enough, Jaspar reversed the flow of the liquid to blow bubbles in the bottom of his cup.

She said, "My father went away when I was quite a few years older than you, and I still miss him."

Jaspar stopped his blowing. "Did he die?"

I don't know, Sylvia thought. After all these years, I still don't know what happened, why he walked out and left us. She reached for words of safety. "He got very sick," she said.

"Cancer," Jaspar said.

Sylvia nodded. "A kind of cancer."

Jaspar stared at her and his eyes seemed to pierce her skin. "Did you say good-bye?"

I never forgave my mother. Sylvia said, "It took me a long time to realize it wasn't my fault. I thought maybe I had caused him to go away. But I didn't." She reached across the table and took Jaspar's hand. "Jaspar, did you ever wish your daddy was gone? Like sometimes when you got mad at him for some reason?"

Tears welled up in the child's eyes.

"Because that's a normal thing to wish. But it didn't make him sick. It did not make him sick."

That sentence kept running through Sylvia's mind while she dropped Jaspar with his mother and drove to her own house.

In her kitchen, she unpacked the groceries as a few feathery snowflakes began to fall against the window. She stared out at the river and the dark shape of the Calidros' house in the distance. Her neighbors were gone until after New Year's, visiting family in Colorado.

From the kitchen door, she called Rocko, who materialized immediately at her feet. When she reached down to pet him, he slipped under her hand. "Hey, big guy, what's up? Long day?" He ignored her and trotted right on by. When she straightened and looked back at the window, she noticed that the mobile Jaspar had made her for Christmas was gone.

Puzzled and uneasy, she followed the terrier down the hall toward the bedroom. Rocko stopped abruptly and sniffed along the edge of the carpet. A deep growl rumbled up from his chest.

The paper mobile—crushed and torn—was a tiny pile on the floor.

Suddenly, the dense, suffocating smell hit her in the face.

Sylvia stared at the open bedroom door. Blood was spattered on the wall, on the bed, the floor, even on the door itself. Rocko was inside the room whining and turning circles. Sylvia didn't make a conscious decision to continue down the hall, but she found herself by the edge of the bed. The world seemed to slide into half-time as she stared down at the crumpled, bloody duvet.

A pair of black brocade heels were blood-stained as if someone had taken a brush dipped in scarlet ink, and whisked it violently.

They were positioned next to her bed, just like the shoes that Lucas Watson had left in her room so many weeks before.

This time it wasn't Lucas. It must have been Billy living out his brother's nightmare. Then another name registered in Sylvia's mind: Duke.

TWENTY-ONE

IN THE GLARE of the Volvo's headlamps, fresh snowflakes spiraled in a wild vortex. Sylvia drove too fast, and Rocko was tossed side to side by the car's motion.

Traffic was light on Agua Fria Street—the reds and greens of the traffic signals put on their show for almost empty roads—and the trip from her house to Osage Drive lasted less than twelve minutes. At Osage and Hopi, she hesitated. From here it was six blocks to the Sanchezes' home or a half block to Matt England.

The grounds of Salazar Elementary School were dark and deserted. It took a moment to spot the trailer. It was set back from the asphalt play area, forty feet west of the main school building.

The double chain-link gates were open and Sylvia guided the Volvo onto the school grounds. She pulled up next to Matt England's Caprice and a pickup truck. Before she was out of her car, the door to the trailer opened and light spilled out.

England jumped off the porch, and approached the Volvo. "Sylvia?"

Rocko growled and pressed his nose against the passenger door window.

"My house—" Sylvia took a breath to steady herself and closed the car door to keep Rocko from escaping. He began to bark hysterically.

"Someone got in again. There was blood all over my bed, on the walls—"

"Did you see who it was?"

She shook her head. "I know who it was."

"Come on. Bring the mutt."

Inside the trailer, Rocko backed his tail into a corner in the small living room, and his constant growl was punctuated by single explosive barks. Fueled by excess adrenaline, Sylvia paced in front of the couch and described the scene in her bedroom. She said, "It has to be Billy."

"What about Duke? He could've hired somebody—"

"It's possible as part of some psychotic family pattern. Believe me, I've seen sicker things."

Several different scenarios were running through her mind while Matt spoke with the state police dispatcher. "—get an officer over to the dead end, state route 32, a one-story adobe. That's right, the same one." He answered a series of questions with yes or no, then said, "And tell Hansi to bring a mop, there's lots of blood." He hung up.

Sylvia contracted her muscles to control the tremor that had begun twenty minutes ago in her bedroom. She dropped onto the couch.

Matt said, "We've got about four minutes before we need to go back to your house." He set two mugs of water into a microwave, closed the door, and set the timer for two minutes. "If it was Billy, how did he know about the shoes?"

"It has to be something he and Lucas talked about; it's part of a ritual. A ceremony centered around their mother's death. I think it was a *folie à deux*—" She stopped, shook her head in apology, and started again. "The two brothers shared their psychosis, and Billy has taken over where Lucas left off."

The intensity of Rocko's growl increased when the microwave bleeped. Matt busied himself with a jar of instant coffee. He carried both mugs from the kitchenette and handed one to Sylvia. He glanced at his watch as his long legs straddled the end of the couch.

Matt said, "I talked to Hansi Gausser at the crime lab. He just matched the shell casings—same Army-issue .45 A.C.P.s—at two very different Santa Fe homicide scenes."

"A.C.P.s?"

"Automatic Colt pistol. During World War Two, special ball ammo was manufactured for the army. Each casing had a headstamp that equaled the factory. For instance, Frankfurt Arsenal. Very distinctive."

Sylvia set her coffee on the floor and scratched Rocko's back to quiet the animal. "And ammunition from the 1940s still fires?"

"This stuff sure did. Hansi's expert says that as long as it's been stored at moderate temperatures, no great fluctuations in humidity, it's fine." Matt stood up again. He was wearing faded Levi's and an old sweater. He was barefoot.

"So . . ." Sylvia tipped her head and closed one eye.

Matt kept moving, a shift of feet, a few steps back and forth just to keep the blood flowing to his brain. "The first homicide was a tattoo artist, Tony Regis, who got whacked two days ago—aka Gideon."

"Gideon? That's who did the Virgin on Lucas's chest. He's dead?"

"Shot in the head, one through the back of the neck, one through the mouth."

Sylvia burned her lips when she sipped the scalding coffee.

"Then a retired couple, a dentist and his wife, were shot in their home last week. Guess who used Dr. Ortiz as the family dentist?"

"The Watsons." Sylvia felt jittery and the coffee didn't help. She set the cup down and wrapped her arms around her shoulders. As Matt talked, he took a small crocheted blanket from a shelf and draped it over her shoulders. She murmured her thanks.

He said, "The point is, Duke Watson and the dentist Henry Ortiz were business partners. They owned a parcel of land they tried to turn into Blue Mountain Business Park. The development hasn't really caught on yet, but Mr. Ortiz had his home on the land and that's where the murders occurred." He checked his watch again. "You're the expert on weirdos. Why would Duke or Billy want to whack a dentist and a tattoo artist?"

"I don't know." Sylvia sank deeper into the soft couch. She felt much younger than her thirty-four years. She was at a loss. It was as if all her years of study and training had let her down, left her flat. And hyperactive. And exhausted. She had to force herself to think.

She said, "You kill because someone has some power over you. At least, that's your perception. Even the sociopath is dealing with power issues." Her eyes glazed over and she disappeared inside herself for a moment. "All the usual motives . . . blackmail, love, revenge, or the need to eliminate a witness . . . those are the externals, but the internal issues have to do with rage, self-esteem, power." She brushed a strand of hair from one eye. "And control."

Matt had been watching her closely and he realized she made him uneasy. There was something that happened to her face, her energy when she got caught up in her mind. The only way he could describe it was a sort of manic gleam.

He said, "Let's go. I'll get some shoes on." He finished his coffee in one swallow and stood, and Rocko let loose a series of yips. "Dogs usually like me."

"It's your testosterone," Sylvia said flatly.

—

WHEN SYLVIA WOKE it took her a few moments to orient herself. Pale green and yellow wallpaper, blue net curtains capturing direct sunlight, a turquoise bedspread, and a framed Helen Hardin print on the wall. The Inn at Loretto. Room 213.

Something wet kissed her cheek: Rocko. She hugged the terrier to her breasts, then she pushed him away. Last night, in her bedroom, he'd had his nose in blood.

She pictured the gory scene and felt the pressure of sudden anxiety in her chest; depression would follow if she didn't do something to interrupt her emotional spiral. If she had been dealing with one of her clients, she would suggest simple steps, positive action: a hot shower, a nutritious breakfast, take the dog for a walk, talk to a friend.

She pictured Matt England: Levi's, sweater, barefoot, looking rumpled like he'd be good . . . After the trip to her house, he had offered to let her stay the night.

You can have the bed or the couch. Alone—I mean, I'll—

She had declined. But the offer was nice. And off-limits. The last thing she needed to do was get involved with a cop. The last thing she needed was to get involved with any man so soon after Malcolm's death.

Still, she was looking forward to their date; six o'clock at the Coyote Café.

After she was dressed, lipstick and sunscreen applied, she used her remote code to check her answering machine. Duke Watson had left a message.

"Dr. Strange? I'm having a social gathering at my home this afternoon for a few dozen friends and supporters . . . to celebrate the new year . . . I'd be flattered if you'd accept this invitation to join us."

There was a pause, a long hesitation as if he didn't like to commit himself to tape. He finally continued, "I'm thinking very seriously about dropping the complaint against you. All I ask is a few moments of your time."

She was astounded by his call. She was also suspicious, skeptical, a little frightened, and sorely tempted to accept the invitation. She'd give a lot to have the complaint, and the lingering threat of a lawsuit, erased from her life.

She called Juanita Martinez at the firm; her lawyer was in her office, working. Juanita listened patiently to Sylvia's report, then she said, "Are you fucking insane? You want to go to Duke Watson's house?" She didn't wait for a response. "I had a chat with his new lawyer yesterday. Maybe that's why . . ."

"It's a party, Juanita. He can't do anything to me." As Sylvia spoke calmly to her lawyer, a voice in her head screamed, *What the hell are you doing? What's happened to your judgment?*

"That's what you think. Come to think of it, I got an invitation a few weeks ago. It's a gala with a chamber quartet or quintet or whatever the fuck they're called. Lots of strings."

"So, I'll be safe."

"Never." Juanita tapped the phone with something hard. "Want me to come along?"

"You don't think he might get defensive if I come armed with my lawyer? Especially *you*."

"My best advice is, do not go." Juanita sighed. "Since I've worked with you before, and I know you somewhat, my second-best advice is, keep your mouth shut! Listen to any offer, but don't say a word, and get everything in writing whatever the fuckety-fuck you do!"

—

ON THE INTERSTATE, a single seam had been cut by an early snowplow. La Bajada was slick where snow had melted from the touch of hot rubber and then refrozen. Sylvia kept herself focused on the strip of asphalt that stretched down into the snowy valley. She passed the turnoff for Santo Domingo Pueblo. Twelve miles later, the sign for San Felipe Pueblo was only a white blur. She could barely make out the orange stucco community center to the west. At the off-ramp to Bernalillo, she slowed to twenty miles per hour and steered toward the descending parade of mesas. The trees lining the course of the Rio Grande stood like distant, snowy hoodoo formations.

She followed the river road until she passed the graveyard, the site of Lucas Watson's funeral. Every mile or so she saw a car with headlamps glaring, but not many people were braving the blustery weather this afternoon. She had to rely on a state map to find the county road where the Watsons lived.

The large house was set off a lane about a mile and a half from the main road. It was a rambling ranch-style structure painted a glossy white. The roof was covered with red-stucco tiles. Carefully trimmed and tended Navajo willows lined the gravel drive and the front door faced a wide turnaround where fifteen or twenty cars were parked.

Sylvia slowed the Volvo and let the engine idle. A teenage boy stepped up to the driver's door. He wore clean blue jeans, a cowboy shirt and boots, and a tuxedo jacket that was three sizes too large.

"Valet parking?" Sylvia asked in surprise.

He nodded sheepishly.

She surrendered her car, walked gingerly over freshly scraped snow to the front door of the house, and entered.

A huge fir tree dominated the foyer. It was covered with antique ornaments and twinkling white lights. The branches were so symmetrical, the tree looked artificial, but the delicious scent of fresh pine was unmistakable.

One wall of the foyer was lined with mirrored tiles. Sylvia caught her own reflection severed and graphed into gilded rectangles. Her hair was in disarray, and she fluffed it quickly with her fingers. She couldn't do anything about the dark shadows under her eyes. A waiter appeared at her side and offered her a sparkling beverage. She accepted, glad to have something in her hands. It tasted like quality champagne.

She followed the waiter away from the Christmas tree toward the sound of voices and music. Juanita had been right about the string quartet.

In the living room, the musicians were arranged in front of a very large and perfectly square fireplace. An audience of forty, perhaps fifty coiffed and manicured guests seemed to be enjoying the chamber music. The spacious room made it difficult to gauge the size of the crowd. People stood in small groups or sat on settees, love seats, and delicate chairs. Sylvia recognized the governor and his wife seated near a violinist. The governor smoked his trademark cigar. The governor's wife smiled at Sylvia.

"Thank you for coming, Dr. Strange." Duke Watson had a soft voice with a Good Old Boy twang. When Sylvia turned, he took her hand graciously. She wondered how he'd recognized her, then she remembered the photographs.

Duke Watson's face was smooth, clean-shaven, and set off nicely by neatly layered graying hair. His expensive tweed suit fit him impeccably and gave him a look that was conservative but not priggish.

He said, "I'd like to introduce you to some of my friends, but perhaps we should talk privately first?"

She followed him from the room, back across the foyer, and down a dimly lit hall. He stopped and was about to enter a room when a young woman hurriedly approached from the other end of the house.

"Senator? Can I whisk you away from your guest for sixty seconds?" She waved a typewritten page. "Your speech—"

Duke Watson turned to Sylvia. "I'm very sorry. Will you excuse me for just a few minutes?"

Sylvia nodded. "I'll wait in here." Before Watson could steer her elsewhere, she stepped around him and entered what appeared to be a library. She closed the door, pleased to have a few minutes to explore.

It was a medium-size room, and the long view revealed bookcases filled with dark leather volumes, a crackling fire burning in the ornate fireplace, and three glass guncases each displaying firearms of varying shapes and sizes.

Sylvia walked quickly to the fireplace mantle to examine the array of photographs. She scanned the faces and figures and recognized the stocky shape of Duke Watson shaking hands with governors and senators. Other pictures showed him playing golf, mounted on a blue-ribbon quarterhorse, and ascending in a hot air balloon. There were several shots of a young and rather shy Billy. And one of his smiling sister Queeny in what looked like a prom dress.

At one end of the mantle, almost hidden behind other frames, was the portrait of a lovely woman. Even in its worn condition, the photograph revealed striking features: thick, dark curls framed high cheekbones, the chin reached a soft point, the lips were full, the eyes deeply lidded and gently almond-shaped. It had to be Lily Watson. Both boys had inherited her perfect bone structure.

Beside the portrait, another photograph drew and held her eye. This time she was looking at Duke Watson, Lucas, and Billy. Sylvia guessed the shot was more than ten years old. The man and both boys wore orange hunter's caps, wool jackets, and high leather boots. Each of them cradled a rifle in his arms. A freshly killed buck lay prone in the foreground. Behind the animal—standing over its rack—Duke presented himself to the camera as a virile, arrogant Hemingway type. Next to him, Lucas had the haunted look of a boy in his first week of boot camp. Around the edge of his cap, his hair was shaved military-style and the cut made his ears look unnaturally large. His eyes gleamed with characteristic cloudiness, but a trick of the camera made him sightless. His shoulders were narrow and he was too thin for his height. What struck Sylvia most was the way he shrank under the weight of his father's arm; he was both an extension and a shadow of Duke. He was the anointed fuck-up. Finally, Sylvia's gaze moved to Billy. He must have been nine or ten. He stood slightly apart from the others and his face disappeared behind a huge grin.

"You don't grow up in this house without carrying on the fine family tradition of the second amendment."

Sylvia started.

A bleached blonde gazed up at her from the lap of a brocade armchair. She appeared to be in her mid-forties. The first four buttons of her silk chambray blouse were undone, and Sylvia glimpsed the cleavage of large breasts hanging loose. Making no effort to cover herself, the woman pulled on a long cigarette. She examined Sylvia carefully, her eyes tiny slits between the shutters of her lids.

Sylvia extended her hand and introduced herself.

"Everyone calls me Bea." The woman offered a Mona Lisa smile. "Are you tired of the festivities so soon? The party's just started." She blew a veil of smoke toward Sylvia. "I think family pictures are so revealing, don't you? They give the whole show away if you know how to look at them."

Sylvia sized her up. When she stepped closer to Bea's chair, she smelled musk, alcohol, and perhaps, the scent of sex. Duke's lover? Not his wife; the senator had never remarried after Lily's death. Sylvia's curiosity was cut short when the door to the library opened and Duke entered.

He took in the tableau of the two women and kept his hand on the open door. "Bea? This is a business meeting."

"It's been a pleasure, I'm sure." The woman rose languidly from her chair, shot Sylvia an enigmatic look, and ignored Duke Watson completely. When she walked into the hall, the senator closed the door firmly.

He rubbed his hands together in a hearty, *Let's get down to business* gesture. His eyes brushed over her. He began with a question. "Were you surprised when I called?"

Sylvia spoke quietly, in part to hide her nervousness, but also because the room seemed to sap her energy. "My lawyer advised me not to come today."

"Of course. Please, won't you sit down?"

"I'm fine."

Duke nodded and casually eased himself into a leather armchair and crossed his legs. It was thirty seconds before he spoke, but Sylvia followed at least part of her lawyer's advice and kept her mouth shut. She'd had endless practice with therapeutic silence.

Duke studied the floor beyond the tooled needle-nose of his cowboy boots, and his voice was muted. "It occurred to me, if you and I had worked together, Luke would still be alive. If I had followed up on your recommendation for a transfer . . . if I had pushed my weight around a bit . . ." He sighed.

His next words threw Sylvia off completely.

He spoke softly, but with a matter-of-factness. "They had to piece together parts of my son before they could put him in the coffin." The tenor of his voice became more unsteady. "They say that for parents, outliving your child is the worst thing that can happen. I think I agree. But I can't begin to describe what it's like to know your son suffered degradation before he found peace in death."

He closed his eyes, touched his chin with his thumb, shook his head. "How can I explain this? Luke had terrible guilt. It began when he was sentenced to prison. He thought he had harmed my political career. He became obsessed with the notion that I would never be able to forgive him."

"Was he right?"

Again, the senator sighed. He raised a finger to his temple in a gesture of contemplation. "No. Of course I forgave him. But I never denied that he was a disappointment; he fell so brutally short of his potential. He wore the mantle of his mother's problems." Duke's fingers massaged the arms of his chair as he spoke. "It's hard to have a mother who kills herself."

"That can devastate a child," Sylvia said.

Duke Watson spoke slowly in a faraway voice. "Yes. That's

something I'll have to learn to live with." He walked to a small old-fashioned rolltop desk that stood alone in a corner of the library. The rolling mechanism made a comfortably aged sound when the top was raised. Duke Watson lifted several brown manila envelopes and scanned their labels. He selected one and walked to Sylvia.

He clasped his hands—and the envelope—behind his back and gave her a sharp look. "I'm not the only one who is carrying around guilt. I believe you attended my son's funeral? And perhaps you made some statements in the heat of the moment to Herb Burnett?"

His hands came into view and he waved a finger at Sylvia. "I'll drop the complaint on one condition."

She waited without taking her eyes off the senator from Bernalillo and Sandoval counties.

"You leave my family's business alone. Respect our privacy." He gave her a sad smile. "And no more funerals."

He opened a plain brown envelope, pulled out an eight-by-ten photograph and studied it; his mouth curved up derisively.

Duke Watson's voice was louder and more confident now. He said, "Let's you and I forget that part of our lives. The past three months never existed." He offered her the photograph.

It was the same picture she'd seen in Herb's office. She looked down at herself, at her pouting mouth and her exposed breasts. Then she raised her head and stared at Duke Watson.

He said, "I'm sure you'd like to forget this. Take it with you. Get your life back on track."

Sylvia felt enraged; Duke Watson had made her feel cheap and small—and he took pleasure in the humiliation. She crushed the photograph in one hand and said, "You and your family have made my life hell."

More words came out of her mouth before she could stop them. "If any one of you comes near me, I'll slap a lawsuit on you so fast, you won't know what hit you." She turned, left the room, and left the house.

Outside in the cold, she signaled the valet for her car. While he anxiously searched up and down the small rows, she steadied herself.

She found a cigarette in her purse and lit it with trembling hands. After three hits, the nicotine began to sooth her nerves.

The valet drove up in her Volvo, and accepted two bills with a big smile. Sylvia climbed behind the wheel. She almost choked on her cigarette when her passenger said, "Do you have another smoke?"

"Get out." Sylvia instantly recognized Duke Watson's daughter. Queeny was lash thin with skin the color of paste. Every possible part of her face had been pierced. Silver rings speared both nostrils, her upper lip, her chin, and, of course, each ear had multiple holes adorned with a variety of bangles, feathers, and beads.

"No." Queeny's hands traveled from limp hair to settle against tight jeans. She was barely recognizable as the face in the prom portrait.

"I said get out. Now."

The girl looked disappointed. "Don't have a shit fit. I only want a ride to the road."

Sylvia realized her fingers were clamped around the steering wheel and she was gritting her teeth. She took a quick breath, released her muscles, and nodded. "Fine." She gave Queeny what was left of the burning cigarette, and the girl smiled gratefully. Her face looked almost pretty when she was genuinely pleased.

As they drove off the property toward the main road, Queeny examined Sylvia through a curtain of smoke. "Are you here about Billy? He doesn't live here." Queeny's fingers slid over the radio dial. "You don't have a CD player?" She shook her head as if the concept of a car radio was amazing. "You could be here about the riot. My other brother died in that. His balls were cut off. They had to search for all his parts to put him in the coffin." She gnawed ferociously on her thumb, almost as if she was sucking. She cocked her head curiously and raised an eyebrow. "I bet that's why you're here."

They were approaching the main road and Sylvia slowed the Volvo. She glanced at Queeny and said, "I bet your nipples are pierced."

"No shit." Queeny grinned. "And so is my you-know-what."

"Your father hates it," Sylvia said. She smiled at the girl.

"Yep." Queeny's grin widened. As the Volvo pulled to a stop at the intersection, she opened the door and balanced one leg outside the car. "You know, he's a bastard. You shouldn't have wasted your time."

Sylvia nodded and pulled the new pack of cigarettes out of her purse. She tossed them to Queeny. "Do you have enough money?"

Queeny's eyes shone. "Oh, money isn't the problem in my family. See you." She slammed the door and began to walk up the road and around the corner.

Sylvia accelerated. Queeny smiled at her, raised her right hand, and separated her third and fourth fingers in a Trekkie salute.

—

THE COYOTE CAFÉ was a creamy blend of poured concrete, cut crystal, and wide open space. It was also an acoustical nightmare; the noise level became frantic as Sylvia climbed the curving stairway to the dining area. A woman and two men, all wearing pale linen suits and ponytails, turned to watch as Sylvia passed by. She felt self-conscious in her contour-hugging dress and high heels. She stopped next to a man she assumed was the maître d' and surveyed the room. Matt England wasn't visible at the small bar. Sylvia questioned the host, and he led her to a table hidden by a low wall. Matt England looked up blankly and then recognition flashed across his face. "Do you know how many quarts of blood one chicken holds?"

Sylvia caught the glances of the couple sitting at the next table. She said, "I take it the blood wasn't human?" The maître d' excused himself abruptly.

He grinned. "Right. You look fantastic, by the way."

She smiled and said, "Thanks. So do you."

Matt spread both hands on the breast of his leather jacket. "I don't know why the hell I picked this place."

Sylvia studied his face, caught the slightest gleam in his eyes, and said, "Maybe you wanted to impress me."

"Maybe."

A very thin, very white waiter appeared suddenly and took drink orders. Matt was already nursing a beer. Sylvia asked for a vodka martini with olives.

"Duke Watson invited me to his house today."

The restaurant was full, and Sylvia could hear snatches of conversation from nearby tables, but she hardly heard England above the din. "You didn't go?"

"My lawyer's going to kill me." Sylvia made a face and kept silent while a waiter delivered her martini.

When the waiter was gone, Matt eyed Sylvia sharply. "Tell me about it."

Briefly, she relayed the details of her visit to Bernalillo. She said, "I'd call it a heavy mood swing from destroy the bitch, to let's kiss and make up, and then back to wreck her career. Basically, he'll drop the complaint if I forget he and his sons ever existed."

"You can't. Not until Billy Watson's in custody."

Sylvia snorted. "Yeah, well, the whole deal was off after he brought out one of the photographs Billy took. I truly wanted to kick him in the balls and watch him suffer."

Matt thought about his own visit to Watson's office and his conversation with Rosie yesterday afternoon. He considered Sylvia, watched her expression, and kept his voice low, "Duke has some business with a C.O. Jeff Anderson. Remember him?"

"*Jeff Anderson?* That's who Herb meant? What kind of business?"

Matt said, "What we have is a C.O. driving a thirty-thousand-dollar car on an eight-dollars-an-hour salary. I think he's doing some extracurricular activities for the senator."

"What's your theory?"

"It's all speculation. But this is interesting. Jeff's father was Duke Watson's caretaker; he's the one who found Lily's body."

Sylvia stared at him. "I'd like to be there when you talk to Anderson."

"Not a prayer." His expression clearly read *end of subject,* and he opened the menu. Crab enchiladas with mango salsa, and duckling egg roll resting in a bed of broiled endive were advertised as the evening's specials.

Sylvia felt her stomach turn uneasily, and she gulped at her drink. When she looked up, she realized England had been gazing at her and not at the menu.

He finished his beer and raised an eyebrow. "What are you hungry for?"

"Actually . . . an enchilada or a burrito, Christmas chile, and a good Mexican beer. What about you?"

He nodded. "Sounds better than peach chutney on organic corned beef." He pulled his wallet from his pocket. "Do you think eight bucks will cover a beer and a martini?"

Sylvia shook her head.

He dropped a ten on the table. "Let's get out of here." He guided her gently into her coat and led the way past the frowning host and down the stairs.

El Chamaco was one of the last downtown holdouts amid the trendy newcomers. It was a tiny restaurant just two blocks east of the Coyote. Inside, there were three customers.

England knew the owners Rita and Al Yaquib, a Lebanese couple newly arrived to Santa Fe via Los Angeles and Albuquerque. They cooked the food and waited table. The evening special was an enchilada and tamale plate. Matt and Sylvia ordered two and fed quarters into the jukebox. Willie Nelson and Waylon Jennings sang while Rita brought a candle to the table in a Pacifico bottle. When a robust Navajo man paid his bill and ushered his two companions from the restaurant, Sylvia and Matt were left alone except for occasional visits by Rita or Al.

"So how long have you lived here?" England asked after a long silence that seemed oddly comfortable.

"I was born here." Sylvia smiled. "In the house I live in now."

"You never traveled around?"

She paused, then said, "After my father left, we moved to California. When I was twenty-seven, I came back to finish up my thesis and found the house for sale."

"What did your father do?"

They were both silent while Rita brought their dinners on steaming plates. The compact, handsome woman fussed around the table briefly and then disappeared. Sylvia played with the enchilada that sizzled in a nest of lettuce, tomatoes, beans, and *posole*. A memory of Malcolm coalesced briefly, dissolved, and was replaced by one of her father.

"He was an electrician. He was also in the Army Reserves, and when everyone started draft-dodging, he enlisted for a tour of Vietnam." She took a small bite of food. England was watching her, his face intent. "After that, he tried to farm."

Matt swallowed a mouthful of tamale and chased it with cold beer. "Was he wounded?"

"Not on the outside. They called it War Neurosis in those days. A label left over from World War Two. Or worse, it was diagnosed as simple schizophrenia or paranoid schizophrenia. They didn't know about post-traumatic stress disorder until mid-Vietnam." Sylvia held up her empty beer bottle and Al smiled from the kitchen alcove. "So what about you? Rosie says you're a good poker player."

The fact that Sylvia had changed the subject without any pretense of conversational tact was not lost on Matt England. He followed her lead, focusing on the most interesting part. "What else did Rosie tell you about me?"

"Just that you're old friends; she thinks you're a good man."

England took another bite of food, but his eyes followed the line of Sylvia's cheek to her neck and breasts. The tightly knit fabric of her dress clung to her body, the rich copper shade set off her skin.

Under his gaze she blushed and took a sip of the beer Al had just set on the table.

England finally spoke. "I came to New Mexico eighteen years ago this May." He leaned back in the chair and ran his hand through unruly hair.

Sylvia knew his wife and son had been killed in a car accident. She debated whether to broach it; if they weren't going to see each other again, it was better to leave the subject alone. She said, "I'm sorry about your family. Rosie told me."

He nodded but kept silent.

The beer had relaxed her movements, and Sylvia stretched out, her legs grazing against something under the table. When Matt England responded with a slight smile, she readjusted herself and said, "You must like it; you've stayed so long."

"I enjoy investigations." He narrowed his eyes and said, "I was in Cruces for a while and then Gallup, but for a state cop, I've been sedentary. Most officers are transferred every couple of years." He paused, eyed her speculatively, then said, "Rosie told me you were married before."

Damn you, Rosita. "Oh, that. I was a kid. Nineteen. I was just coming out of my juvenile delinquent phase, and I needed an escape."

Matt didn't blink. "How long did it last?"

"Being a delinquent? Or the marriage?"

"Both."

"I was an angry adolescent; I spent some time in juvenile detention and psych units." Unconsciously, she rubbed at the thin scar that began at the outside corner of her left eye and ran a lateral inch. It was a reminder of the shadowy days of her adolescence, a souvenir of an early battle with authority. "My husband and I were divorced when I was twenty-one. I dealt with it by going for my doctorate."

They had both finished their meals. Sylvia sifted through a small pile of beans with her knife. She set both elbows on the table and looked Matt England directly in the eye.

He grinned. "Rosie says you know all there is to know about cannibals."

Sylvia laughed.

Matt said, "I like you."

"Well, that's a switch."

"Yeah, I guess it is." He swallowed, and his Adam's apple jumped. His eyes searched hers, then without words, he pulled out his wallet. Sylvia reached for her purse and Matt raised one hand. "You get the next one."

Outside, the air was bitter cold, the sky clear. Sylvia pulled her coat close and began to walk. England kept pace. At the entrance to her hotel, he stopped and faced her. In her heels, her eyes were level with his.

"So?"

"So . . ." Sylvia said. She made a soft sound. The food, the drinks, his company had a tranquilizing effect. The sensation of relaxation after weeks of stress was intensely pleasant. "I think you might be dangerous for me."

He brushed his fingers along her cheek.

She stepped toward him, felt his thigh against her leg. His arm was around her shoulders and his fingers pressed her spine. The level of her desire carried her forward, but panic elbowed its way past her other emotions and sensations. She stepped back just as he pulled her to him. The warmth of their kiss contrasted sharply with the cold air.

His tongue filled her mouth, and she responded with her entire body. Her hips and breasts crushed against him; she opened her mouth to let his tongue probe deeper, then she was forced to break away, to breathe. She bit his lip, pushed him back against the adobe wall.

The hotel's glass doors swung open and hot air splashed against cold. Sylvia pulled away from Matt and brushed her hair from her face. A young couple walked by and the man smiled at the flustered lovers.

"Nice night," the man said.

Sylvia grinned, "I've got to go."

Matt said, "What are you doing tomorrow?"

"Moving out of my house. Temporarily."

"I'll meet you there. What time?"

"Four o'clock."

TWENTY-TWO

THE SCISSORS WERE stiff in Billy's hands, and dark hairs lined the sink and the bathroom floor. He'd cut close to the skull, and he'd punctured himself once. A thin seam of blood had dried from forehead to crown. He set the scissors on the toilet tank and switched on the electric razor. His eyes narrowed in concentration, his tongue caught between teeth like a worm snake. Hairs stung his neck and face. In two weeks, he'd dropped eight pounds. His face was a series of hollows and shadows.

When Billy was finished with the razor, he brushed his scalp with a towel and read the directions on the box. Included in the package were plastic gloves and spoon. When he shook out white powder and mixed it with liquid, chemical fumes scorched his nostrils. The directions said he should do a test patch on his hair. Instead, he slathered white cream over his skull and stared at his face. In a few minutes, he would be blond. He tried a smile in the mirror, and the crown flashed. His gums were red and swollen around the base of the soft metal, but he didn't care. He grunted in satisfaction. The only thing left to change were the eyes—too dark, too big. But maybe that was right after all. He was the bearer of darkness now, and his eyes reflected his soul.

Billy studied the tattoo on his bare chest and ran his fingers over the Madonna's face. She felt rough, still scabbed from the needle, but her expression was angelic. Merciful.

He caught himself and reached out to touch the man in the mirror. That wasn't how Billy would think. No, the thought belonged to Luke.

He pulled back his fist and smashed it into the glass. It shattered into a thousand pieces, and Billy Watson's face was finally, and forever, obliterated.

—

DISINFECTANT, SWEAT, SUGARY urine—the smells in St. Claire's Rest Home assaulted Sylvia's senses. The house had been lovely once, with a glassed-in porch, sunroom, wooden floors, and generous dimensions. Time had worn away the paint, shine, and plain elegance, and replaced those with institutional fervor, religious penance, and the asceticism of old age.

Elderly people filled the living room. They played cards at a folding table, stared like robots at the cartoons on television, or peered vacantly into space. It took Sylvia a moment to pick out the sister bending over a man in a wheelchair. The woman approached with a smile. "I am Sister Genevieve."

Sylvia held out her hand and the other woman took it briefly. "I'm looking for Ramona Herman."

Sister Genevieve nodded and her large green eyes creased into triangles of concern. "Ah, yes. You're not a relative?"

"No. I'm a doctor. My name is Sylvia Strange."

"Ramona has suffered six strokes since she's been with us. She has almost lost her power of speech." The sister hesitated. "It's a painful effort."

"It's extremely important or I wouldn't ask."

After several moments, the sister nodded. "At the end of the ramp you'll find a hall and four rooms. Ramona is in number twelve. Please don't tire her."

The ramp had been built for wheelchairs and walkers. It was scuffed with rubber from tires, cane tips, and therapeutic soles. Sadness seemed to permeate the air of the rest home as thickly as the smell of chemical cleansers. The door to number twelve was shut. She knocked twice and then entered. It was so dim, it took fifteen seconds for her eyes to adjust. An old woman lay on the bed next to the window. A frayed lace curtain covered the glass and a small yard was barely visible behind the house.

"Mrs. Herman?" Sylvia moved slowly to the bedside. There was one straight-backed wooden chair in the room. She carried it to the bed and sat. "My name is Sylvia Strange. Your daughter told me you were here."

Sylvia had found Ramona Herman listed in the Bernalillo phone book. Although the woman had recently moved to St. Claire's, her daughter Lucille hadn't changed the listing in the directory. Lucille seemed pleased that somebody wanted to visit her mother.

Ramona Herman blinked.

Sylvia leaned closer and she could smell the sour odor of the old woman. "I like your room." Beside the bed, Jesus hung from the cross in eternal agony and seemed to be staring out the window. "It's so nice you have a view of the garden."

Sylvia waited for at least a minute. When she had given up hope of response, the old woman turned her head very slowly and moaned. It took another minute for her ancient brown eyes to focus on Sylvia's face. When she did, the eyes were lucid. Her hand lifted a half inch from the sheet and then collapsed.

Ramona Herman moaned again. Her hand fluttered and fell, fluttered and fell.

"Do you need something?" Sylvia stood and adjusted the bed covers gently. As she did so, she saw a child's magic writer. The plastic cover on the gray board was curled at the edges, but the pencil was sharp and attached to the writer by a piece of twine. "Ramona, can you write with this?"

Ramona Herman nodded and the effort twisted her face. Sylvia placed the board in the woman's gnarled fingers.

"I need to ask you about something that happened a long time ago. You knew the Watson family. You worked for them in Bernalillo. You were their housekeeper. Isn't that right?"

Ramona whimpered.

"You knew Duke Watson and his sons and his wife, Lily. You were working for the family the year that Lily killed herself." Sylvia was about to go on when Ramona Herman made a frantic gurgle.

Sylvia waited, then said, "The night of the suicide—why did the boys stay with you?"

The letter *N* followed by an ululation. "Oohhhuuuu."

The woman was in obvious pain but Sylvia had to continue. "The newspaper story said both boys weren't at home that night. They were with you?"

B-I-L.

"Just Billy?"

Ramona Herman hesitated and then etched a small *Y* on the board.

"Where was Lucas? Was he with his father?"

Mrs. Herman etched a tortuous question mark.

"You don't know? Was Duke out of town?"

"Noouuuuu." Mrs. Herman raised her pencil and her hand shook wildly.

Sylvia's pulse had risen, an artery throbbed in her throat. "Is there someone I can talk to? Did you tell anyone else?"

"Noouuuuu."

"Why not, Mrs. Herman?"

"Neevvver assskkked." Mrs. Herman lay still on the bed, her eyes closed. She was breathing rapidly, a shallow inhalation. Sylvia touched her palm to the woman's forehead and held it there; the skin was cool and damp. Ramona stirred and struggled to raise her hand without result.

Sylvia moved away from the bed and paced the tiny room in frustration. There was so much she wanted to ask about Luke's childhood and his family, but there wasn't time. She turned back to Ramona Herman and said, "Did Duke Watson kill his wife?"

Now Ramona Herman's breath came in painful gasps, but she formed a second big question mark on the board.

Sylvia leaned over the bed to touch her cheek to Ramona Herman's withered skin. The old woman's fingers closed around her wrist. Her breath fanned Sylvia's hair. "Earl' morn af—ter Lily dead . . . Duke . . . came . . . my houzzzz."

Mrs. Herman's dark eyes flashed at the memory and then closed. "Brought Lucas . . . wuzzz sick . . . foun' blood on him." A tear rolled over her cheek. It coursed along the side of her nose and settled in the corner of her misshapen mouth. When she took a deep breath her chest rattled. She had gone to sleep, or into some twilight place.

"Thank you," Sylvia whispered. And although the words felt foreign, she added, "God bless you, Ramona."

Sylvia closed the door quietly and left St. Claire's without speaking to anybody. The home was tucked between Lead and Silver avenues on a shaded side street in Albuquerque. The neighborhood had seen better days and was also the location of missions, blood banks, and shabby rental units. The sidewalk was crusted with ice, and Sylvia's breath condensed into clouds. She pulled her coat around her throat.

Three scruffy winos who were huddled in a doorway called out to Sylvia, and she paused to pass the time of day. She left them with a five-dollar bill. Since they had little else, they might as well enjoy the fortified warmth of the bottle.

Sylvia had parked the Volvo around the corner in a lot. Rocko would be waiting patiently to settle in her lap for the drive home. As she walked the last hundred feet to her car, her thoughts latched on to the Turner case in Massachusetts. Twenty years after the fact, when Sue Turner was twenty-five, she claimed to have recovered repressed memories: she remembered witnessing her uncle murder her best friend. He was currently serving a life sentence, and the verdict had been based solely on the evidence of his niece's memories.

Repressed-memory therapy had triggered an intense debate among mental-health practitioners. Accusations of childhood sexual abuse and satanic ritual abuse stemming from "recovered" memories had unleashed counterclaims of false-memory syndrome. The debate had even triggered a change of statute of limitations in many states. Some therapists believed absolutely in Freud's definition of repression. Others believed that certain details of an experience can be lost through amnesia, but that trauma victims usually have trouble *forgetting*.

Sylvia's own experience was that the mysterious twists of memory affected each life in startling, often amazing ways.

It was possible that Lucas had witnessed the murder of his mother, repressed that memory only to begin the process of recovery seventeen years later. But Sylvia believed that it was much more likely that Lucas had not repressed the memory, per se; instead, fragments had been displaced . . . and he had reinvented the memory to suit his needs.

That might explain why, in their first interview, he had asked her about remembering something bad from the past.

If her theory was correct, it gave Duke a motive to silence his son. But it didn't help to explain why he would have killed his wife in the first place.

TWENTY-THREE

THE HOUSE WAS filled with shadows, and the faint smell of blood still lingered in the air. Sylvia locked the dead bolt on the front door and switched on the light. Rocko bounded through the living room, down the hall, back to the kitchen. Her terrier seemed satisfied that they were alone. She felt better, but she walked to the window and checked the road. There was no sign of Matt's Caprice. She noticed the wind had picked up and so had the snowfall.

She checked the back door, the windows. Everything was shut tight. Sleet tapped out a staccato rhythm against the windowpane.

She had to prepare herself before she could face the bedroom.

In an effort to gain entrance, Rocko had left vertical scratches on the closed bedroom door. Perhaps he was attracted by the blood.

She turned the knob and pushed. It looked like it had on Sunday night except the bloody duvet had been stripped off the bed and some of the spatters had been scraped off the wall.

Quickly, she changed into jeans and a T-shirt and began the job of packing. She had two suitcases filled when a low rumble began in Rocko's throat. He cocked one ear toward the living room, then he barked, and skittered down the hall. Matt had arrived.

She lugged her suitcases to the living room where Rocko was woofing excitedly. Through the sliding glass door that opened onto her patio, she saw that the snow had become a whirling mass. At four o'clock, night had already fallen.

"Quiet!" Sylvia snapped.

She took her hand off the cold glass of the door and switched on the outside light. A man was staring in at her.

For one instant, she saw the waxy features, the clouded eyes, the matted hair, and scabbed skin. His face was clearly visible, then just as suddenly it disappeared, completely obliterated by snow.

Rocko began to claw at the glass, and Sylvia ran to the hall closet where she kept a loaded shotgun. She hefted the gun, and snapped off the safety as she darted back into the living room. She pressed the stock against her shoulder and aimed squarely through the glass.

She screamed at her dog, "Rocko, get back!"

She heard a voice calling, "Sylvia!"

Again, the man materialized behind glass.

Rocko's tiny body bounced against the sliding door like a tennis ball, and Sylvia's finger tightened as she lowered the barrels and fired a warning shot. The blast tore a fist-sized hole in the adobe wall next to the door. The explosion made her ears ring.

"Shit! Sylvia, it's Matt!"

She recognized his voice and staggered to the door to release the lock. Sleet pelted her skin when Matt slammed it open. He knocked her backward as he entered the room.

He caught her and she dropped the shotgun. His leather jacket was cold and wet next to her skin, and she trembled violently. He shut the door with one arm and moved her toward the couch.

"It was Lucas." Her teeth chattered and she could hardly speak. She saw the disbelief on Matt's face.

He spoke deliberately as if she were a small child. "Someone was in your house?"

"No, outside. In the snow." She picked up the shotgun.

"Wait here, lock the door. I'm going out to check," Matt commanded. "Where was he?"

"There." Sylvia pointed toward the patio. "Didn't you see him?"

Matt shook his head and eyed her curiously. "That was me. I tried the front door, but you didn't answer."

"No, before. Lucas was there."

Matt slid the door open and stepped out. Rocko darted between his legs. Sylvia locked the door after them. While she anxiously waited for Matt's return, she reloaded the shotgun.

A few minutes later, he was back. When he shook his head droplets of water sprayed off his hair. "Your back gate was open. That's all."

"You didn't see anyone? No footprints?"

"The wind's blowing so hard there's nothing on the ground. It's gathering in drifts." He pulled his coat collar from his neck.

"I'm telling you it was Lucas." Sylvia could see it written all over him, the worry, the embarrassment, the concern for her, and the uncertainty.

"Maybe it was Billy." Matt didn't sound convinced.

"You think I'm over the edge." Sylvia imagined what she looked like—a crazed, overwrought woman. A woman who had lost touch with reality. One of her own clients.

She was suddenly aware of the thin T-shirt she wore over mud-stained jeans. No doubt her face was as pale as paper. She tucked foot behind knee and balanced on her right leg.

England said, "How could it be Lucas?"

"Maybe he didn't die in the riot?"

"Then who did? A body was buried. And how did he escape from the pen? North was crawling with guards, the National Guard, our guys, the press. In spite of that, let's say he managed to get out alive. Where is he now?"

Sylvia bit back the anger and shook her head. "He could be hiding out in the Calidroses' house. They're out of town until New Year's."

"Fine. I'm going to call a unit and have them search the area thoroughly." Matt ran his fingers through his hair. "Are you ready to go?"

Sylvia stared out the sliding glass door.

"Don't open it," Matt said, but she had already unlocked and opened the door. She felt Matt's hand on her arm as Rocko ran inside and shook snow off his wiry fur.

Matt reached over her head and closed the door.

Sylvia dropped her chin to her chest.

Matt sighed. "If it was Lucas . . . if he rose from his grave . . . why would he be doing this?"

"Because he's delusional. He believes I love him." Rocko began to sniff around Matt's legs.

Sylvia snapped, "Rocko, stop!" The terrier sat and fixed her with his black eyes. His head moved with her; she was pacing now and she continued, "Letters, calls, spying, stalking—you're my destiny sort of stuff."

Rocko yawned, thumped his stub-tail against the floor.

"John Hinckley and Jodie Foster. Erotomania. Hinckley worshiped her. He fixated on her to the point he believed they belonged together, they were made for each other. Psychotic transference is a basic element of erotomania." She finally looked directly at Matt. "I think I was supposed to be his savior. I think he witnessed his mother's murder."

Matt frowned and said, "I want to make sure the house is locked up tight."

Sylvia followed him as he checked every window and every door. When they were in the hall and he was satisfied the house was secure, he said, "I can get someone to keep an eye on the property if you don't come back for a while."

Sylvia nodded mutely. She let her weight slump back against the wall, and Matt took her gently by both shoulders.

He whispered, "You're exhausted."

Her face belonged to a stranger. For an instant, he felt he couldn't breath. The intensity of her gaze, the depth of the mahogany pupils seemed to pull him under.

He ran his fingers through her disheveled curls. His gaze dropped to her breasts, her nipples erect against the thin fabric of the silk T-shirt.

Sylvia lifted her mouth to his and tasted coffee. Her arms dropped to her side as if paralyzed by fatigue, fear, grief, and the intensity of her need.

He let his hand follow her arm, tracing the elbow, then down to her wrist. He pressed his palm against her belly, waiting for resistance. When he didn't sense it, he slid his fingers under the T-shirt along her skin until he reached the soft weight of her breasts. His tongue touched hers lightly and then with more insistence.

Sylvia ran her hand up the rough nap of England's jeans until she reached the zipper. Her fingers labored with the metal until he reached down to guide her. She bit his ear with sharp teeth and they both stumbled.

Rocko growled and Sylvia pulled away. "Wait."

Matt's body stiffened.

"Not here." She took a blanket from the linen closet and led Matt to the study. There was a moment when they both stood watching each other in the dim light. Then Sylvia slowly pulled her shirt over her head. She felt the scratch of his whiskers as his mouth brushed her skin. His tongue circled her nipples, then his teeth delicately closed over the erect flesh.

Together, they dropped down onto a slightly threadbare Navajo rug. Light from the doorway cast shadows overhead. Matt pushed Sylvia gently back against a small, embroidered pillow, and he reached for the waistband of her pants. He fumbled for a moment with the snap, and then slid her pants down her legs. The tips of his fingers brushing against the inside of her thighs almost made her skin burn.

She opened her mouth to whisper his name and then caught herself. Malcolm; she had almost called for her old lover. She took a deep breath, but the thought was chased away by the immediate sensation of skin, hair, and heat.

She heard Matt make a sound that was closer to a growl than a moan, and his tongue flicked lightly against her clitoris. Sylvia caught her breath. She could smell the scent of both their bodies as she drifted into the languid inertia of sensuality. Her body met his in a rhythm all its own until she was teetering on the verge of orgasm, suspended by pleasure.

She came with a rush, suddenly under water, every inch of her body sensitized to the point of pain. While her muscles were still caught in the contractions of orgasm, Matt plunged deeply into her, his breath escaping in short gasps, his face slack with abandon. When he reached climax, his teeth chattered, he arched his body, until finally all tension left his muscles.

They lay with limbs intertwined like roots growing into each other. Minutes later, when Sylvia stirred, she heard Matt's breath deep and regular, and she saw that they had moved to opposite sides of the rug. She had her mouth over him, kissing, caressing, before he was fully conscious, and he seemed to slide from half-sleep to sex without waking. This time, she climbed on top.

TWENTY-FOUR

He was the watcher—a different person now—hiding behind air so cold, his breath left his mouth in ghostly clouds. He stood at the window, every cell absorbing information, and his muscles twitched methodically in the twenty-degree temperature. He saw them through the slatted blinds.

She rode the cop like a horse, her body twisting and thrusting, her head thrown back, her mouth open wide. Her hair tangled and curled in the wet heat. Beads of sweat glistened on her olive skin. The warmth of both their bodies steamed the windows and he viewed them through a soft mist. But he heard when she cried out.

And the sight of what she did to the cop after that made him sick.

He stumbled away from the window and vomited.

When he looked up again, the house loomed like an obscure monolith behind the shelter of two giant cottonwoods. It had eyes and it seemed to speak to him. It whispered, *Wait. Be patient. You are the watcher.*

His eye was on the front door when it opened. He saw them both. The sound of their voices reached his ears. His hands gripped the club.

She said something and walked back into the house. England carried a suitcase down the porch steps and walked toward the two cars parked in the drive. His Chevy was behind her Volvo.

His own breath came in ragged spurts now. He forced it back down his throat and kept it prisoner in his belly. He crouched low, the club in his hand. The dead lawyer's blood had dried black against wood. He could not see it in the darkness, but he knew the taste. He would do to this man what he had done to the lawyer— teach him to stay away.

He took four steps, raised the weapon, and heaved it downward with all his strength just as England turned instinctively toward his attacker. The club grazed flesh and England stumbled to his knees. Again, he raised the club, but he was thrust off balance by the force of the cop's elbow back-jabbed at his belly. Something small and black hurled itself at his ankle. He let a growl surge up from his gut, tried to shake the thing off: her dog. He could feel its teeth break his skin.

He saw the cop swaying in front of him. He kicked England— sent the dog flying instead—but the cop retaliated with a left elbow to his face. He raised his club for a third time, swung and missed. England faced him now, kicked, and shoe connected with groin. The dog was back, lunging. He felt himself weaken, knew that he had to finish it all with his last blow. He heaved the club upward.

Just as his motion reached its apex, he heard her voice. She was running down the steps with the shotgun in her arms. There was a blast and pellets stung his shoulder. He screamed in pain and smashed his weapon down. He felt the club crush bone, and the cop crumpled to the ground.

He turned, faced her, saw her backlit by the artificial light cascading through the open door.

"Matt!"

He was torn between the desire to finish the job and the need to avoid her eyes. Like a racer thrust forward at the crack of a pistol, he sprinted toward the icy river where he could cut back to the road and safety.

—

Dr. Turner held out a hairy hand. "Mrs. England?" His eyes were bloodshot like the liquid globes of a bassett.

"Sylvia Strange."

"Ah. It's a serious concussion, but his vitals are strong, and I hear he's a fighter." The doctor shrugged and patted his pockets. "He's doing as well as anybody can do after getting bashed. I'm waiting for the neurologist to get here. We'll know more later." They were both silent for a moment until the doctor said, "Look, we can't let you see him, so go on with your day, keep yourself busy." As he turned away, he smiled gently and the skin crinkled around his face. He already had a good start down the hall when he said, "We may have some news in a few hours."

Sylvia nodded to his back.

"Dr. Strange? I'm Agent Osuna."

Sylvia found herself staring blankly into the intelligent eyes of Terry Osuna. "Yes, I remember you. Did you see him?"

"No. They couldn't tell me much. He sustained a heavy blow to the head, but his shoulder took some of the force, thank God."

Osuna's dark brown eyebrows rose. She stared down at the polished toes of her boots and then continued, "Our guys haven't located the weapon at the scene, but the doctors picked some rough wood splinters out of the wound." She lowered her voice. "I'm not forgetting that Herb Burnett was clubbed."

Sylvia swallowed and her mouth was dry. "I saw him."

"Was it a man?"

"Yes."

"Anglo? Hispanic?"

"White."

"Did you see his face?" Agent Osuna kept her eyes on Sylvia. "It was dark. What makes you think the assailant was a white male?"

"I saw his face for an instant, in the light."

"What did you see?"

Sylvia's voice was low. "Lucas Watson."

Osuna gazed unblinking at Sylvia. After a silence, she said, "Lucas Watson's dead, Dr. Strange. We have an A.P.B. out on William Watson."

A woman's voice, paging a party to emergency, interrupted the normal hum of sound. Osuna stretched her neck in a gesture of irritation. "It's not a good idea for you to stay in your house right now. Not for a few days."

Sylvia bit off her next words. "I've already packed. I need to find my dog."

"I'll drive you back," Agent Osuna said on her way out the door. She seemed relieved that Sylvia hadn't pressed the subject of Watson.

Skirting exhaust-stained patches of ice, they crossed the road to the parking lot, and Sylvia saw a familiar figure approaching. Rosie Sanchez was shivering in high-heeled boots, a wool skirt and short jacket, and a scarf. Her normally meticulous makeup was askew. She immediately hugged Sylvia and held her for several seconds. When she stepped back, Rosie's eyes were filled with tears.

"They've called in a specialist," Osuna said.

Rosie spoke quietly. "The man is a lion. He'll pull through."

Agent Osuna kept her head turned away and mumbled, "I just want to nail the sonofabitch who did this." She walked angrily across the lot to her car and Sylvia began to follow.

Rosie reached out and caught Sylvia's sleeve with her fingers. "You'll stay at the house with Ray and me until they catch the guy."

Sylvia nodded. "Was there an escape from North the night of the riot?"

Rosie stared at her.

"It was Lucas Watson." Sylvia turned and walked back toward Agent Osuna's car. As they drove out of the lot, she saw Rosie still standing in the cold, staring open-mouthed.

Sylvia was grateful that Osuna kept the volume on her police radio aggressively loud during the drive to La Cieneguilla. She didn't feel like talking.

At the house, a small fleet of cars was parked on the road near the driveway. Uniformed and plainclothes officials were at work.

Inside, Sylvia sat down to answer Agent Osuna's questions. She told the woman that someone had been outside her house before the attack on Matt. But she didn't mention Lucas Watson's name again.

When Osuna had almost exhausted her questions, a uniformed officer arrived at the door.

"I wrote down the number where I'll be," Sylvia said, handing Osuna a business card. "Rosie Sanchez's."

The officer cleared his throat and said, "We checked the house across the river. There was a broken window with some cardboard taped over the glass, but no sign of occupants."

"That's the Calidroses' house," Sylvia said.

The young officer shuffled his feet and frowned at the interruption. "We did search the outbuildings in a thorough manner."

Agent Osuna nodded. "Anything?"

"No, ma'am."

"What about the windmill?" Sylvia asked.

"Uh." The officer looked uncertainly at Agent Osuna. "We checked that, too."

"And?" Osuna's voice was sharp.

"There's some bottles like Thunderbird and stuff, like winos maybe hang out there."

The officer scraped the heel of his boot against the floor and said, "We did find this by the mailbox." He carefully held out a torn piece of paper.

Osuna used her thumb and middle fingernails to take the page. She scanned it, said, "Jesus," and set it on the table.

Sylvia read the scrawled words.

> *I think about this every waking second.*
> *As if I'm preparing for some turn.*
> *A reunion in the catacombs.*
> *You of all people should know*
> *it will cause you pain to regain yourself.*
> *We should accept pain and surrender.*
> *Do you know what it's like to breathe*
> *here in darkness?*

"You better watch your back until we get this bastard," Osuna said. "Stay close to your friends."

—

"SHIT." DOWNTOWN, AT her office desk, she had to try three times before she punched in Lucille Gutierrez's number correctly. Her movements were jerky, and her heart still pumped too fast. The room had a glare, a painfully bright aura, and she recognized the beginning of a migraine.

Her mind refused to settle and her thoughts tumbled over themselves until she didn't think she was capable of speech. It had almost killed her to leave Matt lying in the snow—blood gushing from his nose, mouth, and scalp—while she called for help. She feared the minute she left, he'd be attacked again. She'd packed snow on his wounds, and cradled him until the ambulance arrived. The wait had been endless.

So many people were dead. And Sylvia was convinced that all the violence around her had its genesis in Lily Watson's death. If she understood more about the woman who had been Lucas Watson's mother, perhaps she could put an end to the nightmare.

She thought of Ramona Herman in her bed at St. Claire's. She wondered if Lucille had inherited her mother's strength of will. After a dozen rings, Sylvia was going to hang up when she heard a child's voice.

"Hi."

"Hello. Is your mom at home?"

"Hi. Hi."

"May I speak to your mother?"

The child's rhythmic breath grazed the receiver for several seconds and then there was a click.

At first, Sylvia thought the child had hung up, then she heard voices in the background. Moments later Lucille Gutierrez reached the phone.

"Yeah?"

"Lucille Gutierrez?"

"Un huh. Who's this?"

"I spoke to you last week. I'm a doctor, and I visited your mother at St. Claire's. She asked me to get in touch with someone for her: Belle Nash? Your mother used to work for her sister many years ago."

After a lengthy silence, Mrs. Gutierrez spoke again, suspicion clouding her tone. "What kind of doctor are you?"

"I'm a psychologist."

"Who hired you? Does this have anything to do with the will?"

Sylvia was about to deny any connection when she changed her mind. "Probably not, but it will make things flow more smoothly if we can reach Ms. Nash." It was possible that Albert Kove and the Board of Psychologist Examiners would have quite a bit to say to her in the future, but she didn't give a damn at the moment.

"Why?"

"You know how complicated legal matters can become, and since Mrs. Herman expressed this desire, it might be in your interest to speed the details along, however routine they may be."

"Yeah, right. So what do you need from me then?"

"I need an address for Ms. Nash."

"Look in the phone book!"

"She's not listed. Is Belle Nash married?"

"No." Lucille Gutierrez screamed at a child named Ruby without removing her mouth from the receiver. "Why should she get married? She seems to be happy with what she's got."

"Excuse me?"

"She's a housekeeper."

Sylvia was puzzled by the information. Somehow domestic helper did not fit her image of Belle Nash. "Do you know where I can reach her?"

"Sure." Lucille Gutierrez spit the words out. "Try Duke Watson. She lives with him."

TWENTY-FIVE

THE WOMAN NAMED Emma clutched her small vinyl handbag to her stomach and stared up at the thick round tower ahead. This was not her first trip to the penitentiary, but it always felt that way. The huge tower was one of the reasons visits were unpleasant. That, and the wire that topped the steel fence like a giant slinky with razor blades. And the guards who sneered as she passed by. And the sight of her brother. Emma couldn't lie to herself. It had become too much after so many years. Reform school had stunted his spirit at sixteen, then the Army, and now prison was draining his soul. Emma's mother had stopped visiting her son after her stroke. Two years later she died, and Emma had come to tell her brother the news. After that, she took her mother's place, but the visits were becoming difficult. Only something very urgent could induce Emma to enter the Penitentiary of New Mexico today.

At the security desk, she explained to the guard; she had not come to visit her brother; she needed to see Ms. Rosie Sanchez.

It took fifteen minutes to track Ms. Sanchez down by phone, and the guard was angry by the time he let Emma pass through the electronic gate and back into daylight. A plump black-and-white cat meowed from behind the parallel fence and Emma murmured hello. Inside Main Facility, the air warmed considerably with each step she took.

Ms. Sanchez was waiting just behind the gate to the right. Although it had been years, Emma recognized the other woman immediately and thought how pretty she was. They shook hands after the gate opened, and Ms. Sanchez touched Emma gently on the shoulder.

"It's very nice to see you again."

"You remember?" Emma was so used to being invisible, she could hardly believe a woman as important as Ms. Sanchez would retain a nobody in her memory.

Rosie Sanchez smiled. "Of course. How are you doing these days?"

"So-so, Ms. Sanchez. That's why I'm here."

"Rosie."

"Rosie." The halls and stairs disappeared in a blur of dull green as Emma allowed herself to follow the efficient click and swish of Rosie Sanchez.

Inside the office, Emma sat low in a big chair while Rosie made tea in the lounge next door. For several minutes, Emma examined the office through the thick lenses of her glasses and clucked appreciatively at two paintings by inmates of statuesque women dressed only in snakes. She found them innovative.

Rosie entered with a mug and a Styrofoam cup and saw Emma almost enveloped within the folds of her heavy woolen coat. Emma smiled timidly as she accepted the tea; her eyes blinked myopically behind glasses. Both women sipped the steaming beverage for several minutes. Emma spent the time allowing herself to relax in Rosie Sanchez's presence now that her mind was made up. Rosie disciplined her curiosity and let the other woman unwind.

"I thought of you because you were so helpful when Mother died," Emma said finally.

"I'm glad you felt free to come," Rosie said. "I'll do anything I can to help you again."

Emma nodded. "Have you seen my brother recently?" Her voice communicated interest and dread simultaneously.

"Actually, I may see him today," Rosie said.

"Ahh." The syllable escaped as a poignant whisper. "About anything in particular?"

Rosie let her index finger trace the rim of her tea mug but kept her eyes on Emma. The woman was becoming increasingly upset although she struggled to maintain a calm exterior. "Why don't you tell me why you came here today?"

Emma took a sip of tea, and her hand shook as she lowered the cup and set it on the desk. She opened the clasp of her purse. Her gray hair obscured her face for several moments while she hunched over her handbag and reached inside. She retrieved what appeared to be a packet of neatly tied envelopes and handed them to Rosie.

"Letters from your brother?" Rosie asked after examining the bundle. Emma nodded, and Rosie took that as a sign to read the first letter, which was neatly written on the penitentiary's inmate stationery.

My dearest Em,

I hope this letter finds you in excellent health. It is always an extreme delight to read the fine literature, such as the magazines, you send me. Sister Em, your thoughts are marked by a worldly outlook, an abundance of faith. I only pray that my science will put the world at your doorstep. One is impressed by the frenzied dance of organisms within their natural environ-

ment. If we increase our knowledge of biology, ecology, and Supreme Responsibility, we will discover the Glory and the Truth and the Perfection of God's Architecture. The Holy Spirit of science is at work, even as you sleep. This is my mission. I need not tell you when this happens. The *New Mexican* will carry the story.
  Your devoted brother

The letter was dated December 20, and it was the most recent. Rosie skimmed through the others. There were nine total dating back through the last year. The message in every one was similar but the heat and passion of delivery intensified like a fever when the letters were arranged chronologically.

Rosie looked at the woman's worried, frowning face and said, "I'm very glad you brought these to my attention. Do you have any idea what his 'mission' might be?"

She shook her head solemnly.

"Can I keep these for now?"

Emma seemed to sink even deeper in the folds of her coat as she nodded. "I know . . ." She hesitated, reached toward the Styrofoam cup with its tepid contents, and then returned her hand to her lap. "My brother is a gentle man, Rosie. He would never do harm to anyone."

Rosie enjoyed the irony of the description. She glanced at the packet of letters, fingered the red twine that bound them, and returned her gaze to Emma.

"Why did you come?" Rosie asked softly.

Emma looked down at her handbag and swallowed as if her throat hurt. She couldn't bring herself to mention the $3,500—folded in brown paper—that had arrived in her mailbox. Her brother had told her it was from a friend, an Army debt finally repaid. Emma didn't believe him, but the money was so helpful. It would allow her to finally make a pilgrimage to India. For almost thirty years, she'd dreamt of visiting the erotic temples of India. She said, "Mildred Spoon always tells me what her son tells her."

Rosie raised her eyebrows searching her memory for clues. She had no idea who Mildred Spoon or her son were.

As if reading her thoughts, Emma added, "Joseph Spoon's mother. Well, they call him 'Greasy' Spoon, he works in the kitchen, I think. Mildred Spoon?"

"Ahhh." Rosie nodded with understanding.

"She's very old, older than me, and I visit her because she has no one else and I'm good with old people."

Comprehension was dawning, but Rosie kept her face neutral. "Yes," she said.

"Mrs. Spoon says that Greasy thinks—" She paused to look left and right as if some eavesdropper previously undetected might be hiding behind file cabinets or paintings. "He thinks my brother is doing some things that aren't healthy, and besides, Greasy says there's no more room." Emma rushed through the last sentence breathlessly.

"Room?"

"That's what she said he said." Emma stood with effort and her small white hand emerged from her coat sleeve to shake Rosie's hand. "I know you'll help him. You're a kind woman." As she left, Emma said, "I know you'll make everything okay."

Alone, Rosie sat back in her chair and touched the tips of her polished nails together. She shook her head; at first glance, Emma's brother made a very unlikely jackal, but his name had been highlighted in the files that Sylvia had given her at the gym. He was a Vietnam vet. He could easily have been a soldier at My Lai, maybe even a medic. He'd gotten a medical discharge for psychiatric reasons. Damn those Army records . . .

Acting on the tip from Bubba as well as advice from Colonel Gonzales, Rosie had placed a phone call to the Department of the Army at the Pentagon. *Sorry, ma'am, but we can't even talk about this unless we have your request in writing.* So Rosie had sent a letter Special Delivery. (Why not just send it by camel?) *Sorry, ma'am, but there is no set roster of Charlie Company because companies aren't stable things—people come and go.* So then, Rosie had talked to a friend who also happened to be a congressman, and he had called the Pentagon to make the request. They said, Fine, but it's going to take a few months.

It was Colonel Gonzales who had saved the day. He'd suggested she call an old buddy of his: the journalist who had written a book on the My Lai incident. The writer had agreed to copy the roster from his files and send it by Federal Express.

Rosie gnawed a fingernail. Even if she got confirmation on her man, she'd need proof. Bobby Jack Hall's missing arm had turned up tucked behind pipes in the wall of the warehouse. The penitentiary investigator was the only person who didn't think gang members had hidden it there.

She had the very queer feeling that the puzzle of the jackal was much more complex than she'd ever imagined. She grunted and tore off a sliver of red polished nail. Bubba had linked Jeff Anderson to the jackal; and now, Matt had seen C.O. Anderson visiting Duke Watson.

She picked up the phone and called the shift commander. He told her that Jeff Anderson was due at work at 3:00 P.M.

Rosie said, "No, don't give him a message. I'll find him myself this afternoon."

There was something else on Rosie's mind: her brief exchange with Sylvia. She knew her friend was under horrible emotional stress; she'd probably been in shock this morning. Rosie blamed herself for not forcing Sylvia to see a doctor immediately. For the last hour, she'd been unable to reach her by phone.

She had other reasons to be worried; nothing relieved the sense that she wasn't getting all the information she needed from Warden Cozy. Doubtless there was some smooth political maneuver going on that had everything to do with suppressed information.

——

MATT EXAMINED THE water-stained pattern on the lime-green hospital walls for the umpteenth time. A jazz quartet had taken a gig in his brain and the drummer was on a roll. At intervals, the pain forced him to shut everything down, hold his breath, and wait until he could exist again. But little by little, the periods without pain were becoming longer.

He tasted blood in his mouth and lifted a tentative hand to his nose. All he could feel was misshapen mush. Numb. Not familiar. He sighed. Broken for the third time.

They'd given him drugs, at first just codeine. The I.V. currently dripped Valium into one vein. Through the haze of chemicals, he should be drifting into never-never land.

But he couldn't relax. Between Coltrane jazz riffs, something tugged his brain for attention. The knowledge that Sylvia was in danger made his skin crawl. He had to do something. He'd asked to see her, but they wouldn't let him have visitors until tomorrow. St. Vincent's was more like a prison than a hospital.

Matt raised his head and took several deep breaths before the knife pains in his neck convinced him to ease himself back on the pillow. But it was a beginning.

He tried again a few minutes later. This time, he made it all the way to his elbows.

—

RAPHAEL'S SILVER CLOUD was deserted except for the bartender and two young women playing a video game. Sylvia was sure they were both too young to be in the bar. She wondered once again why Belle Nash, Lily's sister, had selected this spot for their meeting. Thirty miles south of Santa Fe, the roadside bar was a watering hole for road crews, motorists with car trouble, and thirsty refugees from nearby—and dry—Pueblo land.

Roughly two hours ago, Sylvia had decided she had nothing to lose from a phone call to Belle Nash. Nash had answered after two rings. When Sylvia identified herself and said, "I have some things to ask you about your sister's death," Belle Nash had simply named the place and time for a meeting.

The video game bleeped, and bells and zingers went off while the girls exclaimed loudly. The large round clock showed 2:13 and Sylvia began to think that Belle Nash had never had any intention of meeting her.

The bartender swirled his rag within inches of Sylvia's orange juice. She lifted the glass and he nodded.

"Noisy," he said, raising his eyebrows in the general direction of the girls.

As Sylvia followed his cue, a woman walked through the door. She stopped a moment to adjust her eyes to dim light, and then she walked slowly in Sylvia's direction. It was Belle Nash.

"Didn't recognize me, eh?" Nash slid onto the stool next to Sylvia and snorted. "When you came to see Duke, that wasn't one of my better days."

"What can I get you?" The bartender let his eyes linger on the cleavage visible above Belle's low-cut sweater.

"Double bourbon, neat," Belle Nash said.

"You want another OJ?" the bartender asked Sylvia.

"Fine." Sylvia tried to guess the other woman's age. She must be close to fifty, and she had good genes. Her bones were finely chiseled, and her skin was firm and bronzed.

Belle Nash pulled a long cigarette from her purse, lit it, and inhaled. She screwed up her eyes against the acrid smoke and squinted at Sylvia. "After you came to the house, I got curious about you."

Nash waved her cigarette up and down in the direction of Sylvia's body. "You don't look like any of the shrinks I've seen—the short men in suits. You've got tits."

Belle grabbed the glass of golden brown liquid the bartender had just delivered. The red polish on her fingernails was chipped. After she swallowed half the drink, she shot Sylvia a look and said, "You called me, remember?"

"Yes." Sylvia took a sip of her orange juice and let the silence lengthen. When she looked up, Belle Nash was watching her. Sylvia tried a wry smile and said, "Could I bum a cigarette?"

Belle Nash kept her eyes on Sylvia for another ten seconds and then she nodded. She pulled a Benson & Hedges Gold from her purse and flicked the pack twice. A single cigarette nosed its way out. Sylvia took it and drew in smoke when Belle Nash held up her lighter.

Sylvia's voice was soft and husky from smoke. "What was Lily like? I've tried to imagine her . . ."

Belle's sharp features seemed to darken for an instant but her suspicion was quickly replaced by other, more powerful emotions: sadness, affection, yearning.

"She was very special. When we were young, I always thought she was a princess or some exotic species of flower. It seemed like we weren't related. For my parents, she was their daughter, I was—" Belle shook her head and took a long drag on her cigarette. She looked directly at Sylvia for a moment. "Let's just say I wasn't the perfect daughter and Lily was."

Sylvia tapped her cigarette against the tin ashtray the bartender had set on the bar. She let herself absorb the other woman's words. An image came to her of two young girls playing in a field near an old cottonwood. The younger girl sat on a wooden plank and with her hands she gripped the thick ropes that anchored her to the tree as she flew. She was pale, dark-haired, and delicate. She had a liquid laugh.

The older girl stood behind the swing and pushed her sister higher and higher. She was sturdy with tawny skin and golden hair, and she was firmly rooted on the ground. With each arc of the swing, the younger girl screamed and the sound of her voice was a blend of delicious fear and wild abandon.

Sylvia didn't know where the image had come from, and she let it dissipate. Belle Nash was eyeing her curiously.

"You've seen Lily's picture?" Belle asked.

Sylvia nodded. "On the mantle."

Belle took another breath and inhaled smoke and oxygen. "She was beautiful wasn't she? Why do you want to know about her?"

Sylvia rested her chin on her hand and considered her response. She was treading into a gray area as far as psychologist/client confidentiality issues were concerned; but the truth seemed like her only option. "I evaluated her son."

"Luke is dead."

"I still have questions."

Belle Nash smiled at her cigarette. "You have a way of not telling the truth, Doc." She took another drag on the cigarette and her skin blanched around her lips. "You withhold . . . isn't that what shrinks call it? Withholding?"

Sylvia placed both palms flat on the bar. "Lucas invaded my life . . . from the first moment I met him, he wanted something from me." She looked at Belle. "The day before he died, he asked to see me. We met briefly."

"What did he want?" Belle asked.

Sylvia shrugged. "I think he wanted my help . . . he wanted to solve a puzzle." She set her smoldering cigarette on the edge of the ashtray. "Something about his past. It had to do with his mother's death."

Belle signaled the bartender for another round. Her eyes settled on the myriad signs hung over the bar; nonsense slogans and silly rhymes that made sense when you were drunk. She tapped her finger against the glossy wood of the bar top.

The bartender set a fresh bourbon in front of her. He didn't touch her first drink; there was still a quarter inch of liquid in the bottom.

"It was a happy marriage at first." Belle drank, then continued. "They were in love. Duke gave her security, someone to depend on, he made the decisions for her. Lily gave him social connections. Believe it or not, our family was prominent. We had money in those days."

Sylvia remembered her cigarette burning in the ashtray. It was down to a half inch of tobacco and then filter. She took a tentative drag.

"Later on, the marriage soured; he had some affairs, and she . . ." Belle attempted to smile and failed. Her eyelashes quivered suddenly. She stopped their motion with her fingertips.

"In her own way, Lily loved her husband. But when Luke was born, she worshiped him. Luke was her firstborn, and the moment she laid eyes on him, he owned her soul. So then Duke spent more time with other women, and Lily turned bitter. It got so she was stoned all the time . . . vodka, then Valium, then more vodka . . . more pills. It was bad for Duke's political career and bad for his family. Sometimes Duke took the kids away from the house so they wouldn't see her like that."

"Is that what happened the night of her death?"

Belle frowned. "They were at the housekeeper's."

Not true, Sylvia thought. According to Ramona, only Billy had spent the night. She didn't want to interrupt Belle's narrative. "And Duke?"

"He was in Denver." Belle Nash stayed still as a tree.

The noise level in the bar increased when a group of construction workers entered and found a table close to the door.

Sylvia said, "I know that's not how it was, Belle."

Nash didn't put up a fight. She set her glass down and took a tired breath. "He was in Albuquerque with another woman that night."

"How do you know?"

"Because I'm the other woman." After several moments, Belle continued in a soft voice. "I loved my sister, but I didn't understand her. She let people take her life from her and she wouldn't fight back."

The jukebox blared suddenly and Tammy Wynette sang, "Stand By Your Man." Belle Nash mouthed the words, her face twisted with irony.

Sylvia's eyes burned and she closed them for a moment. She said, "You were always the other woman, weren't you?"

"Yes. I loved him." For an instant, she looked ashamed. "He was such a bastard in so many ways . . . Duke demanded perfection. He was strict with the boys like they were in the Army instead of just kids. And he got meaner because of Luke's fits." Belle sighed. "Luke's temper was awful. He'd scream at Lily—he always took his anger out on her. He turned beet red . . . she used to lock him out of her room."

"How old was he?"

"Four, five, six. It seemed like he had them every few weeks."

"What about Billy? Healthy?"

Belle smiled suddenly. "Billy-bo was always healthy."

Sylvia stared at the melting ice in her glass.

Belle shook a second cigarette from her pack and stabbed it against the bar. On impact, the cigarette collapsed in the middle, tobacco scattering from the paper wound. Nash crumpled the cigarette pack in her fist. "I'm here because of Queeny. She's my daughter."

Sylvia found that she wasn't surprised. Unconsciously, she'd made the connection between mother and daughter.

Belle's hands trembled around the glass. "I've seen them destroyed . . . first Lily, now Luke, and Billy in his own way. The evil must come from Duke . . . where else could it come from?" A dry sob escaped her throat. "I'm afraid for my girl. But I'm not strong enough to stop him."

She looked at Sylvia and her large eyes implored. "You work with darkness, don't you? You work with evil people, so you know. Eventually, they destroy everything they touch."

———

SYLVIA WASN'T READY to face anyone so she drove to her office and parked under a street lamp. She'd called the hospital from a pay phone, but the switchboard cut her off twice. It was 5:30 and the streets were dark. She let the engine idle, warmed her fingers in front of the heater vents, and then locked up the Volvo. Tall cottonwoods ribbed the sky, and the gravel beneath her feet was crusted with ice. The two-story adobe building looked frayed around the edges. Frost gleamed from the wrought-iron gate that opened into the courtyard. Sylvia walked quickly, moving under two antique lanterns and past an old wagon, a relic of the Santa Fe Trail. She climbed the stairs to her office two at a time, and held her coat tight at the throat. The open hallway felt more frigid than the air directly outside. She heard faint laughter from the courtyard below, then nothing.

She was still thinking about the disturbing meeting with Belle Nash.

Sylvia reached her office and slid her key into the lock just as she heard a faint whisper. She turned back to the hall and found herself staring at Lucas Watson.

TWENTY-SIX

SYLVIA TURNED TO run, but he caught her by the arm and forced her backward. She fell and slid along the floor of the hall. Her head struck the porcelain drinking fountain. There was no pain, but she couldn't get her muscles to move, to propel her body out of his range. He stood over her, scowling down through a shadowy haze. She wanted to tell him she'd known all along that he'd come back for her. A rush of nausea sickened her and she choked on vomit. Her muscles jerked into motion, she scooted forward to gain traction so she could stand. She was halfway up when she felt a sharp pain in her thigh. He kicked her again before she twisted and grabbed for his ankle. The impact of her body forced him sideways and he stumbled, cursing.

She protected her head, tightened her abdominal muscles, and anticipated another attack. Nothing happened. She began to inch herself onto her elbows. In response, he moved his body over hers —he was straddling her—and his ragged breathing marked the seconds before he spoke.

"Who am I?" he whispered.

Sylvia peered up at his face, tracing bone structure, coloring, searching for the tooth, the tattoo, road signs along a deserted highway. Then she saw his eyes, and the darkness pulled her in where an icy blue should have been.

"Billy." Her voice was a raspy whisper, but he heard it and jerked her forward by her hair.

"No, bitch!" He slapped her face. "Who am I?" A gun protruded from his fist.

She opened her mouth—to tell him to put the gun down—but nothing came out. Just a shudder, a sigh.

"Who am I?" His fist connected with her abdomen, and she collapsed from the pain.

She waited for the next blow. When it didn't come, she used her hands and the wall for leverage. The adobe felt cold. The shadows in the hall had thickened.

"Billy—"

"Who am I?" The butt of the gun sliced her lip.

"Lucas."

Billy was shivering; he whispered in an effort to control his voice. The words spilled from his lips in an eerie monotone. "I've come back for you."

She put up her hand to block the next blow. She saw a dark shape in the distance. It was night, the dream, her father calling to her from his prison inside the cave.

Billy dragged her back from the dream. He fell on her body, tore at her coat, at her legs. She could smell the sour sickness of his fear. Terror clogged her throat until she thought she was going to pass out.

She thrust her palm into the base of his nose and pushed with all her strength. His teeth sank into her skin. She saw him as Lucas, and her rage gave her new strength. She screamed. She stabbed his eyes with her fingernails, bit his wrist, and pummeled his kidneys with her fists. She thought she might have knocked the gun from his hand.

Mustering all her power, she drove her knee into the hardening flesh of his groin and heaved him sideways. He cried out in pain.

Then someone else filled the hallway, a great ship of a man. Suddenly the weight was lifted from Sylvia, and she could breathe. She saw two faces in half-light for one instant: Billy—transformed into Lucas—and someone else who was familiar. She fought the dizziness that threatened to pull her down.

———

MATT ENGLAND KNEW Sylvia was conscious and breathing. He didn't want to leave her, but Billy was getting away. He wanted to pound the little sonofabitch until his ears bled. As Matt ran toward the stairs, his knee jammed the mud wall and his fingers razed splinters from the level banister. Billy was twelve feet ahead of him speeding down the stairs.

Another thought flashed through Matt's mind—he was forty fucking years old and a fugitive from the hospital—but he wasn't feeling sorry for himself. He whooped as Billy Watson lost his footing and flipped headfirst down the last few stairs.

Matt gained ten feet while Billy scrambled painfully to his feet. When Watson took off again, he was limping. Both men hobbled up Grant Avenue, but Billy stumbled right at Johnson Street. Puddles of light from street lamps illuminated his reckless progress.

Matt's heart felt as though it would pump its way out of his chest. A woman stared with golf-ball eyes as he charged past. He gave a hopeful grunt when he saw Billy slide on ice and go down.

He gained ten yards before Billy clambered to his feet. Matt caught his own ice patch and both legs shot out from under him.

Billy took off again, sprinting across Johnson and slamming through the back entrance to the Eldorado Hotel. A few seconds later, Matt was up, following Billy into the hotel. The sound of Matt's footsteps reverberated off the wide tiled hallway. He saw Billy skidding around the corner in the direction of the Eldorado's main lobby.

Mood music floated out from the lobby bar. As Matt slid on the tile and abruptly hit carpet, he stumbled and knocked over a small Christmas tree. At that instant, he saw Billy crashing past crowded tables. The bar was filled with happy-hour drinkers crooning along to "Feelings."

Matt scrambled to his feet and launched his body forward, but Billy Watson had too much of a lead—he wasn't going to catch him.

A woman yelled as Matt knocked her cocktail out of her hand. He was huffing his way toward the Eldorado's reception area.

When he was almost to the main desk, he saw a security guard. The man was a great hulking Sikh complete with turban and he had Billy Watson in a choke hold.

Matt called out, "Police! He's under arrest!" Then he collapsed.

———

ROSIE DICED A tiny *habanero* chile and sliced cheese for two whole-wheat tortillas. She placed the quesadillas on the rack of the toaster oven, then closed the door, flipped down the switch, and licked her finger. "Watch out for my cooking."

Without asking if Sylvia wanted more, she refilled coffee cups and sat down. She gazed at her friend with concern. Sylvia's face was swollen, her eye purple and red, her mouth raw. She had a cracked rib and a torn shoulder ligament. But she was in good shape compared to Matt England. He was back in the hospital—

this time for at least three days. His fellow investigator, Terry Osuna, threatened to have him arrested if he followed any more hunches.

Rosie said, "I talked to Terry just to make sure all the bases were covered. They're doing a thorough job. Last night, when I saw Billy during the interrogation, I couldn't believe it; he bleached his hair, had his tooth capped, starved himself, and that tattoo—it's all so eerie."

"To take over where his brother left off," Sylvia said quietly. "In Billy's case, I think his transformation into Lucas gave him the psychic energy to *act*."

"He would have murdered you," Rosie whispered. Tears formed at the corners of her eyes, and Sylvia hugged her.

Rosie said, "Thank God Matthew has a hard head." She stepped away from Sylvia and set her hands on her hips as if she packed a pair of six-guns. "Go see him."

The toaster oven gave out a sudden squawk, and Rosie opened the glass door to rescue bubbling quesadillas. "Ouch!" She juggled one tortilla onto a plate and set it down in front of Sylvia on the plastic floral tablecloth. "Eat your food."

Sylvia smacked a fist on the tabletop and coffee sloshed over cup edges. "For two months I've been goddamn harassed, stalked, and brutalized. I've had my integrity attacked, and I've lost the job that I wanted." Her voice had risen an octave and the Sanchez cat jumped off a stool and streaked from the kitchen. Sylvia started after the animal and then turned back abruptly to face Rosie. "I've been to too many funerals, my goddamn dog won't stay home, and I can't stand another hospital. I hate hospitals!" Her eyes shone with tears.

"Oh, look at you! It's about time you lose some of your damn control! You lock your feelings inside of you like somebody's going to steal them." Rosie brushed a wild strand of hair from her face.

The women faced each other nervously. Rosie stood almost two heads shorter than Sylvia. The seven-year age difference between friends felt more like twenty. She paused for a moment, made a face, her expression tentative. "I remember your dad."

"So?"

"Don't go all defensive again. He was a kind man . . . but he had so many problems. And he left a giant hole in your life when he disappeared . . . I don't want to see you spend your life haunted by him. I don't want you to waste good years searching for a ghost in every man you meet." She smiled shyly. "I love you, Ray loves you, Tomás and Jaspar love you . . . You know what the old people say? *El muerto al pozo y el vivo al retozo.* Stick the dead in their hole and let the good times roll! What I mean is . . . Matt isn't your typical cop. Don't pass up a good man."

Sylvia grinned, lowered her chin, nodded. The silence between the two women was not uncomfortable. A beam of sunlight bathed the kitchen in butterscotch warmth. The cat had returned to curl up in her chair.

—

THE HOSPITAL ROOM was dark with just a slash of sunset visible through white blinds. Sylvia entered quietly, afraid she would disturb Matt England's sleep. But he was awake, sitting up in the elevated bed, and he attempted to smile when he saw her.

"Hey," Sylvia said. She kept her voice light, but the sight of his face upset her. His lips were swollen, his eyes were bloodshot, his skin pale and rough with two-day-old stubble. His hair disappeared under a thick bandage.

"Hey." He spoke slowly. "Don't worry, you look worse than me."

"Thanks." She smiled.

"That bad, huh?" Matt patted the edge of the bed. Sylvia sat down and he took her hand. His mouth curved into a smile. "We finally caught the bastard."

She leaned over and kissed him on the cheek; then she moved

her lips to his mouth. After a longer, much more demanding kiss, Sylvia said, "Are you sure you're ready for this?"

"No." He moved his head to kiss her again and then groaned. His hand fell against her breast and she let it stay there, even when he peeked one eye open to see her reaction. He said, "You're not an easy woman to keep up with."

"I'm glad you did." Sylvia reached for the call button just as a nurse arrived. She moved out of the way while the other woman lowered the bed, set a white cup of pills on a tray, and glanced at a chart.

"It's time for me to go," Sylvia whispered to Matt. He took her arm gently.

"We'll take up where we left off later," he said.

She smiled. "Get some rest. I'll come to visit tomorrow."

Matt nodded. "Hey," he said as she reached the door. "I hope this doesn't happen every time we make love."

—

IT WAS TOO early for lunch, but Rosie followed the noisy complaints of her stomach to the cafeteria. In honor of New Year's Eve, the fare included pressed turkey breast, mashed potatoes with gravy, and gelatinous cranberry sauce, an exact clone of the Christmas Day meal except for the absence of sweet potatoes pureed with marshmallows. How fortunate that particular dish had been scratched from the menu. Rosie took it as a positive sign of the new year ahead.

Afterward, she finished reviewing a stack of incident reports, wrote a note to the compliance monitor at the D.O.C., and rewound her tape of yesterday's interview with C.O. Anderson. The tape might as well have been blank. Anderson had led her in circles for an hour. She sat back in the chair, slid her shoes off, and stretched her toes.

Rosie had decided to give herself another hour at the office and then call it a day when the phone rang. She picked it up and snapped, "Sanchez here."

Pat O'Riley, security wizard, laughed just like a leprechaun. "It doesn't sound like you wanna be. You should take a vacation like I just did. Montana was heaven."

"It's even colder up there," Rosie exclaimed.

"You get used to it." Pat O'Riley suddenly sobered. "Listen, I need to know something. You read my report?"

"What report?"

There was a long silence on the line. Rosie could hear a tapping sound that she assumed was the drum of Pat O'Riley's fingernails on something hard.

"What dark and dingy water hole would you care to meet me in?" O'Riley said finally.

—

ALL OF THE bar stools were occupied at Molly's when Rosie walked in at 2:15. The smoke stung her eyes, and she squinted through the gloom in search of a familiar face.

Pat O'Riley was tucked in the corner booth nearest the rest room, nursing a beer. Rosie slid her rear end along the red vinyl bench and faced him across the table.

A waitress appeared.

"Ginger ale," Rosie said.

The waitress had a stride worthy of a trucker.

Pat placed a large white envelope on the table. "Take a look."

Rosie glanced at the bar where everyone's attention was focused on the large television screen suspended from the other end of the room. Oprah Winfrey was interviewing five transvestites.

"I know, you feel like a spy," Pat said. "This is my report, and it went to the warden and his compadres. You were supposed to get a copy."

She peered into the envelope and then let the thickly bound report slip onto the table. The first thing Rosie saw was the large CONFIDENTIAL stamp in red ink at the top of the page, and next, the title.

"I saw this two years ago. It's the vulnerability appraisal."

Pat wiped some beer foam from his mouth and shook his head. "This is my follow-up—as an independent contractor—hence the date."

"Ten days ago."

"Righto."

"I don't understand. Who called you in?"

"Top brass from the governor's office. They wanted to make sure the security systems could be put back into working order without mucho bucks. And they were anticipating the lawsuits that spring up after a riot like pigpen daisies after a summer shower."

Rosie held up her hand and began to skim the pages. Like the original assessment, there was an introduction with a brief history of institutional security systems, a system description, and diagrams. Escape scenarios followed, some of which Rosie recognized from actual attempts by inmates in the past. On the last ten pages, she found the addendum, undoubtedly the portion that had upset the administration so deeply. Rosie felt her upper lip prickle with barely suppressed rage. How dare they withhold this kind of information from her? She bit her lip and continued to read.

> Normally, escapes attempted from prison interiors present potential escapees with more impediments than attempts originating from exterior prison areas such as yards and sally ports. However, the conditions that existed during the riot, and the evidence collected in North Facility following the riot, show that the possibility of a successful escape effort generated from the interior, not viable under normal conditions, must be thoroughly investigated.

Bound in plastic, the report slid easily off the varnished wood surface of the table into Rosie's lap. She stared at Pat O'Riley and her skin lost its color.

"Are you telling me that someone actually got out that night?"

—

THE CHANGING OF the guard was in full swing when Rosie entered the pen for the second time on New Year's Eve. As she passed the waiting area for visitors, she saw an old man sitting alone. Something about his posture—perhaps it was his worried expression— stopped her. She tiptoed to his chair.

"Are you being helped?"

"Necesito encontrar mi hijo."

"¿Quien es? ¿Cómo se llama?"

"Se llama Juan Gabaldon."

John Gabaldon. Rosie didn't remember that particular inmate. Perhaps he was new? She asked the old man, but he insisted that his boy had been incarcerated for nine years. When was the last time he had visited his son? Six months before. The old man explained that he'd been hospitalized for a minor stroke. He'd been in a hospital in Las Cruces when the riot occurred.

"¿Cuantos años tiene?"

"Veinte-ocho."

A twenty-eight-year-old inmate named John Gabaldon was missing. Rosie questioned the man in Spanish for several minutes. She believed him when he said he'd written letters to the governor, the Department of Corrections, the warden. He thought no one had responded because they didn't like his Spanish. She asked him to go home for the day. She promised to have an answer for him by Saturday. She watched him shuffle to the main door. His body was stooped into a question mark, his pants sagged off bony hips.

Rosie walked past the lounge where a half dozen C.O.s celebrated New Year's Eve in a cluster around a white sheet cake. The sharp smack of pool cues marked a counterpoint to the click of Rosie's heels.

Locking her office door behind her, Rosie switched on the lights but nothing happened. Her digital clock gleamed from the opposite wall, which meant the light bulb had probably blown. There was just enough daylight to illuminate the files. It didn't take long to find; John Gabaldon was released in October 1994.

Had he been released? Or had someone lost track of Gabaldon's release date? It had happened before; guys doing a hitch, and their release date finally rolled around, and they didn't remember and neither did their caseworker.

Reluctantly, she walked toward her desk to phone the deputy warden. When she was almost there, she stepped on the Fed Ex packet that had been slipped under the door. It skimmed the carpet like a skateboard, and Rosie landed hard on the floor. Without moving, she tore open the seal and pulled out the list of names she had been waiting for. The members of Charlie Company. On the second page, she found the jackal. He had served from 1966 through 1969; he'd been at My Lai.

—

TRAFFIC WAS SURPRISINGLY light as Sylvia drove home. She felt tired and relieved; she wanted to sleep in her own bed, and she wanted to find Rocko. When she reached her house she left a message at Rosie and Ray's and then she called her mother in California.

"Sylvia, is that you?"

"I got the package. Thanks." It had been waiting on her front stoop. A Christmas gift. There was a note inside, a smiling Christmas angel with a message: Thought you'd want this. Love, Mom.

Now, embedded deep in Styrofoam snow, her fingers found the silver frame of a family portrait—her mother and father holding the baby Sylvia between them. The picture had dressed the *nicho* in the living room for years. There was something else, a smaller package wrapped in tissue paper and ribbon—her father's Silver Star, awarded by the Army for bravery in battle, and a tiny silver pendant that had been his good luck charm.

She blew particles of Styrofoam from her fingers and fingered the chain.

After the slightest hesitation, her mother said, "I thought you might like them."

"I do." Sylvia shook her head, frustrated, trying to send feelings through the phone lines. "I love them, Mom."

"I'm so glad."

The two women talked for fifteen minutes, catching up, communicating for the first time in years. After they had covered the subjects of various relatives, Sylvia's career, and her mother's social activities, they even touched on the idea of a visit.

After the phone call, she spent forty-five minutes cleaning house. The rooms weren't really dirty, but scrubbing, sweeping, and dusting were all part of a small ritual to reassert her control of territory.

Dinner was toast and soup, and then Sylvia concentrated on reviewing files and preparing for her postholiday push. It felt good to focus on her work. She was beginning to accept the fact that the nightmare of the past few weeks was finally over. The only thing that bothered her was Rocko's absence. The runty terrier had not shown up since her return, and the bowl of food she'd left behind the day before remained untouched. He'd been known to stay away for several days, but that was usually when the weather was much warmer.

At seven o'clock, Sylvia answered the phone to Monica Treisman's breathless soprano. She could hear Jaspar in the background asking to speak with her, and she smiled with pleasure. When Monica explained that her aunt had lapsed into a coma, Sylvia immediately offered to watch Jaspar.

"Should I come over?"

"Let me drop him off with you. It's just as easy. He's been talking about you and Rocko since Christmas."

Sylvia hung up the phone without mentioning Rocko's absence. She didn't have the heart.

TWENTY-SEVEN

LIQUID GREEN LIGHT; the upper hallway of Main Administration glowed in the semidarkness. Behind their frosted glass window panes, all the offices on the floor were empty. Even Rosie's office was illuminated only by the small tensor lamp she kept at her desk. Every few minutes, the growl of thunder vibrated against the old institutional walls. Neither Rosie nor Colonel Gonzales said a word. She leaned anxiously against her desk. The colonel sat in a chair and smoked. He had agreed to back Rosie up; she felt a confrontation was necessary to get the information she needed, but her methods for the evening were unorthodox to say the least.

It was Rosie who sensed his presence at her door. He had come at her request. She stood, moved around her desk, then held a finger to her lips and reached for the doorknob. It was time to meet the jackal.

When she stepped out into the hall, Bubba Akins nodded. "Miz Sanchez."

"Mr. Akins." She closed the office door firmly and Rosie dismissed the correctional officer who had accompanied Bubba from North Facility. "We're fine here. Check back in fifteen minutes." The C.O. seemed happy to leave.

"Night of the Jacka' . . . a good nigh' fo' travel," Bubba slurred.

Rosie said, "You'll be on your way soon. The transport vehicle should be here in forty-five minutes."

"I wan' thank you fo' keepin' your word."

They both turned when they heard footsteps on the stairs. C.O. Anderson's skin took on an odd purple cast from the green reflection. Shuffling along beside him, Elmer Rivak's egg-shaped head barely topped the buckle of the C.O.'s belt. Rosie thought of a ventriloquist's act she'd seen recently on television. These two made believable stand-ins for the comedian and his dummy.

When they were within earshot, Rosie said, "That's close enough, gentlemen."

"I thought you wanted to interrogate him?" C.O. Anderson's voice had an unpleasant edge magnified by an echo in the hall.

Rosie nodded. "I do." As she opened her mouth, a crack of thunder exploded overhead. In the electric stillness that followed, Elmer spoke.

"Thunder . . . unusual in winter. The gods are angry tonight."

"I agree with you, Mr. Rivak." She paused, then said, "Elmer, do you know why the gods are angry?"

"Oh, yes."

Rosie raised her eyebrows, folded both arms across her waist, and watched him with interest.

"All the waste," Elmer said.

"I'm not sure I know what you mean."

"Him." He pointed to C.O. Anderson. "And him." To Bubba. "Such a waste."

"He's crazy," C.O. Anderson mumbled, but the words were swallowed up by another crack of thunder. He was stepping from foot to foot like a shadow boxer.

Bubba said, "Wha' make you so nervous, Butt-fuck? This lady, she lookin' for whoeve' kill the devil dog."

It was the first time Rosie had heard the expression, but devil dog seemed an appropriate description of Lucas Watson.

Thunder didn't faze Bubba. "Why don' you tell her 'bout Lucas? Why don' you tell her 'bout all that moola from the senator who wan' a job done?"

C.O. Anderson lurched toward Bubba.

"That's enough, boys." Rosie turned to Elmer. "I understand you were at My Lai."

"Yes."

"You saw a lot of waste in Vietnam?"

Elmer nodded. "Waste. Broken men. Organicity."

Rosie kept her voice so low it was a whisper. "Do you mind if I ask you a personal question?"

"Not at all. The Lord told me you'd contact me soon."

"Why did you need Angel Tapia's pinkie?"

"Ah, because I didn't have one, did I?"

"Did you have a hand but no little finger?"

"Yes."

Rosie shot Bubba a look when he laughed. Although she didn't smoke, she found herself filled with the sudden desire to light up. "What else do you have?"

Elmer looked surprised at the question, as if Rosie had somehow not lived up to her role as hostess for an otherwise pleasant evening. "Everything."

"You mean arms and legs?"

"Oh, yes."

"How many exactly?"

"Well, actually I have one extra arm. I haven't decided which one to use."

"For what?"

Elmer frowned again and seemed abruptly tired. He spoke to Rosie as if she were a rather slow child. "Construction. Organic architecture."

"Ahhh . . ." Rosie's words were simultaneous with another bolt of thunder. "You're building a body. I mean a person."

"Of course," Elmer said.

"I tol' you," Bubba snorted. "Doc Frankenstein."

"What about the head, Elmer?" Rosie tensed suddenly. "Whose head do you have?"

C.O. Anderson stepped forward but Bubba Akins's meaty hand slapped the guard's belly. Anderson stopped.

The jackal said, "God gave me Lucas Watson's head."

Rosie nodded to Bubba.

"No, he didn'," Bubba announced.

Anderson looked amazed.

"Yes, he did," the jackal said.

"No."

"Yes."

They went on like schoolboys until Rosie said, "Enough. Bubba, whose head does the jackal have?"

Bubba peered at the small man named Elmer Rivak and grinned. "Accordin' to my mouth, ya'll got John Gab'don's head."

Three things happened simultaneously. Bubba exploded in laughter, lightning hit the building and crackled down the hall, and the jackal charged C.O. Anderson.

"You told me I'd get Watson's head!" The jackal's eyes were level with Anderson's neck, and he could watch his own fingers tighten around the hack's throat.

Anderson fell backward; his skull smacked the wall just as the jackal changed gears. He lowered his head and bounced off Bubba Akins's grotesque belly.

The door to Rosie's office flew open and Colonel Gonzales emerged in time to see the jackal and Bubba grappling in the dark hallway like two titans. Their shadows climbed the walls and bounced off the ceiling. Although the jackal was outmuscled, he was amazingly fierce. Before Rosie's eyes, he transformed from a mousy porter into a ferocious combat vet, a guerilla fighter.

The jackal bit off a piece of Bubba's ear and the big man roared. Pain and anger thrust him forward, and he trampled C.O. Anderson's semiprone body. Colonel Gonzales helped Anderson out of the way.

The impact of Bubba's next tackle sent the jackal flying. His torso smacked the door to Rosie's office and glass shattered. When Rosie saw him reach for a glass shard, she stomped on his wrist with her stiletto heel. The jackal howled in pain.

Bubba was wheezing, walking in circles. He glared at Elmer Rivak. "You're not the real jacka'."

C.O. Anderson moaned, "Shut up."

Bubba turned to Rosie. "Senator Duke Watson. He's the King of the Jacka's. He paid these boys to kill Lucas. But you'll never prove it."

At that moment, the guard who had accompanied Bubba from North topped the stairs and turned into the hall. He stopped, and his eyes widened in amazement.

Rosie's head was swimming. She spit out a command. "You know where to take Mr. Akins."

She turned to Jeff Anderson. "We got some talking to do, mister."

Finally, she said, "Elmer Rivak. Help me, and I'll help you, because the Lord talks to me, too. Now take me to this damn head."

Elmer stood carefully. Every vestige of the savage combat fighter was gone. Now, with his flyaway hair and his myopic eyes, he truly appeared to Rosie like an elfin Dr. Frankenstein. Colonel Gonzales stood by, ready for action.

Elmer said simply. "It belongs to Lucas Watson. You'll see."

—

SYLVIA TURNED OUT the lights in the kitchen and balanced a very full cup of cocoa in her hand as she walked toward the bedroom. Several drops of the chocolate mixture slopped over the side and onto the floor, but she managed to keep the cup upright. Jaspar was tucked under the duvet, his eyelashes fringing sleepy blue eyes. He blinked back a tear when he saw her. "I'm sorry."

"Jaspar, you don't have to be sorry; you didn't do anything wrong."

"I made it wet."

"You had an accident. Everyone has accidents, especially when they've been going through such a hard time. I bet you've been really sad and angry."

Jaspar nodded slowly.

"Did you have one of your dreams about the bad men?"

"I think so. One bad man came, and I got so scared I couldn't move. I froze."

"Why don't you tell me some more about the dream?"

"I want to read now."

Sylvia set the cocoa on the bed stand and adjusted the lamp. "Are we going for dinosaurs?"

"I think so."

Sylvia gave Jaspar a peck on the cheek and then she picked up two books for review. "This one?"

"Nope."

"How about this one?"

"Yep." He squirmed deeply under the duvet.

Sylvia opened the book jacket and began to read. She was four pages into the story when she heard a sharp, faint noise.

"What?" Jaspar asked sleepily, his eyes almost shut.

"Nothing," Sylvia said. She continued to read, but much of her attention was straining outward, waiting for the sound to recur. For a moment, she had been sure it was Rocko's bark in the distance, in the storm.

—

Accompanying Elmer and Colonel Gonzales down the hall, Rosie wondered once again how they could encounter so few correctional officers. They had been walking for several minutes, and she'd used her keys to open two manual grills. Once, passing the cell blocks, someone had laughed. After that, it had been too quiet. Their shadows bounced off the walls of the deserted hall.

Elmer turned and entered the cavernous area of the cafeteria. Rosie could smell turkey and canned peas. The colonel switched on a flashlight. Chairs, tables, a drinking fountain emerged in garish light.

The kitchen was a gleaming space of stainless steel and tile. Great kettles, cans, and double boilers stood mute watch. Rosie saw that the jackal had suddenly covered his eyes.

His voice was barely audible as he recited the words like a litany: "Look not mournfully into the Past. It comes not back again. Wisely improve the Present. It is thine."

Rosie froze in her tracks when something streaked by. Elmer sucked in oxygen beside her as a dark form shot across his path. A cat. Colonel Gonzales let the flashlight beam play over the institutional surface, but could not find the stray trespasser. They continued toward the bowels of the kitchen, the giant walk-in freezers.

Rosie had to try twelve keys before she found the cut that fit the padlock. The great door swung open and the overpowering smell of Freon filled her nostrils. Elmer sneezed. When Rosie looked up, he was already inside and headed toward the back of the freezer, shuffling past crates of frozen corn and hunks of meat. She flashed her beam so it hit the wall fifteen feet away. Elmer motioned to her from the corner; childhood fears of hell and death in tight spaces washed over Rosie. She prayed softly and entered, followed by the colonel.

"Here," Elmer said when she stood by his side. He seemed very much at home as he pointed to a lumpy, undefined mass wrapped in white freezer paper. Rosie swallowed hard. Her throat hurt. She ran through a mental checklist of possible body parts that might match the size and shape of the package. "What is it?" she asked wearily.

Elmer began to unwrap. The paper fell off piece by piece. Although logically there would not be much odor, Rosie held her breath as the paper cracked open.

She paused for a moment to see if the uneasiness in her stomach would become more violent, but she managed to examine the object before her with clinical detachment. It was a leg, or more exactly half a leg. She was staring at a slice of human thigh, scorched and scarred with deep burn marks, the flesh turned greenish-black from time and decay. Rosie swallowed quickly to force down the bile rising in her throat.

"Elmer?" Her voice sounded surprisingly normal. "The head. Do you have it?"

Elmer nodded and set down his precious thigh carefully. He began to rewrap and Rosie spoke quickly. "Could we see the head first?"

Elmer considered the question. "That's irregular," he said finally.

"I know. But this is an emergency."

Elmer struggled to lift a wrapped sphere from a fruit crate. Rosie tried halfheartedly to help, but he wouldn't let her near. Again, he went through the painstaking procedure of unwrapping the parcel. This time, the inner layers of wrapping were stained with blood and the seepage of other bodily fluids. There was an unmistakable odor of flesh. A sheet of paper crumpled away and a cloudy fishlike eye stared up at Rosie. She put her sleeve in front of her mouth and motioned for Elmer to remove the rest of the covering.

The head was really a pulpy brain mass, no longer round, no longer contained by bone structure. The hair and scalp were singed to charcoal and the throat blackened by the flame of the blowtorch used to sever head from body.

Rosie realized her eyes were six inches from the skull and the mouth that gaped open in a rictus grin. There was no gold cap covering either canine. In a raspy voice she whispered, "Juan Gabaldon."

—

Sylvia watched Jaspar sleep until her own breathing matched his. The dinosaur book had fallen to the floor. The boy clutched a fabric cat next to his chest. When she stood, carefully so he wouldn't wake, her muscles ached from the effort. She picked up the cup of cocoa and walked back to the kitchen. As she washed the liquid down the sink, again she heard the distant cry.

She flung open the kitchen door and stood listening. After a few seconds, the sound rose once more, a piercing howl.

"Rocko," Sylvia said under her breath. A faint streak of lightning illuminated the sky, and the ridge gleamed like a great fossil animal. She stepped outside and bitter flakes of snow burned her face and hands.

"Rocko!"

The dog's cries were steady now, coming from a place halfway up the ridge. She could reach him quickly if she ran. She found a flashlight under the kitchen sink and started back to the bedroom to wake Jaspar when she realized that didn't make sense; if Rocko was badly injured, she didn't want Jaspar to know.

Her windbreaker was draped over a chair, her keys in the pocket, but she couldn't remember where she'd left her gloves. She closed the kitchen door and stumbled as she began the run up the rocky hillside.

Bolts of electricity brightened the sky every thirty seconds, but not every one was intense enough to illuminate the path. Flashlight in hand, she groped her way over ice and shale.

After three or four minutes she stopped abruptly and shone her light on the large pile of boulders thirty feet ahead. Shadows danced against rock.

She moved in bursts and fits, calling and listening, gaining ground. Her chest burned with every inhalation. "Rocko!"

After each stroke of lightning, the night seemed darker and more silent. Sylvia used her hands, fingers numb with cold, to feel her way along the path.

The soles of her shoes were slick. She felt her shin crack soundly into a ridge of granite and she went down, tumbling five feet over rock. When she stood again, her ankle ached and she was disoriented. She closed her eyes and strained to hear Rocko once more.

This time the cry seemed close, coming from behind a boulder roughly eight feet away. She skirted a skeleton of cholla and limped to the rock. Her hands slid over the porous surface, she stumbled around the ledge, and choked off a sound when she saw him.

Rocko stared up at her, wet, shivering, his back leg abnormally twisted. When she knelt down, the dog moaned and his tongue came out automatically to lick her hand.

There was blood on his head, over much of his coat. Rocko whimpered, and Sylvia bit her lip as she scooped her wounded dog in both arms.

The storm was almost on top of them now. Electric streaks of light and color came so fast the effect was one of implosion. Wind whipped her hair in her eyes, and the cold was wearing on her body.

She was a third of the way down when she saw her house illuminated by the soft glow of lights. The man cast a deep shadow as he entered through the kitchen door. Moments later a shotgun blast echoed off the ridge.

TWENTY-EIGHT

THE SHOTGUN WAS gone. Lucas Watson had taken it from the top shelf of the linen closet. The ammo box was on the floor, shells scattered underfoot. There was no way of knowing how many loads he had.

The phone was dead; it had been blasted to pieces, the wires blown out of the wall. The house was empty. She left Rocko bundled on the bed and stepped outside. There was one set of footprints in the fresh snow.

She moved quickly past the Volvo—its hood gaped open. Moonlight made it easy to follow his trail. At the road, the tracks continued directly toward the creek.

When she reached the barbed fence that kept strays off the road, Sylvia saw a child's footprints scattered next to a man's shoe print. They'd gone under the wire.

It took her two minutes to reach the icy creek; it felt like ten. There was a footbridge a quarter mile upstream, but the tracks did not veer, they led straight into the water. She slid over rocks and stumbled up the opposite bank where the snow gave way to sheltered earth and clumps of weed. She'd lost their trail.

Across the field, to the northeast, the Calidroses' house was dark. Straight in front of Sylvia, roughly an eighth of a mile away, stood the rotted wooden frame of the old windmill. She caught her breath—they were in the windmill.

The electrical storm had blown itself south, and distant lightning zigzagged across the sky. A soft, steady snow had begun to fall on Santa Fe.

Her pace quickened until she was ten feet from the windmill and then she stopped. The silence was broken only by the distant drone of a jet. The hum of great engines increased and then faded away.

She froze when the tip of the shotgun jabbed her spine.

"You came." Lucas Watson's voice was cold and flat. "I knew you would come."

He was behind her, maybe three feet away. She saw no sign of Jaspar. *God, let him be alive and unhurt.*

"Put your arms behind your back."

She followed his orders slowly and deliberately.

He yanked her windbreaker from her shoulders and twisted the slick fabric into a makeshift knot around her hands. She swallowed; her tongue felt swollen. "Lucas," she began.

"Shut the fuck up." He thrust the shotgun into her side, right above her kidney. She groaned in pain and stumbled forward.

She whispered, "Where's Jaspar?"

A small voice reached her from inside the wooden structure. "Sylvia?"

Lucas jerked her back by her hair. He put his mouth to her ear and spoke softly. "Shut up and walk."

She stumbled over a wooden doorway; inside, the floor was uneven, half dirt, half rotted planks. The air was sour with the smell of wet ashes. Between slats and missing boards, moonlight poured into the windmill. Her eyes slowly adjusted to the milky light and shadows became a bale of straw, a pile of boards, a child.

Jaspar whimpered. He couldn't move; he was terrified.

Sylvia fought back tears.

The child watched her, then his eyes shifted. Sylvia felt Lucas directly behind her. He said, "Sit right where you are. Get back against the wall."

When she had done what he asked, she looked up at him. He stood in the center of the floor with the shotgun clutched in his right hand. There was a festering wound where his thumb had been. His face was gaunt and yellowed, and his skull was covered with thick, dark scabs. His cloudy eyes had gone almost white.

Jaspar whispered, "The bad man came."

Sylvia locked eyes with Jaspar and saw his courage and his will to survive. She felt oddly reassured.

Lucas moved in front of her and blocked the moonlight with his shoulders. He gazed down at her without emotion. "Tell me what happened. The night she died. Help me wash away the badness."

This was what he'd wanted all along—to know the truth about his mother's death. "I can't do that, Lucas. I wasn't there."

Lucas smiled and tipped the shotgun toward Jaspar. "Talk to me or I'll kill the little fuck-up."

She took a breath, and part of her detached itself from the darkness, the horror, and began the job of gathering details from memory. She knew enough about Lily's death to begin the story. But the details were hers—not his—and the wrong cue could be fatal.

When she saw his finger tighten on the trigger, she began to speak woodenly, forcing the words out. "Your mother was home that night. And so were you. Billy went to stay with your housekeeper, with Ramona."

"Why?" Lucas insisted.

Jaspar tried to change position; his arms were thrust painfully together behind his back.

Sylvia kept her eyes on Lucas, alert for any reaction. "Because your mother—"

"Lily!"

"Because Lily was drinking too much, so Ramona took your brother away. But you didn't go."

"Why didn't I?"

Sylvia thought he sounded tortured and desperate. For an instant, her mind went blank, and she panicked. Then the picture began to coalesce in her mind. She took a guess. "You were working up to one of your tantrums."

Lucas nodded. "I hid her pills. I should be punished. I was born bad."

Sylvia said, "You were afraid you'd lose your mother."

"I wanted to stay with her."

Sylvia spoke slowly, waiting for Lucas to finish the story on his own. "So you went to get the pills . . ."

"That's right," he whispered. "I sat and cried in a corner. I watched her, and the pills and the bourbon did what they always did—they made her go to sleep." He stopped speaking. Anger and confusion flashed across his face.

At that instant, Sylvia had a sickening realization—Duke had not been in the house when Lily died.

Lucas sighed. "I wanted to punish her . . . and my daddy taught me how. I took the High Standard, the .22." His eyes glazed over and he disappeared inside himself. "I walked back to Lily's room, and I stood by her bed. She smelled bad from the nasty drink . . . but her hair was so pretty. I put the .22 against her head, and I pulled the trigger."

Sylvia fought to hide her shock—Lucas had murdered his mother.

Behind her back, she worked one hand free of her jacket.

Tears streamed down Lucas's face. "I took her ring . . . and then I lay down beside her . . . Will you help me, Mama?" he asked in a child's voice.

"I'm not your mother, Lucas." Sylvia knew that in Lucas Watson's mind, she and his mother were merged into one woman that he both worshiped and hated—merged in psychotic transference. She also knew he'd try to kill Jaspar as a sacrificial lamb—to purge his sin.

"But I can help you." She twisted her other hand free of the binding fabric.

For a few seconds, he appeared almost lucid, calm. "You found me," he said. "I knew you'd come back." He pulled the shotgun up and swung the barrel toward Jaspar.

She propelled herself away from the wall to shield the child with her body.

Lucas fired, emptied both barrels, and the shot tore a hole through wood.

Sylvia lunged forward screaming, "Run, Jaspar, run!" She threw herself at Lucas. Her force knocked them both to the floor, and Lucas flipped her over, pinning her down.

The child streaked toward the doorway and into the darkness.

Lucas kept his lips just inches from Sylvia's mouth. His sour breath poured over her face. He whispered, "Mama?"

"She's dead, Lucas."

His eyes rolled up in their sockets, and his voice turned high and shrill. "Mama!" He raised his torso and brought his fists up.

Sylvia wrenched herself partially free and braced for the shock of impact. She saw his face contort in agony, his hands contract like talons ready to strike.

There was a great report. His throat exploded and he was thrust back by the blast. Where he fell, a widening pool of dark liquid spread across the old wood floor.

For a moment, Sylvia did not recognize Rosie Sanchez. Slowly the other woman's features came into focus. She could smell the acrid scent from the gun in Rosie's right hand.

She forced herself up from the ground, reached for Lucas, and pressed her jacket against the gushing wound that had been his throat. Instantly, the fabric was soaked with blood. She shook her head, gazed up at Rosie, and mouthed, "Jaspar?"

The other woman's face was pale, almost white, and her dark eyes were huge. "He's outside. He needs you. I'll take care of Lucas."

Sylvia stared down at the dying man, then she stood with effort.

She found Jaspar waiting fifteen feet from the windmill. His teeth were chattering, he was shaking, but he reached out to hug Sylvia. She wrapped the child in both arms, and neither of them moved until two men brought a stretcher and the static of official voices surrounded the old windmill.

TWENTY-NINE

When Billy Watson walked out of the Santa Fe Judicial Complex, the sun was so bright it seemed to sear his eyes. He pushed dark shades over the bridge of his nose and hunched his shoulders. After nine days in a cell at the Santa Fe Detention Center, he was a free man. He was also a man who was filled with newfound resolve.

The Honorable Judge Cooper had presided at the brief preliminary hearing. The charges included aggravated assault, battery, and three counts of capital murder.

The prosecution presented its case, and the judge heard all the evidence. There was very little to hear. The murder weapon—an

Army-issue Colt .45—had disappeared from the evidence locker at state police headquarters. So had the shell casings found at both crime scenes. The hairs and fibers taken from the victims and the scenes were mislabeled—no chain of custody.

Billy's lawyer (a hotshot suit from Ruidoso hired by Duke) smiled sadly when he approached the bench to explain that the validity of the entire investigation was now open to question.

At the end of the hearing, Judge Cooper had no alternative. He dismissed the murder charges, and set bail on the lesser charges at $200,000.

Duke Watson's lawyer didn't even blink.

Queeny had the Corvette illegally parked next to a red curb. Beastie Boys poured out of the stereo and she was humming along. Her rangy soprano strayed off-key.

Queeny didn't smile at Billy when he opened the door. But he noticed her eyes before she slid over to let him drive. Her pupils were dabs of ink floating in green-gray orbs, and they blazed with an odd sort of respect.

She turned off the music, stabbed out her cigarette in the ashtray, and wrapped her long arms around her bony knees. "Hi."

Billy said, "Where is he?"

"At the capitol."

He drove slowly, but even so, they reached the state capitol Roundhouse in less than four minutes.

They parked in a lot across the street, and Queeny gave him the velvet purse she'd been holding on her lap.

Billy opened it and took out the High Standard single action semiautomatic. He smoothed it gently with his fingers. It was the first gun that Duke had ever owned. It had been a gift from his father passed down to Duke when he turned five years old. Duke had given the very same gun to Lucas on his fifth birthday.

One year later, when Billy turned five, he had received shooting privileges, too. Both boys had cut their teeth on that revolver. It was light enough—had a small enough grip—to accommodate a child's hand nicely.

The Standard took .22 long rifles, but only six because the spring was old and didn't feed properly. Billy loaded it.

The legislature had been in session for five days, and the streets were busy with men who wore dark suits and cowboy hats. They walked stiffly the way men in tight-toed, high-heeled cowboy boots often do.

Billy kissed Queeny on the cheek, climbed out of the 'vette, and watched while she drove away. Then he followed a quartet of the men up the long tree-lined walkway toward the main entrance of the Roundhouse. The sky was beginning to cloud up, but the rays of sunlight still had the strength to melt snow and ice. Three smiling women passed Billy on the steps. Their brightly colored coats reminded him of candy. They looked familiar; maybe one of them worked for the senator. Billy stepped through heavy, eight-foot-tall doors and entered the building's rotunda.

For an instant, he was lost, disoriented by dim light and echoing sound. He regained his bearings and followed the same four men past the information desk toward the Senate chambers. He knew his way—he'd probably been here a hundred times to watch his father at work.

The rotunda was live, and sound strained up toward the stained-glass ceiling, bounced off the walls, and tumbled back to the floor.

Two of the men suddenly veered off in front of him. He kept going behind the other pair. They opened the narrow doors to the chamber and passed through. Billy was only four paces behind.

His eyes took their time adjusting to the dusky light. Gradually, he recognized the rows of smooth walnut desks and the speakers podium. And the senators who occupied their assigned seats.

He heard his father's deep voice before he picked out his thick-set body. Duke's chin and barrel chest were thrust forward while his butt stuck out just slightly in a way that reminded Billy of a strutting baboon. Duke had the floor, and his voice didn't just carry, it commanded.

"—an impossible task? Some would like to convince us of that, but the fact is, we can't afford to be pessimistic. The children and youth of New Mexico have been cruelly neglected by this body, ladies and gentlemen. The numbers back me up on this—"

Billy heard the words for a few seconds and then he shut them out. He shut out the myriad mundane sounds that human beings are always making: the constant breath and expiration, the movement of muscles, the rustle of papers.

Billy began his walk down the center aisle that would lead him directly to his father. Several faces turned his way with expressions of bland curiosity.

Billy felt as if he'd been launched irrevocably on a course. When he was five yards away, he saw the Duke waving pages in the air.

"Don't cheat the young who will carry on the torch. They are the ones who will be casting votes in 2016," Duke said.

Billy saw laughter on some faces. He slipped the revolver from inside his jacket and let his arm drop to his side. His finger brushed against the trigger.

"—federal funding isn't enough; it's never enough. Nor is the—"

When Billy was seven or eight feet away, he picked up his pace just a bit, extended his arm, got his father in his sight the way he'd been taught, and began the lazy squeeze on the trigger.

Duke turned, saw the man who approached, and a slow look of recognition shifted his features like a light breeze over wild grass.

Could there have been a fleeting sense of coming face-to-face with the unavoidable? There was definitely reproach, but it was the condemnation of a man who has seen everything around him fall too far short of perfection.

Billy squeezed off six rounds. Three bullets lodged in Duke Watson's chest, one penetrated his neck, and two hit the senator in the head. Billy had been well taught.

THIRTY

Sylvia pulled on her sweater, shook out her hair, and glanced at herself in her bathroom mirror. Under artificial light her skin was wan, and she had deep circles under her eyes, but the bruises were gone. Considering the events of the last month, she thought she looked pretty damn terrific. She switched off the light, and walked into the living room.

Only thirty-six hours had passed since Billy Watson shot and killed his father. He hadn't resisted arrest; he was in custody at the detention center.

It had been almost two weeks since Lucas Watson's death, and the endless questions by investigating officers.

Sylvia wrapped her arms around herself and gazed out the living room window. The sun was just about to crest the Sangre de Cristo Mountains.

"Why don't you come over here and give a guy a break?"

Matt England was stretched out on the couch watching her. "Earth to Sylvia," he said softly.

Sylvia welcomed the strength of his arms around her. "I'm so glad you're here," she said pressing her body into his. "It's frightening to be so needy."

Matt gripped her tightly, and she settled onto his lap. When she turned her face and pressed her lips to his, he tasted the salt of her tears.

—

OUTSIDE MAIN FACILITY the sun was shining and the air had bite. Rosie led the way to her car and opened the door for Sylvia. Without explanation, Rosie maneuvered the Camaro over rough asphalt onto dirt. Five minutes later she braked to a stop and switched off the ignition. Sylvia stared out at the large arena directly ahead. Even with the ground frozen solid there was a cloud of dust as several inmates in blue shirts and jeans worked to separate one skinny bay horse from the rest of the herd.

"I'm so glad you came," Rosie said. "How's Jaspar?"

Sylvia took a deep breath. "He's coming out of it slowly. Children are amazingly resilient."

"And Rocko?" Rosie smiled.

"Johnny Rocko is an outlaw to the end. He gets his cast off tomorrow, and he never leaves Jaspar's side. They're like this." Sylvia wrapped two fingers around each other. She returned Rosie's smile. "I think I've lost myself a dog."

"I think you've gained yourself a boy. Now, how about a horse? You can adopt." Rosie gestured to the arena. "From the inmate's wild horse program."

One stocky man, the color of carbon, had his halter over the bay's neck when the horse bolted and the man hit the dirt. The other inmates were laughing while they moved to intercept the manic horse.

"I'm glad it's a new year," Sylvia said. She turned to Rosie and smiled. "I wouldn't want to do the last one over again."

Rosie said, "When are you coming back to work?"

"At the pen?" Sylvia shrugged. "Juanita Martinez wants me to evaluate one of her clients next week."

"And will you?"

"Maybe. Probably." Sylvia let her head fall against the glass of the window. She raised her eyebrows and smiled at Rosie. "You know I can't stay away." She watched a chestnut colt scratching the earth with front hooves as steam escaped from its flared nostrils.

Sylvia reached around her neck and removed a delicate chain. She held it out to Rosie.

"What?" Rosie took the hand-carved silver pendant in both hands. There was a miniature unicorn delicately cut into the metal.

"It belonged to my father." Sylvia smiled slowly. "He said it brought him luck in battle. I want you to have it, if you'd like."

"I'm honored." Rosie mouthed a silent prayer in Spanish and squeezed Sylvia's hand. "But you don't owe me a thing, *jita*."

"Oh, yes, I do."

Rosie held up the glimmering unicorn.

"It's a start," Sylvia said, smiling.

There was a cry of victory as the stocky inmate grasped the trailing end of the halter once again. He dug his feet into the ground and pulled against the bay with all his strength. Rosie heard the small gasp of air as Sylvia held her breath. Both women nodded with satisfaction when the bay lowered its head and kicked rear hooves skyward. The man on the end of the rope landed butt first on dirt as the horse bolted for freedom.

ABOUT THE AUTHOR

SARAH LOVETT has worked inside correctional institutions as a paralegal and researcher. A student of the criminal justice system and author of more than twenty nonfiction books for adults and children, she is currently pursuing a degree in criminology. She lives in northern New Mexico.